Beginnings

Beginnings

Penny Jo Shoup

E-BookTime LLC
Montgomery Alabama

Beginnings

Cover artwork by Colleen Duffey Shoup

Library of Congress Control Number: 2004116243

ISBN: 1-932701-57-5

Published November 2004
E-BookTime, LLC
6598 Pumpkin Road
Montgomery, AL 36108
www.e-booktime.com

Contents

Acknowledgements

Writing *Beginnings* has been a life process and I would like to offer heart felt thanks to my family and friends for their encouragement, patience and inspiration. Two people diligently offered their professional knowledge of the law and medicine and I would like to thank Dr. Jeffery Kirkpatrick and Mr. Edward Lancaster for sharing their knowledge with me. *Beginnings* would be much less eventful without the encouragement of a good friend Jeff High. I would like to offer gratitude to him and encouragement to him to follow his dream. The book wouldn't be the same without the patient corrections of my editor Virginia Yeoman. Thanks, Ginny.

My gem of a sister-in-law, Colleen Duffey Shoup, took my vision for the cover and made it a reality! Thank You Colleen!

My continuing dream is for *Beginnings* to speak to you of God's love as you read it!

CHAPTER 1

"Britany! Help!" A young lady in teal scrubs came rushing through the door of the nursery pushing a crib containing a bluish-colored infant. Britany flew across the room. Her heart raced as she immediately realized that the baby wasn't breathing. She briskly shook the infant and yelled out orders as she guided the crib under an empty warmer. "Hand me the oxygen mask. Turn on the flow meter!" The infant gasped and took a deep breath. She placed the mask over the baby's mouth and nose. Britany listened with her stethoscope. She heard a faint heart beat. She could hear the weak heart beat speed up.

"I need a heart and oxygen monitor!" yelled Britany. Jeanne was already at her side with the monitors and quickly attached them to the infant.

The commotion brought immediate attention from the rest of the busy nursery. "I paged Dr. Goldstein stat." Shelly, the charge nurse, called into the room. "He is still over at Peds. I'll get some IV tubing ready!" Britany appreciated Shelly's efficiency. Shelly was good person to work with in a time of crisis.

The infant started breathing regularly. The heart rate steadied and the oxygen readings increased. Britany was removing the oxygen mask from the baby's face as the tall stately Dr. David Goldstein appeared at the door. He determinedly crossed the room with an air of authority.

"What's happening? I heard the page." His black eyes scanned the scene with a look of anxiety on his face.

"This infant stopped breathing and was blue. He pinked up with stimulation and oxygen. His heart rate was down but increased when the breathing resumed," reported Britany. Dr. Goldstein stood beside Britany, looking intently at the baby. Even though he was bent over slightly he stood almost a head taller than Britany. His short black hair was starting to gray at the temples. He reached over for Britany's stethoscope and listened to the infant's heart and lungs.

"I was doing vitals on my babies," added the tech, Heather as he looked up. Her shiny black hair reached to her waist in back. "He was just fine one minute, and then I turned around and noticed he was blue and not breathing. I rushed him over here for help."

"Did he choke?" asked Dr. Goldstein.

"He didn't appear to," replied Heather.

"There wasn't any spit-up on his blanket, and he didn't cough when he took a breath as I shook him. It looked like he simply stopped breathing," Britany said. Her green eyes were filled with concern. "Heather reacted quickly. I was really proud of her."

Heather's young face smiled at the compliment. She had only been working a short time. She was especially pleased that Britany praised her in front of Dr. David Goldstein because she knew it was hard for a new person to gain his respect.

"I have his chart here," said Shelly. "He's Baby Caleb. He weighed seven pounds, eight ounces. He's eighteen hours old. No complications at birth, normal pregnancy. He was eating good up until the last feeding when his mom said he was too sleepy and wouldn't eat." Several strands of brown hair with gold highlights managed to escape the barrette and fell across her chubby cheeks as she spoke.

"Well, I guess we better start an IV and antibiotics. We'll draw blood cultures and do a lumbar puncture to check for infections. Get a chest x-ray and an EKG, too," Dr. Goldstein said briskly.

Shelly left to order the items on the computer. Jeanne crossed the room to close the blinds so the procedures could be done without visitors watching. Her short dark hair bobbed as she moved rapidly.

Britany set up the trays with Jeanne's help. Needles, syringes, tubing, alcohol, betadine and tape were laid out on a clean tray along with sterile gloves.

Britany, Jeanne, and Shelly had worked together for the last fourteen years. At thirty-five Britany Becker was the youngest of the three, but only by a few years. Jeanne and Shelly were more than just co-workers: they were Britany's best friends. Jeanne Oakley had lost her husband to a car wreck three years earlier. Her faith and trust in God were strong, and Britany had been amazed at the calm with which Jeanne had faced the tragedy and bravely raised her six-year-old daughter on her own. When Britany had a spiritual dilemma, it was Jeanne to whom she turned. Jeanne was there sometimes even when Britany didn't want to hear God's will, but she was always honest and open and Britany appreciated and loved that in her. Shelly Cambell was fun-loving and vivacious. She believed in Jesus but didn't have a strong trust in Him. She let too much human thinking color her choices. Her husband Stan was a stabling influence in her life. Britany had been saved as a young child and loved Him with all her heart, but she was used to being in control, and it was hard for her to put her trust in God without wanting to help.

Caleb remained pink as they worked, but he didn't protest. Britany held him for the procedures. He felt weak and lifeless. He offered little resistance when the nurse from the IV team drew blood in a tiny vein in his foot and proceeded to start the IV in the same vein.

Britany spoke reassuringly to the baby as Dr. Goldstein prepared to draw the spinal fluid. She placed Caleb on a high bed with a heat light directly over him. The sides of the bed were glass, and they folded down to make it easier to reach the baby. Britany's long slender left hand held the infant's head and shoulders. Her right hand held his legs and buttocks. She folded him into a crescent position to make it easier for Dr. Goldstein to get the needle between the vertebrae of the back. The heat from the warmer felt hot on the back of Britany's auburn curls as she bent over the infant to get a better hold on him. She prayed for Dr. Goldstein as he inserted the needle. The procedure was difficult, and she asked God to guide him as he worked. The needle pierced the skin and went smoothly into the gap between the vertebrae. A drop of spinal fluid trickled into the collection tube.

"I would like it better if he cried a little. I think he's a sick little boy," remarked Britany with concern.

"It certainly does appear so. We will know the preliminary results in a few minutes," Dr. Goldstein said. He swiftly removed the needle and applied pressure to the insertion site. He looked at Britany, his dark eyes serious.

"Go ahead and start the meds IV. I will be at the nurses' station for a while if you need me." He peeled off his sterile gloves and tossed them in the trash can as he left the room. Britany cuddled Caleb and wrapped him in the blankets. She then placed him back in his crib and proceeded to clean the warmer and treatment trays. She carefully labeled the tubes of fluid.

"Shawn!" called Britany from the door of the treatment room. The ward secretary hurried over from the desk. Her light blue eyes eagerly waited for Britany to continue. "Please take these to the lab. We need the results ASAP."

Shawn turned quickly and sped out of the nursery. Shawn reminded Britany of a cheerleader with her bubbly personality and petite figure.

Jeanne had received another baby from labor and delivery, a little girl. She was busy admitting her as Britany wheeled Caleb back into the room.

Shelly followed her in and said, "X ray is coming down the hall. You put on the lead apron, and I'll start getting Caleb ready." Britany held Caleb over the x-ray plate while the technician took the pictures. She looked up to see a young lady dressed in a white lab coat and tan slacks pushing a cart with a machine that looked like a printer with lots of wires. The young lady with short curly blonde hair stopped at the scrub sink and was ready to hook Caleb up for his EKG as the x-ray technician finished. Britany pushed Caleb's crib under a warmer to conserve his energy during the EKG. The EKG technician finished and was wheeling her cart out the door when Dr. Goldstein entered. His slender frame fit easily between the cart and doorframe.

"Let me have a look at the rhythm strip," he said, reaching out toward the young woman in the lab coat. He studied the paper with the tracings and then handed it back to her. "Thank you," he murmured and dismissed the technician without another glance. Looking up, his dark eyes showed relief.

"The rhythm strip looks normal," he said to Britany. "The lab called and said it appears Caleb has strep in his blood. The antibiotics we started should cover it. We will need to keep him on meds for a full seven days. Keep him on the monitor. Continue the IV fluids for twenty-four hours until he gets enough strength back to eat. If he acts hungry, you can try to feed him, but don't worry about it if he's not. The mom can come down to see him, but keep him in for now. I'll be back this evening. I'm going to talk to the mom now. I'll tell her he's in good hands." He paused, looked intently at Britany and said, "By the way, good work."

"Thanks, he sure gave us a scare." She met his gaze. "It was nice of him to do this while you were still in the hospital," Britany said with a smile.

"Yeah." He smiled and turned to leave.

Nursery 1 was filled with crying babies when Britany was finally able to turn her attention away from Caleb. Jeanne was working on an admission. Britany hurried to take several infants to their mothers for feeding. She wheeled the infants down the hall and found herself thinking about David Goldstein. He was strangely handsome. Anyone else with the same features might appear awkward, but the way he carried himself made his looks flow together. Her thoughts returned to the present as she entered the nursery. Jeanne was sitting at the counter filling out charting on her admission as Britany walked in from taking the last baby to its mother. Britany took the stool beside Jeanne and sat down with a sigh. Jeanne was an inch or two taller than Britany but thinner. Her frail frame belied her strong personality.

"This morning has been a bit more exciting than I had hoped for," said Britany. "I'm still a little shaky. It always waits until later to hit me. I could use a breather."

"He looks a lot better. I hope Dr. Goldstein was right," said Jeanne.

Britany caught sight of David as he entered the nursery. He nodded his head slightly, indicating he wanted her to come speak to him. She followed him out into an adjoining empty room.

"How is the mom doing?" Britany asked. Her eyebrows lifted in concern.

"She's fine." He waved his arm as if to pass it off. "I came back because I wanted to talk to you. How about dinner tonight?"

Britany sighed in relief. "Is that all? I thought something else went wrong."

"You really know how to deflate a man's ego fast." His dark eyes saddened.

"It's hard to shift gears so fast. You know that." She reached out and touched his arm. "I didn't mean anything against you, although I guess it did sound rather bad!" Britany said with a light laugh.

"I take that as a yes. I'll pick you up at seven." David's dark eyes brightened.

"Dr. Goldstein! Are you asking me for a date?" asked Britany.

"Shhh... Not so loud. The whole nursery will hear. Let's just say it's a meal between friends. I know you don't like to date."

"In that case, could you make it six? I'll be starved by then. It doesn't look like we will get any lunch."

"If I can get out of the office on time six would be fine. I'll tell the nursing supervisor to bring you a lunch so you won't waste away," he continued with a twinkle in his eye.

"Oh, to have such clout!" she sighed in mock admiration.

He laughed and turned to leave. Britany returned to the nursery, smiling slightly.

Jeanne looked up with concern as Britany entered. She pushed her glasses back on her nose.

"What did he want? Is something else wrong?"

"No, he just wanted to take me to dinner," Britany said and walked over to mark on her worksheet.

"From the way you are smiling, I take it you said yes," Jeanne said a little coolly.

"Jeanne, not again." Britany looked up and frowned. "We are just friends. We always have been, and we always will be and that is exactly what he called it, a meal between friends!" Britany shot back.

"You know you are just encouraging the relationship to go further than that. You are compromising your values. You are a Christian and he is a Jew," Jeanne said emphatically, putting her hand on Britany's arm.

"We believe in the same God!" Britany said in exasperation. "Besides, he's a good friend, he's kind, considerate. At least most of the time, as long of none of us nurses makes a mistake. He even said it wasn't a date, just a meal between friends." She looked down at her worksheet and made some more marks. "Crystal's going to be gone soon, and I don't want to be left alone," Britany finished so quietly that Jeanne only heard her because they were such good friends that she knew what Britany was thinking.

"Britany, God has been with you through every stage of your life. He will be with you now. If He wants you to marry, He will provide the right person," Jeanne said giving Britany's shoulder a squeeze.

"I guess from the sound of these babies we had better get back to work," Britany said lightly. She stood up and hurried to busy herself. She loved Jeanne dearly, but sometimes her friend could just get too serious. She made her face issues she didn't want to face.

Dr. David Goldstein arrived at Britany's apartment shortly after six, He wore the suit he had had on earlier, looking stern but attractive.

"I hope I haven't gotten here so late that you've waisted away in hunger," David said as he escorted her to his car.

"Actually I didn't expect to see you quite so soon. How is Caleb doing?" asked Britany.

"He ate a little, and his color and breathing looked good," David said, opening the car door for Britany.

"That's great! By the way, where are we going?" she asked.

"That's my surprise!" he said with a smile and closed the door behind her.

He took her to an elegant restaurant, and they talked freely. Britany enjoyed hearing of the encounters at the office. He returned her home fairly early.

"Thank you for a wonderful evening," he said quietly taking both her hands in his as they stood on the landing to her front door. She smiled up at him exposing a dimple in her right cheek.

"Thank you. I really enjoyed it," she said.

He took her in his arms that easily encircled her slender waist. She lifted her hands to his shoulders and looked up into his eyes, then laid her head on his chest. He felt warm, secure and friendly. Well, what is so wrong with friendly, she thought as he kissed her goodnight. At least she wasn't alone.

CHAPTER 2

Britany drew her coat closer as she opened the car door Friday morning. The Ohio breeze was still cool with a touch of lingering winter. The brisk walk to the building felt good. Britany enjoyed a last moment of quiet before entering the busy schedule of another day. The sun was trying to push away the dark with a soft glow of violet over the Miami Valley. She wished it would also push away the uncertainty that seemed to be trying to consume her. Looking up, she could see the impressive height of Dayton's Centennial Hospital in front of her, ten stories high with three wings off to the side. Lights in several windows glowed like eyes and gave the building a sense of animation.

In a brief prayer Britany asked God for guidance, protection and wisdom as she was about to start the day. There was no need to remind herself of the impact, good or bad, her actions had each day. Wrong actions could mean life or death to those under her care. She took one last deep breath of fresh air as she entered the building. The walk down the hall and up the four flights of stairs was as familiar as the back of her hand. She had worked here for fifteen years. Entering the locker room, she picked an appropriate set of teal green scrubs, hung her coat on a hook, picked up her white sneakers, and entered the main area of the brightly lit changing room. There were only a few ladies dotted around, but before long there would hardly be room to turn around.

"Hi, Betsy! Are you ready for another exciting day?" Britany addressed a pleasant looking lady in her early sixties. At five feet four inches she was the same height as Britany and was slender in build with short, softly curled gray hair streaked with brown.

"I could do with a little less excitement than we've been having lately! How is your daughter Crystal doing? Does she have senioritis yet?"

"Does she ever! I could use a little of her enthusiasm! She's going to visit Ohio State this weekend with her friend Sabrina. They left this morning to drive up and stay until Monday afternoon. She has a friend on campus they are staying with. That will give her two days to observe classes and two weekend days to observe college life. I wish she were going to a smaller university, but my brother talked her into his alma mater." As she spoke Britany slipped her feet into the legs of her scrubs and pulled them up over her hips to tie the drawstring at the waist. "He has a lot of influence over her. I can't complain though. He's been the father she never knew." Her voice was a little muffled as she brought the scrub top over her head and bent down to tie her shoes. "I'm glad he was older before he got married and started his own family."

Britany finished as three more co-workers came rushing into the room. Within moments, greetings and good-natured teasing filled the locker room. Britany quickly ran a comb through her hair and reapplied a touch of light rose lip-gloss. She wanted to look good on the outside whether she felt it on the inside or not. She pushed her purse into the locker containing her street clothes and made her way out the door.

The cool air of the scrub room felt good against her hot cheeks. Any mention of Crystal brought tears to her eyes. It was really hard to have her go. Britany was not sure what her own future held for her. It had been just the two of them for the last seventeen years. She dreaded the thought of spending the rest of her years alone. "I'm only thirty-five!" She thought. "Well, no time for reflecting there is work to be done." She performed her two-minute scrub, then went through the heavy door that led to the nursery. The sound of crying babies met her ears as she entered. Nurses in teal green scrubs hurried about trying hard to finish tasks to prepare for the start of a new crew. Four separate rooms opened from the large middle area where she stood. The common middle area consisted of a nurses' desk for the secretary and charge nurse to her right. Two smaller rooms for treatments and exams, a storage room, and a visiting room for mothers whose babies had to stay were off to her left. Straight ahead was the door that led to the first of four nurseries. Each nursery contained windows on the outside walls for parents and visitors to view the babies from the surrounding halls.

The night nurse in charge quickly reviewed each baby's condition. The day nurse, Shelly, gave out assignments. "Jeanne and Britany, cover Nursery 1," Shelly said and turned to inform others.

Britany was pleased. New admissions were her favorite task and Jeanne was her favorite person to work with.

"Come on, comrade, let's see what adventures are in store for today!" Britany said as she placed her arm over Jeanne's shoulder and walked with her into the first nursery. The nursery was set up to receive babies from labor and delivery as they were born. Seven overhead warming lights lined one wall. The opposite far wall contained five heart-rate monitors with screens. A crash cart containing resuscitation supplies and medications was in the corner between the two. The room was set up for emergencies and had seen quite a few in its short history. The nursery and maternity part of the one-hundred-year-old hospital were only six years old and were part of the new east wing of the hospital.

Entering the room Britany noticed that there were five babies. The night nurse had reported four or five babies were expected to deliver before 3:00 p.m. That would make for a normal day if no complications occurred, but Britany knew that was the exception rather than the norm.

"If we can get vitals on these five babies before they bring us new ones, it will really help," said Britany as she again washed her hands and reached for a stethoscope.

"Yeah, two of them are almost twelve hours old, and if their vital signs are stable they can over to the next nursery," responded Jeanne. "By the way, how did your date go last night?" She was looking over the infant, counting respirations.

"I enjoyed it. He took me out to eat, and we had a very nice conversation. It was fun," Britany said nonchalantly, removing the stethoscope from the infant's chest. She gently changed the infant's diaper.

"Britany, I think you need to be careful. Things could go further than what you want," Jeanne said as she finished listening to her infant's heart rate.

"Jeanne, I know you're a friend and just trying to help, but, honestly, he is just a good friend. That is all. It's nice to have someone around once in a while. It gets lonely at times when Crystal is gone so much of the time. Besides, I like to be pampered a little. The dinner was very nice." Britany shrugged her shoulders and continued working.

Britany was listening to the heart rate of the next baby and watching the normal rise and fall of the baby's chest when she glanced at the door to see a very pleased-looking young man gingerly carrying a little bundle wrapped securely in several blue blankets. She chuckled quietly and motioned to Jeanne to look toward the door. Even though she had seen the same scene hundreds of times, it never ceased to warm her heart to see a proud father carry in his newborn baby.

"If you could just hold him as he is, I'll loosen the blankets and weigh him," She said. "What are you going to name him?" Britany asked as she gently reached up to loosen the blankets and extract the naked baby from his father's arms. Firmly grasping his legs with one hand and his head with the other, she lifted the baby and placed him on the scales. The father watched with concern on his face, fearing she might drop his son.

"Joshua," the father stated simply.

"Nine pounds, five ounces. He's a beautiful little boy! I need to keep him under the warmer for two to four hours. We will monitor his heart rate, breathing and temperature each hour, and then he can have a bath and go out to Mom if all is OK. You're welcome to watch, but you may want to tell Mom his weight first."

"Wow! Yeah, I guess I should do that!" he stammered. He looked down at Joshua and then hurried to see his wife.

Britany placed the infant under the warmer and secured a probe with a patch to his abdomen. The probe regulated the warmer with the baby's temperature. Joshua lay quietly looking around, occasionally moving his arms and legs in a gentle fashion. Britany drew up the injection of vitamin K that each baby received at birth. Joshua protested the injection with a loud yell. She also pricked his heel for a drop of blood, since babies over nine pounds were routinely checked for a drop in blood sugar following birth. As she finished, the father appeared and stood on the opposite side of the crib from Britany. She listened to Joshua's heart and lungs with a stethoscope, then proceeded to do the head-to-toe physical, explaining observations to his father as she went along.

"His head is a little molded, but that will correct itself in a week or two," she said as she felt the baby's little head, which was covered with brown hair matted down with blood from the birth. The sutures of the skull were a bit separated at the top and soft to the touch. "The shape of his head is all a part of God's plan to facilitate birth," she explained "The skull has amazing resilience in a newborn and can mold into different positions during birth without harm to the brain."

"If your wife plans to breast feed, I think he's more than eager!" Britany said.

"He nursed a little before we brought him over," the father responded with pride in his voice.

Continuing the exam, she looked at his perfect fingers while his hand closed firmly around her own finger. His skin was soft and velvety, and, although still a bit violet with pink undertones, she knew he would soon be pink all over. His abdomen puffed out slightly on the sides like a frog's, and his umbilical cord was still fat and creamy. She examined his legs and then finished her exam by measuring his head, chest, and length.

"Everything looks fine," Britany said as she crossed the room and sat on a stool at the counter to chart her findings. As she glanced up at Joshua and his father, a wave of sadness swept over her. She longed for another baby and a husband with whom to share the joy. At thirty-five with not even a boyfriend, she knew her longing was an impossible dream.

Britany's charting stopped as she thought about the past eighteen years. Crystal's father had broken off all contact with Britany when she became pregnant in the middle of her senior year of high school. He was a promising athlete and had a full college scholarship in baseball. He was good, and had gone on to play in the pros. He now had a wife and two boys. He hadn't been mature enough at the time to make a commitment. Britany had thought she loved him, but after Crystal was born she realized what true love was. He had never made any attempt to contact Britany or see Crystal, for which Britany was grateful. She had buried herself in Crystal and in her nursing career. That had always been enough, but now, as she faced the reality of Crystal leaving, a new desire was overwhelming her. Britany shook her head as if to bring herself back into the present, and she resumed her charting.

The rest of the day continued to be busy, but with no major problems. Dr. Goldstein came in on his lunch hour to check on Baby Caleb.

Britany was bent over a crib when he put his hand on her shoulder. She looked up, startled, and the stethoscope clanged against the side of the crib.

"I'm sorry, I didn't mean to startle you," he said.

"I guess I was engrossed in my work. Don't feel bad, it wasn't your fault," Britany said. What she failed to mention was that he was part of the reason she was so preoccupied. She knew he would be in to check on Caleb and she wanted him to ask her out again. At the same time she wasn't sure she should go if he did.

"Some friends of mine invited me to a dinner party this evening, and I was wondering if I could interest you in attending with me. I would really like your company," he said as he looked down at her.

Her lip quivered slightly as she thought. Should she or shouldn't she? She wanted to go, but her better judgment told her not too. His face looked so compelling and innocent, like a little boy asking his father to take him fishing.

"I was planning to go to my parent's place in the country this evening and spend the weekend," Britany said. She wasn't lying. That would be a good excuse. She tried to convince herself that she was doing the right thing.

"Could you call them and tell them you will be there first thing in the morning? It's important to me. I need a date, and I really want it to be you," he said as he reached over and laid his hand on her shoulder.

Britany couldn't resist his sad eyes. "I guess I could," she heard herself say. She had wanted him to ask her out, but a small voice deep inside said she should have said no. She ignored it. "It really doesn't matter when I get there, as long as I have time to ride on Saturday. I'm taking my horse to a horse show in June, and we have a lot of things to work on," Britany said.

"Great! I'll pick you up at seven!" David smiled and reached out to pat her back and left.

Britany hurried home after work. She had a purple velvet dress that she hoped would be nice enough. She showered and dried her hair. She wished that Crystal was home to help her with her hair. An uncontrollable anxiety was making her hands unsteady. She had purposely avoided serious relationships for the last seventeen years. She had had many inquiries from men, but she had always managed to brush them off and find some excuse to avoid intimacy. She had wanted to keep her life simple with just her and Crystal. She had her daughter, her job, a horse and wonderful parents. Crystal was about to change all that, and now Britany no longer wanted to be alone. But that meant she would have to let down some of the wall she had built. The thought was disturbing.

She finally managed to swoop her hair up into a swirl, but a few strands escaped. She used the curling iron to shape them into ringlets framing her face and then told herself to relax. David Goldstein was a wonderful friend, and that's the way things would stay. The doorbell rang as she finished, and she hurried to answer it.

"You look great!" Dr. Goldstein said admiringly. The soft velvet dress touched her shape lightly as it flowed to her knees. Rhinestones edged the demure scooped neckline and continued along the daring v-shaped back where a satin bow rested near her waist.

He kissed her cheek lightly, trying not to disturb her make-up. She blushed when his hand touched the bare skin of her back. Britany wished she had made another choice in dresses. She excused herself to get her purse and coat. Maybe I will end up wearing my coat all night, she thought as he helped her put it on.

"You know, Britany, since this is our second date, maybe you should call me David instead of Dr. Goldstein," he said as they turned leave.

"But it seems a little disrespectful-too personal," Britany stammered foolishly.

"It is my name, and maybe I want it to be a little more personal," David looked deep into her eyes.

Britany smiled back hesitantly and looked away.

Before she knew it she was standing nervously in front of a spreading estate belonging to one of David's colleagues.

"Relax, Britany. Just be your charming self. Don't let the size of the house intimidate you," he said with a protective arm around her.

"I didn't realize my nervousness showed so much."

"I can tell when you're nervous. Your lip quivers slightly." He reached up and softly placed a finger on her lips. "Not a lot, and most wouldn't notice, but I've seen you work under pressure when a certain obstetrician comes in the nursery and starts demanding immediate help."

"I thought that was anger!" Britany said, unconsciously taking a step back. "Is your home this magnificent?"

"No. Pediatricians don't make nearly as much as vascular surgeons," he laughed. Britany looked up quickly as the butler opened the door to allow their entrance.

"David! So glad to see you! Who is this beautiful lady at your side?" came a woman's voice from another room as David and Britany stepped past the door that the butler held. The woman walked gracefully toward them and held out her hand in welcome. Before David could speak, a distinguished-looking man stood beside the woman and added his opinion.

"Wow, David, where did you find this gorgeous little lady?"

"This is Britany. She is a nurse at the hospital. She works in the nursery," David said. He started to introduce the hosts to Britany when another man broke in.

"She's got brains too. David, you had better hang on to her!"

The same comments seemed to flow whenever David tried to introduce her by the time dinner was over Britany was angry and didn't feel like she could handle another comment. She grabbed David's hand and pulled him into a secluded room.

"What is it with all these comments about my looks!" she whispered fiercely. She didn't want to attract anymore attention that what she already seemed to be getting.

"Did you invite me here as some kind of trophy? Is that what you had in-mind to have someone who looks good to accompany you on your social functions? And, of course, I qualify as brainy, too, since I am a nurse!"

"Britany, you sell yourself short. You aren't just good-looking--you are beautiful!"

"Being beautiful isn't exactly the reason one wants to be invited to a dinner party," Britany blurted out and turned sharply to leave.

"Britany, stop. Please wait. I'm sorry I got carried away. The fact is you are beautiful, and people notice. I didn't mean to make you feel bad. My friends didn't either. They meant well. Most women would take it as a compliment," David said, grabbing her arm to get her to stop.

"Maybe most of the other women you date don't have brains to go with their beauty!" Britany's eyes flashed with anger and indignation.

"Now, that's not fair, Britany," David said sternly and stared coldly at her.

"I want to go home now, David," said Britany, not backing down from his stare.

"Fine!" he shot back and went to get their coats. He excused himself and Britany and walked her to the car.

The ride home was full of tension. Neither David nor Britany said a word. David dropped her off and promptly left. Britany was too angry to try to sleep. She got in her Saturn and drove to her parents' farm. When she arrived, she went straight to the barn. The smell of fresh hay greeted her, and her horse Misty whinnied as she opened the door. She quickly crossed the length of the barn to Misty's stall. Entering, she buried her face in Misty's warm, soft neck, threw her arms around her horse, and cried.

"Why did I agree to go to that dinner party? Why do I even care? Oh, Misty, I'm so confused. I really do want to have a husband and a family. I don't want to be alone the rest of my life, but it is so hard. It scares me. Why can't I find someone to love me? I really thought he cared, but if he did, he wouldn't have gotten so angry." Misty nuzzled her shoulder as if in understanding. Britany dried her tears and turned to go to the house. "It looks like it's just you and me now, girl."

CHAPTER 3

Britany awoke the next morning to the sound of her mother preparing breakfast. She heard her father come in the back door. She hurriedly threw on some jeans and a T-shirt, and then she went downstairs to the kitchen.

"Are you finished with the chores already?" Liz Becker asked in surprise as her husband, Charles, leaned over and peered into the pan of eggs she was frying. Charles Becker kissed his wife's cheek, snatched a slice of bacon from a plate on the counter, and shook his head as he ate.

"The feeder calves still need to be fed, but I thought Britany might help me finish. Misty wants to see her pretty bad," said Charles with a smile at his daughter.

"Sure, you know I love to help." Britany smiled back and hoped her parents didn't notice that her eyes were swollen from crying and the lack of sleep.

She crossed the room and gave a warm hug to each of her parents. Her father was a handsome man at sixty, with broad shoulders, gray hair and blue eyes that twinkled when he laughed. He smelled of outdoors, and his chin was rough with stubble. His beard grew fast, and Britany always remembered him with a slight shadow even after a fresh shave.

Britany and Charles left the farmhouse and crossed the gravel drive to reach the barn. The white house with green shutters and the red barn stood as majestic and proud as they had one hundred years ago when they were first built. Their presence gave Britany a feeling of security. They had seen many hard times and still stood strong.

The barn was dark as Britany and her father entered. The rays of dawn hadn't reached the windows yet. The smell of sweet hay permeated the air. Britany could hear the munching of the cows. It was a warm, inviting atmosphere. Charles switched on the lights, and the sound of bawling calves anxious for their meal poured forth. Britany climbed the ring ladder to the loft and threw down several bales of hay which her father started to distribute. She loved the barn and the cows. It was peaceful here. The cows were never in a hurry, and it compelled her to relax. She had spent many hours in the barn sorting through troubled thoughts, much as she had the night before. She hurried back down the ladder and helped spread the hay and grain to the hungry calves.

Misty heard her voice and whinnied a familiar greeting. Charles looked at her, smiled and said, "Go ahead, I'll finish. Someone else is glad to see you."

With no hesitation Britany crossed to the other end of the barn where the stalls were located. Misty looked eagerly at her, her eyes large and dark as she tossed her head in anticipation. The horse's beautiful blond mane bobbed up and down and revealed a lustrous copper-colored head and neck. Britany gave her a fond pat and emptied a scoop of grain into her manger.

She lovingly brushed Misty as the horse ate. Britany had to stretch to reach over Misty's shoulder as she groomed her slender body. She then cleaned the stall. It opened to the outside, and Misty was able to spend a good deal of time outside in the pasture. That made it easier for Britany's parents to care for her. They simply fed the horses twice a day when they fed the cows. Britany came several times a week to clean the stalls.

When she had finished she went over to the other stall that contained her friend Jeanne's black gelding, Trigger, and a pinto pony called Sissy. The gelding was a huge thoroughbred mix which Jeanne rode for jumping. Britany fed them and cleaned their stalls so that there would be more time to ride when Jeanne came later.

Crystal called the farm and talked to her grandmother while Britany was in the barn. She assured her grandmother that she and her friend had arrived safely. She told Liz that she and her friends were busy and not in their room much, so it would be hard to reach her. "Tell Mom that I am fine and will see her Monday night," she told Liz before hanging up.

Jeanne arrived around ten as Britany was preparing to saddle Misty.

As the car came to a stop, a little girl pushed open the car door, ran to Britany, and threw herself into her arms.

"Britany! Mom brought a picnic. She brought my favorite juice and said I could ride to your favorite spot and drink it!" Her dark eyes sparkled. She wore a big smile that radiated across rosy cheeks. Even at six she felt light as Britany lowered her to the ground.

The little girl was Amy, Jeanne's only child. Since Jeanne's husband had died three years earlier, Jeanne and Amy had come out to the farm often and spent many weekends with Britany and her parents. Britany's parents adored Amy, and she called them Grandma Liz and Grandpa Charles. Jeanne's parents lived far away and were rather reserved and stiff. Jeanne rarely traveled to see them. Amy was very close to her father's parents, but they were also far away. They visited frequently and loved to have her spend a week with them each summer.

Liz appeared from the barn and called out, "Amy, I haven't gathered the eggs yet or fed the goats. Would you like to help me?"

"Sure," answered Amy as she ran to give Liz a big hug, her brown hair flying in the wind.

Britany looked at her mother and smiled. She knew her mother had purposely waited for Amy to arrive to do those chores. It would give Jeanne and Britany time to do some riding before Amy joined them on her pony.

Britany mounted Misty as Jeanne headed for the barn to get ready to ride. Misty was prancing about, anxious to run. Britany held her to a posting trot until Misty warmed up a bit and relaxed. The cool breeze brushed Britany's face and played with her shimmering hair. Misty's muscles rippled across her shoulders as her feet rhythmically fell in sequence. Britany worked her in circle eights and then in several circles of various sizes. With each direction change Britany bounced twice in the saddle and then resumed posting in sequence with the horse's rise and fall. She then pushed slightly with the heel of her outside foot, the one closest to the rail. Misty immediately broke into a smooth canter. Misty enjoyed it as much as Britany. They were a team and looked graceful as they performed together.

After working on walk, trot and canter, Britany stopped her parallel to the rail and guided her with her hands and legs to do a turn on the forehand. Pivoting her back end around while her front feet stayed in place, Misty executed the turn expertly. Britany then walked her to the center of the ring and signaled for her to go sideways by crossing the feet over each other. The first time she went sideways, but not by crossing the feet over each other. They tried several times without success and Misty started to prance and shake her head.

"Ok, girl, let's relax and try later," Britany spoke to Misty. They circled again, on the third time they were successful. Britany shouted enthusiastically and bent down to hug Misty's soft warm neck. Jeanne had entered the ring in time to see the new trick, and she vigorously cheered for them.

"Since you think you're such hot stuff, how about a race to that tree in the middle of the pasture?" challenged Jeanne.

"You're on! Just give the signal," responded Britany, accepting the challenge.

"Ready! Go!" yelled Jeanne.

Britany and Misty quickly took the lead, but Misty's agility was no match for Trigger's speed and strength. He soon pulled past them to establish a firm lead. Both women yelled and shouted as they flew past the tree and pulled their horses down to a slower canter back to the barn.

Amy was leading her pony out of the barn, and Liz walked beside them. Liz's work-boots peeked out from under blue coveralls that made a swishing sound as she walked. Her big smile was framed by short brown hair mixed with a touch of gray, and a ball cap sat on her head. Except for her definitely feminine curves, she could be mistaken for a man.

"Grandma Liz helped me saddle him up," Amy piped up. "Can we go for a long ride?"

"Let me get the lunch I packed for us, and then we can have a picnic. It's warm enough today," said Jeanne. She dismounted gracefully and handed the reins to Liz, who gladly accepted and petted Trigger on his velvety nose. He nuzzled her hand, looking for a treat.

"Sorry, Trigger, I don't have any carrots today," said Liz warmly.

"He looks so disappointed," said Britany with a laugh.

The ride was a leisurely one. Each rider pointed out budding trees, green patches of vegetation or an occasional rabbit or squirrel. The songs of various birds filled the air as they found the trail down by the small winding river. They crossed where the water was shallow. The horses picked their way through the water, splashing their riders' pant legs. They had ridden a short distance after crossing the river when the horses suddenly stopped, and their ears shot to attention. Britany could feel Misty's breathing increase, her body tense and tremble. Britany's eyes scanned the woods in the direction the horses were looking, and she could see two deer behind several trees.

"It's ok, girl, it's only some deer. They aren't about to hurt you." As Britany spoke the deer stopped and looked at them.

One had a good-sized velvet rack. He snorted loudly, which made Misty jump sideways and kick up her heels as the deer ran off into the woods. Britany's heart skipped a couple of beats as all of a sudden she felt air under her instead of a horse. She grabbed a clump of Misty's mane to pull herself into the saddle as she struggled to control her balance. Jeanne's horse was prancing about, and she had her hands full to keep him from bolting in the opposite direction. Amy's pony quietly stood and watched as if to say, "What are you two big horses so afraid of?"

"I thought you two were going to be on the ground," giggled Amy. "Weren't they so beautiful!" she continued with a touch of awe.

"They were beautiful, all right, but I'm afraid I didn't get to see too much of them," replied Britany with a laugh.

"I think we need a break. How about lunch?" asked Jeanne.

"Sounds great!" both Amy and Britany agreed.

Lunch consisted of juice, grapes, crackers and cheese sticks. The horses grazed as their riders sat on a log and relaxed, taking their time and chatting as they ate. When Amy had finished her lunch, she wandered off to explore the area.

"Britany, you look like things didn't go too well last night. What happened?" Jeanne asked as they munched grapes. She was always straightforward and honest. Britany appreciated that in her.

"I was hoping it didn't show too much," Britany said meekly.

"Well, we are close, and I can tell things when others can't, but you would have to be blind not to see something is bothering you. Your forced smile can't hide those swollen eyes."

"I've dated so many guys that liked me for my looks or wanted more than I was willing to give. I thought he would be different," Britany said, staring at the ground with a look of disgust on her face. "We've always been good friends. I thought he liked me. He just wanted to show me off at the party we went to and make himself look good."

"Wait a minute, Britany!" said Jeanne sitting up to face Britany. "I thought you and Dr. Goldstein were just friends and that you were just having a meal between friends, as I remember being told."

"I'm sorry, Jeanne. He took me to a dinner party last night on a, quote, official date." Britany shrugged her shoulders. "I knew you told me not to go, so I didn't tell you. You were right. I am getting too involved, or let's put it was. Last night he burst my bubble, so to speak."

"Well, the fact that you didn't tell me is beside the point. I'm not trying to be mean. I just don't want you to get hurt." Jeanne waved her hand emphatically. "I guess it's a little too late for that, but what you described doesn't sound like Dr. Goldstein," Jeanne said thoughtfully.

"His name is David, and I didn't think so either, but I found out different," Britany said angrily and kicked at a clump of dirt with her boot.

"Tell me what happened," Jeanne said quietly.

"We went to the party, and the first thing out of the host and hostess was how pretty I was and how I was such a good catch. Then someone found out I was a nurse, and they decided I was smart, too." Britany snapped a twig and threw the pieces to the ground. "'Brains and beauty, boy, David, you had better not let this one get away!' I was getting so angry I took him aside to talk to him. I told him I didn't appreciate being brought to the party because I was pretty. He said I wasn't just pretty, I was beautiful! I got really mad and insisted he take me home." Britany rested her head on her hand as she sat Indian-style on the ground. "Then he got mad. We didn't say another word to each other the rest of the night He dropped me off, and I came straight to the farm."

"Britany, you know that I don't think it is good for you to get romantically involved with Dr. Goldstein, but it is not because of his character. He is a very sensitive man who is truly devoted to his career. I think he's in the same situation you are. He is probably at the point in his life where he feels that if he doesn't find someone soon he never will. I'm sure his expectations are high, but I just can't believe beauty is one of them. He respects you, and you both get along very well. I think you jumped to conclusions. I'm sure he didn't feel very flattered that you thought he was only interested in you because you are cute."

"So you think I should rethink my attitude toward David and his friends?" Britany asked, doubt crossing her face.

"Most definitely," Jeanne nodded.

"I will try. I guess maybe I jumped to conclusions because I'm scared and confused. I just want to be loved, Jeanne. I want to find someone who loves me! I've always had Crystal to be concerned about, but now she is grown and doesn't need me anymore. I always thought I would find someone who loves me and someone I could love in return. We could have a family together, but I thought it could wait. Maybe I waited too long. Now it looks like I'm going to be an old maid," Britany said sadly. She looked off into the distance, only half seeing Amy playing with some sticks as the horses grazed nearby.

"Britany, you are trying too hard to control the circumstances in your life. God will show you when the right man comes along, and if He wants you to be single, then He will help you be content with that. Don't try to make it happen," Jeanne said.

"Jeanne, you had a wonderful husband. How do you survive knowing you loved someone so much, and then he died?" Britany asked in frustration, and then was immediately sorry. She suddenly felt ashamed for complaining while Jeanne was the one who had faced the real heartaches.

"God was with me then, and He still is now. It is only through Him that I live day by day. Of course, it helps to have a great friend like you," Jeanne said. She reached over and gave Britany's hand a squeeze.

"It is so like you to help me see things more clearly. Please don't ever leave. I need you," Britany pleaded.

"I don't plan on going anywhere for a long time," her friend smiled in response.

"Except maybe back! I think the horses have finished off what little bit of grass was here," Britany said. Jeanne called Amy, and they all mounted up and rode back.

Sunday morning dawned bright with promise. Britany stretched her slender arms and legs as she enjoyed a minute more of the warmth and coziness of her old bed.

Praise the Lord, all the earth. All that has breath Praise the Lord. I lift my eyes to the hills, where does my help come from? My help comes from the Lord, maker of heaven and earth. He who watches over you will never slumber or sleep. Portions of Psalms 100 filled her heart. She reached her hand toward heaven and squeezed an unseen hand and whispered softly. "Thank you, Jesus, for your never-ending love."

Donning a sweatshirt and jeans she headed downstairs to make breakfast for her parents who were at their chores early to be done before church.

Liz watched Britany as she drove out the driveway Sunday afternoon to return to Dayton. It had been easy when Britany was little to help her when she was hurting, but life was a little more complicated now. When Britany became pregnant with Crystal she started to wrap herself in a protective shell and only let a select few in. Men were excluded from her private circle, except for her father and brother. Liz had been praying for a husband for Britany to share her life with since she was old enough to sing lullabies to. From the look on Britany's face during the weekend Liz was afraid the husband Liz had prayed for wasn't the one Britany had on her mind. Liz shook her head sadly as the car disappeared in the distance.

CHAPTER 4

On Monday morning Britany pushed through the heavy door of the scrub room, using her shoulder to keep her hands clean. She had given it much thought, and Jeanne was right. She had been too hard on David. She had known him too long to accuse him of being shallow. Now she just had to find the right way to apologize. He would be in soon for morning rounds, and Britany's stomach was in knots about what to do.

"Wow! Someone must be pretty special!" said Britany as she walked up to a large bouquet of red roses sitting on the nursing desk.

"I wonder who that someone could be or what that someone did to deserve those," said Shawn, the secretary. Her blue eyes twinkled with mischief. Britany walked up to the roses and breathed deeply of their sweet aroma. There was a card in the midst of the roses, and it had her name on it.

"Are you going to share with us why you are so special?" Shawn asked and winked.

"I'm afraid I wasn't so nice, and this should be from me, not to me," Britany said solemnly. She knew who the flowers were from even before she opened the card.

Britany looked up to see David looking on from the door of Nursery 1.

"I'm sorry," she said quietly as her eyes met his. She walked over to where he stood. "I acted pretty stupid. The roses are beautiful, but I really don't deserve them."

"Britany, you are a very special person, and you deserve better treatment than what I showed you," David said quietly. "Could we start over again with dinner tonight at seven?"

"Sure, that sounds nice," Britany answered lightly.

"Thanks," said David. "I'll see you then. I think we are making a scene." He looked over her shoulder and grinned at the crowd of nurses gathered at the nurses' desk watching them.

Britany laughed. "I'm sure we are. See you at seven." She turned and went to the desk to join the others for report.

The day went quickly, and Britany was soon heading for her home. Crystal wasn't home when Britany telephoned before leaving work so she went to the YMCA to exercise. Crystal still wasn't home when Britany arrived at her house. She missed her and hoped she would be home soon.

Britany had just stepped out of the shower when she heard Crystal's exuberant voice.

"Mom, I'm home!"

"I'm in the shower. I will be right out!" Britany shouted.

Britany wrapped her hair in a towel and slipped into her bathrobe.

"Well, how was the campus?" asked Britany as she gave Crystal a hug.

Crystal's gray-green eyes shone as she excitedly chattered about all her adventures.

"The campus is huge, and the stadium is unbelievable!" Crystal was taller than her mother and bigger built. She took after her father's side.

"That's how I felt the first time I saw it!" said Britany.

Crystal sat on the couch, her lovely blonde hair spread across her shoulders.

"It was hard to remember how to get back to where we were staying! I hope I can find my classes all right," said Crystal.

"That could be a definite problem," said Britany. She could remember the wave of black gowns and hats marching across the field at her brother's graduation. From where she had been seated she could barely see them. They had looked like the little plastic graduation person on top of a cake. She had marveled at her brother's ability to get around campus and graduate with his masters. Now her Crystal was going to be living on that massive campus!

"We were able to see some of the classes," Crystal said, bringing Britany back to the present. "I loved the labs with all the new equipment. You wouldn't believe the computers they have! They can do things I never dreamed computers can do. We went to a fraternity party Friday night and met the cutest guy. His name is Ron. He's six feet tall with the broadest shoulders!" Her beautiful blonde hair seemed to emphasize her outgoing personality. Crystal reminded Britany of her father when he was that age. Britany often prayed for Crystal as she started college that she would temper her zest for life with a bit more responsibility than her father had.

"He has blond hair and blue eyes," Crystal continued. "We talked and talked Friday night. Then he picked me up on Saturday at noon, and we walked along the river. The grass was green and soft and there were some tulips blooming. There were also a few trees with green buds. Oh, Mom, it was so romantic! We bought sandwiches and had a picnic. Then Saturday night he brought some friends, and the girls and I went with them to the movies."

Britany walked around the counter to give her daughter a big hug.

"It all sounds wonderful, but it seems to me you were more impressed by Ron than the campus!" laughed Britany.

"Oh, Mom. He was great, but he lives across state, and I may never see him again! I do have his address, though."

Crystal was still chatting when Britany noticed the time.

"Oh my goodness ! It's almost seven," said Britany, jumping up. "David will be here any minute. Crystal, I hate to do this, but I have to go get ready," said Britany.

"Mom! Who is David?"

"Dr. Goldstein. He is taking me to dinner," Britany said looking back over her shoulder as she hurried to her bedroom. "Have you eaten yet?"

"Sure, we ate on the way home. I thought I was the one who was supposed to run out on you. I'm not so sure I like the idea of you leaving me!"

"Crystal, stop that mock pouting. Your turn is coming soon enough. You were probably planning on going out tonight anyway."

"Actually, you are half right. Sabrina and I were going to study. She is coming here, though. I don't plan on going anywhere."

"Good. You talk to David for me if he gets here before I am finished."

Britany rushed to her room to get ready. Fortunately David was late, and he arrived just as Britany was applying the final touches. He smiled warmly when she answered the knock at the door and she wondered how she had ever accused him the way she had.

She welcomed him in. "David, you know my daughter, Crystal," said Britany, smiling at Crystal.

"Sure! I heard you went to visit the big campus this weekend," said David, crossing the room to shake Crystal's hand.

"Yeah. It was great! So you are finally taking my mother on a date. It's about time!" laughed Crystal.

"Sh! She doesn't date, remember?" David whispered in her direction. "We are just going to a friendly dinner," David continued.

"Gotcha!" Crystal nodded. "Well, have fun and have her home before midnight. She's a working Mom, remember."

"I'll be sure she's not out too late," agreed David.

"Good night, Crystal!" Britany said and gave her a sideways glance. "I'll remember this if Ron ever comes to visit."

"Mom, you wouldn't!" Crystal grabbed her mother's arm in protest.

"Come on, David. I'm hungry!" Britany laughed.

"I'll try to put in a good word for you, Crystal," said David as they left and waved good-bye.

Britany was surprised when he took her to his place instead of to a restaurant. His house wasn't as grand as the mansion they had gone to for the party, but it didn't fall too far below it in splendor. They walked through a chandeliered entry to a dining room with cherry furnishings and an elegant oriental rug. The table was set for two. Glowing candles accentuated the warmth of the brown red color. Britany looked at David questioningly.

"Don't fear," David spoke up when he saw her puzzled look. "I had my housekeeper fix the meal. I didn't plan on cooking tonight although I do so very well, if I can be so bold as to brag. I wanted tonight, to be special with someplace where we could be alone to talk."

"I think that is a wonderful idea! It seems a lack of communication kind of got us in a tough spot last time."

He seated her at the table and left through the side door. Soon a neatly dressed elderly lady appeared following him back through the door with a tray of food.

"Britany, this is Edith. She's been with me for several years and is like a second mother to me," said David. "Edith, this is Britany."

"It's nice to meet you, Edith," said Britany. "The table and food are lovely."

"Thank you. Enjoy your meal." Edith continued to serve them food until the dinner was finished and the dishes collected. Then David dismissed her for the night. He led Britany into a large living room lit by a warm fireplace burning at the other end. He guided her to a leather sofa and asked her to sit, taking a seat beside her.

"The meal was lovely," Britany told David with a smile. "I think your idea of being alone together was a very good one. It's hard to get time alone to talk, and our last date was rather complicated by the other people involved," she finished.

"My thoughts exactly. I want you to get a chance to know me for myself and not for what others may seem to think or say," David replied.

"David, we have been friends long enough that I feel I have a pretty good idea of what you are like." Britany looked down at her hands resting in her lap. "I'm just sorry I let the circumstances color what I thought of you instead of relying on what I knew in my heart. Please forgive me." She looked up into his dark eyes. He took her hand in his, and she looked down at his long fingers. They were clean with well-shaped nails. She had seen his hands work many times and appreciated the skill with which his long slender fingers could agilely perform procedures on tiny newborns.

"I'm glad it happened," he said quietly. Britany looked at him in surprise.

"Sometimes I think we get along too easily, and it was good to know we can work through difficulties. Britany, have you given much thought to the future?"

"It seems that is all I think about these days. My daughter is leaving in less than six months, and for the first time in my life I am going to be alone. The thought scares me to death," Britany said, looking into the fire as the orange and yellow flames danced around.

David released her hand and placed his arm around her shoulder, pulling her close.

"You know, Britany, working in the nursery and being around babies all the time, do you ever think about having more children?" he asked.

"I think about it. I love babies, and it's hard not to think about it."

"I know a way in which you wouldn't have to be alone and could have more children," David said and softly kissed the top of her head. Her hair was soft and smelled fragrant. "I've been alone for a long time, and, to be truthful, I am quite tired of it. I want someone to share my life with me, and I very much want a family. You are a wonderful person, Britany. I can't think of anyone who would make a better wife or mother." Britany was stunned. What was he saying? Did he actually mean what he said? Her heart raced and her chest felt tight.

"Don't you think you're rushing things a bit?" Britany stammered. "We have only dated a few times."

"We've known each other for fifteen years. Do you think more time is going to make a difference?" David questioned. He looked at her with sincerity in his eyes. She looked back at him and turned slightly to face him.

"No, I guess not," she said quietly. She looked into the fire and then back at David. "You seem to have thought about this, and perhaps you have put me on a bit of a pedestal, but you didn't mention love. Is love involved in this proposal?" she asked firmly. Her palms outstretched toward him.

"Do you love me?" he asked, taking both her hands in his. His hands felt warm and secure and even though Britany knew she didn't love him romantically she did feel something for him. She felt very confused.

"David, I don't know. You are a wonderful friend, and in that way I love you dearly, but I'm not so sure it is in a romantic way." She looked up at him helplessly. Her bottom lip quivered.

David placed his hand under her chin and kissed her warmly.

"I'm not asking you to love me that way. A lot of marriages have romantic love and end up disastrous. We have something many marriages never find." He removed his arm from her shoulder and reached into his pocket. He drew out a black velvet box, and opened it to reveal a dazzling diamond ring.

"Britany, will you marry me?" He took her hand, and his black eyes seemed to bore right through her.

She looked at the ring. He was making her an offer, a logical well though out offer. It was much different from any proposal she had ever dreamed of. She sat in silence for a very long time. "No!" her heart screamed inside her. This isn't what you want! But I may never get what I want, and this is very close to it, she argued with herself. She closed her eyes and then opened them and looked at the ring again. During her silence he took the ring out of the box and placed it on her finger. It fit perfectly.

She looked at him in amazement.

"How did you get it to fit?"

"This isn't the first time I've thought of this; it's just the first time I have actually had the nerve to go through with it. I've seen your hands and your fingers many times. I'm a doctor. I notice things. I know this may not be the romantic proposal you have dreamed about or even deserve, but I love you and want you for my wife," said David, continuing to hold her hand.

"Your love for me is as a friend, too, isn't it?" she asked.

"Yes, is that bad?"

"I don't know. It just seems almost too logical. You must really care for me, though, to go through with all this and be careful enough to get the right size!" Britany said almost pleading.

"Britany, I do care. Please marry me! We can make it work. I'm sure of it!"

David took Britany's other hand and held them both tight. "Say yes."

Britany looked at the ring and then up at David. She couldn't bring herself to say yes, but at the same time she couldn't bring herself to take the ring off and give it back. He was offering her what she wanted most in life at this time: an escape from the fear of loneliness, a husband, a family. How could she logically turn it down? "Ok, I guess we can make it work," she said quietly. David smiled and held her tight. A tear streamed down the side of her face, and she wasn't sure if it was from joy or sadness.

Later, at home, Britany stared at the diamond ring as she lay in bed. She thought of David and what he was offering her. His sensitivity and caring touched her heart. Maybe he was right. Maybe it would work. She touched the ring lightly and reached over to turn off the light. Tonight she felt excited and just a bit confused, but the ring offered her the security she had been looking for.

The next day at work she carried the ring in a little pouch tucked securely in her pocket, but she didn't show it to anyone or tell anyone of the proposal. She needed time to think, to sort things out. To her relief Jeanne was working in a different area. Jeanne would have been able to see right through her and know something was going on.

Britany invited David for dinner at her place when she saw him on morning rounds.

"I guess maybe you had better sample my cooking. You may change your mind," Britany said.

"I'm sure you are a great cook, but it wouldn't matter if you aren't. My housekeeper cooks wonderfully and I couldn't bear to put her out of a job after all these years," David said with ease.

How can he seem so calm and nonchalant, thought Britany, when every inch of me is a bundle of nerves?

Britany's anxiety only worsened as the day wore on and it was time for supper. Crystal helped Britany with the meal. Britany kept the ring tucked away. She wasn't ready to tell even Crystal yet. Crystal excused herself shortly before David arrived, stating that she had homework to work on at a friend's house. Britany knew she used homework as an excuse to give her mother some time alone with David. Britany wished she would stay She wanted desperately to confide in Crystal but didn't feel it was time.

The doorbell rang, and Britany hurried to answer it. The anxiety faded as she looked up into David's smiling face. There was comfort in his presence that she was beginning to appreciate.

"It smells good!" said David as Britany led him into the room.

"Crystal helped me with the meal but then left to go to a friend's house I think she thought we might like to be alone," Britany offered him a seat on the couch. "Would you like some iced tea?"

"That sounds good," David said as he sat on the couch. "Crystal was very thoughtful, although I was hoping to get to know her a little better."

"I hadn't thought about that, or I would have tried to get her to stay. I don't imagine she thought about it that way," said Britany as she poured the tea over ice.

"Where is your ring?" asked David, a bit concerned. He walked up beside her.

"Oh, I'm sorry. It's in this little pouch." She withdrew the pouch from her pocket and placed the ring on her finger. "We aren't allowed to wear rings at work and I wanted to keep it safe. I just hadn't put it on yet."

"That looks better. I was a little worried,." he said as he wrapped his arms around her. "Apparently you didn't tell anyone at work about our engagement."

"No, if I said anything to anyone everyone would know, and I wanted at least one day before the commotion started. I hope you don't mind."

"No, I like sharing the secret between ourselves. You are right about everyone knowing. That is exactly how I knew you didn't tell anyone. I was kind of afraid I was going to get mobbed as soon as I entered the nursery. Instead it was reasonably normal except for the fact that I couldn't help looking for you the moment I entered the door." He pulled her close, kissing her on the cheek.

"You are sweet," Britany answered.

The meal went well, and Britany felt some of her anxiety melt away. He was kind and considerate, a perfect gentleman. He was thoughtful of her feelings. Maybe they were just good friends now, but there was always the chance that love would grow. At least she wouldn't be alone.

They finished dinner and talked easily. David walked over and looked at some of the special treasures Britany kept on a bookshelf in the corner. He picked up a little plastic replica of praying hands that glowed in the dark.

"I know it doesn't look very impressive, but Crystal got that from Bible school when she was five years old. She recited the Lord's Prayer, and that was the reward. I was very proud of her," said Britany with warm memories of Crystal at age five, her chubby hand grasping the prize and her cheeks glowing with excitement.

She looked at David and suddenly realized that he wasn't smiling. In fact, he wore a strange expression.

"Britany, I think there is something we need to talk about," he said solemnly.

Britany panicked at the look on his face. Whatever could she have said to cause him to react this way?

He replaced the treasure and continued. "It just occurred to me that we haven't discussed one very important issue. I respect the way you believe, and I sense the same from you, but, Britany, I don't believe in Jesus other than He may have been a knowledgeable man. I don't mind that you believe in Him--that is up to you--but I wouldn't want you telling our children about Him. We can share the Old Testament and teach them from it, but the Messiah hasn't come yet, and I wouldn't want you filling their heads with anything else." He stood in front of her, and looked down at her with his hands on his hips. His black eyes were stern.

"You mean I couldn't tell my babies about Jesus? I couldn't teach them the song Jesus Loves Me?" Britany looked up into his stormy eyes. "I couldn't take them to Sunday school with me or Bible school in the summer? David, I couldn't do that!" Britany said horrified. "Jesus means more to me than anything, and there is no way I could not tell my children about Him. It is part of my being a mother. I just can't separate the two!" Britany looked from the praying hands to David. She couldn't believe what she had heard. She had thought a little about the problems the two of them might encounter, but she had never once considered the children they had talked about. Now she could see what Jeanne had tried to warn her about. Even if they never had children, she and David would never be close. How could they be close when she belonged to Christ, and David didn't even admit He existed?

"It won't work will it?" Britany said hoarsely.

"Not if that is how you feel and I can't change your mind," he said. He sat beside her and took her hand in his. He squeezed gently. His eyes softened. "Britany, are you sure you can't accept me and not insist on making Jesus an issue?"

"I'm sorry, David, I can't. And even if I did, I wouldn't be the same person that I am now." Britany looked up at him with a tear in her eye and conviction in her heart. She reached down and quietly slipped the ring off her finger. She placed it in his hand and looked up into his eyes. "You keep this for your partner in life. Someone who can share your views, someone you can love for more than just a friend. You are a very unique person and will make someone a wonderful husband."

"I'm sorry, Britany. Do you think we can still be friends?" His dark eyes were moist, and his hand trembled slightly.

"I think that is what we are best at! We will never stop being friends." Britany kissed him on the cheek and rested her cheek against his. He sighed and stood up.

"Goodnight, Britany," said David and reached down to kiss her on the forehead.

"Goodnight," said Britany as she watched him walk out the door.

She heard the car start and listened to the sound as it drove off into the night.

She dropped to her knees and prayed.

"Dear Lord, I am so sorry I didn't listen to You. The fear of being alone the rest of my life became more important than listening to what You had in store for my life. Lord, if You want me to remain single for the rest of my life, I will." She paused and looked up, then added in anguish through blurred eyes, "But Lord, please don't ask me to!"

CHAPTER 5

Britany knew she had made the right decision as she prepared for work the next morning, but she felt lost and alone. She had trouble concentrating on work during the day. Even though she had felt hesitant about David's proposal, it had offered her a sense of security and feeling wanted. She found it harder than ever to face the prospect of spending the rest of her life alone. That night she went to the YMCA and worked out with a vigor borne of frustration.

Crystal was busy and came home late. They talked before going to bed.

"Mom, can I spend the night at Sabrina's tomorrow night?" Crystal asked. "We have a term paper due, and we're working on it together."

"Crystal, it's a school night," Britany protested. "And you've been gone all night tonight."

"Mom, I'm going to be on my own in a few months. I don't think staying overnight at someone's house on a school night is a big deal. Besides, I promise we'll go to bed early and not stay up all night."

Britany looked at Crystal. How could she possibly tell her the reason she didn't want her to go to Sabrina's house was that she didn't want to be alone?

"Mom, you could invite David over, and I won't be around to bother you."

Britany grimaced, but tried to hide it. She realized that she needed to sort things out before she told Crystal that she was no longer dating David.

"I guess it's all right. If you promise to go to bed early," Britany said.

"Thanks, Mom," she said and gave Britany a peck on the cheek. "Good night. You have a fun evening tomorrow night."

"Good night, Crystal. You, too."

Britany dropped into a chair when Crystal left the room. "Dear Lord," she prayed. "I know I was trying to fill the emptiness on my own and not waiting for you. Please forgive me. I am feeling more alone now than I did before. Please give me the strength and courage I need to get through this time. Amen."

The next day at work was very busy. Shelly was off for the day, and Britany took her place as charge nurse. The morning passed quickly, to Britany's relief. It gave her something to occupy her mind. Every time she thought of spending the evening alone she cringed. Labor and Delivery brought eight babies before noon and stated that there were more on the way. Britany looked at the schedule for the next shift during lunch. There was not enough staff scheduled to care for the number of babies they had. Britany picked up the phone and called the nursing supervisor, Lee Anne.

"Lee Anne, this is Britany from the nursery. We are getting babies faster than we can handle and there are more on the way. I looked at the staffing for afternoons, and it is definitely short. Are there any nurses available from one of the other floors?" asked Britany.

"I've been on the phone calling people already. I knew you would be needing some help. So far there is no one available. The other floors are busy, too. I'll keep trying. Check back with me in about an hour," Lee Anne said.

"OK, thanks, good luck." Britany hurried to help with a new admission in Nursery 1.

At one o'clock a nurse called in sick for afternoon's. Britany sat looking at the schedule. She called the nursing supervisor.

"I hate to tell you this, LeAnne, but a nurse called in sick for afternoon's. Have you had any luck finding someone to come in?" Britany asked.

"No. We have gone through the list, but no one is available. I think I can find you someone to float, though. Orthopedics is slow tonight."

"How does Peds look? Could you spare someone from there? They have several nurses who have worked here before."

"I'm afraid not. They aren't in much better shape than you are."

"One float would help, but we really need two. We need at least one who knows babies."

Britany looked at the schedule in front of her and thought about the situation. Actually she didn't want to spend the evening alone. This looked like the perfect solution.

"If you will OK it, I will work a double," Britany offered.

"That would be great. Sure, I'll OK it."

"Good. Let me know who is going to be floating when you find out, and I will get back to work on the next shift's schedule," Britany said. She felt relieved that it would work out, although she was tired already. She hadn't slept well since the night David had proposed, but she really didn't think she would be able to sleep even if she did go home on time. At least at the hospital she would be busy.

The night was busier than she had even expected it to be. She didn't get a chance to go to supper until seven, and when she did she just looked at her food. She hurried back to the floor and continued on from where she had stopped. Her feet hurt, her legs ached, and she was starting to get a headache. It still felt good to be needed, and she threw herself into her job.

Finally it was ten o'clock, and she only had an hour to go. She was busy admitting the newest baby girl when Dr. Goldstein arrived at the door. He was dressed in scrub clothes and held a tiny bundle in his arms. She looked up startled. He looked at her just as surprised.

"What are you doing still here?" he asked. "You should have gone home hours ago."

"We were really busy, and I worked a double. I'll be going home shortly."

He looked at the infant in his arms. "We need to weigh this infant quickly and get her under the warmer. I got called in on this delivery because the mother was early. She's small, but she is a trooper, and I couldn't see any immediate reason for her to go to the neonatal unit."

"Three pounds, eight ounces," Britany said as she weighed the baby. "They will probably want her to go to the unit if they find out she is here." She quickly took the infant from the scales to the warmer and placed her in the warmed crib.

David was at Britany's side examining the baby and listening to her heart and lungs. Britany did her own assessment as he worked.

"She's breathing well, and her heart is strong, although she has a loud murmur," Britany said. "Is she 34 weeks?"

"She's supposed to be 38 weeks, but I agree she looks more like 34. They were worried that the mother was measuring small, but it looks like maybe the dates were off. She went into labor on her own, and it went fast. I think the murmur is the foramen ovale which hasn't closed yet. That should close in the next few hours." David looked at her, half apologetic. "I know you have put in a big day and are short-staffed, but could you possibly keep her and give her a chance to see if she can hold on and not have to go to the unit?"

"Sure, I'll stay right with her. My last admission is almost done, and she is doing great." Britany took off her stethoscope and hooked it to the edge of the crib.

"The mom says the baby's name is Lauren. I have some charting to do. I'll stay in the hospital for a couple of hours to be sure she is doing all right before I leave." He suddenly looked older.

"You must be getting tired, too. You didn't get here much later than I did this morning," Britany said.

"It's my job. Besides I don't sleep much lately anyway." He looked at her.

Britany felt a lump form in her throat as she met his eyes, but didn't speak. He turned resolutely and left the room.

Britany did another quick set of vitals on Lauren. She was small but looked around attentively. Britany placed her little finger in the infant's palm to watch her hand close around it. "You are a precious little thing," she said quietly. The little fingers were dainty and tiny. They barely encircled Britany's finger. The infant's forearm wasn't any bigger than Britany's index finger.

Assured that Lauren was doing fine, Britany turned her attention to the other infant she was admitting and finished the admission. She sat down on the stool at the desk to chart on both babies. Suddenly she heard a rasping sound. She looked at Lauren and ran to her side. The infant was gasping for breath, and her color was ashen gray. Britany could see each individual rib with every breath she struggled to take.

"Dr. Goldstein!" Britany yelled. She turned on the oxygen and placed it to her face. She quickly took her stethoscope to listen for heart tones.

David appeared at the door in an instant and joined her.

"Her heart tones have shifted from the left to the right," said Britany.

"Quick, get the chest tube tray. It looks like a right pneumothorax," he said as he took the stethoscope and listened.

Other nurses were quickly in the room helping arrange supplies. Dr. Goldstein expertly inserted the needle between the tiny ribs, allowing the air to escape and allow her lungs to function again.

The infant's gasping breath relaxed to an easy inhale and exhale. Her color returned to pink.

"Order a chest x-ray to check placement. I guess we should call the neonatal unit for a transfer," said David. "I was really hoping she would do fine, but it's time for her to change homes."

Immediately nurses were running to follow the orders. Britany remained at

Lauren's side, refusing to take her eyes off her for an instant.

David stood with her until someone from x-ray appeared and took films.

"Don't leave her," David said to Britany. "I need to go to x-ray and read the films. The unit should be here shortly."

"Don't worry. I'll be here!" Britany listened to Lauren's chest again to check her lungs.

He had been gone about fifteen minutes when a resident from the neonatal unit came to get the infant. He was not much taller than Britany and had black hair slicked back on his head. He walked quickly with stiff movements.

"Where is this infant I am supposed to get?" he asked, looking past Britany.

Britany wasn't sure, but she thought his accent sounded as if he might be from New York. "She's right here," said Britany. "I'm sorry. I didn't catch your name."

"Dr. Macer," he said. "I don't see what the big deal is. She looks like she is doing fine to me."

Britany didn't recognize his face or his name but it did match the nametag he wore that identified him as a neonatal resident. "We aren't set up to take care of chest tubes," said Britany sternly. "It's routine that infants with chest tubes goes to your unit."

"Wrap her up and I'll take her," he said.

"Don't you want report?" asked Britany.

"I can read the chart." He grabbed Lauren's chart from the crib and flipped it under his arm.

"Where is the transport crib? And the oxygen?" Britany asked. She was getting perturbed at his abrupt behavior.

"If you would just get her wrapped up, I'll take her over there," he ordered loudly.

"You can't just take her," Britany said, upset by his arrogance and ignorance. "If she gets cold it could stress her and cause the other lung to blow!"

"You nurses are always trying to tell me my job. Move out of the way." Dr. Macer waved his arm in front of Britany to motion to her to move.

"No!" Britany exclaimed and moved to stand between him and Lauren. "You can't take her that way!" She stared at him.

"Go back to the unit and get the transfer crib and oxygen. Make sure it is warm!" Britany was surprised to hear Dr. Goldstein's stern voice coming from behind her.

The resident turned without another word, but his eyes glared at Britany and David as he left.

David put his hand on Britany's trembling shoulder. "Are you all right?"

"No, he was a jerk!" she exclaimed, her fists clenched tight.

"And you were right to hold your ground." David started to pull Britany close and then stopped and removed his arm from her shoulder. "Believe me, his attending will hear about this. This little girl needs to be handled with care, not just toted around. His actions could have been disastrous."

"You came back at just the right time. I don't know what else I could have done," Britany said, taking a deep breath to calm herself.

"Knowing you, you would have thought of something." He smiled. "Relax, the tube is in well, she is doing fine, and the unit should be back shortly. I will stay right here until she is safely transferred," David said.

It was a good half hour before someone came to get Lauren. The night shift had arrived, and Britany reported off on her other babies. She waited with Dr. Goldstein until they arrived. This time a nurse came, and she had the proper equipment.

"I'm sorry Dr. Macer acted the way he did. He gives all of us a hard time, and hopefully he won't be around too much longer," the nurse said.

"I think after I talk with the attending, his stay will be considerably shorter. He was endangering my patient's life," said David.

Britany's legs felt feeble as the infant was safely transported by the nurse with David as an escort. She knew her weakness came partly from exhaustion; partly from the excitement of the infant's condition, and partly from the arrogant resident. She made her way to the locker room without saying anything to anyone. She was too tired.

David was waiting for her as she left the locker room. "You look like you could use a friend," he said.

"You're right. Thanks," she smiled weakly. She felt extremely tired.

"I could give you a ride home," David offered.

Britany stopped and looked at him.

"Do you think we make the right decision?" he asked.

"Yeah, It's been hard, though," she said honestly.

"Yes, it has," he said. He looked tired. Britany took his arm, and together they walked down the hall to the elevators.

"Crystal is spending the night at a friend's house, and it seemed too lonely to spend the evening alone," Britany said softly.

"Is that why you worked a double?"

She nodded, "It was a good way to not be alone. It was also good to feel needed," Britany said.

"I'm glad you stayed. I don't think someone else would have reacted as quickly with that resident. Lauren will thank you."

Britany laughed, "Lauren will never know what went on, and neither will her mother."

"No, but we do," David said solemnly.

They left the building and walked to the parking lot.

"Thanks for the offer of the ride home, but I think I will be fine," said Britany.

They reached the car and Britany turned to face him. She reached up and softly kissed his cheek. He drew her tight in a long embrace.

"Good night, Britany," he said as he released her.

"Good night David." Britany unlocked her door and got into her car. David waved and watched as she started the car and backed out.

The drive home was short and soon she was home. She was very tired as she fell into bed. Sleep came swiftly, and soon the alarm was ringing. The night was a blur as she prepared for work.

"Britany, what in the world happened to you?" asked Jeanne as Britany entered the locker room.

"I worked a double yesterday."

"I'm sorry Britany, but you look like it is more than that." Jeanne put her arm around Britany's shoulders. "Do you want to talk about it?"

"I'm afraid it will take more time than we have now," Britany said quietly.

"I will meet you for break, and we will go some place quiet to talk," Jeanne said.

Britany saw David shortly after she received her assignment. He looked tired too.

"I just came from seeing Lauren. She did well through the night. They put her on a pip machine to help her breath. It looks like in a couple of days she will be able to get the tube out and will be breathing on her own. If she does well she will go home next week," David said.

"That's great! I'll go see her later."

"Did you sleep better last night?" asked David.

"I slept great it was just too short. I guess the excitement was good therapy," said Britany.

"I think that working together was good therapy."

"So we're going to help each other get through this time?"

"Why not? Who else would know any better what we are going through?"

"I guess you're right," said Britany.

"See you later. I have rounds to make. No working over tonight!"

"And no late night calls!"

"Right. I'm off tonight," said David and then left with a wave.

Jeanne, and Britany, went to lunch together. Britany told Jeanne everything that had happened.

"Britany! Why didn't you tell me?" asked Jeanne.

"When he gave me the ring I was too stunned to tell you," Britany said, as she shrugged her shoulders. "Later I felt too embarrassed. You tried to warn me."

"Oh Britany, of course I objected to you getting involved with David, but do you honestly think I have never done anything that went against my better judgment?"

"No."

Jeanne laughed and then added, "I warned you because I didn't want to see you get hurt, but I can understand why you did what you did, he's a wonderful person."

"Wonderful just isn't enough," sighed Britany.

Jeanne gave Britany a hug.

"You're going to get through this, just give yourself some time. You made the right decision."

"Thanks, I needed to hear that," Britany said with more confidence than what she felt.

CHAPTER 6

Jeanne was right. Each day seemed a little easier. Britany began to sleep better and her appetite returned. Crystal spent the weekend with a friend, and Britany was relieved to find that she didn't panic at the thought of being alone. She used the time to ride and enjoy having some time to herself. By the middle of the next week her confidence returned, and she felt she could begin to face the future again.

Britany awoke with the sun just beginning to color the sky. She showered and dressed, grabbed her gym bag and went downstairs to prepare breakfast. Crystal joined her for breakfast and together they read the Gospel of John, chapters seven and eight, for their morning devotions. Before leaving, Britany gave Crystal a quick hug, and reminded her that she would pick her up after school to go to the health spa.

Shelly was already in the locker room when Britany arrived at the hospital.

"Did you have a nice three-day weekend?" Britany asked Shelly.

"It was fun. Stan and I went to Lake Erie to check on our boat and be sure it wintered OK. It looked fine, and the weather was great. If this keeps up, we may put it in the water Easter week-end," answered Shelly, as she took off her blouse and exchanged it for a green surgical gown.

"Sounds nice. Some of the lucky ones get Easter off while the rest of us slave away," teased Betsy who was also getting ready for work.

Britany was finished changing, and together she, and Shelly walked to the scrub room. They continued their conversation during the two-minute scrub.

"How is Baby Andrew doing?" asked Shelly, opening a package of betadine scrub.

"Great. He's hungry all the time, and is not shy about letting us know it," said Britany light-heatedly, as she dried her arms with a towel.

Entering the main nursery, Britany smelled the aroma of fresh roasted coffee and noticed that someone had brought doughnuts.

"Hey what's the occasion?" asked Shelly as she and Britany joined the other nurses, who surrounded the coffee and doughnuts.

"We're having an in-service on heart-rate monitors," explained Carol, who had been in charge of the night shift. "We're trying a new company and the rep is here to give us training on how they work. He will give classes every two hours until five o'clock." She continued to give important information on the status of the nursery.

Report was fast, and soon Britany was entering the admission nursery with Shelly, who had been assigned with her. Britany was caught off guard as her gaze fell on a man bent over a heart-rate monitor. It took her a moment to realize it must be the representative whom Carol had mentioned.

Shelly leaned over and whispered, "He's cute," as they took their places on the high stools beside the counter for individual report from the two nurses who had worked admissions during the night. Britany answered with a brief nod of agreement.

As the four finished report, the man approached with a smile.

"Hi. I'm Michael Kiezer," he said as he extended his hand to Shelly. "I'm here with HEART-LINE. I'll be giving the inservice today," he said.

"Good morning. I'm Shelly," responded Shelly as she shook his hand. "We're grateful that you could come and thanks for the doughnuts."

"I'm Britany," said Britany, as she slid off her stool, and reached out to shake his hand.

Britany noted that she had to look up slightly to welcome him, but not so far that it hindered direct eye contact.

"I'll be in and out of this nursery as I'm getting the machines set up and making sure they all work. Please let me know if I'm in the way at all," said Michael as he turned to leave, and start class in the conference room.

"I think this class is going to be fun," teased Shelly with a giggle. The morning was busy and neither Shelly nor Britany had a chance to go to the eight o'clock class.

Around nine the nursery received a call from labor and delivery informing them that there was a baby to be born shortly, that showed a severe abnormality, and, if at all possible, the baby was going to come to them. Shawn, the unit secretary, had received the call, and she came into the nursery where Shelly and Britany were working to tell them. She was a usually bubbly lady, but now she wore a solemn face that warned them of the ominous message.

The call put everyone in the nursery on edge, not knowing what to expect. The charge nurse came into the nursery to double check the emergency equipment while Shelly and Britany worked feverishly to finish vitals, and get the babies to their mothers to nurse in case they were tied up for a while with the new arrival.

At nine-thirty, Britany unwrapped a beautiful little girl to put her on the scale. She weighted five pounds, fourteen ounces. Wispy golden hair that was barely visible covered her head. Her eyes were attentive, and alert to all that was going on around her. Her arms and legs were shaped perfectly and tiny fingers grasped Britany's as she examined her. The diminutive infant had an air about her that seemed to draw Britany to her. Her lips were daintily defined, and she appeared to smile. She had pink translucent soft skin and appeared perfect in every way except one. When Britany tried to take a rectal temperature she had no place to put the thermometer. Britany had not heard what the ultra sound during pregnancy had shown, but she did know that something was wrong. She notified Dr. Riley of the baby's arrival. He promised he would be right in.

The little girl did well. Britany and Shelly kept a watchful eye on her as she lay under the warmer, wearing only a diaper. Something about the little infant reminded Britany of an angel, and she called her Angel while caring for her.

Britany bathed the tiny, wiggly body and combed her wispy hair as they waited for Dr. Riley. Michael Kiezer entered the nursery as Britany finished the bath. He was finished with his first class and wondered if he could try his new monitor on the new infant.

"Yea, I guess it would be all right," Britany agreed. She looked at Shelly questionably, and Shelly shrugged her shoulders. She and Shelly observed as he attached three small electrodes to the infant's chest and explained the new monitor. Britany was relieved to see the heart rate make a normal tracing across the screen. Michael seemed unaware of their apprehension, as he eagerly demonstrated the new equipment. Britany admired his skill in working with the machine and the intensity with which he worked. She smiled and chuckled to herself as she watched him so fully engrossed in what he was doing, looking from infant to machine, making alterations in the intensity of the lines and giving explanations as he worked. She looked over to see Shelly smile, trying to conceal a laugh.

"She's a beautiful little girl. She almost seems to smile," commented Michael as he finished the task at hand and became aware once again of his surroundings.

"I thought so, too. I'm nicknaming her Angel," Britany said quietly and patted the infant's wispy hair. "There just seems to be something special about her."

"She is very pretty. I have a little boy. Well actually he's not little anymore. He's nine years old now. He never was pretty! He looked more like a battered fighter when he was born." As he spoke, Michael bent over to look more closely at Angel, and put his finger in her tiny hand and watch her fingers close around it.

Britany watched his hand with the tiny fingers grasped around his large, strong one. His fingers looked stout and masculine next to Angel's dainty ones.

"Well, how is she doing?" asked Dr. Riley as he approached drying his hands with a paper towel. "Did she have some rhythm problems?"

"No, she is doing fine," said Britany. "Dr. Riley, this is Michael Kiezer. He is demonstrating new monitors to us, and wanted to try one out on a real patient to give us a better understanding of how they work."

"Glad to meet you," Dr. Riley greeted as he extended his hand to Michael.

"My pleasure, Sir," said Michael shaking Dr. Riley's hand.

"So you're trying to make our job easier around here?" Dr. Riley walked to the side of the crib.

"Yes Sir. The right equipment can be a big help." Michael's light, brown eyes sparkled.

Dr. Riley said as he gently lifted Angel, "Just make sure you teach these nurses how to take care of it. I've been around a few too many years to feel comfortable with this new fangled stuff. Half of my patients are the offspring of babies I treated when I first started practice."

"I'll do my best to be sure the nursing staff understands the equipment, but a sign of good equipment is that it is easy to use," said Michael.

"Good," replied Dr. Riley.

"Actually, her heart and breathing are doing fine," Britany explained. She liked Dr. Riley. He was a very understanding man who was deeply involved with his patients.

Dr. Riley continued his exam in silence. He looked up at Britany when he got to where her anus should be. They shared an unspoken worry. Michael saw the look of concern pass between the two. When Dr. Riley finished he ordered some tests and stated that he would be back in several hours to read the results.

Britany escorted the delicate infant down to ultra sound and X-ray. She took stabilization items in case of an emergency. Angel did well, and soon they were both back in the nursery awaiting Dr. Riley's return. The nursery seemed unusually quiet when Britany returned, and she realized that another class had started and many of the nurses were at the second class. She felt a twinge of disappointment that she had not been able to go.

Shelly was admitting a new infant. She paused as Britany entered. "Britany I've been doing some snooping, and I found out he isn't married," Shelly said smiling.

"Who isn't married?" Britany's brow wrinkled in confusion as she placed Angel in her crib.

"Michael, the sales rep!" Shelly exclaimed.

"But you are Shelly. He's cute but not that cute!" Britany frowned at Shelly.

"Britany, get with it. I didn't mean for me. Who is it who doesn't want to be alone the rest of her life?" asked Shelly with a twinkle in her eye.

"I'm sorry. I'm kind of preoccupied with Angel," Britany said with a sigh as she took a seat. "I'm hoping maybe surgery can correct her problem, but something seems to be wrong, and it has me concerned. She is such a beautiful little girl. It's easy to get attached."

"You get attached to the neighbor's stray cat, but if you want to get attached to a man you had better pay closer attention!" Shelly said and patted Britany on the back.

Britany carefully positioned Angel back under the warmer, did a quick set of vital signs, and proceeded to help with other babies.

Dr. Riley appeared shortly with a dismal look on his face. His hunched shoulders gave him a defeated appearance, and he suddenly looked old. Britany felt her heart skip a beat, and her chest tightened slightly as she waited for him to speak.

His voice was grim. His gray eyes filled with compassion, and he looked close to tears as he spoke.

"It appears that the original ultrasound was correct in its findings. Baby Angel has no stomach, small or large intestines. There is nothing we can do. There is no possible way to provide the nutrition she needs to live, let alone to grow. All we can do is provide comfort measures for her until her time is up. Fortunately, we didn't start any IVs. Legal issues would require us to continue treatment. We don't need to continue any heroics that we haven't already started. I will make phone calls and get other opinions, but for now there is no hope beyond keeping her as comfortable as possible. I already talked to the mom, and she would like to see her. I told her you would bring her out," Dr. Riley said. He turned and walked out.

Britany and Shelly stood in a daze as he left. Britany walked over to Angel's crib and looked down at her perfect little face. How could it be that anything was wrong? She looked so normal and healthy. Gently she dressed her in a T-shirt and diaper and wrapped her in double pink blankets. She combed her hair and spoke softly as she lifted the bundle to her face to caress her silky cheek against her own.

"You get to see your mama now, little one. You need to look your best." She looked up at Shelly as she placed the infant back in her crib. Shelly wore a pained expression that she was sure reflected her own.

"Are you going to be able to do this?" asked Shelly quietly.

"I've had the privilege of taking many babies to see their moms for the first time on the happiest of times. It would be wrong to not accept the bad when it comes. God will give me the strength I don't have," Britany stated much more calmly than she felt. "Thanks for your concern."

Michael stood at the door of the nursery as Britany was leaving with Angel. The class had ended a short time earlier, and he had been coming to check on his equipment when Dr. Riley had arrived. Seeing the doctor's expression, he had decided to wait and not to interrupt. He had heard Dr. Riley's prognosis and stood quietly as Britany passed. He looked from Britany to Shelly, feeling totally helpless, yet wanting badly to comfort them in some way. He was not involved, yet somehow he felt as if he were. Sadly, he watched Britany's back as she left. He wanted to reach out and touch her hand, but he didn't. He had heard her reply to Shelly and admired her courage and reliance on God. Michael was strong, but he couldn't remember ever needing more strength than what Britany would need now.

Britany prayed silently as she wheeled the crib to the mother's room down the long, busy hall. "Dear God, I know you are right beside me. Please help me know what to say and do to help Angel and her parents during her short life. I don't know why this is happening, but give me words to help the parents cope," she finished as she came to the mother's door. Knocking quietly, she took a deep breath and let it out before she entered the room.

A pretty young lady with short black hair wearing a light blue gown was sitting up in bed with the blankets covering her legs. She reached her arms eagerly toward the infant speaking enthusiastically.

"There's my baby. Isn't she beautiful! Come here, darling."

"Mrs. Debra West?" Britany asked and discreetly checked the mother's wrist bracelet to ensure the correct identity, and then nestled the infant into the mother's waiting arms.

Debra didn't seem to notice Britany as she admired her baby.

"Isn't she beautiful, Brian!" Debra looked towards who appeared to be her husband. "Dr. Riley said you've been calling her Angel. She does look like an angel. It's a perfect name. I think we'll call her that, too," Debra said without looking at Britany.

She continued to speak to the infant, fully engrossed in her baby. Brian, a man in his early twenties, sat on a chair in the corner. He stared at the mother and baby with a confused, tormented look on his face.

"If you like, you are more than welcome to keep Angel with you, or I can take her back. You can have her as much or little as you wish," Britany said quietly.

"I want to keep her. Our time together is limited, and I want to cherish it as much as possible." Angel's mother spoke to Britany, but her gaze remained on the baby.

A low gasp escaped from Brian. Britany looked up. His shoulders were shuddering, and he was struggling to keep his composure.

Britany stood silently, looking from one to another. She searched for words, but none came. She felt helpless and turned quietly to leave the room. She was struggling to keep her composure, too. She wasn't sure what she had expected, but it certainly wasn't a beautiful mother happy and excited about her new baby. She felt a flood of emotions threatening to close over her. She needed some place to escape for a moment. She remembered the mother's room in the back of the nursery. She walked swiftly down the hall and entered the nursery. Everyone looked up rather concerned, but no one spoke as she walked past and entered the room.

Fortunately, it was empty. Lamplight provided subdued lighting as a radio played softly. She collapsed into the large, soft couch, and the tears broke loose. Her thoughts tumbled over each other. How could this happen to such a caring family? Why would God bring a precious life into this world to have it starve to death? How could the mother be so happy? Tears flowed unchecked for several minutes. Then she tried unsuccessfully to wipe at them with the back of her hand. She went to the small sink by the door and looked in the mirror above it. She looked horrible. She ran cool water over a washcloth and used it to cover her eyes to try to get the redness out. A knock at the door startled her. The cloth dropped. Before she could answer, the door opened, and in walked Michael.

"Are you OK?" he asked in a compassionate voice as he reached his arm around her shoulders.

Without thinking she took a step toward him and felt his strong arms encircle her. She relaxed into his embrace and felt comforted by his strength. Her cheek lay against his clean white shirt. He smelled of expensive aftershave. After several seconds she backed out of his embrace and looked up into soft brown eyes that were filled with concern.

"Thanks, I needed that," Britany said gratefully, continuing to look into his warm brown eyes.

"My mom always says we need at least eighteen hugs a day, and I thought maybe you could use one of them now," Michael said with a smile. He looked at her gentle face and found himself attracted to her caring spirit. Her green eyes glistened with lingering moisture.

"Your mom sounds like a real smart lady." Britany wiped at her cheek to dry a tear.

"Well, I think she is. I turned out pretty well, and she had a lot of work to do to smooth out the rough edges," he responded lightly, the smile still across his face.

Britany smiled back and dabbed at her eyes.

"Don't worry," said Michael. "You look fine."

She suddenly felt self-conscious and took a step back. "I look horrible!" she exclaimed.

"In that case I'd love to see you when you look good!" said Michael and patted her shoulder.

"I guess I'd better get back to work," said Britany "I'm sure a lot of things need to be done."

"They are covering for you, don't worry. And as for what they think, a little gossip always seems to liven things up," Michael said with a chuckle and wiped a last tear from her face.

She smiled back. Britany appreciated his quick wit and relaxed nature.

"Maybe so, but I'm fine now. I had better get back. Thanks again." Britany turned and led the way out the door.

She felt rather self-conscious as she came out, but no one stared or seemed to notice. Shelly looked up and smiled as Britany entered the nursery.

"I would have gone instead of you if I had known Michael was going to be so concerned. Some people get all the luck! Seriously, though, how did it go? You looked pretty shocked when you got back."

"To be quite truthful, I don't know how it went," Britany said with a shrug of her shoulders. "Angel's mom seemed so happy, it was kind of spooky. The dad looked awful. I don't think he knew what to think of the mom's behavior either. She was excited to see the baby. She's going to call her Angel."

"Do you think she's going through denial?" asked Shelly. "That would be expected and normal in a case like this."

"It could be a form of denial, and at first I was sure that's what was happening, but then she said she wanted to keep the baby as much as possible because their time was limited. She wanted to enjoy Angel for as long as she could." A small wrinkle took its place on Britany's forehead.

"Wow, I see what you mean," said Shelly, taking the stool beside Britany "Either she has accepted the situation amazingly well or is walking on pretty dangerous ground. We had better keep an eye on her and talk with the nurse taking care of her."

"Yeah, either way, the dad is definitely not feeling the same way, and I would imagine he is feeling very confused right now. I'm going to go talk to Mrs. West's nurse," Britany said. She slid off the stool and walked toward the door.

The nurse caring for Debra was equally concerned about her attitude. The nurse said the father would leave and then return, but stay only briefly. She was sure he was very worried about the mother but could only handle seeing the mother and baby together for a short time. Britany returned to the nursery.

The rest of the shift flew by, and soon Britany and Shelly were quickly finishing last-minute duties to get ready for report.

"I'm going to give Crystal a call at school to let her know I'm going to be late," Britany said, walking toward the phone in the nursery. "We're going to the Y tonight to work out, but I would like to go to the in-service after work. It's been too busy to go during work." After the quick call, they reported off and went to the classroom.

"I'm glad this day is over as far as work goes. I can use a breather. It feels good to sit down," said Shelly.

"I couldn't agree more. I'm kind of looking forward to this class," Britany said, taking the seat beside Shelly.

"I can understand why!" teased Shelly.

"That's not what I meant! I like to work with monitors," Britany responded quickly.

"OK, then, you watch the monitor. I'll watch the guy."

"Sh, he's coming," Britany whispered. She could see his blond hair through the window in the door.

"Hi, ladies. Looks like a small class," said Michael as he entered and looked around.

"I think everyone came earlier, and the second shift came in before they started work," explained Britany.

"I already covered some things with you two. It won't take too long. How is little Angel doing?" he asked as he handed instruction sheets to them.

"She is still with her mother," said Shelly. "But I guess she is as good as expected."

Michael quickly covered the information, and soon it was time to go.

Britany rose to leave, picking some papers up from the table. Michael reached out and touched her elbow.

"Could I speak with you a minute?" he asked.

Looking up into his brown eyes, Britany felt her heart skip a beat, but calmly answered, "Sure."

"My plane doesn't leave until morning, and I was wondering if you would join me for supper. Then maybe afterwards you could show me a little of your town. I'll be back in two weeks to check on the monitors, and it would be nice to know my way around."

"I'd love to, but I'm picking my daughter up from school, and we were planning to go to the Y to work out."

"This is embarrassing." Michael touched his temples and hesitated. "I thought you were single."

"I am single, but I have a seventeen-year-old daughter." Britany paused and considered whether to go on. Somehow she wanted him to know the rest. "I never married her father. We were both too young at the time." She glanced at the floor.

"Whew, you had me worried for a while," said Michael, looking genuinely relieved.

Britany smiled, "Do you like racquetball?" She asked, surprising herself as she spoke.

"I better warn you, I play a pretty mean game," Michael said.

"I love a challenge! How about the loser buys dinner?"

"You're on. You win, I buy dinner. I win, my treat. But only if your daughter joins us," he said and extended his hand.

"Do you always drive this hard of a bargain?" Britany asked and shook his hand in agreement.

"Only with someone as cute as you," he said, smiling slyly.

Britany knew she was blushing and looked down to try to conceal it.

"I'll go change. You can get your equipment and meet me at the elevators just outside the nursery," said Britany, pointing toward to her left.

CHAPTER 7

Britany quickly entered the locker room that was empty. Shelly had already left. She wasn't sure if she was disappointed or relieved. It would be fun to share her excitement, but at the same time it was nice to cherish it to herself. She quickly changed her clothes. She combed her hair loose, and the gentle waves fell just below her shoulders.

She met Michael at the elevator. He was sitting on a bench, and he stood to meet her as she approached.

"You look lovely," he said simply, with a touch of awe in his voice.

"Thank you," said Britany as she reached for the elevator button.

She realized as the elevator arrived that she had no idea where Michael was staying and that he probably didn't have a way to get to the Y.

"I just remembered you flew in," said Britany, as they entered the elevator, and she pushed the light for the ground floor. "If you don't mind riding with me to the school, we could go pickup Crystal, and then I'll stop by where you're staying so you can get a change of clothes," she suggested. The elevator landed, and the door opened.

"If it's not too much trouble, that would be great. It's not too far from here," answered Michael as he held the door open.

"My car is in the back parking lot. We nurses get the royal treatment. We get to park as far back as you can get!" she said with a quick smile.

The air felt cool as they left the building. The sun was bright, and it took a few moments for their eyes to adjust to the light.

"Nice car!" exclaimed Michael as Britany unlocked the door to her red Saturn. "This car is made in my neighborhood."

"You're from Tennessee?" Britany asked in surprise as she got behind the wheel. Somehow she hadn't pictured him being from the south. He had a northern accent.

"My base office is located there, and that's where I live, but I'm originally from Michigan. A loyal Blue and Gold fan," he answered as he took his seat and fastened his seat belt.

"I didn't realize you traveled so far!"

"I go all over. I love to travel," he said, watching the sights as they drove along.

"This is called the Miami Valley," Britany pointed out as they reached a crest that overlooked a prestigious-looking area. The road ahead wove down among established homes with meticulous lawns and then back up again in the distance. A light haze off in the distance gave the area a soft, inviting look and signaled the approaching sunset. The lawns were a lush green with tulips and daffodils scattered throughout.

Britany pulled up in the circular drive of the high school. She saw Crystal depart from a group of youths and wave behind her. Her blonde ponytail bobbed as she sprang lightly to the car.

Crystal chatted eagerly as she scolded her mom for being so late. She greeted Michael cheerfully during introductions and continued reviewing the main events of the day. She ended her dissertation by breathlessly saying it worked out great she was late because she finished her homework and still had time to talk with one of her friends.

Britany laughed lightly as Crystal finished and said, "OK, if you're through, Michael has offered to take us out to dinner later at the place of our choice."

"That's great! There's the best Mexican restaurant just down the road. Believe me, you won't be disappointed! That is, if you like Mexican food," Crystal quickly interjected.

"I love Mexican! It sounds as if it's settled, if your mom approves," answered Michael as he half turned in his seat to look back at Crystal and smile.

"How could I not approve? I already knew what she would say when I mentioned it. Besides, their prices are just as good as their food."

Britany was pulling up to the motel. Soon Michael had his things, and they were on their way. The Y was close to her condo, and Britany pointed out the street where they lived as they passed.

The Y was a fairly new building with a beautiful pool and hot tub. They signed in, and Britany showed Michael the locker room. Then Britany and Crystal went to the ladies' locker room.

Britany was expecting the barrage of comments that started as soon as the door closed.

"Mom, he's a hunk! Who is he?" Crystal asked.

"He is a sales representative from work. He is in town for the night and asked me out," Britany said as she pulled off her shoes.

"Is he married?" Crystal asked. Britany looked at her in shock.

"Crystal, do you really think I would go to dinner with a married man?"

"I was just checking." Crystal shrugged her shoulders. "Where is he from?"

"He is from Tennessee."

"If he asked you out, why am I here?" Crystal asked as she gestured with her hand.

"I told him we were planning to go to the Y, and it just kind of ended up the way it is."

The locker room smelled of a mixture of chlorine, perfume, and shampoo. A back door exited to the pool. Britany changed into royal blue, knee-length spandex shorts and T-shirt while they talked.

"If you say anything embarrassing in front of Michael you will be in deep trouble!" Britany threatened.

"Mom, what would I do that would embarrass you?" Crystal laughed.

"I don't know, but I'm sure you will think of something," Britany said and pulled her hair back with a headband. "Let's go. Please behave!"

"I will, Mom, don't worry." Britany cast her an anxious glance and pushed through the door.

Michael was setting on a bench in the hall. They went to the front desk and got the balls and rackets. Crystal went on to the pool.

"Do you come here often?" asked Michael as he served the ball. The serve was easy, and Britany skillfully returned it.

"We like to come whenever we can, but it's not that often that I get a partner to play racquetball." She picked up the ball and hit it toward the wall. He jumped for the return, and they volleyed back and forth. Then they started a game.

Michael was impressed with the skill with which she returned his serve, and he returned the next ball off the wall. She returned it.

"You aren't going to make this easy for me, are you?" he asked.

"Not if I can help it," she quickly replied and got back into position.

Soon the game became more intense with the score going back and forth. Britany noticed Michael played racquetball with the same strong concentration that she had seen earlier in his work.

"Wow! You have a wicked serve," said Michael as he dove to save it. The muscles under his T-shirt rippled as he reached toward the ball.

Britany missed the ball as it came back toward her. She had lost her concentration when she found herself watching him instead of the game. She played harder.

"You play this game well!" said Michael at the end of their games. He was impressed with her ability and the grace with which she moved.

"Well, if I play so well, why did you win every game?" Her green eyes sparkled with enthusiasm. Her smile was inviting.

"Because I'm so good!"

Tired and sweaty, Michael suggested that they use the pool and then the hot tub.

Crystal was in the pool when they dived in. She loved to swim and had already lapped one fourth of a mile. Britany swam leisurely for a while. Michael did various dives off the board as Britany and Crystal watched and cheered.

Michael popped up from under the water right beside Britany following one his dives and startled Britany. Water droplets dripped from his face and he gave his head a shake.

"You look much more relaxed than you did earlier. Are you still thinking about Angel?" he asked.

"A little. You looked like a little boy sneaking up behind me like that!" Britany splashed water in his face and dove under the water to swim away.

He easily caught her and lifted her to the surface by her waist. Britany laughed as her head came up.

"If you weren't so pretty, you would be in big trouble. Not many people get away with dousing me like that. Are you ready for the hot tub? It looks like Crystal is already taking advantage of it."

"Sure," said Britany.

There were several other people in the hot tub when they got in.

Crystal kept the conversation lively during dinner, and filled Michael in on her plans for the fall.

"I graduate in two months. We are having the graduation at my grandmother's farm. They have cows and goats, plus my mother has her horse out there," chatted Crystal.

"My son Ben likes animals," said Michael.

"How old is your son?" asked Crystal.

"He is nine. And he is curious about everything."

"I kind of grew up on the farm," said Crystal. "My mom and I lived with Grandma and Grandpa when I was young and she was going through nursing school. We lived with them several years after that until she got enough money to move into town. We still go to the farm a lot.

"I have a marvelous idea! Why don't you come to my graduation and open house? My grandmother loves visitors. You and your son would have a chance to spend some time on the farm," Crystal said.

"My son would love that. He hasn't spent much time on a farm," said Michael.

Britany wished she could sink into her chair and not be seen. Crystal had a tendency to unknowingly put her on the spot, but Britany couldn't remember when she had done it in such a big way. How could she be so forward! Michael seemed nice, but she really didn't know him yet.

She tried hard not to show her distress, but she knew she always got a funny little wrinkle on her forehead when she was worried. She didn't dare take a bite or a drink for fear she would choke. Fortunately Michael's attention was on Crystal, and he didn't seem to notice Britany's distress.

"I'll check my calendar and see if my schedule is free. That sounds like a lot of fun!" He seemed genuinely interested in Crystal's offer. He casually stretched back in his chair and pushed his plate to the side.

"I think your mom is done," said Michael, looking up at Britany. "I've certainly had enough. You were right about their food. It was muy deliciosa!"

"Thank you. I have enjoyed the meal very much. Please excuse me for a moment," said Britany as she got up and went to the powder room. Crystal excused herself and followed her in while Michael paid for the meal.

"You promised not to do that!" Britany spoke sharply as Crystal entered.

"Mom, relax. You're making a big deal out of nothing. Besides, he likes you, I can tell," said Crystal matter-of-factly as she fixed her make-up in the mirror.

"Sometimes..." Britany fumed lamely.

"You look like a schoolgirl Mom. He's good for you," said Crystal, giving her mother a hug. Then she turned and walked casually out the door.

Crystal informed them that it would be best if they dropped her off so she could work on her accounting. Britany agreed readily, since she wasn't sure what else to expect from her daughter.

"Your daughter is lovely, almost as lovely as her mom. She's a wonderful girl. I'm sure you are very proud of her," said Michael after they dropped Crystal off.

"Thank you. I love her dearly, but she can have her moments," said Britany.

"If it's not too late, I'd love to have you show me more of your town. It's very interesting." Michael looked at Britany and smiled. Britany looked over at his curious grin.

"I'd love to," replied Britany, and she started the car, glad to change the subject.

She drove him past the art institute and downtown past the old stately buildings. They followed the curvy street to the river's edge, where there was a scenic park.

"I know it's a bit chilly," said Michael, "but would you like to go for a walk along the river? The lights are fabulous!"

"Yes, I'd like that very much."

The lights reflecting off the river were beautiful at night. The river was calm and peaceful. It looked like thousands of stars bouncing off the water, adding to the millions of stars in the sky. They walked in silence as they enjoyed the beautiful night. The river lapped occasionally onto the shore. The smell of spring and water filled the air. Michael put his arm around Britany's shoulder. She fit snugly in the crook of his arm, soaking in his warmth.

"Tell me a little about your son. He sounds very interesting," Britany said as they walked along.

"He looks like me, most people say, but he takes life a bit more seriously. Of course, he's had a rather rough road. His mother and I never got along very well, and then he had to go through the divorce."

"I'm sorry. That must be hard on you, too," Britany said.

"I keep pretty busy with work," Michael said. "His mom gets him every other weekend, but she has a family of her own now, and his step dad doesn't like him too well. He claims he reminds him too much of me."

When they reached the end of the boardwalk Michael turned her gently to face him and kissed her softly on the lips.

"I had a wonderful evening. Thank you," said Michael, looking down into her deep green eyes.

"Thank you. I enjoyed it, too. Thanks for being there this morning," she said softly, smiling back.

He was tempted to kiss her again, but something about her made him change his mind. Instead he turned, and they walked back to the car with his arm around her shoulders. Britany noticed a change in his attitude after he kissed her, and she felt puzzled. Both remained silent amid the sights and sounds of the night as they walked.

The phone rang the next morning as Britany was stepping out of the shower. Wrapping a towel around her, she hurried for the phone in her bedroom.

"Good morning." Britany was pleasantly surprised to hear the familiar male voice on the other end. "I wanted to tell you again that I had a wonderful time last night. My plane leaves this morning at seven thirty, and I needed to say a last goodbye."

"This is quite a pleasant surprise! I had a great time, too. Have a safe flight." Britany wasn't sure what to say and was at a loss for words.

"I was wondering," the velvet smooth voice continued, "if you would accept my offer to a real date when I return in two weeks?"

"I'd love to," she replied.

"I'll call to confirm the place and time. Have a nice day."

"You, too." Britany slowly and deliberately hung up the phone, staring at it. Suddenly she realized she was dripping wet and still needed to prepare for work. She hurried to finish getting ready.

Britany tried hard to concentrate on her work the next several days but found her thoughts drifting back to Michael. Each night when she got home she hoped he would call. She scolded herself for acting like a schoolgirl. Wednesday she and Crystal drove out to the farm and went riding.

She was pleased with the progress Misty was making. An important horse show was scheduled for June, and it looked as if they would be ready. Britany rode hard, pushing Misty more than usual. Misty looked back at Britany at one point and shook her head as if to say, "Give me a break."

"I'm sorry, girl. You're right. I am being a bit rough. I just thought if I rode hard it would get my mind off Michael. I'm not seventeen anymore, and yet I'm acting like I am. I just can't stop thinking about him. He's cute, sweet and thoughtful. Masculine, yet caring. Very sensitive. He is so easy to talk to. I feel as if I've known him all my life, and yet I've only met him once. I have never felt this way about anyone before, and I'm not sure what to think about it. There is no way I am going tell anyone how I feel. They would think I have fallen off the deep end! I tend to think so myself. At least I know I'll get to see him again, even if he does change his mind about the date. He will be back at work in just over a week. This is totally crazy!" Britany exclaimed as she hit her head with palm of her hand. "Not only am I acting like a teenager, I'm telling my horse all about it!"

"Come on, Misty. Let's go for a run across the pasture. We both need a break." As Britany finished speaking she reined Misty over to the fence and leaned over to unlatch the gate. Off they raced across the soft, tender grass of spring. The horse's mane and Britany's hair flowed out behind them. Britany leaned forward in the saddle, the wind whipping at her jacket and whizzing in her ears. She breathed deeply of the brisk spring air. She could feel Misty's rippling muscles beneath her and the pounding of the hooves as they met the ground. Misty's nostrils were flaring, and her breath was hard and loud. Britany reined her in after they had covered the smooth lane and took it much easier as they rode into the woods.

A hawk screeched in the trees above, and its majestic body soared overhead as it sought to distance itself from them. Squirrels cried out their protest to the intrusion and scurried up trees to turn and look back at them. Dried leaves left over from fall crackled underfoot and seemed to echo throughout the woods. Soon the trees would be full of leaves, but now the branches were bare with only swollen buds to hinder the view of the sky. The musty wood smelled of the dead branches mixed with the fresh spring scent of new growth drifted around them. The sky's orange and blue color was evidence that dusk was near. Britany turned and took a more leisurely ride back to the barn.

It was dark by the time Britany finished in the barn. Her mother and Crystal were busy getting supper. Britany quickly cleaned up and helped finish.

"Crystal tells me you met a new friend and that she asked him to her graduation," Liz said as they were preparing the meal. "She also told me he's very good-looking and seemed quite taken by you."

"Mom, you know Crystal tends to get a bit carried away. He was very nice, and we had a good time. I was very embarrassed when she asked him to her graduation. He lives in Tennessee, so I'm sure he won't be able to come. Did she also tell you she invited him to stay here at your place?"

"Yes, she did, and I told her he would be very welcome. Crystal is a good judge of character. If she thinks it will be OK, then it's fine with me," Liz said, dishing out mashed potatoes.

"Mom, you are so sweet, but I think Crystal has you wrapped around her little finger," Britany answered, kissing her on the cheek.

"Grandma just knows and trusts me, that's all!" Crystal interjected and patted Britany on the shoulder. She smiled a taunting smile.

The meal was delicious and made Britany want to curl up and sleep instead of drive home. She sat in a chair by the fireplace and watched the blaze of the fire. Her mother sat beside her.

"It's been a long time since I've seen that sparkle in your eye," Liz said.

"Dad has a nice fire going. I thought I would enjoy it a while before driving back," said Britany absently.

"The sparkle I see is not the reflection from the fire. It's the excitement I read in your eyes every time someone mentions Michael," Liz said quietly, looking intently at Britany.

Britany looked at her, startled. The fire cracked in the background, and Britany could hear her father in the next room tuning the radio to farm market reports and futures.

They sat quietly watching the fire, Liz waiting patiently for Britany to respond. "You know, it's scary." Britany searched her thoughts. "I do like him, but what if what I like about him is only a dream? What if he isn't at all what I think he is once I get to know him? Part of me really wants to see him again and part of me is afraid."

"Britany, life is full of surprises, and sometimes you just have to live it to find the answers." Liz looked at Britany, and saw a faint wrinkle between her eyes, as Britany continued to stare into the fire.

CHAPTER 8

On Thursday Debra West was dismissed from the hospital, but Angel had to stay in the nursery. As she left, Debra smiled and told her tiny daughter that she would be back first thing in the morning.

Britany watched quietly from where she worked on a new admission. Jeanne came over to speak to Britany as the mother disappeared into the elevator.

"It hurts to see Debra so happy," Jeanne said sadly. "I can understand how she can pretend that everything is all right. Angel looks healthy. She's beautiful and is easily contented with a pacifier. It's easy for me to forget what will eventually happen, but it is just not healthy for the mother to behave this way."

"You're right," said Britany. "I find myself avoiding her, but I just don't know what to say. She doesn't really seem to have any type of bond with any of the nurses. It seems like we are the enemy, making the whole thing up."

"Maybe by putting the blame on us it makes things easier to accept. It's hard to tell, it's so confusing," said Jeanne with a sigh. She sat down and worked on charting.

"I'm caught up with my work. How about going to lunch?" asked Jeanne, looking from her charting to Britany.

"That sounds like a winner. Give me just a minute, and I will be ready," said Britany as she wrapped a baby in its blanket.

Soon the two friends left the nursery and headed toward the stairs. "Did Michael call yet?" asked Jeanne as they descended.

"No, but then again I wasn't home, so he might have tried. I went to the farm to ride," answered Britany, grabbing the railing and swinging herself down the last two steps.

"Was Trigger all right?" Jeanne asked, copying her actions.

"He was fine. Do you think you will be ready for the show coming up?" Britany asked as she held open the door.

"I think so. Trigger is always ready to jump. I'm glad we're going to have this weekend at the farm to work with him." They went through the cafeteria and got juice and muffins.

"Misty is doing well, but we can use all the time we can get. Is Amy excited about Easter?" Britany asked as she broke off a piece of muffin.

"Yes, but not any more excited than you are for Michael to call!" Jeanne said with a tease.

"Jeanne!" Britany exclaimed and gave her a light shove.

"Britany, don't feel bad. I think it is cute. I didn't get to talk to him much at the in-service. Did you get a chance to find out if he is a Christian or not?"

"Not yet, we really didn't get a lot of time to talk about serious things."

Britany answered. She didn't want to tell Jeanne that she was afraid to. She wanted very much for this relationship to progress, and she knew that if he wasn't a Christian she would have to stop seeing him. It was too scary to face.

Britany felt weighted down as she left work. It had been a tiring day. The nursery had been busy, and they had gotten behind in discharges, causing parents to wait to go home with their babies. One of the doctors came in late, causing all of his patients to wait until after lunch to go home. Two fathers had yelled at Britany because they were eager to go and felt things were too slow. A swim would be relaxing, and she was glad it was the night for Crystal and her to go to the Y.

The workout and swim were relaxing, and as she left she felt rejuvenated again. They went to the nearby mall where Crystal helped Britany pick out a pair of white shoes for Amy to go with the new dress Jeanne had gotten her for Easter. They also purchased a pair of shoes to go with Crystal's Easter dress.

"Mom, this is so darling!" said Crystal, holding up a dress for Britany to see. "You could use a new dress for Easter. Try it on, please," Crystal coaxed.

"It is cute. I don't need a dress, though," said Britany as she turned to leave.

"Oh, Mom, loosen up. It would also be perfect for my graduation."

"Yeah, it would work well for that," Britany answered as she stopped and looked at the dress to consider it. It was navy and white in a new style with a high waist and bright silver buttons down the front.

She tried it on and was pleasantly surprised. It fit as if it was made for her, and she fell in love with it immediately. She modeled it for Crystal, who eagerly approved. Together they picked out a pair of white and navy heels to match.

They were both in good spirits as they entered the drive to their condo. The telephone was ringing as Britany fumbled with the key to unlock the door. She felt both nervous and excited as she picked up the phone just in time to hear the party on the other end hang up. Her heart sank as she tried to convince herself that it probably wasn't Michael, and if it had been he would try again. She busied herself by fixing a bite to eat and doing some laundry.

Finally she prepared for bed and picked up her Bible for nighttime devotions. She read about the last supper and Jesus' agonizing prayer in the garden. It was wonderful reading the prayer Jesus prayed for future believers. His love for them was so rich and full. His desire for them was that they might know Him fully and share in His oneness with God. It was hard for Britany to understand how God could love her so much and actually desire her love for Him in return. Next to Him she was nothing, and yet to mean so much to Him was beyond her grasp of understanding. It was also hard to understand how, knowing He was to die the next day, He could think of those around Him and those who were yet to come. As she read, it was as if she no longer needed to understand it, because it was part of her and beyond understanding with human logic.

Her thoughts were interrupted with the ring of the telephone. She jumped with a start from where she was seated in bed, with the covers over her legs. She reached for the phone beside the bed.

"Hi! You are not an easy person to reach!" The welcome voice came through the telephone.

"I'm sorry. I guess I'm not. I went out to the farm to ride last night and went shopping after working out tonight. Did you have a nice flight home? How have you been?" She sat upright and toyed with the edge of the blanket. She wished she could see him as he talked.

"It's been busy. I was in Kentucky yesterday, but got back tonight so I will be home for Easter. My son Ben and I are spending the weekend with my parents in Michigan. We fly out tomorrow. Ben is excited. He loves his grandparents. I'm planning on being back at your hospital on Thursday. Would you still be interested in going to supper Thursday night?" asked Michael.

"I'd love to." She was relieved that he still wanted to see her.

"I've been asking around, and a friend of mine says there is a quaint little theater that has marvelous plays. 'Singing In The Rain' is playing. Would you like to go?" asked Michael.

"How did you know I love the theater! That particular theater is my favorite! The acting is always good, and their productions are super. You must have been snooping around. Did you call Shelly?" Britany asked with suspicion.

"No, honestly, I didn't. I love the theater, and I was hoping you would too. I guess my hoping proved effective. So, it's a date then. I'll be looking forward to it." Michael felt pleased at her enthusiastic response. She sounded fresh and alive, not artificial and shallow like some of the girls he had dated.

"If you like, I can drive you to the airport on Friday. It's my day off because I work the weekend."

"In that case I'll get a later flight out, if you would like to do something together during the day on Friday,." Michael said, hoping she would agree.

"That sounds like fun. I'd love to," Britany replied.

"I had better say goodnight now. I'll see you next Thursday, bright and early." Michael spoke sincerely.

"It's a date. I'm looking forward to it. Thanks so much for calling. I'll see you then. Goodnight," answered Britany, hating to say goodbye.

Michael sat back in his chair and grinned. He could see Britany's warm smile and the way her golden brown hair waved over her shoulders. He liked her laugh and her innocence. She made him feel important and strong, by the way she looked at him admiringly. He smiled. He thought about being single, and how it was lonely at times. He used his job to keep him busy.

He dated often, but any relationships he developed were shallow. He made sure of that! If a lady seemed too serious he quickly put an end to the relationship. He had made a promise to himself at the time of the divorce to not get involved with anyone again and he had worked hard to keep that promise.

He sat up straight and ran his hand through his hair. "Keep your head on straight Michael," he said to himself. "Don't let this one make you break your promise!" He walked to the bedroom and looked in the mirror. A boyish grin that revealed straight white teeth looked back at him. "I don't think there's too much to worry about old boy," he answered himself. "She's five hundred mile away. That seems like a safe distance!"

The next day seemed to fly by, and soon Britany and Crystal were on their way to the farm. Britany felt a special glow that she knew was because of the phone call she had received the night before. Despite her excitement, a sadness prevailed. It was Good Friday. The air was cool, and the sky cloudy. Britany had expected it to be so. She had never seen a Good Friday that didn't at least get cloudy for a part of the day. It was a reminder to her of the pain and suffering Jesus went through for her.

On Saturday night Jeanne and Amy joined Britany at her parents' for the weekend. That evening, when Amy was snugly tucked into bed, Crystal hid jelly beans and colored eggs while Jeanne and Britany prepared Easter baskets. Charles loved malted milk balls, so they were placed in his basket along with a pecan log. Liz and Crystal both liked the chocolate eggs with fruited cream filling. Britany had white chocolate in the shape of a bunny, and Jeanne couldn't resist a solid chocolate rabbit. Amy had both a small chocolate bunny and white chocolate lamb. They also placed the new shoes for Crystal and Angel in their baskets. They then retired early so they would be able to get up for sunrise service.

The alarm went off at 4:45 a.m. Britany rose, quietly slipped out of bed, took her Bible and went to the window. She looked out into the star-studded night. Millions of stars danced in the sky. When she was young she would look at the stars and imagine that one of the stars represented the boy she would marry. It was the star farthest up in the sky that she could see from her window. It stood out because it was brighter than those around it. She looked for it out of habit. She quickly found it, but she was surprised to see that it seemed brighter than usual. A thought flashed across her mind and then was quickly lost so that she was unable to quite distinguish it.

She sat on the floor, turned on a small light, and picked up her Bible, turning to the nineteenth chapter of John. She read about the crucifixion of Jesus. Pain filled her heart as she read about the horrifying experience. Thinking of her beloved Jesus on the cross in pain and agony was more than she could bear. A single tear moistened her eye as she put the Bible down and once again looked into the sky. The star was still shinning brightly and seemed to have a message for her.

"Dear Jesus," she prayed, barely audible. "I'm so sorry You had to go through all the pain, all the suffering, all the humiliation. I thank You that You did. You made the ultimate sacrifice for my sin once and forever. You gave your life that I might have eternal life by believing in You. Without Your presence, life would have no meaning to me. Guide me and keep me tucked beneath Your wing." She smiled up to the stars and then went to take a shower and prepare for the service.

Everyone looked nice in their new Easter outfits, and Britany was glad Crystal had talked her into the new dress. Amy was clicking the heels of her new shoes, pretending they were tap shoes.

"How can you be so alert this early in the morning?" Britany laughed and gave Amy a big hug. The sky was still dark as they drove to the church.

The church was dark except for the candles in the windows. Everyone was quiet and greeted each other in subdued voices. The air seemed to be permeated with reverence and anticipation. They slipped into their usual pew near the center of the church. Britany heard a slight commotion beside her and was pleasantly surprised to see her brother, his wife and two boys standing at her side, waiting for her to move so they could slide in. She smiled to each as they took their places. It felt wonderful to have her whole family beside her.

A lovely vocalist sang "I Come to the Garden" to the accompaniment of a mellow organ. Britany could feel Jesus' presence through the song. As she sang Britany could picture Jesus in the garden speaking to Mary that first Easter morning. The scriptures were read of how the tomb was found unguarded with the stone rolled away. The tomb was empty as the women went in to prepare Jesus' body for burial. They feared someone had stolen the body, but inside they found the angel who told them Jesus was alive. They quickly ran back to tell the disciples. Mary stayed behind and mistook Jesus for the gardener. He spoke her name and she recognized Him. The same Jesus who spoke to Mary that first Easter morning was still alive and speaking to Britany. She felt honored that even though most of the people mentioned in the Bible were men, Jesus had been born of a woman and first appeared to a woman following his resurrection. It assured her that men and women do have different functions in God's plan, but that a woman is no less important than a man. She closed her eyes and listened to His message of love.

Sunlight began to filter through the windows as the candles burnt low. A vibrant "Up from the Grave He Arose" finished off the service. Britany's heart filled with joy as they sang.

There was a breakfast served afterward and then a break before morning service.

It had been a wonderful day, and both Britany and Crystal were in high spirits as they headed for home later in the evening.

CHAPTER 9

Some days it was hard for Britany to remember why she liked her job so much. Monday was one of those days. It was nine o'clock, and already she was far behind in her work. Baby Cooper was screaming to eat, but his mother was presently in the shower. Mrs. Hollister had been insistent on leaving immediately and then burst into tears when she was told she would have to wait several hours because her baby's doctor needed test results before releasing the baby. Dr. Sawyer came in to do circumcisions and Britany assisted. He decided to do two more that she helped with. She felt as if she were in high gear as she prepared the area for one and then quickly cleaned another table for the next one.

Mrs. Blake was having difficulty feeding her baby, and she asked for help. Britany tried all the tricks she knew to get the infant to nurse, but he continued to fall back asleep. Britany tried to assure the mother that most babies are sleepy for the first several days and not to worry, but Mrs. Blake wouldn't give up. Finally Britany suggested taking the baby back to the nursery for an hour to let the mother shower and change, and then she would help her again.

By ten, Britany was extremely hungry and decided that if she didn't take a break she might scream a little bit, too. On her way out she saw Debra West in the hall coming in to see her little girl. Britany had noticed a change in Angel over the weekend. Her cry was weaker, and her eyes seemed too big and a little sunken in. She felt too tired to approach Debra, and she knew that Debra didn't really want to see her anyway, so she continued down to the cafeteria. On the way there she heard her name called and turned to see Shelly hurrying to catch up.

"Britany, wait! Are you too busy to have a break with a friend, or what?" Shelly asked teasingly.

"I'm sorry! It was so late I figured everyone else had already gone to break and was back by now. Lunch breaks start in an hour."

"Well, I've been real busy, too. I guess it's just been one of those days. By the time we get back from break the bilis results will be back, and we should be able to send quite a few home. Maybe the day will be a bit nicer then."

"I think you're dreaming. This day has already gone past the point of no return, and I'm sure the only way to save it is to have it pass quickly," responded Britany a bit of dramatically. "If the moms only realized how many babies we draw bilis on each day and how very seldom does one have trouble, maybe they would relax a bit when we tell them their baby needs one. Maybe they should warn the moms on their hospital tour."

"You know, you can tell a mom over half of the babies get a little jaundice and that it won't hurt them if it's managed well, but when it is actually their baby it takes on a whole different meaning and suddenly seems like a disaster," reminded Shelly as they found a table.

"You're right. I need to be a little more understanding, thanks."

"Well, did Michael call? I've been dying to ask," Shelly asked, her eyes sparkling.

"He called, and we have a date lined up for this Thursday to go to the theater and dinner. Doesn't that sound fabulous?" responded Britany, suddenly not feeling quite so tired.

"A real date! That does sound fabulous!" Shelly exclaimed with a sly smile. "I'm so happy for you. I hope he turns out to be as nice as he seems."

"So do I! It makes me a bit nervous. I only met him once, and he's on my mind constantly. I feel like a schoolgirl," Britany said. A small wrinkle appeared on her forehead.

"Don't worry too much. He's brightened your life up already. Enjoy it," Shelly commented and gave Britany's shoulder a little squeeze. It didn't take long for them to finish their muffins and juice. They decided they should cut their break short and get back to work a little early.

The results of the bilis were just coming to the floor as they got back. Britany breathed a sigh of relief when she saw Baby Hollister's was low enough for the baby to go home with his mother. Mrs. Hollister was so excited she gave Britany a warm hug. Britany said a silent prayer for Baby Blake as she took him out for feeding again. Britany was more excited than the mother when after fifteen minutes the baby finally seemed to figure out what was going on and began to eat. The day suddenly seemed to fall together and go much more smoothly.

On Wednesday Debra West seemed a bit agitated. Britany was caring for Angel when she arrived. The smile was gone and in its place the mom wore a strained appearance. Angel had not been as happy the day before and was starting to take on the appearance of an old lady. Her legs were swollen and her cheeks were sunken, making her eyes appear even larger. Her cry was weak and bird-like. It was heart-breaking to listen to.

Dr. Riley had ordered some medicine to ease her agony, but it was hard to be sure how much could be used since her kidneys were probably not working right. It seemed that sips of water would help ease the dehydration, but Dr. Riley had reminded them that in a state of dehydration the pain sensors aren't as acute, so she was better off as she was. Britany could read on Debra's face that Angel's deterioration had an effect on her. Britany cleansed Angels face and wrapped her snugly, preparing to hand her to Debra when the mother broke down.

"Can't you just leave us alone! You are always fussing with her and waking her up. She's my baby-just leave us alone," Debra said harshly.

Her change in manner caught Britany off guard. Britany looked at her, startled. She realized it was probably a step in the right direction and didn't reply. Maybe now she would start to understand what was happening and begin to work through her feelings. She handed Angel to her and quietly left her alone.

It wasn't long before Angel's mother came out of the mother's feeding room with Angel in her arms.

"She's in pain. Give her something!" she demanded.

"I just gave her some medicine a little while ago," said Britany mildly.

"But can't you see she's in pain!" The look on Debra's face was agonizing, and Britany reached out to touch her arm. Debra jerked away, causing Angel to flinch.

"Of course, I will get her something for pain," said Britany. "You're right, she looks very uncomfortable." Britany turned to prepare a small dose, and then gave it. Britany reasoned to herself that Debra needed some control in a very uncontrollable situation, and the medicine would definitely not hurt Angel.

Debra fussed about a couple of other things and then left. She had only stayed for thirty minutes. It was quite clear that she was starting to comprehend the severity of the situation.

Britany went over and picked up little Angel. She held her upright and looked into her large blue eyes.

"You have a rough road to travel for one so small, and your mother is very confused by all this. So are the rest of us, honey. It just makes no sense at all, and I'm not going to try and reason it out. You're a beautiful child, and I'm privileged to have a part in your short life." Britany cuddled her as she spoke and rocked her gently for as long as time would permit.

Britany went to the farm to ride after work and once again lost the concerns of the day in the thrill of riding. Angel's face continued to make an appearance in Britany's thoughts, and she realized that it was bothering her. She hoped she wouldn't be caring for Angel the next day. Michael was coming back, and she was very excited to see him again. She didn't want to be depressed when she saw him.

Finally it was Thursday, and Britany went to extra trouble to get ready for work. She expected Michael to be there already as she entered the nursery, and couldn't help being disappointed when he wasn't. The suspense was more than she cared for when he wasn't there at ten o'clock. Jeanne went to lunch with her, and she was glad for the company. It was two before she caught a glimpse of him entering the nursery. He was smiling and looked as attractive as she had remembered. She forgot to be nervous as she went to greet him. He reached for her hand as she approached.

"It sure is good to finally be here. My flight was delayed for fog. I was afraid I wasn't going to get here before shift change. You---" Michael stopped as he realized they weren't alone. In fact, there were several other nurses around them. He let go of her hand and greeted the others

"Well, how are the monitors working out?" He addressed those around.

"Great, thanks to your thorough instructions. They are wonderfully easy to hook up and don't pick up erroneous information like our others. It saves us a lot of steps running to check false alarms," Shelly spoke up.

"Well how many do you want to order?" asked Michael proudly.

"I think you'd better talk to the boss about that. I just hang out here No authority what-so-ever," Shelly responded. She threw up her hands and shook her head as if to wave off responsibility.

"You know better than that. Don't try to make him feel sorry for you," Margaret, the department head, said as she came up from behind. "Seriously, though, I think we had better talk about this in my office." She extended her hand toward her office.

"That would be just fine," Michael answered. He turned to Britany and whispered, "See you shortly," as he left.

He was in Margaret's office the rest of the shift. Britany hurried to finish work and change into her street clothes. Michael was still in the office as she returned, so she waited quietly in a chair close by. It felt good to be off her feet. In a few minutes the door opened. Britany could see Margaret, sitting at her desk, her gray hair neatly in place. Michael walked out and looked at Britany with a smile.

"I thought by the sounds of things that the new shift must be here. I won't be needing to take the monitors with me, so I guess we're ready to leave," he said. He touched the back of Britany's shoulder to escort her out the door.

"So how is Angel doing?" asked Michael as they stepped into the elevator.

"She's hanging in there, but she is definitely losing ground," Britany said as the elevator arrived at the ground floor. Michael looked so sad as she spoke that she reached out and squeezed his arm gently.

"I was really worried when you were so late. I'm glad it was simply delay due to fog," Britany said to change the subject.

"Yeah, it was a pretty boring morning. I think I read every version of the news they had. I'm glad I had my laptop computer with me. At least I got some work done."

They were soon through the hospital and at Britany's car. "Do you mind if I pick up Crystal and go to the house for awhile before we go out? I would kind of like to freshen up a bit," Britany asked.

"That would be fine. We have three hours before the play begins."

They settled into light conversation as they drove to the school. Crystal was as breezy as ever when she got into the car.

"Well, Michael, are you going to be able to come to my graduation? I got the OK from Grandmother," she asked.

"I checked, and I happen to be free." Michael nodded. "If it's OK with your mom and grandparents, I would be honored to come."

Britany felt a surge of delight instead of anxiety this time as they spoke of Crystal's graduation, and she was quick to respond.

"We would be the ones honored to have you come. The farm certainly isn't elegant, but it is very warm and inviting, and my mother dearly loves children. I hope Ben can come."

"I'm sure Ben would love the farm. It would be good for him to get out of the city for a few days. He's never been to the country, and I'm sure he would love it. Speaking of which, I was wondering if possibly we could go there tomorrow," Michael suggested. "I would like to see your horse that I've heard so much about. I like to ride, and it's been ages since I've been able to."

"That could easily be arranged, if you think you could stand my company without Crystal being with us. She has school tomorrow."

"I don't think that would be a problem. I kind of figured she would." Michael smiled at Britany as he spoke. Her heart fluttered as she read in his eyes more than his words had spoken.

'"Hmm..." said Crystal clearing her throat. "Don't forget I'm still here guys."

Britany glanced back at her through the mirror and smiled. "Don't worry Crystal. I would never forget you are around, but you do seem quiet."

"I'm rather tired," Crystal said, and sank back into the seat. "Besides its fun listening to the two of you talk."

Britany turned her attention back to Michael. "I hope you know how to ride fairly well. Jeanne's horse is not for a beginner." Britany glanced at him quickly, with concern, as she drove.

"I haven't ridden in quite awhile, but when I did I was fairly good at it. I would love a spirited horse," said Michael.

"Well, I can almost guarantee Jeanne's horse would be spirited enough for you. She rides cross-country jumping events. He is a hot horse and has lots of energy, but actually he is quite controllable. I think he would give you a good ride."

Britany continued. "I would let you ride my horse, but she is just getting broken in and can be unpredictable. She is really gentle and wouldn't hurt anyone intentionally, but her inexperience makes her more volatile She is also quite light on the reins, and if you would happen to get too rough she just might dump you."

"Jeanne's horse sounds great. Would she mind if I rode him?"

"No, my brother rides him quite often. Jeanne works tomorrow and won't be out to ride, because she also works the weekend. It will be good for him to get the exercise. My horse needs it, too. We have a horse show coming up in four weeks, and they both need a lot of work to be ready." They pulled into the drive as Britany finished speaking.

"You have a nice place here," Michael commented as he got out and held the door for Crystal to get out.

"We like it. It's small, but we're not here much, and we have all the space we need at the farm."

Britany showed him the living room and left him sitting comfortably chatting with Crystal while she excused herself to get ready.

She took a quick shower, reapplied her makeup, and slipped into a stylish, colorful dress to match the festive occasion. She dabbed some perfume on and took a glance in the mirror to check her appearance. Feeling somewhat shy, she entered the living room where Michael and Crystal where talking. Michael stopped in mid-sentence and smiled as she entered.

"You look beautiful," Michael said with awe as he rose and took her hand.

"Thank you. You look pretty handsome yourself," Britany replied softly, meeting his gaze. After a short pause she said, "I guess we can leave now."

They said their good-byes to Crystal and were soon on their way.

The weather was perfect. The sun was taking advantage of the time it had left until dusk. Britany felt as if everything was a little brighter than usual, and all her senses seemed to be a little keener. Michael smelled manly with an aftershave that she was sure would be a favorite of hers. Her car was small, and his nearness seemed comforting. They talked easily. Normally she hated first dates because she felt uncomfortable and stiff, but with him there was none of the stiffness and formality. She felt as if she had known him a long time.

He chose to take her to an elegant restaurant that Shelly had suggested to him. The carpeting was lush dark green with bold, rose-colored flowers. Chandeliers hung over each table and were dimly lit to cast a glimmer of light on the gold accents that reflected back a cascade of richness. Michael moved his chair a bit closer as they were seated at the table. Soft music played in the background. The marvelous smell of food floated all around them. Britany ordered shrimp, her favorite. Michael ordered the catch of the day. They both laughed after the waiter left, knowing that there wasn't a decent place to fish nearby and the fish certainly had not been caught that day.

They ate and talked. The lights danced on Britany's hair, shining on the gold highlights. Her dark green eyes sparkled and lit her soft-featured face. Her smile was warm and inviting. She was greatly enjoying herself, and her pleasure radiated all about her. Michael felt captivated by her warmth and charm and delighted in her presence.

Michael offered her his arm on the way to the car. The air felt cool and brisk. The sun was just visible between buildings as it disappeared on the horizon. Streetlights flickered, and car lights filled the street as they rushed by.

The play was delightful. The characters sang beautifully, and the dancing was captivating. Water cascaded from the ceiling during the "Singing in the Rain" scene. A few of the front row audience got wet, and they laughed. Britany leaned over and gave Michael a spontaneous kiss on the cheek while he was laughing. He squeezed her hand and smiled back at her.

They discussed the play and laughed again at the raining scene on the way to his motel.

"I'll be back at eight to go to the farm. Did you bring jeans and boots, by any chance?" Britany asked as they pulled up to the building.

"Actually I did. I was hoping to go riding. Would you like to come in?"

"I'd better not," Britany said. "I'll see you in the morning."

"Yeah, you're probably right. See you at eight," Michael said and leaned over to give her a quick kiss.

"Thank you for a wonderful evening," she replied softly. She started the car and looked behind her. She knew she would see him again in a few short hours, but she felt lonely as she drove away.

Michael went down the lobby to his room. The room felt cold and empty in comparison to the company he had just been in. He had looked forward to their date, but he was impressed by Britany more than he wanted to admit. She was different from anyone he had ever met, and the realization was a bit scary. He didn't have time for a serious relationship, especially not long distance. He had a promise to live up to. He was confused and not too happy at what he was feeling; yet at the same time he was compelled to be with her. What is happening to me! he thought as he fell into bed.

Michael saw Britany as soon as she entered the lobby, and he jumped to his feet. When he had awakened earlier in the morning he had thought of calling her and canceling their ride, since he was afraid of the feelings he was having, but as soon as he caught a glimpse of her smiling face he was glad he didn't. He gave her a fond embrace that lifted her to her toes, and he kissed her softly on the cheek. He was dressed in jeans with cowboy boots and carried a small gym bag. His arm remained around her shoulder as he escorted her to the car.

"If you like you can drive," Britany offered. "I'll be sure to tell you when to turn."

"You trust me to drive your new car! I must really have your confidence You don't even know if I'm a good driver."

"Well, are you a good driver?" she questioned.

"Truly I am, although I have a tendency to speed. I would love to drive I've always wanted to drive a Saturn, but if it's OK, I'd rather drive on the way back. I'd like to see all of the countryside I can." He opened the door for her.

"Sounds great," Britany said and took the driver's seat. Michael walked around to the other side and buckled himself in. He opened the window slightly and let the spring air in.

"I found out when I called my parents last night that they will be gone," Britany said as they drove. "They have a farm machinery sale to go to. They buy and sell farm machinery along with farming. They have done that since I was little. Mom and Dad buy machinery that needs to be fixed. Then they repair it and resell it hopefully at a profit. They mostly deal in horse-drawn equipment and sell it to the Amish people. It's getting hard for the Amish to find decent farm equipment they can afford, so my parents are helping them out in a way. My dad is such a softy that if someone needs something and can't really pay as much as he could get elsewhere, he will go ahead and sell it for less. He also has quite an impressive collection of old machinery and tractors. Tractors are his favorite. I know he would love to show you his collection. But I'm not sure whether or not they will be back before we leave."

"Your dad sounds like quite an impressive fellow."

"I think so, but then my view might be a bit distorted," stated Britany as they drove out of the city and into mile after mile of pancake-flat farmland.

Michael watched the farms breeze by as they drove. Tractors were in the field at almost every farm they passed. The planters made neat rows the length of the field. Small clouds of dust followed the tractors as they moved. Dark green wheat fields were scattered in the midst of the brown newly planted fields, giving a patchwork appearance to the land. The scent of fresh soil filled the air as they drove along.

Shortly they pulled into the farmyard, and Britany gave Michael a quick tour of the farm before they went to see the horses. He was interested in everything about the farm, and Britany enjoyed answering his many questions.

The horses nickered as they approached the pasture, and they ran to the fence for their treats. Britany gave them each an apple and a welcome rub behind their ears. They pushed into her pockets for more with their noses, and she laughed, gently pushing them back. She placed the halters on their heads and led them to the tack area in the front of the barn. Michael led Trigger; talking to him while they walked.

"I think he will get used to me faster if he hears the sound of my voice before I hop on his back," Michael said to Britany. Amy's pony whinnied and ran from side to side in the pasture.

"Will the pony be OK?" asked Michael with concern.

"Sissy always acts like that for a few minutes when we first leave, but then she quiets down. She will be fine," responded Britany as they reached the tack area.

She began brushing the dust out of Misty's coat, letting the lead rope fall to the ground. Michael watched and copied her actions. Both horses stood quietly for the grooming.

"Do you know how to saddle him up?" Britany asked.

"Sure, just show me his equipment. I think I can handle it," Michael answered with confidence.

"Would you rather ride English or Western?"

"Western please. I don't care for those English saddles. I don't know how you get used to them."

"They aren't hard at all to get used to. They let you feel the horse under you and help you know how he is going to move. You can also control the horse's movement with leg pressure. Never fear though, Trigger does well with both saddles," Britany explained and showed him where the saddle was kept along with the blanket and bridle.

Michael finished saddling Trigger at the same time Britany finished Misty.

"I'm impressed. I was afraid you may have told me you know how to ride when you actually didn't. Trigger is too much of a horse for someone who has never ridden before," Britany said as she checked the cinch of the saddle and made sure the bridle on Trigger was correct.

"I really have ridden quite a bit. Horses are quite popular in Tennessee and Michigan. An old friend of mine used to raise horses," responded Michael.

"Girl friend or guy friend?" Britany blushed as the words came out before she realized it. Why did she say that! she thought to herself.

"Does it matter?" He quickly turned to mount Trigger. Michael felt a little defensive. Why shouldn't he have girl friends? I've been divorced for a long time.

"No, not really. Just curious." She tried to hide her blunder. Britany felt resentment in his words and vowed to herself to think first before she spoke. She quickly mounted also.

They warmed up the horses in the arena. Misty pranced along as if she were showing off. Trigger obeyed Michael easily. After a short time Britany was assured that they were both fine, and she concentrated on working Misty. Britany noted after a while that she was working Misty alone. Michael and Trigger were in the middle of the arena watching them. She pulled in beside them.

"You make a beautiful team. Please don't stop. I was enjoying watching you work," Michael smiled.

Britany reined Misty back on the track, and together they performed some of the maneuvers they had practiced. Michael watched quietly. He was amazed at the ease and agility with which they moved. With no noticeable movement from Britany, Misty turned or changed paces. The horse and rider appeared to flow as one. Britany's hair was loose and flowed behind her, waving rhythmically up and down as she rode. Misty's golden mane and tail, slightly lighter in color than Britany's hair, streamed out behind them. Britany's slender form matched the horse's slender build, as she sat straight and tall. Her hands were expertly placed above the pommel of the saddle; her legs were slightly bent and steady. Michael watched and felt a growing fondness. The resentment he had felt was pushed aside.

Britany pulled up beside him.

"Are you ready to take the trails? They are beautiful this time of year Just stay away from logs, puddles or any thing that would give Trigger the least bit of reason to jump, or you will be over it in a flash. He was born to jump and takes every opportunity he can."

"Thanks for the warning. I might just try a jump if it looks reasonable. Don't worry about us. We will do just fine," Michael responded and reined Trigger around to follow Britany's lead.

The ride was marvelous as they went through woods and fields. New leaves were just beginning to peek through, adding a touch of green to the stark brown gray of winter. Birds sang, and squirrels scurried through the trees. A few wild flowers were making their appearance, but it was still too early for most. Michael tried Trigger over a jump once and was thrilled with the burst of energy. The next time Trigger caught him off guard as he flew over an indentation in the ground that was barley visible.

"You weren't exaggerating when you said he would jump at any opportunity I think he made that one up," Michael laughed as he straightened himself back in position on the saddle.

"Give yourself credit. You did well; I'm impressed. There hasn't been anything about you that I'm not impressed by," Britany said teasingly but honestly.

"You had better be careful. My ego can get out of control at times." Michael looked over and laughed.

They continued over the trail. Misty gingerly stepped around rocks and sticks while Trigger trudged along. Britany led the way down toward the river and dismounted at the bank. She ground-tied Misty, and let her pick at some of the sparse grass on the bank.

"You can do the same with Trigger. They won't head for home or go far. I thought maybe we could have our lunch here by this tree," she said, pointing to a tree that was leaning out over the river.

The river was small and flowed slowly, making a soft gurgling sound as it passed over rocks and around fallen trees. They spread a blanket over a moss-covered area that overlooked the river, arranged the food on it and sat down.

"This is so peaceful," said Michael. "I love being back in the saddle, and Trigger makes an excellent mount. The countryside is beautiful. I have a wonderful companion to share the day with. What more could a person ask for?" Michael took a drink and then stretched out on his back with his hands behind his head.

"How about a sandwich?" Britany asked, kneeling beside him holding out a sandwich. "I'm so glad you like it here. Its always been one of my favorite places."

He leaned up on his elbow facing her. As he reached for the sandwich his gaze caught hers, and instead of the sandwich he reached for her wrist and pulled her close. He kissed her gently, and she softened into his embrace. He kissed her again, longer and more passionately. She felt the strong masculine curve of the muscles across his back and shoulders as he embraced her.

Here was someone special. She felt she had known him all her life. She felt trust and confidence; a peace and oneness she had never felt before He kissed her cheek, her chin and continued in a path down her neck. A voice inside her warned, Be careful Britany. You trusted before, and remember where it got you. Reluctantly she withdrew her arm from behind his back and placed her hand on his chest. Then she pushed herself from his embrace and sat up.

"I think maybe you forgot your sandwich," she said with a coy smile, and retrieved it from the blanket where it had fallen from her hand.

"I guess maybe I did, but you looked a whole lot better."

"I kind of gathered that. You had better eat. It's a long way back to the farm."

He reached over and kissed her again lightly.

"Since you insist, I'll eat, but you still look much better." Michael smiled at her mischievously then settled back into a comfortable position and began to eat.

Britany felt a joy she was unable to explain as they rode back. She watched Michael as he rode. He was strong and confident. Nothing missed his keen sight. She couldn't seem to drink in the sight of him enough.

Her parents were back when they reached the barn. Britany introduced them to Michael. They visited for a short time, but it was soon time to go back in order for Michael to catch his flight. They freshened up before leaving the farm, then said good-bye and were off.

The ride back was bittersweet for Britany. She had enjoyed a wonderful time, but soon Michael would be gone again. He was driving, and she looked over to find him stealing glances at her.

"You look troubled. Is something on your mind?" he asked her.

"It's kind of embarrassing," she replied. "I feel sad to see you go. I've really enjoyed having you around, and I'm going to miss you." She looked up at him sadly.

"Come here," he said softly as he pulled into the parking spot at the motel and turned off the car. She leaned toward him and he comfortingly embraced her as much as the limited space of the car would allow.

"Come inside. I need to get my things together. I'll behave, I promise," he whispered in her ear, then kissed her cheek and released her.

She smiled back at him and said, "OK."

She waited seated on a leather chair while he packed his things, shaved, and cleaned up. She felt nervous and unsure of what to say as she waited for him. She squirmed in the chair and looked around the room, trying hard to act relaxed.

"I'll be back in three weeks for the graduation, you know," he said as he came out of the bathroom donning his shirt.

There was something intimate about sitting there watching him, and Britany felt herself blush slightly. He noticed and smiled. He walked over and lifted her out of the chair to her feet. The smell of after-shave filled her senses as his arms moved around her, and her cheek was drawn against his bare chest.

"You're blushing," he said with his cheek against her hair.

"I know. I'm just being silly. Sometimes I feel a bit off guard around you."

"Good, I like to surprise you. Keeps you wondering. I will be back in three weeks, and you will be very busy between now and then. I'm anxious for you to meet my son. I think you'll like him."

"That's right!" Britany exclaimed and took a step back looking up at him. "I'm anxious to see him, too! I'm sure I'll like him, especially if he's anything like you."

"Well, he looks like me. Outside of that I'm not so sure." He glanced at his watch. "Are you hungry? If we hurry we can eat at the airport while I'm waiting for my plane."

They drove to the airport and found a restaurant for supper. Britany walked with Michael to the terminal. She watched the airplane depart, again feeling the bittersweet feeling. An ache filled her heart as she watched the plane get smaller and smaller. Soon it was out of sight, and she turned to leave.

Michael settled into his seat, trying hard to relax. The flight was fast, but not as fast as his churning emotions. Maybe he was wrong to promise to go back in three weeks. Maybe it was safer to stay in Tennessee.

CHAPTER 10

When Britany arrived at work the next day Angel was much worse. Debra West came in, quiet and subdued. She held Angel in the rocker as tears flowed down her face. She stayed only twenty minutes and then left, never speaking. Two hours later she was back. She wrapped Angel gently in her little pink blanket. Angel's eyes were no longer bright, and she was too weak to smile or even cry. Her wispy hair was almost gone, and her cheeks were gaunt and hollow. She had a gray-green coloring, and her arms and legs were nothing but skin and bone. Angel's mother picked her up gently and sat in the rocker. This time she sang softly to Angel.

It took all Britany's reserve to care for the other babies and not dissolve into tears. Her eyes burned, and she noticed tears on the faces of the other nurses. More than once her work mates would excuse themselves and come back with noticeable redness to their eyes. They watched discreetly, not wanting to interfere, but each feeling deep empathy for the mother and love for the baby, who had been with them for quite a while.

Jeanne approached Debra. "Britany could go with you to get something to eat, and I will hold Angel," she suggested.

"No, thank you. I'm not hungry," she said softly and continued singing.

At one o'clock Britany called Dr. Riley to inform him that Angel's conditioned had worsened. He arrived just minutes before Angel took her last breath while in her mother's arms. Jeanne stood by the mother's side with her hand on her shoulder. Dr. Riley stood beside the two of them. No one spoke as the mother held the infant tightly in her arms. They remained that way for quite some time before the mother finally looked up and said, "At least she can rest now and feels no more pain. I'll see her again some day, and she will be whole and complete."

Jeanne and Dr. Riley nodded softly in agreement. Britany called the father and grandparents to tell them about Angel and to ask if someone would come and be with the mother. She also made the necessary phone call to the funeral home where the arrangements had been made. Britany then called the family's pastor.

The father arrived within ten minutes looking very lost and confused. Jeanne and Britany escorted both parents to the family room where they could spend a few last minutes with Angel. The grandparents and pastor arrived soon afterward. Britany showed them to the room where the parents were.

Jeanne waited an appropriate amount of time and then asked if she could take the baby. Together she and Britany bathed and prepared the body in a separate room. Tears flowed freely as they bathed the shell of a body that had once been a beautiful baby.

"It's really hard to understand how God could let something like this happen. She was such a beautiful baby, with loving parents," Britany said accusingly.

"I learned a long time ago not to question God," Jeanne responded. "Every life to Him is valuable. Some are just on this earth longer than others, is all. God's ways are not for us to reason out. Our wisdom is foolishness to God. We just need to accept life and realize that God is in control no matter what it may seem to us. We will only confuse and frustrate things if we continually ask why," Jeanne finished with a peace that Britany wondered at.

"I wish it were as easy to believe as you make it sound. It still seems cruel to me," Britany said, shaking her head sadly.

Britany felt depressed and dazed as she proceeded through the day. In the evening Michael called. At the sound of his voice a heavy weight seemed to lift slightly from Britany's shoulders. She told him of Angel's death. It was comforting to have him share in her sorrow.

"Are you all right? Is there anything I can do?"

"You already have. I'm sure I will be fine. I just need some time. I felt pretty involved in her little life," she responded in a subdued voice. "It's going to be hard to accept that she's gone." A muffled sob escaped her lips, followed by silence. "I'm sorry. It's hardly fair to involve you in this. It's comforting just to know you're concerned, and it's so nice to hear your voice. Thanks for being concerned."

"You take care of yourself. I'll see you in three weeks. If anything comes up, call me." Michael hung up the phone and shook his head as if to clear it. What was it that drew him to her so? How could she be so vulnerable and yet so strong? He had called to tell her work had changed his plans about the graduation. When he heard about Angel he couldn't bring himself to tell her. Now he didn't want to change them. He wanted more than anything to see her again.

It was raining hard Sunday morning, and Britany felt relieved. She didn't want to try at any false cheerfulness. The rain seemed quite appropriate. She watched it patter against the windows, total darkness as a backdrop. She ate breakfast and read the twenty-third Psalm. She pictured little Angel in Jesus' arms like the sheep the psalmist spoke of.

The space where Angel's crib had been seemed empty and was a constant reminder. Every glimpse in that direction brought a sharp stab of pain. In unspoken agreement no babies were put in that spot. It was reserved in respect for Angel.

Britany and Jeanne left work an hour early to go to Angel's funeral. The room where Angel lay was full of flowers and smelled like carnations. Debra and Brian stood beside the casket as family members and friends spoke to them. Britany thought Debra's face looked softer and less stressed. Britany was surprised when Debra reached out and hugged her as she came near.

"Thank you both for coming. The two of you cared for my Angel deeply. I know it was almost as difficult for you as it was for Brian and me. You know, I just kept thinking everything would be all right-that God would reach down and heal her." She dabbed at a tear in the corner of her eye with a tissue. "Then when

I realized that He wouldn't, I was so mad. I know I wasn't very nice to the two of you, but you helped me more than you can ever realize."

Debra reached out and took Jeanne's hand. "Jeanne, your faith never wavered, and your acceptance of God's will helped me through this. I may never know the reason Angel died, but I'm ready to put it in God's hands, and be reassured that He loves me and that He loves Angel even more than I do. Thank you."

Jeanne reached her arm around Debra's shoulder. Britany thought of how frail Jeanne looked physically, but how strong she was spiritually. Her long slender frame and short wispy hair were a stark contrast to Debra's short, full stature; yet she was strong were it counted and was giving strength to others. Maybe someday Britany's own faith would be so strong.

Britany was amazed at Debra's words. It had seemed that most of the time she never recognized they were around. She thought back to her prayer asking God to help her comfort Debra. She realized that God had answered that prayer even though Britany had felt inept. God definitely worked in a mysterious way.

She thought about God as she went home and prepared for the next day. She went to work in the morning feeling a peace about Angel after speaking with Debra. The day seemed almost normal, and it went faster than she expected.

At the end of the day Britany was preparing the work area for the next shift to come in. Jeanne was across the room stocking the shelves with new supplies. A noise startled Britany, and she glanced up to see Jeanne standing by the shelf with a blank look on her face. A box of diapers was lying at her feet. Britany jumped to her feet and ran toward her. Jeanne touched her forehead as if to clear her thoughts and then noticed the box of diapers beside her feet.

"Clumsy me," Jeanne said as she bent to retrieve the diapers.

"Oh, no, you don't. You come and sit down. I don't like the look on your face," Britany said with authority as she grasped her shoulders and led her to a rocking chair.

"Are you OK?" Britany questioned.

"Really, I am fine. I guess Angel's dying bothered me more than I realized," Jeanne tried to assure Britany.

"You just sit here for a while and let me get you a drink." Britany rushed out to get some water.

Jeanne looked fine when Britany returned. The confused look was gone. She handed Jeanne the water and then sat down beside her in another rocker.

"Can you tell me what happened?" questioned Britany leaning forward slightly.

"Things just seemed a bit fuzzy for a while. The next thing I knew you were beside me and the box was on the floor. It was probably from the stress and reaching up over my head to put away the boxes. I have low blood pressure. I'm sure that was it," Jeanne tried to reason.

"Has anything like this happened before?" Britany continued to question with a look of concern.

"No, and I am just fine. I told you it was from reaching over my head," Jeanne insisted. "Now we had better get back to work or the next crew will be here, and we won't be ready."

"OK, but you sit and do the paper work. I'll do the rest of the stocking. I also want you to see a doctor and tell him what happened."

"Sure, Mom, whatever you say," Jeanne said with a tease in her voice.

Jeanne was fine the next several days, and the incident was all but forgotten.

Britany and Crystal spent the next weekend with her parents to help with preparations for graduation. Jeanne and Amy joined them on Saturday and Sunday.

Britany, Crystal, Jeanne, Amy, and Liz worked hard to prepare the house for the graduation. Britany's mother wanted the windows washed, the carpets cleaned, some simple repairs done and new draperies hung in the dining area.

"Mom, I know I can't really complain because you are doing this for me and Crystal, but do you truly think we can get it all done?" Britany asked.

"We can do it. If we don't get it all done today, I can work on the remainder during the week," Liz said. "That reminds me. The back bedroom needs cleaned out, too. You be sure and tell Michael he and his son are to stay here. I don't want them to travel all that way just for Crystal and then stay in a motel," she continued, working steadily.

"Don't worry Grandma," said Crystal. "I already told Michael he was to stay here. He was excited, too. He said it would be good for his son to be on the farm for a day or two."

"Yeah, and she did that the day we met! What if I didn't like him or he turned out to be a creep!" exclaimed Britany.

"Mom, you just don't trust me enough. I knew he was a great person when I first met him, and there was no doubt from looking at you that you liked him," Crystal said with full confidence, shrugging her shoulders slightly, her blonde hair flipping lightly across them.

"She's right there, you know," Jeanne said. "We all knew there was something happening between you two. We are glad for you, so stop pretending to be upset with Crystal and be grateful. You now have a definite time when he will be coming again." She patted Britany on the shoulder. "I think maybe we had better get to work."

Britany and Crystal started with the carpets. Jeanne and Amy worked on the windows. The day was sunny and warm. A breeze came through the open windows and drove out the staleness of winter, while the cream lace curtains billowed in the wind. They worked hard, and by the time Liz announced it was time for a break, they were well on their way to finishing the tasks. Liz had fresh baked sugar cookies with a golden crust and homemade lemonade waiting for them on the front porch.

The old farmhouse was white with green trim. A large porch adorned the front. Original Victorian scrollwork decorated the posts supporting the roof of the porch. A swing hung suspended from the ceiling. White wicker furniture with green stuffed cushions added to the charm and sense of repose.

Britany and Jeanne sat on the swing. Amy jumped up and sat between them. She pushed the swing with her toes. Britany's dad, Charles, joined them when Liz called to him in the barn. He strode up and sat in the chair next to Liz. He relaxed back, his lean leg folded ankle over knee. Taking his hat from his head he ran a hand through his gray hair.

"I see Mom's got you working hard," he said to Britany, who was tickling Amy.

"You should see all the things she has planned for us to do!" Britany exclaimed, giving him her full attention. The porch swing swayed in a frenzy from Amy's trying to escape Britany's tickles.

"I don't have to. I know your mom. When she starts spring-cleaning, there is no stopping her. At least she feeds you good!" he said, reaching for the glass of lemonade and cookies Liz held out to him. The ice clinked against the clear glass as he took it. A fresh pair of slacks and cool summer top replaced the coveralls Liz normally wore. Her eyes sparkled at the compliment.

"Yeah, these cookies are great! Do you think I will be able to make cookies like Grandma Liz when I grow up?" Amy piped in. The swing was once again in a rhythmic motion.

"Grandma will be glad to teach you. I think I was around ten when she taught me," Crystal said.

The little group worked hard into the day and finished in time to go horseback riding before falling exhausted into bed for the night.

Michael called when Britany returned from the farm on Sunday. She had just changed into an oversized T-shirt that she slept in when the phone rang. "I'll get it!" Britany called to Crystal. She hoped that it was Michael. She wasn't disappointed as his voice came across the wire.

"I was worried about you and wondered how you have been doing," Michael said.

"I'm doing fine. We were at the farm getting things ready for the graduation. It was a lot of work, but we had a great time. Mom wants me to be sure to tell you that both you and Ben are to stay at the farm when you come," Britany said cheerfully as she pulled back the covers of her bed and seated herself comfortably, leaning back on the headboard.

"To be quite truthful, Ben and I have been looking forward to staying there. He can't stop talking about riding the horses and maybe getting to milk a cow."

"I'm sure we can arrange that. It's kind of funny. I was dreading this graduation. Now I'm looking forward to it. Well, not the graduation itself but getting to see you again and meeting your son. The graduation is still going to be hard, but having you there will make it easier."

"I can't even imagine the day when Ben graduates. It's hard to think of him grown up when he is only nine," Michael replied.

"It's hard now for me to picture Crystal when she was nine, but in a way, it seems like she should still be nine. I guess things change. All we can do is just hang on for the ride and watch them. I think we had better change the subject. I'm getting a bit nostalgic," Britany suggested.

"OK. How would you like to go boating for a weekend?" he said, trying to make it sound like an everyday type of question.

"Are you serious?" exclaimed Britany as she bolted to an upright position.

"Very serious. Shelly called and asked if we could join her and Stan on their boat the weekend after the graduation. She felt it would be good for you to get out instead of being at home worrying about Crystal. She called me first to see what I thought and if I would be able to fly up. I thought it was a great idea, and I get enough frequent flyers that the flight is no problem. The only problem I see is you: if you will agree, and if you can get the time off work," Michael explained lightheartedly.

"I've filled in enough for others and have enough vacation time that it should be no problem getting the time off. I will check when I go in tomorrow. I'm still not sure why Shelly asked you first," she said quizzically as she once again relaxed against the headboard.

"To be quite truthful, she felt you would be hesitant to ask me, and she also felt you might not think it was proper. She assured me, though, that we will be adequately chaperoned---much to my dismay."

Britany laughed and said, "You know she is right. Sometimes I think she knows me a little too much. That sounds wonderful. I'm going to call her right away and thank her."

"You may want to wait. We've been talking quite awhile. According to my watch, it's midnight there."

"Oh, my goodness! You're right! I guess I had better go. I hate to, though. Thanks for calling and brightening up my day," responded Britany. She wanted to add, "Thanks for brightening up my life," but held back the words.

"I'll see you soon. Sweet dreams," came the alluring voice over the phone.

"You too," she replied softly.

She reached over to hang up the phone on the nightstand and turn off the light. Then she slipped under the covers and turned to her side snuggling into the pillow. Her last thoughts were thanksgiving to God and warm feelings for Michael.

On the other end Michael was confused. Last week he was hesitant to see her again; now he had just asked her to join him for the entire weekend. The funny thing was, he was as excited as she.

CHAPTER 11

The next several days focused primarily on Crystal. She had received a last minute invitation to the prom from a close friend of hers. She wasn't dating anyone regularly and neither was Noah, so they decided to go together.

Britany and Crystal spent two evenings shopping for a prom dress. Dresses that Britany felt looked pretty Crystal turned her nose up to; things that Crystal loved were either too low-cut or not in her size. The cost was also a definite factor. Britany just couldn't bring herself to pay the extravagant cost of many of the dresses. Most things that they did together they both enjoyed, but this was definitely not going well. By the end of second day Britany decided something had to give. The next day she sent Crystal off with one of her friends and a list of stipulations to buy a dress. Britany drove out to the farm to ride and to try to recover some of the patience she had lost. For the present, having Crystal away at college didn't sound like such a bad idea.

Britany arrived home before Crystal, much more relaxed than when she had left. She was just finishing a load of laundry when Crystal and her friend came home. Britany smiled as their excited voices entered the house.

"Mom, I finally found one! Tabitha knew of a place were she got hers that she thought I would like. It's an expensive shop, but they had a display dress in just my size, and it is gorgeous! It's not too low in front and it fits like it was made just for me. I'm going to try it on, and don't look until I tell you to," Crystal exclaimed as she hurried to change into the dress.

Crystal looked radiant as she waltzed into the room. The dress was an emerald green with a v neckline, and an off the shoulder sleeve made up of a ruffle. The bodice and waist were fitted with a skirt that flared out to just below the knee.

"You were right. It's beautiful, and you look just stunning!" exclaimed Britany as she crossed the room to give Crystal a hug. "I wonder how much it would cost to have shoes dyed to match."

"We already have some ordered. We took the dress so we could match it and we ordered them. They really weren't too much. We can pick them up Friday. I hope you don't mind."

"Considering that you got the dress for less than we had planned, it should be fine. Turn around again so I can see. Then you had better take it off and hang it up. We don't want anything to happen to it."

Saturday arrived before she realized it. Britany shared Crystal's excitement as they spent the morning getting last-minute details finished and doing light housework. Britany left around noon to pick up napkins and favors for the graduation. She had a very strong urge to go shopping for herself to have something new to wear on the boating trip. She kept telling herself that it wasn't necessary, and that she had already spent enough this month, but she just couldn't get it out of her mind. Finally when she had all the errands done sooner than planned, she gave in and took a side trip to the shopping mall.

The stores were bursting with new styles for summer. She wasn't at all sure what to wear for a boating trip. She chose white denim shorts with a red and white striped sailor top. She also got a new pair of white canvas shoes. She looked for a new bathing suit but was disappointed with the new styles. They seemed too skimpy or too expensive. She shrugged as she took one off the rack and then replaced it. Maybe another time she would have more luck. She was pleased with what she had and hurried home

Music filled the air as Britany entered the house. Crystal was playing the piano. The sound was beautiful as she put things away. A pain of sadness touched her, as she thought of how soon it would be before Crystal was gone, and she would be all alone. Tears came to the corner of her eye and she stubbornly brushed them away. I will be fine, she reminded herself. God has always been there for me and with me when I needed him. He won't stop now.

Crystal was in her room when the doorbell rang at six. Britany escorted Noah into the living room and offered him a glass of cola while he waited. She had always considered Noah to be a cute boy, but as he waited dressed in his black tux, she realized that he was becoming a handsome young man.

"I guess since Crystal's dad isn't here to intimidate you and scare you on your first date, maybe I should fill in for him. Do you have any pointers to help me out?" Britany teased as she sat across from him in the living room.

"Maybe if you stood on a stool and spoke real deep it would help," Noah joked back. "I don't think it would do much good, though. I've known you too long to be scared. Besides, I don't know how anyone could be too scared of you, Britany."

Crystal entered the room. Noah rose as she came in. She looked stunning in her emerald green dress, her blonde hair waving over her shoulders.

"You look lovely, Crystal." Noah's eyes shone. "Here, I brought these for you," Noah said as he handed her a wrist corsage with red roses and a green ribbon that matched the dress.

"How did you know the color!" Crystal exclaimed.

"I have my sources," Noah said as he placed it on her arm.

They made an attractive couple. Britany made them pose for pictures until they protested and insisted that they would be late if they didn't leave. She watched them leave with feelings of love and tenderness. She was sure Crystal was going to enjoy the prom, even if Noah was just a friend.

Britany filled the evening by making banana bread for the graduation to keep in the freezer. She also started baking several layers for the cake. By ten o'clock she was worn out and fell asleep on the couch. Around one o'clock Noah and Crystal came home so Crystal could change to go to the after-prom activities. They were bubbling and full of descriptions of the events of the night. Britany was able to wake up enough to join in the excitement. They left shortly after, and Britany went to bed. She was going to get up at four to go and help with the breakfast the parents were serving to the prom-goers.

Work was unusually calm during the week, for which Britany was grateful.

She needed all her energy to prepare for graduation. The open house was on Saturday with the actual graduation to be on Sunday. Michael and Ben were arriving at seven-thirty Friday night.

By Friday she was very keyed up. She had lists and double lists of things to be done. She was excited about seeing Michael again and meeting his son. She felt pride and nostalgia, mixed with a sadness over Crystal. She felt overwhelmingly nervous about the open house. All the feelings seemed to tumble over each other, and she was never sure which feeling was going to surface at what time. Fortunately all the excitement took the form of nervous energy, and she was able to do the tasks that needed to be accomplished. Crystal didn't share all the jumbled emotions Britany felt, or at least she didn't appear to. She was involved in all the fun and gaiety surrounding graduation and took every opportunity she could to partake in it. Britany was glad to see her enjoy herself. She wanted this to be a happy time in her life.

Friday finally arrived. Britany and Crystal were anxiously waiting at the airport terminal for the arrival of Michael's flight. The last few minutes seemed like hours for Britany as they watched the planes land.

"Mom, you're acting like one of my classmates," Crystal teased.

At that point Britany couldn't care less how she was acting. The loud speaker was announcing the arrival of Flight 605 at Terminal Seven, and they hurried to watch the passengers unboard. Britany caught a glimpse of Michael's head and ran to greet him. Michael saw her just moments after she saw him and placed his bag on the floor to free his arms. He swept her off her feet in a huge hug as she reached him, and then kissed her fully on the lips.

"Now, that's how I like to be greeted!" Michael said as he released her back to the floor. "This is my son, Ben. Ben, this is Britany and her daughter Crystal."

"Hi, Ben, I've been eager to meet you!" Britany said as she extended her hand for a handshake and then changed her mind and gave him a quick hug.

The top of Ben's sandy-colored hair reached to Britany's shoulder. His dark brown eyes mirrored his father's only with more reserve, a bit too serious for a child of nine.

Crystal reached a hand out in greeting and in her beguiling way said, "I'm glad to meet you, too. Someone has to help me keep these two in line! They can be quite a handful. I do fine when its just Mom by herself, but the two of them together can be too much."

Britany gave Crystal an exasperated look, but Ben gave her a slight smile, and Michael laughed.

"Crystal, you never cease to amaze me," Michael said. "Come on, you guys. I don't know about you, but I'm starved. Is the food here any good?"

"It's good, but I thought maybe we could go to this place that serves great spaghetti and lasagna," Britany said. "It looks like a railway station. Some of the tables are actually set up inside old railway cars. It's real cute, and I insist, it's my treat."

"I love lasagna, but Miss Britany, my dad would never let you pay for it," Ben said politely.

"He won't, will he? Well, thanks for warning me," Britany said with a smile. She loved the way he said "Miss Britany" and felt a bond toward him that surprised her a little. He resembled his dad, but she could tell instantly that they were quite different.

Ben was impressed with Britany's car. He looked it over and told her some specifics about the car and its engine.

"I guess he's a little interested in cars," Britany said to Michael out of Ben's earshot.

"That's putting it mildly. Cars, sports and hunting, that's where his mind is. He reads a lot and has a memory for statistics," Michael replied.

The conversation was lively throughout the meal and on the drive to the farm. It seemed as if Ben had a question about every aspect of the farm.

"Dad, can we go straight to the barn and see the cows and horses?" Ben asked as soon as the car pulled into the driveway.

"Ben, it's close to ten o'clock. I'm afraid it will have to wait until morning," Michael said.

Britany's parents were still up, and Britany introduced Ben. Liz showed Michael and Ben where they could put their things.

"Are you hungry? Would you like something to eat?" Liz asked.

"Oh, no, ma'am. We just ate before we came out. I'm stuffed. Thank you, though. I've heard good comments about your cooking," said Michael.

The conversation continued until Britany finally said, "I hate to break up the party, but it's late, and we have a big day tomorrow." She was disappointed that she hadn't been able to see Michael alone, but she hoped they would find some time the next day.

Britany heard Liz in the kitchen early the next morning and hurried to help. She quickly freshened up, put on a touch of make-up and tied her hair back with a bow. She would shower and do her hair later. She put on a pair of jeans and a purple T-shirt then hurried downstairs.

Britany and her mom put the ham in the oven and started the potatoes and eggs to cook for potato salad. Britany took the cake layers out of the freezer and started the icing for the cake. It wasn't too long before Michael came out to see if he could help.

"If you wouldn't mind, you could help Britany's dad with the chores when he comes down," responded Liz. "Then I won't have to go out to the barn until later. He will be down shortly."

"I would be glad to help with chores, ma'am."

Thanks. I appreciate it. I saved a little ham to have for breakfast. Would you like some with eggs?" Liz asked.

"The eggs and ham sound terrific," Michael said as he lowered himself into a chair.

Britany smiled over at him from where she was mixing the icing at the counter. He looked handsome in his T-shirt and jeans. His shoulder muscles bulged beneath his shirt as he crossed his arms in front of him. He leaned back in the chair with his legs stretched out, his bare feet crossed at the ankles. He smiled back at her and she felt a thrill run through her. She knew she was falling in love with this man with his calm manner and winning ways. The thought was scary, but she felt she could drink in the sight of him forever.

Liz left the room with an excuse that she needed to get something and

Michael quickly rose and came up behind Britany were she stood at the counter. He placed his arm around her waist and gave her a firm embrace.

"I like waking up to your smiling face. A guy could get addicted to it real fast," he whispered in her ear and then kissed her on the cheek. He returned to his place on the chair before her mother came back. "Your mom seems like a real special lady," he continued once he was seated.

"I think so. She is certainly going out of her way for this graduation. I have always tried not to be a burden to my parents but it gets rough at times being a single parent. Both my parents have been great about being there when I need them. Crystal and my mom have a very special relationship and I cherish that," Britany replied, glad for the conversation change to give her time to compose herself.

Liz returned and shortly Charles appeared ready to start chores. He was jovial, and Britany could tell he was as excited as she about the graduation of his oldest grandchild. Soon he and Michael were on their way out the door. Not long after the door closed a sleepy Ben appeared from the bedroom. His hair was tousled and a lock stood straight up on the back of his head. Britany chuckled to herself but managed to keep a straight face.

"Hi, did you sleep good last night?" Britany asked.

"Where's my dad?" he asked.

"He went to the barn to help with chores," answered Britany.

"Can I go too? I can help," Ben said enthusiastically. He was suddenly wide awake.

"Of course you can go! Liz exclaimed. "They can use your help. Britany will walk out with you. She can show you the horses and you can help her feed them. Later, after breakfast, Crystal can show you how to gather eggs and feed the goats," Liz said.

Ben looked more alert than ever and ran to the bedroom in a flash to get dressed.

"Things are going just fine. You take some time and spend with the boy. I think you are both good for each other," Liz said as Ben ran for the room.

Britany gave her mother a quizzical look but didn't question her. She put down the icing and went to change.

Ben was excited over the cows and pigs, and begged for a ride when he saw the pony. Britany assured him that later, after the open house, she would saddle them up and the three of them could go riding. She suggested that in the mean time he could join the men and help feed the animals. They went back to the milk house where Michael and her dad where finishing the milking.

"I'm getting initiated well. I even smell like a cow," said Michael.

"Boy dad you sure do! Whew!" Ben said as he puckered up his nose.

"That's a good smell Ben. That's the smell of dollar bills. Without those cows we wouldn't be able to afford this farm or the food on our table," Charles said.

Britany wasn't sure Ben fully understood what her dad meant but he looked thoughtful.

Jeanne arrived at eight and helped with breakfast. Amy insisted on going upstairs and waking up Crystal. Britany readily agreed since she felt it was long past time for her to get up anyway.

Following breakfast Jeanne and Britany worked on the cake, while everyone else set up tables and chairs on the lawn. The day was beautiful and a soft breeze rustled the leaves overhead. Jeanne and Britany brought out the finished cake, as the last of the tables were in place, and set it on the center table that was covered in white paper. Everyone cheered as it took the place of honor. Britany fixed another table with pictures of Crystal, as she was growing up, and special achievements she had earned. The rest of the food was set up, and Britany hurried to shower and get ready. The morning had flown and it was time for guests to arrive. She was glad the graduation itself wasn't until the next day. She needed to face one thing at a time.

The rest of the afternoon was a blur of greetings and introductions. Britany was relieved, when she found herself so busy, that there was no time to be sad. Most of the time she simply felt pride in Crystal with all the wonderful comments the guests made. Britany had been fearful many times during Crystal's childhood. She was concerned that she wasn't being the mother she should be. Whether Britany had been a good mother or not, Crystal was doing well. She felt grateful to God for His guidance and protection through the years.

Charles saddled up the pony later after the meal and took the children for rides as he led Sissy. They were all excited and begged to ride time and time again. Michael gave him a break, and led the pony for a while. When most of the other children were gone Ben and Amy were able to ride the pony by themselves. Ben proved to be a fast learner and looked as if he was thoroughly enjoying himself.

Michael came up behind Britany just before dusk and suggested that they sneak off, and go for a walk, just the two of them. Britany readily agreed.

The quietness was revitalizing as they walked along the path to the woods. The soft breeze was still blowing, and it carried the scent of dusk on a warm summer day. The air was beginning to cool a bit, and, even though it hadn't been hot, the coolness felt good. Purple martins darted after bugs calling out as they flew. The sun dropped to the horizon, and resembled a big, brilliant, orange ball. Shades of pink, orange and red mixed with the blue sky to add patches of violet to the scene.

"It's been quite a day," Britany said with a sigh as they walked hand in hand. "You seemed to make quite an impression on my dad," she continued, turning her attention from the sky to look over at Michael.

"I really like him. It was good to work with the animals again. I've always enjoyed that. I wouldn't care to farm myself, but it was nice to help out."

She told him about the feeling of pride and gratitude she had felt earlier in the day. He stopped, turned to face her and said.

"You are special Britany. I've dated a lot of ladies, even married one, but you are different. I feel at ease with you and it's kind of like I've known you for a long time not just several weeks. It's hard to explain, and I'm not sure why I'm saying this."

"You don't need to explain. I feel the same way about you. I keep reminding myself that I just met you, and that I haven't known you forever. It's just that I feel more whole when I'm with you. Like you make me a better person.

I like that, and I like being with you," Britany spoke softly.

He looked deeply into her dark green eyes and then kissed her fully. She returned his kiss and reached around the back of his neck to pull herself close to him. Reluctantly he released her, and slowly they walked back.

During the night Britany awoke for some unknown reason. Soft rhythmic breathing from the other bed assured her that Jeanne was fast asleep. Not sure why she had awoken, she went to the window to look out. Everything looked quiet. Clad in her white cotton gown with lace trim she stood looking out the window. A slight breeze rustled the lace on her gown. She searched the barnyard carefully, then her gaze traveled to the stars above. They were shining brightly, and she smiled. She noticed one star seemed to shine brighter than the rest. She studied it for a while, but she couldn't remember seeing it before. No, wait, she thought. She remembered seeing it on Easter morning. The lustrous star that had shown brilliantly in the spot she had cherished as a little girl. She pondered for a while what would be taking place in the solar system that might be causing it. She didn't remember reading anything about a star being particularly bright this time of year. Then it was just as if a fog had lifted. She remembered that as a young girl she had watched for that one star that would shine radiantly for a special someone. The one who would be her husband. The man God intended for her. Her heart beat wildly as the thought filled her, and tears began to sting her eyes.

"Dear God," she prayed silently as she mouthed the words, not wanting to awaken anyone. "Could it possibly be that the star is shining for Michael? Could he be the one that You have chosen for me?" Her knuckles were white from being clasped tensely as she held them to her chest. Her face lifted toward heaven, her eyes shut tight, she continued her prayer. Her entire body was so taut she felt as if she didn't dare breathe in anticipation of what the answer might be. She wasn't sure how she expected God to answer--she just knew He would. Ever so slowly she took a deep breath and opened her eyes. The star shone brighter than ever, and suddenly the answer was clear, shining as bright as the star. Michael was the one!

She slowly dropped to her knees, her gown folding around her. Moonlight filtered in and shone softly on her white frock. She bowed her head in reverence as the words of Revelation came to her thoughts:

> "You are worthy, our Lord and God, to receive glory and honor and power, for you created all things, and by your will they were created and have their being."
> Revelation 4:11

She felt small and unimportant next to God's greatness, yet very blessed by His touch. A peace filled her, and ever so quietly she got back into bed and fell into a serene sleep.

The next morning they all prepared for church. The house was a mass of activity as they were all trying to get ready. Britany's brother, Phillip, and his wife, Lori, met them at church, and once again the whole family was together, along with their guests.

Jeanne leaned over and whispered to Britany, "Have you asked Michael if he is a Christian or not yet?"

Britany just shrugged her shoulders. She had been putting off the inevitable. Michael never seemed defensive when she talked about Jesus. She felt in her heart that surely he must be a Christian, but was afraid to ask, knowing what happened in the past.

"The fact that he came is a good sign," Jeanne said encouragingly.

Britany smiled.

Crystal sat in the front of the church with the other graduates from various schools in the community. They were all wearing their caps and gowns.

"You have a very warm, caring church. It's refreshing to hear Jesus spoken of with so much love," Michael said thoughtfully as they walked to the car following the service. "Our church is so formal that God's tenderness gets forgotten. You are very fortunate."

"Thank you." Britany's heart soared. "I'm glad you like it so. I've been wanting to ask if you know Jesus, but I wasn't sure exactly how to."

"I guess I've had the advantage. I knew from the first day I met you-when you were taking Angel out to her mother-that you had a very strong faith. That's part of what attracted me to you." He paused for a moment and then continued. "I'm afraid my faith hasn't always been so strong. I've known Jesus since I was little, but I strayed as a teenager. Then I got very bitter and defensive during the divorce. I'm afraid I am still struggling with that now. I guess that is probably why the message of Jesus' love was so touching."

Britany looked up into his eyes and squeezed his hand tightly.

"God works in mysterious ways. You thought you were here for Crystal's graduation."

He chuckled and shook his head. It was a mystery to him why he had come Maybe she was right. Could God be calling out to me! he wondered.

The rest of the family was joining them. They piled into cars and drove into town, where they went to eat before the graduation ceremony began.

During the ceremony Britany sat between Michael and Jeanne. Her heart filled with hopes and dreams for Crystal as she watched her march down the field. It was hard to see Crystal's face clearly, but she could tell it was her. Crystal looked calm and confident as she marched with the rest. The names of the graduates were read, and each filed up to the podium to receive his or her diploma. Britany had known most of them since they were little, and she was amazed to see how grown-up they were. Britany managed to hold back most of the tears during the ceremony, but a few did escape and slide down her cheek.

She prayed silently during the closing that God would lead and guide Crystal throughout her life. She said a prayer for the rest of the graduates as well. It was scary thinking about the things they were going to face. She prayed that if they didn't already know and trust Jesus, somewhere during their lives they would.

It seemed quiet when they returned to the farm. Jeanne and Amy had gone home straight from the graduation as had Phillip and his family. Crystal went with her friends to attend some of the open houses that were being held on Sunday evening.

"Can we please go riding?" Ben begged. Michael looked at Britany and she smiled.

"Of course we can," Britany said. "You can ride Sissy. Go change, and we'll see who is the first one to the barn." Ben was ready and waiting with Michael as Britany entered the barn. They saddled the horses, and then Britany led the way through the trails on Misty. When they got back Britany showed Ben some of the maneuvers she and Misty were working on.

"All right Ben, you come on out, and I'll help you with your riding skills," Britany said as she motioned for him to join her.

"I already know how to ride," Ben said with a scowl on his face.

"Ben, you are just getting started. Let Britany help you," Michael said sternly.

"Oh, all right," Ben said. His head was down as he rode into the arena, and he wasn't very accepting of her suggestions. He felt he knew what he was doing and that he couldn't be wrong.

Michael warned him, "Ben, you pay attention and listen to Britany. Don't talk back." Ben listened, but he wore a scowl on his face for a while. It was getting dark when they put the horses up. The day was almost over, and Britany was amazed how fast it had gone. She drove Michael and Ben back to the airport.

Once again she found herself watching the airplane depart. It seemed that the weekend had been so full that she had not been able to spend any time alone with Michael. She told herself that Friday would come soon, and then she would have Michael to herself, except for Shelly and her husband. Five days seemed like a long time to wait. Three days didn't seem like nearly enough time to be together. After that weekend when would she see him again? She slowly turned to leave as the plane was completely out of sight.

She knew she wanted to marry Michael, but did he want to marry her?

CHAPTER 12

Britany felt tired the next two days. She put all the energy she had into work and then went home to fall onto the couch and nap before she could do anything else. By Wednesday she felt more energetic and drove out to the farm to ride. She felt bad because she knew she wouldn't be riding over the weekend, and the horse show was only two weeks away. She would ride every day next week, she promised herself. Crystal was home with her in the evenings and Britany enjoyed the company.

Michael was waiting when she got to the airport on Friday. He was standing outside and waved her down as she drove past. She caught a glimpse of him, quickly checked her rearview mirror and pulled over to the curb. He threw his gym bag in the back and jumped in.

"Is that all you have?" Britany questioned before she took off.

"That's it. I packed light. No suits this trip. Besides, I didn't figure there would be much room on the boat." He reached over and gave her a quick kiss.

"Am I late? I didn't expect your plane to be in yet," Britany said apologetically.

"No, you're not late. My plane got in a bit early, and I hurried to get here. I thought if I met you it would save time. I'm anxious to get to the boat! The weather is beautiful, and it's supposed to be nice this weekend."

Traffic was heavy, and Britany had to concentrate on the road as they drove through town.

"I hate the traffic on Fridays. It's like a madhouse," Britany commented. "Finally traffic is easing up," she said as they left the city.

"I am kind of getting used to the farms and the flat terrain that seems to stretch forever. It's quite pretty, actually. Some of the crops are coming up that we watched being planted," Michael said.

"I've never been to Tennessee. Is it much different than here?"

"Yes, quite a bit. There are farms, but most of the land is hilly and used for pasture. There are tall mountains, lush forests and rushing streams."

Michael looked at Britany as she drove. He had a strong desire to show her the mountains and streams that he was trying to describe. She glanced over and smiled.

"Are you thinking about something?" she asked.

"No, not really," he lied. He wasn't too pleased with his line of thinking. He was trying to convince himself to keep their relationship casual, but his thoughts were running otherwise. He just wasn't ready for a commitment yet, and the thought scared him.

"Was this week hard, knowing that Crystal has graduated?" Michael asked.

"Actually, I saw her more this week than I have for a long time. She went job-hunting during the day and was home at night. I tend to forget she's not still in school," she answered. She realized in her heart that she was embracing a false security for the present. It was easy to forget that in two months Crystal would be leaving. She wasn't ready to share that with him. If she said it out loud then she would have to admit it to herself. Instead she asked him about Ben.

"He's fine. He's with a friend of his who he stays with often. This is the weekend for him to be with his mother, but her other two children have the flu, and she doesn't want Ben to be exposed," Michael said.

"I'm sorry to hear that. I hope they get over it soon," Britany replied.

"I don't think there is much to worry about. I doubt that they are actually sick at all."

He dropped his last statement as if he hadn't meant to tell her as much as he did. Britany glanced over to see him stare out the window. He remained quiet and withdrawn while they drove. Shortly before they arrived at the marina he spoke.

"From the sign that we just passed there is a convenience store at the next exit. Would you mind stopping, and I'll get us a pop?" asked Michael.

"That sounds great. I could use something to drink. Are you all right?"

"Yes, I'm sorry. It's frustrating that she can still make me so angry."

"It's hard not to be angry when someone hurts our children," answered Britany. She glanced at him as she drove.

Michael felt comforted as she looked at him. The warmth in her eyes melted some of his hostility. He returned to his normal talkative self after the stop and soon they were entering the lakeside town.

The town had the appearance of any other town as they entered, but as they got to the heart, it took on a quaint nautical look. The sidewalks were made of boards. Large posts draped with heavy rope accented the walks at the corners. Shops lined the land side of the road. Docks with schooners, sailboats and yachts lined the side facing the water. Ducks and geese swam in between the boats and dived occasionally for fish. Sea gulls dived and squawked as they fought each other for food.

Britany drove slowly through the narrow streets. The air felt cooler and damp with the moisture from the lake. Britany caught a glimpse of the lake in the background. The Great Lakes never ceased to amaze her.

They entered a narrow stone drive that wound down a hill to the marina. The marina was new, and the board planks on the dock were brown instead of a weathered gray. She parked the car, and they opened the trunk to get her things. They grabbed their bags and headed to the dock. It swayed slightly under foot as they stepped onto it. Tiny fish scurried away from the side of the dock as they walked. Michael reached over with his free arm and drew her close. She was dressed in her new white denim shorts and red and white striped top. Her hair was pulled back and woven in a French braid and secured with a red bow. Michael was wearing tan casual shorts, a short-sleeved cotton shirt, and deck shoes.

Britany saw Shelly waving from several boats down. She waved back and hurried. Michael kept pace. Shelly welcomed them aboard with a big hug. The boat was a large blue and white 26-foot cruiser. There was a deck large enough for six people on the front and an area for several to sit around the captain on the bow. The back area was for fishing.

"Michael, you can sleep on a cot here in the back. In case of rain a tarp conveniently fastens over the top, making the area water resistant," Shelly explained. "The nights aren't cold, so you should be comfortable."

Below deck was elegantly done in soft gray velour with accents of blue. They entered a small kitchenette with a dining table that folded into a bed as they descended the stairs. The bow was arraigned into a couch by day and bed by night. Soft indirect lighting added romantic touches.

"Britany, you can sleep here," Shelly said pointing to the bow. "Stan and I sleep in the back."

Closed off by a curtain was a small bedroom.

"This is really nice. I've been on a lot of boats, but this is nicer than any I've ever seen," Michael said with a touch of awe in his voice. "I can't wait to get out on the lake! I hope fishing is good this time of year."

"We've been catching lake trout and a few steelheads. They are similar to salmon, only they are a bit smaller and are a beautiful silver color," said Stan.

"This is my husband Stan," said Shelly. Stan nodded as she spoke. "Stan, this is Michael."

Michael reached out to shake Stan's hand. Stan stood four inches shorter than Michael.

"So this is the fellow I've heard so much about," said Stan as he heartily shook hands. His belly jiggled as he chuckled. "The weather is perfect, and there is nothing to keep us from taking off, so let's get started. I thought we could fish for several hours and then anchor near the state beach. It's a nice place to swim and have a picnic lunch." His deep dimples gave his face a boyish look.

Britany had known Stan for several years and appreciated his zest for life. His blue eyes twinkled when he teased someone, and if you knew him at all it wasn't hard to tell when he was joking.

They went above deck, and Michael helped Stan prepare the boat for departure.

"I like this, having someone else to help Stan cast off," said Shelly. "It always makes me a bit nervous to help him untie the boat and get it away from dock. One time I almost landed in the lake, and another time I thought my leg was going to get taken off as it got between the boat and the dock when I slipped as we were coming in."

The boat proceeded slowly through the river, making its way to the lake. Old branches and trunks of trees protruded from the water. The sun was getting warm as they traveled slowly in the protection of the river.

Britany could see the mouth of the river open wide, and Stan began to pick up speed. The breeze off the lake cooled her hot skin.

Stan increased the throttle until they were skimming across the open water of the huge lake. The air whipped at their clothes and rushed across their faces. Michael took a seat next to Britany on the starboard, or left, side of the boat. He stretched his arms out across the side and sat back to enjoy the ride. Britany breathed deeply, letting the freshness of the lake fill her lungs. The green-blue water was as smooth as glass as they skimmed across the silky surface. A few times Britany could see the bottom ten feet below. The shoreline became more visible as they went farther out, stretching for miles and miles. Beautiful cedar shake homes dotted the coastline where they had left the river. Further down the coast there were only trees and dunes extending inland from the beach. The beach was silvery white in contrast to the green-blue water that lapped up onto it. The sun radiated off the sand and water in a blinding but beautiful way. A few sunbathers dotted the beach with their beach umbrellas, coolers, blankets and loungers. Children ran in and out of the water under the protective vigil of their parents. They carried buckets of water back to moisten the sand to make sand castles. Their screams of sheer delight were carried away by the breeze.

Looking forward, only blueness could be seen, as the blue of the water joined the blue of the horizon. The farther out they looked, the deeper blue the water became, until it was actually a shade bluer than the sky. The vastness of it was awesome. Being out on the lake away from land and civilization made Britany sense God's presence ever stronger. She marveled at His ability to be able to reign over all this and still be able to care about someone as insignificant as her. The words of Psalm 19 came to mind as she viewed the splendor before her:

> The heavens declare the glory of God; the skies proclaim the work of his hands. Day after day they pour forth speech; night after night they display knowledge. There is no speech or language where their voice is not heard. Their voice goes into all the earth.

She looked back at Michael and found that he was watching her. His deep brown eyes shone warmly as they met hers. She smiled back and felt a warm sensation. From the look in his eyes she sensed that his feelings were matching hers regarding the beauty around them.

Stan drove them several miles from shore to his favorite fishing hole and came to a stop. He let the boat drift and made his way to the back of the boat to get the fishing gear set up. Britany and Shelly both enjoyed fishing, although Britany wasn't sure if she really enjoyed fishing so much, or just the fact that most of the time she went fishing it was on a boat. She loved boating. They soon had their lines in the water, and Stan set the boat to a slow coast to troll. Michael sat back in his chair facing the stern with his feet propped up on the side. Shelly and Britany also relaxed as they waited for something to happen. Stan watched the boat as he fished. He kept checking lines and making various adjustments.

"Stan, relax," admonished Shelly. "We'll get some fish. Just enjoy yourself. It's getting hot!" she exclaimed, turning to Britany. "Britany, let's go below and change into our bathing suits."

"Sounds great!" said Britany. While they were down below they heard an excited yell from Stan.

"Shelly, hurry, you have a fish on!"

"OK, just a moment. You take it for now. I'm not coming up half dressed!" Shelly called back.

Britany laughed and hurried to finish dressing. When they arrived Michael was reeling in Britany's line and Stan was holding on to Shelly's.

"Britany, hurry and reel in my line! If the fish gets tangled in the other lines we will lose it for sure," Stan called out.

Britany was quick to respond. Stan had already cut the engine, and they were drifting slowly with the small waves. Stan directed Shelly, "Hold your pole and reel smoothly. Keep steady pressure on the line." The line went from one side to another as the fish tried to swim away. At one point the line went slack.

"Reel fast, Shelly! You don't want to give that fish any chances to spit the hook!" Stan yelled.

Britany cheered as Shelly fought against the fish. Stan shouted commands. Michael observed in amusement.

"Watch out!" screamed Britany as Shelly lunged forward from the sudden jerk on her line. Britany was sure the fish was going to pull Shelly right out of the boat, but Stan grabbed her by the waist and pulled her back. Finally Shelly got the fish close enough to the boat so that Stan could lower a net to the side and get it under the fish. He carefully pulled it up. In the net was a dark silver, shining fish about three feet long.

"Shelly, you caught a salmon! A big one at that!" exclaimed Stan so proud that one would have thought he was the one who caught it. He brought it on board and held it up by the gills. The strong muscles rippled as the fish struggled.

"Can you set it free? I hate to see such a beautiful thing suffer!" Britany urged.

"You may not like to see it suffer, but I'll bet you'll like how it tastes for supper," said Stan brightly as he held the fish. "Go get the camera, Shelly." She came back soon with the camera.

"Here, you hold the fish while I take the picture," said Stan as he pushed the fish toward her.

Shelly backed up. "I am not holding that fish!" she said, standing firmly where she was.

"Britany, would you take the picture while I hold the fish and Shelly stands beside me?" asked Stan.

"Of course I will," said Britany, taking the camera and getting into position. "Shelly, could you please get a little closer?"

"Shelly, this fish is not going to bite. It's not a shark," said Stan.

"Oh, all right," said Shelly and moved closer.

Everyone's hopes were up after the catch of Shelly's fish. Instead of heading to shore for lunch they decide to eat were they were and continue fishing. Britany and Shelly prepared a spread of fresh fruit, cut up vegetables and lunch meats. Michael's turn to catch a fish came while they were preparing the meal. This time there wasn't as much commotion involved. Stan still got rather excited and shouted out commands. The fish lunged out of the water several times, spinning as it did so. Michael expertly brought the fish to the boat, and Stan brought it up with his net. This fish was smaller than Shelly's. It was a light silver color like new metal.

"It's a steelhead," said Stan. "They are a smaller fish than the salmon, but they still give a good fight."

"I'll agree with that!" exclaimed Michael. "My arms and legs sure ache. That was great! Let's try for some more!"

Britany lay out on the bow to nap after lunch. It wasn't long before the rocking of the boat lulled her to sleep. She awoke to Michael whispering in her ear.

"Are you going to sleep the entire afternoon? I was kind of hoping to enjoy your company. Besides, you're working on a good burn if you keep it up."

"Oh, my, how long have I been asleep?"

"About an hour, but it's been an hour too long. I miss you," said Michael as he took her in his arms and kissed her long and gentle.

"I must say, you have a nice way of waking someone up," Britany said as he released her from his embrace.

"I really didn't come all the way up here for the fishing. I wanted to spend time with you. I must admit though, the view alone is worth the trip. You are very beautiful, Britany."

Britany blushed under his gaze and quickly looked away.

"Maybe you had better work on tanning your front side so it will match the back," Michael suggested.

Britany reclined against the side of the boat and put her legs out to catch the sun. Michael took the same position beside her. Together they listened to the water lap against the boat and watched the seagulls soar on the air currents. It was so peaceful that neither of them spoke. They simply enjoyed the moment.

The rest of the day continued in the same dreamy fashion. The sunset was radiant over the satiny water as they headed in for dock. Michael and Britany sat on the bow of the boat and watched the sunset until the colors were completely gone. Stan and Michael cleaned the fish when they got to shore. When they were finished, Stan suggested they go out to eat since it was getting late.

Britany protested, "I don't have time to get ready!"

"You can wear the same shorts outfit you wore earlier," Shelly assured her. "The restaurant is casual."

They walked the three blocks to the restaurant, an open-air cafe that overlooked the river. In front motorboats and sailboats of various sizes were tied to the dock. Some of the sailboats had colorful lights on their masts. The boats bobbed with the rhythm of the waves and a faint thunk, thunk could be heard as they hit the water.

On the plaza beside the restaurant an artist was painting a watercolor portrait of a little girl. The little girl was about four and wore a serious expression as she posed for the painting, trying hard not to move. The artist caught her image, and the canvas seemed to come alive before his expert touch. Several specialty shops surrounded the plaza. There was a slight wait for a table, and Michael and Britany inspected the stores as they waited. Michael held her hand as they leisurely walked through the stores. One store was full of cut and blown glass items with beautiful colors and designs. Another store had jewelry of various kinds and featured Black Hills Gold. They were looking at the display when a smartly dressed lady walked up.

"May I help you?" she inquired.

"We are just--," Britany began but was interrupted by Michael.

"I would like to have a closer look at that tri-colored gold chain."

It was lovely. Three colors of gold were intertwined. One strand was bright yellow gold, another was rose gold and the third color had casts of green. Britany looked at it stunned, as the lady brought it out for his inspection.

"Do you like it?" Michael asked Britany. She felt rather hesitant to answer. She looked at it a few moments.

"It's beautiful," she finally managed to say.

He proceeded to buy it. He carefully placed the chain around her neck, looking down at her smiling.

"It's almost as beautiful as you," he said softly and kissed her on the cheek. The sales clerk was watching them and spoke.

"It looks lovely on you. It brings out the sparkle in your eyes."

Britany thanked her politely and then looked back at Michael.

"You can't do this. It's beautiful, but it's very expensive," she tried to protest when he stopped her.

"I can and I did, now let's hurry. They must be ready with our table by now." He took her hand. Britany felt stunned as they walked back to where Stan and Shelly were waiting.

"I wondered where you two went. I thought maybe you decided not to eat," Stan said sternly. A twinkle in his eye revealed he was teasing.

"Stan, behave. They still haven't called our table yet. We just got back ourselves moments ago," said Shelly as she lightly punched Stan's shoulder.

"Britany! Where did you get the necklace! It's beautiful!" Shelly suddenly exclaimed as she saw Britany's necklace.

"Michael got it for me from that little shop over there," Britany said, blushing, and pointed to the shop. Shelly came closer to admire it just as their table was called. Britany was relieved that the subject was changed.

Following the meal the foursome walked back to the boat, enjoying the sounds of the night. A soft mist from the lake caressed Britany's cheek as she walked beside Michael, tucked securely under his arm. The whole evening seemed to have taken on a magical effect that Britany wished could last forever.

They played card games once back at the boat. With Stan's jokes and Shelly's quick humor they laughed and laughed until Stan and Shelly excused themselves for bed around midnight.

"This has been such a marvelous day. I wish it never had to end. Thank you so much for the necklace. I will cherish it always. I'm not used to having so much attention lavished on me."

"You're lovely, Britany, not just physically but as a person, too, and I wanted you to know that. I wanted you to have something to remind you of me when I'm not with you. So, see, it was actually a selfish act on my part," Michael said softly with a smile.

"I already think of you when you're not with me. I think of you constantly with an ache in my heart when you're gone," answered Britany sincerely.

"Gee, I could have saved some money!" Michael returned brightly.

Britany laughed and pretended to take a swing at him. Michael caught her arm as it came toward him and pulled her close. He kissed her passionately. She responded and melted into his embrace. Her whole being ached to be with him. He kissed her over and over again. Her hands caressed the muscles across his back and smoothed his golden hair.

He looked deep into her green eyes, "Britany, you mean a lot to me. I hope you know that."

A sudden fear seized her. She tensed up. A picture of David flashed in her mind, then one of Crystal's father. Somehow those words were all too familiar.

She looked into his eyes. They looked warm and sincere. She wanted to believe them.

Michael felt her tense up. What was I thinking? I was the one who didn't want a serious relationship, and here I was just inches away from saying I loved her. He had come close, too close for comfort. Britany's reaction brought him to his senses.

"I care for you, too, Michael. But I can't," said Britany hoarsely as she backed away. "I have never felt this way before. It's a little scary."

Michael looked at Britany. She was warm and vulnerable yet strong in her convictions. What am I doing? he thought to himself. Britany is not someone to take lightly. Michael, you're getting deeper and deeper into this. She doesn't see this as a light affair.

He kissed her cheek, then gently lifted her, and, half bending over because the boat was too low for him to stand, he carried her to the place where she was to sleep. He sat down and cradled her on his lap.

"I know you've been hurt in the past. Please believe me, I won't hurt you. You are too caring and sensitive to have that happen again, and I won't do that. I'm going to leave now while I still have enough control."

"Thank you, Michael," said Britany, looking into his eyes. "You don't know how much I want to give in, but I just can't. God means too much to me to disobey again. I'm sorry."

"Don't be sorry, Britany. That's part of what I like about you. I would be disappointed if it changed," he said quietly and kissed her. He gently placed her on the bed and turned to leave. Britany thought about him as he left and cried softly into her pillow. She was so confused. She loved him, yet she was petrified. How could it be that the very thing that she wanted scared her so? He hadn't said anything about marriage. He didn't even say he loved her. Yet what about the necklace and the fact that he came so far just to spend time with her? She just didn't know. It was so confusing. She had thought she wanted to marry him. God had spoken to her through the stars that Michael was the one, yet she felt insecure. She knew her faith was faltering. She tried to pray, but the fear kept getting in the way.

Britany woke up feeling tense and insecure. The sun shone through her small window, compelling her to look out. The day was gorgeous and competed with the previous one in splendor. The lake was gleaming and smooth except for a few places where gentle waves broke up on the shore. Britany felt herself relax under the mesmerizing spell of the beauty surrounding her. She quickly dressed and joined the others. They left the dock early to fish, and at noon they took time to have a picnic on the beach and to grill the fish they had caught the day before. They anchored the boat a short distance offshore and waded to the beach.

Britany delighted in the variety of people on the sand as she and Michael walked hand in hand along the beach. All ages were taking advantage of the beautiful day. She loved watching the little toddlers running to the water's edge and then back to their parents as soon as the water came up over their feet. Michael noticed the light in her eyes as she watched the children.

"Don't you ever get enough of children? You work with them every day," Michael teased.

"Working with them all the time seems to just make you want one of your own that much more. It's like a void that never goes away," she said, almost trance-like, her eyes focused on a toddler running to his mother.

"I didn't realize you wanted more children," he said softly.

"I'm sorry. I don't talk about it often. It's one of those things you keep to yourself. Have you ever thought of having more children?" she asked, glancing up at him.

"I guess I hadn't seriously thought about it. There was such a struggle between my wife and me when Ben was born. I didn't want to bring any more children into that situation. After she left I was too busy with work and Ben to even consider more children."

They both let the conversation drop at that. Neither felt ready to discuss the possibility of the two of them having a family together. Britany was comfortable and happy being with him. She wasn't ready to see beyond that. She loved to be with him and cherished their time together. For now, that was all she wanted to think about.

Michael and Britany continued their walk on the beach until it was time to return to the boat. They were careful to keep their conversation on a lighter note.

Stan and Michael returned to fishing. Britany and Shelly went below deck to prepare supper.

"Britany, you and Michael seem wonderful for each other. Has he talked at all about getting married?" Shelly asked as they worked.

"Actually, I won't let him." Britany worked on peeling carrots as she talked. "We talked about children today, but then I changed the subject. I truly don't understand, but every time I think about marriage, it scares me. I'm not even sure what I'm scared of. I feel certain that God has placed Michael in my life. I love him, and I love being with him. I have never felt this way about anyone before. I dread the thought of him leaving every time he goes back. I can't wait until I see him again when he's gone," Britany said as she vigorously chopped carrots. "The fear just seems to surface when I think of marriage. I've built this wall around myself for years; now I don't know how to tear it down!"

"Be careful with that knife. It would take us awhile to get you to a hospital, and I don't want you bleeding all over my boat!" Shelly teased.

"Oh, I'm sorry. I guess I am being a little careless." Britany looked at the knife in her hand and grimaced.

"Why don't you take over tearing the lettuce, and I'll do the carrots. It will be a little safer that way," Shelly said with concern.

She took the knife out of Britany's hand and gave her the lettuce.

Shelly continued, "Give yourself a little time. This relationship has gone rather fast, and it takes a while for all of us to get used to adjustments in our lives. You were hurt deeply years ago, and I'm sure this new experience is opening old wounds. Michael seems comfortable with the relationship where it is. Relax and enjoy being together for a while. Don't put so much pressure on yourself."

Britany thought of David as Shelly talked. She hadn't told Shelly about David's proposal and their argument about Jesus. She didn't want to talk about that part of her life. She knew her feelings were much deeper for Michael than they had been for David, yet the memories were painful.

"Maybe you're right. He hasn't said anything about marriage so I really don't have to think about it right now. There is a little problem with intimacy though. It's rather hard to ignore," said Britany. Shelly put down the carrots and looked at Britany. "Did he pressure you?" She asked frankly. "No, not at all. I said I wasn't ready and he said he respected and liked that about me." Britany tore lettuce and dropped the pieces in a bowl.

"It sounds as though you both have things under control." "Maybe until the next time." Britany waved her hands in frustration. "What if I don't say no?"

"Britany, you are always the one to say 'trust God.' Don't you think He will be there to help you? You have always depended on Him before. He won't let you down now."

"You're right, Shelly. I needed to hear that," said Britany, giving her a big hug. "Thanks for this trip. It's been wonderful! How will I ever repay you?"

"I know a way. I was kind of hoping maybe you would let me be one of your bridesmaids, or matrons, as the case may be," Shelly said to a startled Britany. They both burst into laughter.

The foursome watched the sunset from the deck of the boat that evening. The spectacular colors started as light oranges and pinks, then deepened to a rich crimson against a dark violet background as the bright orange ball dropped below the horizon. They headed back to shore with the last shadows of dusk. The lights of boats dotted the darkness.

Stan insisted that the trip would never be complete without a visit to the local ice cream parlor. Once again they walked the plank boardwalk along the shore. They passed the eating place they had visited the night before and continued on for several blocks. The walk was crowded with other people out enjoying the night. The shops that lined the boardwalk seemed busy. It was fun watching the people and looking into store windows with their colorful displays. There was a taffy house along the way. Britany insisted on going in and trying a sample. She bought a pound of taffy to take home for Crystal and a package to send with Michael for Ben.

"I could get a caramel apple for Misty," Britany pondered. "She would love it!"

"She might also get her jaw stuck together as she tries to eat it. You had better stick to a conventional apple," laughed Michael.

"OK, then, I will get one for each of us to eat on the way home tomorrow," said Britany as she went to the counter.

"It will be quite a struggle to get Stan to wait to eat his until tomorrow," said Shelly.

"I don't care when he eats it. I just thought since we were going to get ice cream it would be too many sweets for one night," said Britany.

The ice cream parlor looked as if it came straight out of the 1950's, music and all. The menus even had items from a malt shop, except for the modern items such as frozen yogurt and waffle cones. Britany was delighted with the decor and would have stayed longer, except the rest of them started to leave when they were finished. Britany hurried to catch up and take Michael's arm.

They walked back to the boat and once again played cards. This time Michael was the first to excuse himself, and Shelly gave Britany a knowing look as if to say, "See, I told you it would be OK." Shelly and Stan excused themselves soon after and went to bed.

Britany had no trouble falling asleep, but sometime during the night she woke up and couldn't get back to sleep. She slipped on her sweatshirt and pants over her pajamas and quietly walked above deck. Michael was sleeping quietly, wrapped in a sleeping bag. He looked calm and peaceful. She had no desire to wake him but wanted to watch him sleep for a little while. She sat quietly on the deck about four feet from him and watched the rhythmic rise and fall of his chest under the covers. The waves lapped softly against the side of the boat. He looked peaceful and child-like. His light hair was tousled by the breeze, and his eyes were closed serenely. After several minutes, to her surprise, he opened his eyes and smiled up at her.

"I thought you were asleep!" she whispered, feeling a bit guilty to be caught sitting there watching him.

"I was, but I sensed your presence and smelled your perfume. What a lovely way to wake up. Come here," he said, motioning her to come near.

"I just wanted to see you and print a picture of you in my mind to look at when you're gone." She continued to speak softly as she approached and kneeled down beside him.

"I'm glad you did," he said, propping himself up on his elbow. "I didn't trust myself and thought I had better leave early tonight."

"I kind of thought as much. I'm sorry to wake you," she said again to cover her embarrassment.

"Don't be," he said, reaching out to draw her near.

He felt warm and secure as he pulled her to him.

"You're shivering," he continued and rubbed her back in an effort to warm her up.

"Yeah, I guess maybe I had better go back to bed," she said with sadness in her voice.

"I think that would be a good idea. I don't want you to go back home with a cold. Good night, Britany." He held her close for a while and then gently released her.

"Good night," she replied, rocked herself back to her heels and quietly stood up. She blew him a kiss and then tiptoed back to her bed in the cabin.

Sunday was windy and cloudy, and they decided to go back soon after breakfast. Michael sat in the driver's seat. He glanced at Britany as he drove. What was she expecting of him? He knew she wasn't the kind of person to have a light relationship with. She was much too caring and sensitive to get involved with and then leave, yet the thought of commitment still scared him. His divorce had been too painful. He was afraid the trip had already deepened their relationship more than he had wanted. He needed to back off and let her down easy before it was too late.

"Work is busy right now, and I missed a lot of time with this trip. I really don't know when I will get back to see you," said Michael, finishing lamely.

"Michael, I have really enjoyed the time we've spent together, but Tennessee is a long way from Ohio. It's OK, I'm thankful for the time we had together. If we get more time together, it's great, but don't feel I'm asking for a commitment," Britany said. She had noticed Michael's mood had changed on the ride to the airport and somehow she had expected his words. They hurt, but it was better if they backed off a little in seeing each other.

Michael had thought he would be relieved to be free of expectations, but her reply hurt more than he cared to admit to himself. He wanted to pull her into his arms and say he really didn't mean that, he was just scared. But he didn't.

"My plane's ready," he said.

"Have a safe trip," Britany reached up and kissed him good-bye.

Britany found herself watching the airplane disappear into the dark overcast with a lonely feeling in her heart. She had no reassurance that she would ever see him again. A penetrating pain tore at her heart, and she looked back into the sky for a glimpse of hope. All she saw was threatening storm clouds. Britany didn't realize that the dark clouds were a forecast of the weeks to come.

CHAPTER 13

Monday started fast and furious. Britany clung to work to help her keep her mind from dwelling on Michael. Without realizing she was doing it, she reached up and touched the gold chain around her neck that he had given her. Her dark green eyes glanced at it as she touched it. She had promised him that she wasn't expecting a commitment, but the thought of not seeing him again ripped at her heart. She closed her eyelids tightly as if to squeeze out her thoughts, dropped her hold on the necklace, and dived into her work. The day had started with four babies running a temperature during the night and pediatricians coming in on rounds and writing orders for treatments that needed to be done immediately. Britany helped draw blood. She assisted with lumbar punctures, and held babies for x-rays to be taken. She administered antibiotics and felt flustered as several mothers were crying along with the babies.

One baby had problems that started from the time it was brought from Labor and Delivery. An echo confirmed that the baby only had two chambers in the heart instead of the normal four. A new surgery was available to offer hope, but the baby needed to be taken by ambulance to another hospital. While they waited for the ambulance there was a possibility that a hole between the two chambers of the heart could close at any time, which would mean instant death. While the hole was open it kept the blood in the two chambers mixing, so even though the blood being pumped to the body was lower in oxygen than a normal newborn's, it was enough oxygen for the baby, to survive temporarily. Everyone in the nursery was praying for the baby that he would remain stable until the surgery could be attempted. The atmosphere was tense with an anxiety that cleared only slightly when the infant was transported. Later in the day the Nursery received word that the infant had survived the trip and was in surgery. A silent prayer of thanks was offered by many of the nurses, and some of the anxiety subsided.

Britany's spirits soared when the telephone rang Monday night and it was Michael. He sounded warm and sincere. Britany still didn't have confirmation of seeing him again, but the call brought her hope.

Tuesday was just as fast as Monday had been, and Britany agreed to work four hours overtime. She persuaded Jeanne to go home on time because of Amy. They made a commitment that Wednesday, even if it was busy again, they would go out to the farm and ride. The horse show was Saturday, and the horses needed to be ridden.

Michael sat in his motel room in Indianapolis, Tuesday evening. He picked up a newspaper and thumbed through it. His presentation at the hospital had gone well, and it looked as if they were going to place a large order, but his enthusiasm was lacking. He tossed the paper down, got up and walked to the window. Concrete and asphalt were the only landscape he could see. He felt lonely. He watched as the sun disappeared behind the buildings. It was quite a contrast to the last sunset he had watched with Britany. Her smiling face came to his mind like a warm breeze in springtime.

He had been content with his life before he met her. Not everything had been great, but it had been manageable. Now it felt purposeless. He had been sad since he flew away from her, thinking he may never see her again. It had hurt when she agreed to keep their relationship light, although that was what he wanted and he had been the one to suggest it. The feeling of loneliness was new to him, although he knew there was an emptiness to his life that had been there for a long time. He thought about how easily Britany seemed to trust in God and how she spoke of Him with ease and confidence as if she were talking about a dear friend.

Michael looked at his watch. He realized that it was time to eat. He walked back to the table, shuffled through some papers until they were in order, and then left to get some dinner. When he returned he turned on the TV, but was quickly bored and turned it off. He looked through the dresser drawer and found a King James Bible that the Gideons had left. He leafed through it until he came to what had been his favorite verse as a boy:

> For God so loved the world, that He gave His only begotten Son, that whosoever believeth in Him should not perish, but have everlasting life.
> John 3:16

Michael had prayed as a boy and asked Jesus for everlasting life. He had felt God's presence and known the assurance of salvation. How could I have strayed so far from the God who made me? How could I possibly get back? he thought as he continued reading. He was living in darkness as the scripture described. Why hadn't he seen it before? No wonder his life seemed so empty.

Michael bowed his head and prayed, "Dear Lord, please forgive me. I found You as a child, and then I walked away. I am so sorry. I want to follow You again. Please show me what to do." Michael felt peace and love flow through him. It was wonderful. He suddenly felt the urge to call Britany, and he picked up the phone and dialed.

He didn't tell Britany about his prayer because he was embarrassed to tell her that he had strayed from God as far as he had. He was filled with joy as he spoke, and they talked long into the night.

Jeanne and Britany drove to the farm on Wednesday. It felt good to get away. Amy rode along with them and sang happily in the back seat. Britany and Jeanne were busy in conversation in the front seat. Jeanne was eager to hear about Britany's weekend. Britany was eager to talk about it, especially to Jeanne.

"When do you think Michael will come back and visit?" Jeanne asked during the conversation. The breeze from the open window tosseled her short hair and feathered it against her face.

"I really have no idea. He tensed up as we were in the airport and told me that he wasn't sure when he would be back. I think he is feeling pressured. There isn't any special reason for him to come, and he has been making so many trips lately that he probably could use some time to rest. I was thinking of driving down sometime to visit him since he has been so wonderful about coming up. I can't stand the thought of not seeing him again. Would you like to come along? I could use the company."

"If he's feeling pressured do you think that is a good idea?" Jeanne asked quietly.

"I guess I'm not sure, but he still calls. He called last night, and we talked for hours. That is what seems so funny. He was in a really good mood. Maybe he has changed his mind. I don't know what to think. I could talk to him and feel him out about the idea. If he seems hesitant, we can drop it."

"Sure, it sounds like fun. I would love to see Tennessee. Maybe we could visit Kentucky Horse Park on the way. I have always wanted to go there," replied Jeanne.

"Can I go? Please, can I go, too? I won't be any trouble," begged Amy.

"Would we go and not take you?" asked Britany. She glanced back at Amy through the rearview mirror. "Of course you can go, and maybe we can even talk Crystal into going. The Horse Park sounds like fun. We could make this our summer vacation," Britany said excitedly.

"You know, Britany, this long-distance dating could soon prove to be a problem. Your relationship seems to be getting quite close. Has he mentioned anything about marriage?" Jeanne asked.

"No, and I'm glad he hasn't. You know it seems that God has placed him in my life at a time when I thought my family days were near an end. Now there is a possibility of a husband and a son in the future--the very thing I have longed for. To be quite truthful, I'm scared. I don't understand the fear, either." A crease appeared on Britany's forehead. "I know my life would be totally different than it is now, and there would be a lot of changes. Changes always cause some anxiety, but I don't think that has anything to do with it. This is a fear, not anxiety." She swiped at a few stray strands of hair that blew in her face. "I'm afraid of what life would be like without him now that I know him, yet, when I start to consider marriage, the fear starts. I don't understand it. I've sensed that he's scared, too. I don't think he wants to make a commitment, or feel tied down. His divorce was very painful."

"Britany, do you think God has brought Michael into your life for a reason?" asked Jeanne thoughtfully.

"Yes," Britany answered without hesitation, remembering the night in her room when she saw the star.

"You know, Britany, what you are expressing doesn't sound like a reasonable hesitancy. Being anxious or concerned would be expected, considering that you're thirty-five and this step would change your entire life. What you just went through with David was hard, too," Jeanne commented.

"It's not a reasonable hesitancy that I could deal with and think through. This is fear. It is just there, and I don't know why," Britany said with an edge of frustration in her voice.

"Britany, God did not put in us a spirit of fear, but a spirit of power, of love and self-discipline. I see this fear as coming from Satan. He wants to rob you of your joy. Recognize it as that, and tell Satan to leave you alone," Jeanne said with assurance and faith.

"That sounds a little too simple." Britany shrugged her shoulders as she looked straight ahead at the road. Her hands grasped the steering wheel tightly.

"It depends on how you look at it," Jeanne continued. She leaned her elbow on the window and looked thoughtful. "I guess it does sound simple, but actually it can be very complex. A lot of things we struggle with are actually spiritual battles that seem to be natural battles. Paul tells us in his letter to the Ephesians that our struggle is not against flesh and blood but against the rulers, against the authorities, against the powers of this dark world, and the spiritual forces of evil in the heavenly realms."

"Now that sounds too scary," Britany said with a shiver.

"It is, without God." Jeanne waived her arm to emphasize her point and then reached up to push her glasses back into place. "Without Him we are alone in our struggle. God is stronger than all those forces. He has given us the power to fight them. That's why He tells us to put on the whole armor of God. God will drive out the fear. He is stronger," explained Jeanne. Her brown eyes showed compassion.

"I will think about it," Britany replied and glanced nervously at Jeanne They pulled into the drive to the farm. "Right now we are here! I, for one, am ready to ride." Britany quickly changed the subject and pushed the thoughts that Jeanne had conveyed to the back of her mind. When she wasn't faced with making any decisions about Michael, the fear wasn't present. It was easier to ignore and forget it for the present.

Britany rode Misty, focusing all her concerns on the horse. They went through a warm-up, and then Britany pretended they were at the show. She tested Misty on all the commands she would need to perform. Tired but satisfied with the work out, she cooled Misty down. Jeanne was finishing up with Trigger at the same time.

When they were finished riding, Britany and Jeanne worked on getting the horses ready for the show. They trimmed the hair around the horses' ears with quiet clippers. Trigger stood calmly, having been through the routine many a time. Misty wasn't so calm about it. She rolled her eyes and tried to back away. Britany and Jeanne calmly worked with her until she stood hesitantly, but still. They trimmed some of Misty's golden mane around her ears to make a neat path for the bridle to fit. They also trimmed around the horses' hooves and bottom part of the legs. They left late but felt good about the work they had accomplished.

Britany wasn't sure, but she thought Jeanne had another blank period on Thursday while they were at work. Jeanne had been admitting a baby, and several other nurses were in the room talking. Jeanne seemed to be concentrating on the baby she was looking at, but when someone directed a question to her she failed to respond. They teased that she was getting a little too involved in her work and repeated the question. This time Jeanne responded appropriately, but once again she had that confused look on her face. Britany questioned her about it later. Jeanne dismissed it with the excuse that she was thinking about something else at the time. Friday Jeanne seemed fine, and that evening they drove out to the farm together.

They worked the horses for a while and then took them to the back of the barn for a bath. Misty pranced and fretted at the water from the hose. Britany talked soothingly as she worked. Suddenly she felt strong arms encircle her waist. She screamed, dropped the hose and turned to find herself face to face with Michael. Misty reared into the air and started to bolt. Britany had the lead rope in one hand and was able to get her back under control, but not before being pulled five feet. She proceeded to talk softly and quiet her down.

"That was a little more of a reaction than I had anticipated. I'm sorry I should have been more careful," Michael said. He realized that in his enthusiasm he had been careless around the horses. He had intended to stay away from Britany for a while, but the desire to be with her had won out over his fear of commitment. His yearning to be closer to God had also compelled him to come. He felt closer to God when he was close to Britany. Her love for Jesus was contagious.

"Oh, Michael, don't feel bad. Misty is fine. I think I was more startled than she," said Britany. "How in the world did you get here?" she asked.

"Ben and I drove. It was his idea to come. All I have heard about since the graduation is wanting to ride and seeing the farm again. When I told him about the horse show tomorrow he begged and begged to come. Since I couldn't think of an excuse, here we are." Michael felt that sounded a lot better than the fact that he couldn't stand being away from her.

"Oh, Ben. You are such a sweetheart." Britany kept her speech calm and easy so as to not spook Misty again. She carefully reached out and gave Ben a big hug. He had been standing behind his dad when Michael first came up. Britany hadn't seen him until Misty was back under control and Michael had mentioned his name.

"I picked Ben up at two-thirty when school was out, and off we went. We warned your mom we were coming, but I asked her to keep it quiet. I was surprised you were still in the barn. It is getting rather late."

"We probably won't get done much before midnight. There are a lot of last minute things to do. We do a lot to these horses to get them ready for a show. Some of the judges even look under the tails! I look a wreck," said Britany wiping at a stray hair, "but she is looking great!"

"Don't be so hard on yourself. I think the smell of wet horses and soapsuds are quite becoming! I especially like the wet blue jeans," Michael teased, then quickly ducked to miss a wet sponge coming his way.

Misty shied again, but Britany kept her in control, and the three of them laughed together.

Michael helped Britany while Jeanne, Ben and Amy worked on the pony, Sissy. They were just finishing when Liz came in to check their progress and volunteer to put the two young ones to bed.

"That would be wonderful," Jeanne said gratefully. "We need to get started around six in the morning, and Amy will be worn out before the day begins." Jeanne said gratefully.

"I'll come help, Miss Liz. I still haven't unpacked our things," said Michael as he put his arm around Ben and started for the barn door.

Both children protested, but they were too tired to protest for long.

The alarm went off before dawn, and it took Britany a minute to realize she wasn't at home. When she did, she was wide-awake. Her stomach felt like a pit, and she experienced instant anxiety.

OK, Britany, get yourself under control. If you go out to the barn with that kind of anxiety Misty will pick up on it right away and get nervous herself, Britany thought to herself as she quickly showered and pulled her hair back into a French braid. She put on a pair of jeans and a T-shirt. She spent a little extra time on her make-up. She kept it light and natural. She took her breeches, shirt, jacket, hat and riding boots with her as she went downstairs. Jeanne was right behind her.

They ate a light breakfast and hurried out to the barn. Jeanne brought the pony out of her stall, and they quickly brushed her down. She had a large spot on her rump where she had lain in a pile. Jeanne got a fresh bucket of sudsy water to wash it off. Fortunately the rest of her looked good. They led Sissy to an old wooden door laid on the floor. Carefully Britany urged her up on it, and Jeanne began polishing her hooves. The door kept her feet up out of the dirt until they had time to dry. They began on Trigger, repeating the same procedure. He acted half asleep and easily went along with them. They then proceeded with Misty, who was definitely not asleep. She didn't like the door and tried to sidestep it, but after several attempts, and some bribing with grain, she stood quietly on the door. Britany stayed with the horses as Jeanne went in to get Amy up and ready.

Michael was striding across the barnyard as Jeanne was going to the house, and he called out a greeting. The sun was just beginning to brighten the sky. Barn lights made him blink as he opened the door, and the sweet smell of hay greeted his nostrils. Britany was in the back with the horses, and her father was busy throwing hay to the cows. Michael said hi to Charles and walked the aisle back to where she was.

"Do you need some help?" he asked. Her back was to him as she was checking over the saddles and bridles.

She turned and smiled. "Sure. You can help me load the tack into the trailer. We have the horses all ready to go. Jeanne went in to get Amy ready."

"I saw her going in as I was coming out. Ben is eating breakfast, and I'm sure he will be here shortly. He's not too much for mornings, but today he's wide-awake. He's pretty excited."

"I am, too. I'd better warn you. I get rather ornery when I am nervous, and, believe me, I get nervous before I go in the ring." Britany hoisted a saddle and bridle over her shoulder, and Michael took the other saddle. "Some people just look so calm and collected, but not me. I chew a lot of gum before I go in. That way Misty can't tell I'm so nervous. Everything being new makes it hard on her. All she needs is to sense that I am nervous, and that will be disaster for sure," said Britany as they carried the saddles out of the barn to the waiting trailer.

They unloaded the saddles into the trailer. "Come here, and give me a hug," Michael said. He held out his arms toward her. "I remember another time when a friendly hug relaxed you."

"Yes. I remember," Britany said, stepping into his embrace. "I am so glad you came. I still can't believe you're here. Jeanne and I have been talking about coming down to visit."

"That would be wonderful. Have you made any plans as to when?"

"Not definite, but we thought maybe the middle of next month."

"Oh, Britany, that would be great. I can show off Tennessee to you. I know you will love it."

"I'm sure I will."

Jeanne was coming around the side of the van carrying a cooler as they loaded the rest of the tack and were putting in a bale of hay and some grain. Amy followed behind carrying a basket of goodies, and Ben had a thermos of juice.

"Looks like we're ready to load the horses," Britany said brightly.

"I want to load Sissy!" Amy sang out.

"You go get her, but you will need to let me actually take her in the trailer," Jeanne added quickly.

"OK. Come on, Ben. You can help," Amy said over her shoulder as she ran toward the barn.

"Amy! Don't run in the barn! You will scare the horses!" Jeanne called after her just in time to get her to slow before entering the barn.

Britany followed her to get Misty. They loaded the pony. She jumped readily into the trailer, knowing there was grain waiting for her. Misty loaded easily, too, for which Britany was very relieved. Trigger was an old pro and jumped in when his turn came. Jeanne drove the van and Britany sat in the back. She used the time to French braid Amy's hair.

Jeanne and Britany had purchased the horse trailer and van together several years earlier. Neither one was in perfect shape, but they were safe and comfortable. The van was a conversion van that they could use to stay in overnight on occasion.

The drive was short. Soon they were pulling into a stone drive behind a line of other trailers of various sizes and conditions. Horses were being led around everywhere. Some horses were immaculately groomed, and some were still unbathed, waiting at the wash rack. There were extremely large, powerful-looking horses and some ponies smaller than Amy's.

Loud whinnies could be heard from the trailer as they moved along. Once or twice the van shook as Trigger stomped his foot in impatience.

"Trigger, calm down. We are getting there as fast as possible," Jeanne called out the window over her shoulder.

"Do you think he can hear you?" giggled Britany.

"I doubt it. He knows he is going to get to jump, and he gets so excited about competition. He truly loves to show off," said Jeanne.

Jeanne found an empty spot under a tree and pulled into it sideways, keeping a patch of grass in front of the trailer so the horses would have an area to stand and nibble grass between shows.

They unloaded the horses and took them on a stroll of the area to get them used to their surroundings. When they got back they tied the horses to the side of the trailer and gave them some hay to eat. Michael watched the horses while Britany and Jeanne went to sign up for various events. Britany signed up for two halter classes and two riding classes. She didn't like halter classes, but it would give Misty two chances to get in the show ring before the riding events.

Amy's class was first. Britany brushed the pony while Jeanne helped Amy put on her riding outfit in the van. She came out wearing a hunter green riding jacket with tan breeches and a smart-looking black velvet riding helmet. She had on black riding boots that were fitted up her leg to just below the knee.

Amy led her pony into the first class. She held herself straight and erect and appeared to know exactly what to do. The judge was looking at how the pony was built and how balanced her movements were. It made some difference how Amy showed her, but not much. Jeanne had entered her in this class to get Amy used to being in the show ring.

Britany's turn came shortly after Amy, and she had to rush to change into her show clothes.

"You look very professional!" commented Michael as she stepped out of the van in her knee-length black boots, gray breeches, dark gray jacket and pink blouse with a horse pin at the throat. Her hair was tucked up under her riding helmet, except for a few bangs that were neatly placed.

She led Misty over to the holding area and walked her around. She saw ten other horses in the holding area. After several minutes two others joined them. Britany concluded that these would be the class. She was glad that it wouldn't be too big or small. She walked Misty around to warm her up and to help them both relax. Then she went to the side to talk to Michael and Jeanne while they waited.

"Can I brush Misty?" Ben asked.

"Sure. You can spray on some more fly spray, too," answered Britany.

"Do you need to get Trigger ready?" Michael asked Jeanne.

"I didn't sign Trigger up for halter classes," Jeanne said. "Once he enters the ring he can only think of jumping. I gave up halter classes after the first several attempts when he tried to jump a water puddle in the ring and almost pulled me into it. His classes will be the last thing in the afternoon."

The loudspeaker called Britany's class, and she led Misty over to line up and go through the gate.

Misty pranced gracefully into the ring as Britany jogged beside her. She pranced halfway across the ring. Britany slowed her to a walk as the ringmaster instructed, and she lined her up in the middle of the ring next to the other horses. Misty's nostrils flared from nervousness, but she responded well. The judge motioned to each entrant separately to walk to the side of the ring, turn, and jog back. The judge moved on down the line, looking at each horse in turn, and then came back to Britany. He told her to form a line at the announcer's stand. Britany was in shock. That meant that the judge had picked them to get first place! She turned and jogged the twenty feet to the announcer's booth with Misty prancing nimbly at her side. They made a pretty sight: Britany trim and graceful, Misty flowing beside her.

A young girl in western garb handed Britany a blue rosette and congratulated her. Britany beamed, and Misty preened as if she understood she had won. Britany thanked the girl and then jogged to the exit gate. Michael, Jeanne, Ben, and Amy were all waiting at the gate for her. Jeanne carefully took Misty from her just in time for Michael to sweep her off her feet and swing her around. Britany grabbed for her hat to keep it from falling off.

"You did great, Britany!" Ben said excitedly, and Britany reached down to give him a hug.

"I hope I do that in my next class!" said Amy.

"I do, too, honey," replied Britany, giving her a hug. "It was fun."

"Don't relax too much. You have to go back in as soon as the judge picks the winner of this next class," reminded Jeanne.

"Yeah, that's right. I guess I had better go to the other gate and get in line. Thanks for holding Misty."

"You're welcome. I thought I had better hold on to her and keep her calm during the commotion so she wouldn't spook like before. Besides, I wanted to congratulate her, too. You did wonderfully Misty!" Jeanne said reaching up and giving Misty a big hug around her neck.

"You sure did, Misty. I was so proud of you," said Britany, stroking Misty's nose.

Britany entered the show ring again. Two other horses got champion and grand champion class, but it didn't dampen Britany's spirits.

Amy showed next in showmanship. The judge was judging on the way the handler handled the horse and on the grooming of both.

"Amy certainly has a good start with the appearance of her and the pony," Britany commented from where they were watching from the sidelines. "Sissy shines and Amy is adorable. She is handling that pony as though she has done this for years."

Next came Amy's turn to walk her pony away from the line where they had lined up in the middle. She walked Sissy to the fence and then turned her. Jeanne groaned.

"What's wrong?" asked Michael.

"She's supposed to push the pony away from her in the turn, not pull her toward her," whispered Britany. "I hope the judge didn't see it."

"No such luck," said Jeanne. "I saw him shake his head when she did it."

Sissy broke promptly into a jog on the way back just as Amy directed her, but the mistake had already been made. She took third place. She was all smiles as she came out of the gate because she was holding a big white rosette. She got a big hug from everyone, including Ben, who was genuinely excited for her.

They barely had time to take the pony back to the trailer when it was Britany's time to go back in for showmanship. Britany and Misty did perfectly. She took first place in this class and returned to get reserve champion. Britany felt that she would burst from the pride she had in Misty.

There was a break for lunch before the riding classes began. Britany and Jeanne used the time to ride their horses in the practice arena and get them warmed up. Britany asked Michael to take charge over the lunch that Jeanne had packed in the basket. She grabbed an apple but was too nervous to eat any more than that. Amy stayed with Michael and Ben. Jeanne didn't want her riding in the practice arena because there were too many big horses.

Amy impatiently asked Michael to saddle up Sissy before Jeanne and Britany were done. He led her around and walked them both over to the practice arena. Jeanne and Britany were just finishing up. The judge was getting ready to start the show again. Amy didn't have to wait long before her turn to ride came. She was in a walk-trot class for beginners. She did well and took second.

Britany's turn was next. She didn't feel nervous this time. To her the most natural place to be was on her horse, and she concentrated fully on what she was doing. She kept her hands steady and her heels down. Her riding crop was securely in her hand toward the outside rail. She was careful to post evenly with each stride Misty made. She cued her into a canter with a slight squeeze of the heel on the outside foot. Misty followed her cue perfectly. Michael and Jeanne watched from the sidelines in suspense. The class was coming to an end.

"She's got first place. I'm sure of it," said Jeanne. Suddenly a balloon popped as Misty went past. Misty jumped sideways three feet before Britany could get her under control. The next time Misty went past the place where it had happened, she jumped again. The announcer asked all people to please move away from the rail, but it was too late. The judge said quietly to Britany as he motioned her into fourth place that it was a bad break and that they had both been doing very well.

Misty remembered the incident when she went into the arena for the last class. She shied again in the same spot. Britany held the reins securely and continued firm pressure on Misty's side with her legs as Misty approached the spot. She tried to shy one last time and then relaxed and continued the rest of the show easily. The mistakes had been noticed and counted against them.

"Tough break," said Michael as he helped her unsaddle Misty.

"I am pleased that Misty worked through her fright. I knew that since she is a young horse, and there was bound for something to happen the first time in the show ring. She did very well, except for that one incident."

"Well, I think you both were awesome," said Michael.

"Thanks," Britany said and rose to her toes to give him a big hug. "I'm so glad you could come here with us."

They didn't have too long to wait before it was Jeanne's turn to ride. Michael gave her a boost into the saddle. She looked small on the big horse.

"Take first like Britany did, Mom!" exclaimed Amy.

"Good luck!" said Ben.

Jeanne smiled and turned Trigger toward the ring.

From their seats on the bleachers they watched Jeanne maneuver Trigger over each jump expertly, the horse correctly striding between each jump and then collecting himself, muscles rippling, to rise up and over. Jeanne balanced with each stride and then rested her weight on her legs and stretched her head and shoulders long over his neck as he lifted into the air. They finished the course and waited until the jumps were rearranged for the next turn.

They were approaching the next to the last jump when Britany noticed Trigger turn his head to the side before take off. Britany jumped to her feet and gasped. Trigger failed to clear the top bar with his front hoof. It threw him off balance, and his enormous bulk collapsed in an awkward heap on the ground. He shook his head and blew through his nostrils, then jumped to his feet.

Britany was through the crowd and climbing the fence before she was aware, to her relief, that Jeanne had been thrown clear of Trigger. She was lying crumpled on her side as Britany approached.

"Oh, my arm," Jeanne moaned and started to sit up, clutching her left shoulder. Her hat was still on her head, but her once perfectly groomed jacket and breeches were covered with dust.

"Jeanne, lie still and don't move," Britany said with authority.

Britany gently wiped some of the dust from Jeanne's face as she kneeled beside her.

"Do you hurt anywhere else?" she asked. Michael knelt opposite Britany with Amy in his arms. Amy wrapped herself around Jeanne's waist with tears flowing down her face.

"Mommy, Mommy, are you OK?" she sobbed, clinging to Jeanne.

"Amy, your mom hurt her arm. You might make it hurt more by holding her so tightly. She is going to be fine. Just hold her leg like this," said Britany, gently prying her loose and placing her hand on the knee Jeanne had bent up. Amy obediently responded with a slight nod of her head.

"I am fine except for my arm. Please give me a hand to sit up. I can't use my arm," Jeanne said, wincing.

Britany made Jeanne lie still a little longer until she was assured that she was all right. Then she helped her to sit. Michael whisked Jeanne up and carried her to the van. Britany followed with Amy and Ben at her side. Britany opened the van door wide, and Michael deposited Jeanne on the seat. Amy scrambled in to sit on the floor at her feet. Michael instructed Ben to get Jeanne some water to drink.

Several friends were following behind them leading a shaken Trigger.

"Trigger, you look awful!" Jeanne exclaimed as they brought him close to the van.

"You worry about yourself. I'll see to Trigger," instructed Britany.

"You do look pretty shaken up and dirty." Britany said to Trigger as she removed his saddle and brushed him down. She couldn't see any obvious injuries, and he was moving well. She walked him until he relaxed and began breathing normally again.

Ben and Amy sat with Jeanne as Britany and Michael loaded the horses and tack.

"I will drive you and Jeanne to the emergency room and then take the horses back to the farm and unload," said Michael as they were closing the door to the trailer.

"Mom will be there to help you unload. Thanks, Michael," Britany replied.

"We'll be fine. You take care of things here. Be back shortly," he said and gathered her in his arms before turning to leave.

Britany felt conspicuous sitting in the waiting room, the three of them wearing their riding apparel. Fortunately the emergency room wasn't busy, and they were able to see the doctor quickly.

Jeanne was in obvious pain as she told the doctor what had happened. Britany noticed that she left out anything prior to the fall. A technician came with a wheelchair to take Jeanne to X-ray.

Britany sat in the patient room waiting for Jeanne to return. She thought about the events that had happened. She had an uneasy feeling. Something didn't seem right about the incident from the start. Jeanne had taken Trigger over jumps similar to that one many times. He was an excellent jumper in cross-country where the jumps were much more unpredictable. The accident just should not have happened.

Britany paced the floor. She kept visualizing the jump over and over in her mind. Something had happened prior to the jump that had warned Britany there was a problem. In her mind she kept seeing Trigger's head turn just before his feet left the ground. That would definitely cause him to miss the jump and fall, but what would cause his head to turn? She had heard or seen no commotion. Besides, that rarely bothered Trigger. Then she made a mental picture of where Jeanne had been thrown. She had landed to the right of the jump. Trigger had half taken the jump and fallen to the left quite a distance in front of where Jeanne was. Was it possible that Jeanne was actually falling to the side when Trigger went into the jump? That would explain why his head was turned to the side. She would have had the reins in her hands and been pulling on his head as he went to go up. Britany's thoughts were interrupted as the technician wheeled Jeanne back into the room.

The doctor followed them in. He stated that it looked as if Jeanne had fractured her collarbone. He had called the radiologist in to confirm the reports, and an orthopedic doctor was on her way to set the break.

Jeanne, Britany, and Amy were just entering the waiting room again when Michael and Ben arrived. Jeanne was wearing a white canvas harness across her shoulder with a hospital gown underneath. Her riding jacket was thrown across her shoulders. She looked much more comfortable with the help of some pain medication.

"You look better than you did when we left. What's with the fancy get-up?" Michael asked with a hint of humor.

"They had to cut off my blouse to keep from injuring the shoulder further. Now I get this nifty gown to replace it. How is Trigger?" Jeanne asked.

"He's fine. I think he made out better than you did. Liz is fixing you some soup. She said it will make you feel much better."

"I don't know about you, but I know it will make me feel better," said Britany. "I'm starved. We really haven't eaten today."

Back at the farm, Britany helped Jeanne wash her hair and bathe while Liz got Amy ready for bed. When Jeanne had been made comfortable, Britany showered and cleaned up.

Later Michael and Britany took a walk to be alone. The sky was dark as they crossed the cobblestone drive to the deserted road.

"My, what a day!" sighed Britany. "Now that things have quieted down just a bit I am starting to feel the effects. It was terrifying seeing Trigger crash to the ground and not knowing if Jeanne was underneath. It was scary. I still feel shaky."

"Come here," said Michael as he drew her close. "You're right. Things could have been disastrous! She is lucky if you could call it that to end up with only a broken collarbone, if you could call it luck. She will be fine in no time. After all, she is going to have you to look after her. I must say I am a bit envious. I go back tomorrow to my lonely bachelorhood. Man, I hate to leave you, Britany." Michael looked down into Britany's eyes. She looked lost and vulnerable. Suddenly he had a strong urge to protect her. "When you and Jeanne come down to visit, I want you to consider the possibility of making Tennessee your home. We have lots of horses, and the countryside is beautiful. I think you will like it," Michael said and stroked her back with his hand, his chin pressed gently against her hair.

Fear seized Britany full force. She felt herself tense up and pull away from his embrace. A million fragmented thoughts welled up in her mind. She thought of Jeanne and the mysterious blackout spells. She wasn't sure if Michael was proposing or just wanted her to move near him. This had always been her home. She didn't want to move away. Crystal was leaving, but she was only an hour's drive away. Crystal would be a day's drive away if she moved to Tennessee. Her thoughts swirled in her head.

Instead of sharing these thoughts with Michael, she felt as if a wall had suddenly come crashing down, and she wanted him gone. Why couldn't she tell Michael that she was very concerned about Jeanne, and not because of the fall? Why couldn't she ask him to clarify what he meant by wanting her to move near? What was she so afraid of? Instead of voicing these concerns, she heard herself say, "I don't know now if we will be able to come to visit, since Jeanne has been hurt."

"Britany, don't try to protect her too much. She only broke her collarbone. She will feel fine in a couple of days. You're making it sound like she is desperately ill or something!" Michael clasped her hand and turned back toward the farm. "Maybe we had better go back and get some sleep Things will look brighter in the morning."

Michael got up early the next day. Britany avoided being alone with him and kept all conversation light and away from any mention of a visit or concerns about Jeanne.

Michael noticed that Britany avoided talking to him. He had wanted to go to Britany's church and hear more about God's love, but suddenly he felt pushed out. He wasn't sure what to think about her aloofness. Maybe he was rushing their relationship too far too fast. He knew he was pushing himself too fast. He was so excited about his new relationship with Jesus that he had spoken in haste the night before. His own words had scared him. Whatever had possessed him to say such a thing in the first place! He hadn't even told Britany about his new commitment to Christ.

Now he felt defeated. He had determined to distance their relationship, but he seemed to be drawn to Britany by an irresistible force. Maybe he had mistaken his desire to see Britany as God's leading. Maybe God didn't want them to be together. The last thing he wanted right now was a commitment, and if God didn't want it, then he decided he had better leave. With the excuse that he wanted to get home before dark, he packed their things into the car. He gave Britany a brief kiss and puzzled smile that she returned. Then he and Ben were off for Tennessee.

CHAPTER 14

Liz took Amy to Sunday school but came home before church started. Britany stayed with Jeanne. She insisted that Jeanne stay with her at her condo for several days so that she could help with Amy until it was easier for Jeanne to manage. The three of them headed back as soon as dinner was over. They went to Jeanne's house and packed a few things that Jeanne and Amy would need, then went to Britany's for the evening.

Britany tucked Amy into a sleeping bag on the floor in Crystal's room. Jeanne sat on the bed and watched until they finished and then said prayers with Amy. Amy kissed each of them good night and snuggled into her pillow with her stuffed rabbit in her arms. Britany assured her that Crystal would be home soon. She had spent the weekend at a friend's house.

Jeanne and Britany went into the living room, and Britany started to tuck a pillow under Jeanne's arm for support.

"Britany, you have been wonderful, but, really, I can do most things by myself now that I am getting used to it. The pain isn't bad. You are being a little overprotective. Relax a little," said Jeanne. "I think you hurt Michael's feelings. After the accident you hardly talked to him at all. Maybe you should call him and at least make sure he got home."

"Jeanne, you're right. I am being protective. The problem is, it's not your arm I am worried about. Tell me what happened to make Trigger fall?" Britany had been waiting until she and Jeanne were alone to confront her; now was the time. Jeanne needed to realize something was wrong. Letting it go could end in a more serious accident.

"He tripped as he went into the jump," Jeanne stated simply.

"Do you remember him tripping?"

"I think I lost some of my memory from the fall," Jeanne said lamely.

"Jeanne, think about it. If Trigger tripped before the jump you would have been thrown forward. You were on the ground at the side of the jump. I'm sure Trigger's head was turned to the side before he jumped. I keep going over the events in my mind, and I saw him look to the side just before he went up."

"What are you trying to say? Trigger always concentrates on the jump. He never looks to the side no matter what distraction may come up," Jeanne protested.

"Exactly, and there were no distractions. We would have noticed if there were. Jeanne, I think you had one of your spells and were falling off of Trigger at the time of the jump. You would have had the reins in your hand. When you blacked out you probably pulled Trigger's head to the side as you were starting to fall. Pulling his head to the side caused him to lose his balance, and he missed the jump. That's why you fell on the opposite side from where he did. That would also explain why you don't remember the events leading to the fall. I want you to be honest. How many of these blackout spells have you had, and how long have they been happening?" Britany asked bluntly.

Jeanne looked stunned and frightened.

"Britany, I truly don't know. I never remember anything. I just seem to lose a piece of time. I never feel anything. Dropping the diapers was the first time I can really be sure of. If you wouldn't have been there and told me what happened, I would have just thought I was clumsy. I have noticed that I seem to be dropping things and tripping a lot. I just thought I have been more tired than normal. Sometimes my vision acts strange. It seems like I am in a tunnel. I can only see straight ahead. Migraines can do that, so I haven't been too concerned. Please don't worry so. You can't be sure I actually blacked out and caused Trigger to fall."

"Jeanne, someone needs to worry." Britany was on her feet pacing in front of the couch, her arms flung upward in a gesture of desperation. "What if it would happen while you are driving! You could kill yourself or someone else. You need to go to a specialist and find out what is happening!"

"OK. I will call first thing in the morning, just to make you happy. Right now I am tired and would like to get some sleep. Would you please make us some tea? You really need to calm down a little, and it might help us get some to sleep. Herbal tea, we certainly don't need caffeine. I do promise I will call in the morning," Jeanne said.

Britany called Michael to be sure he had made it back safely. He and Ben had just arrived home when she called. He was very tired, but the trip had gone fine. Britany expressed relief that they were home and safe but refrained from mentioning any reference to Jeanne or her own concerns. She told him that they were settled and that she would go into work late the next day because she was taking Amy to school first. She told him she didn't want Jeanne to drive yet because of her arm. She didn't tell him she was afraid to let Jeanne drive until she had been to the doctor to find out what was causing the blackout spells.

She sensed a distance between them as they spoke that came from more than the miles that separated them. Her heart was heavy and confused as she placed the receiver back.

During the night Britany awoke with a start. She wasn't sure what had wakened her. She hurried out to the living room where Jeanne was sleeping.

"Jeanne, are you all right?" Jeanne was lying on the floor trying to sit up as Britany entered the room. "What in the world happened?" She rushed over to Jeanne.

"Would you believe I fell out of bed?" Jeanne chuckled weakly. "It hurts to try and get up because of my arm."

"Let me help you," said Britany.

"It is so dark in here. It would help if you would turn on a light so I can see what is going on."

Britany assisted her back into bed and then went to turn on the light. She was rather puzzled because she had left the hall light on so Amy wouldn't get scared if she woke during the night. There was quite a bit of light. She started to the kitchen to make tea.

"Britany, please turn on the light. It is so dark. I don't know how you can get around!"

Britany stopped in her tracks. Her heart filled with dread, "O Lord, what is going on!" She lifted a silent plea. She turned slowly and went to kneel beside Jeanne.

"Jeanne," she said quietly. "I did turn the light on." She softly took Jeanne's arm and waited for her to respond.

"Britany, don't do this to me!" Jeanne pleaded. "It is totally dark, and I am not in the mood to joke around."

"Jeanne, I am not joking. The light was never off. I left the hall light on for Amy. Can you see anything?"

Jeanne's face filled with fear as she whispered a faint, "No."

Britany kept her voice calm, although she felt like screaming for help. She wanted to keep Jeanne calm and get her to the hospital as quickly as possible. Should she drive Jeanne to the hospital or call an ambulance? She was afraid something had happened during the fall from Trigger. She could possibly be having a stroke, or maybe there was some bleeding that was building up pressure. Whatever it might be, both situations could be worsened by further trauma. She felt that maybe it would be safer to call an ambulance than to risk another fall. "I am going to call an ambulance, and then go and let Crystal know what is going on. She got home several hours ago. She can watch over Amy and come up to the hospital later with my car."

"Britany, I'm scared. This has never happened before, and everything is so dark," said Jeanne, clinging with her good arm to Britany.

"I am, too," said Britany, giving Jeanne a gentle hug. "Let's pray together."

Britany held Jeanne's hand and prayed softly, "O Lord, You are here with us and You know we are both scared. Please help us and give us strength Give the doctors wisdom as they search for causes to this, and please heal Jeanne of whatever is going on, and restore her sight."

Britany rose and quickly called 911. She then hurried to wake Crystal. She gave her a brief explanation and hastened to throw on some clothes. She was zipping her jeans as she heard the noise of the sirens. She slipped on her shoes and ran to the door to assure the paramedics that they had the right place.

"Andrew!" exclaimed Britany when she saw Andrew, one of the paramedics. He was a mutual friend of Britany and Jeanne from the church. They had known him before he became a paramedic. "It's Jeanne. She fell from her horse two days ago. She woke up and is blind!"

He took control of the situation. Two men in blue uniforms brought in the stretcher. Carefully they lifted Jeanne onto it. Andrew calmly explained what was happening since she couldn't see. He continued talking and asking questions as they lowered the stretcher down the steps and along the sidewalk. The lights from the ambulance cast an eerie red glow. With ease and agility the three men lifted Jeanne into the ambulance and helped Britany up to ride with her. Andrew kept in constant contact with the hospital by way of a handheld radio. When they arrived a doctor was waiting for them. A neurologist had been called and was on his way to the hospital along with a radiologist. By the time the emergency room doctor examined her, the neurologist was there and did his exam. They ran a CAT scan that showed something irregular. The radiologist was present, and they took her to a room to follow up with an MRI.

The room they wheeled Jeanne into was large and white. It was void of everything except a large metal canister with a hole in the middle. Britany got a glimpse of Jeanne being put on a bed in front of the canister before the door closed.

It took a long time for the test to be done. Britany walked up to the nursery. She told the staff what was happening. She went into the office to call Jeanne's parents. Anguish gripped her as she dialed the phone. Jeanne's mother could be a very difficult person to deal with, and she didn't like horses. If the fall was the cause of the blindness, Jeanne's mother would be livid. She was sure to be upset whatever the cause, and when she was upset she could be very unpleasant to be around. The last thing Britany wanted to do was talk to her, especially since she felt partly at fault. She shouldn't have let Jeanne ride, knowing that she had experienced at least one blank spell and who knew how many others? She didn't have too long to contemplate the situation. The phone was answered on the third ring.

"Do you know what time it is!? What could possibly be so important as to wake me at four in the morning!?" came the shrill female voice on the other end.

"Hi, Mrs. Peirson. This is Britany, Jeanne's friend. I am sorry to wake you, but there is something going on with Jeanne that I think you would like to know about. Jeanne fell off her horse during a jump yesterday and broke her collarbone. Everything else seemed fine, and I took her to my place to help her with Amy for a couple of days. During the night she fell out of bed, and when I went to help her back into bed she couldn't see. I called the ambulance, and we are at the hospital now. She is still not able to see anything. She is having a test done right now that will hopefully let us know what is happening."

"Oh, my baby! Oh, how horrible! I knew that horse would hurt her someday. I want that horse shot immediately! My husband and I are on our way down. We will be there by noon. We will call from my cellular phone on the way down. You tell Jeanne her mom is on the way."

"Mrs. Peirson, please don't say anything to Jeanne right now about the horse. She is pretty shaken up already. Please don't say anything to upset her. It won't help Jeanne right now, and she needs us," Britany pleaded.

"Surely you don't think I would say anything to upset her! What kind of mother do you think I am!" the shrill voice retorted.

The kind of mother I am glad I don't have! Britany thought to herself as she hung up the phone. She had an overwhelming urge to pick up the phone and call someone whose voice she wanted to hear: Michael. Something held her back from calling. Maybe it was his words about not worrying so much about Jeanne because she simply had a broken collarbone, that she wasn't desperately ill. Maybe it was her pride. She didn't want to run to him every time something bad happened. Maybe it was the fear that seized her every time things got too involved. Whatever the reason, as much as she longed to call him, she didn't.

The test seemed to be taking forever. She skimmed through some magazines without seeing what was there. She heard a familiar voice come in through the door and looked up to see Crystal and Amy. Britany ran to give them each a big hug. Amy looked small and pale. Britany picked her up and carried her to the seat she had occupied for what seemed like eternity. She set Amy on her lap, and Amy clung to her.

"How are things going?" Crystal asked.

"I have no idea. They took her back to do some tests, and I haven't heard anything. Amy, your Grandma Peirson is coming to see you and Mom. She will be here in time for lunch."

"I don't want Grandma Peirson. I want my mommy. I want her to go home," Amy said with a pouty look on her face.

"Oh, honey, so do I." Britany wrapped her arms around Amy and laid her cheek on Amy's silky hair. "I am sure your mommy does, too. Right now we have to wait. The doctors are trying to help her get better. When she gets better, then we can all go home." Amy cowered her head into Britany's shoulder and after several minutes fell into a light sleep. Holding Amy was as comforting to Britany as it was to Amy.

"Are you hungry?" Britany asked Crystal.

"No, but if you like I could go get you something," Crystal offered.

"I don't feel much like eating, but a diet soda or some tea would be nice. Take some money out of my purse. The cafeteria is open. Bring some juice and crackers back for Amy, too."

It wasn't too long after Crystal came back that the doctor came out and asked Britany to come with him. She gently handed Amy over to Crystal and followed him back to a conference room. Her knees felt weak as she lowered herself into an offered chair.

"Britany, I want to be frank about this," Dr. Hanson began. "Jeanne has a brain tumor. The fall probably had nothing to do with the blindness except for the fact that it may have caused some bleeding or swelling, creating more pressure on the nerve."

"A tumor," Britany murmured. She felt stunned. "A tumor in her brain. That just can't be possible."

Dr. Hanson leaned forward and looked straight at Britany. "Jeanne told me you felt she blacked out and that is why the fall happened. She also told me you felt guilty for letting her ride."

"But how did she know that!" Britany dropped back against the chair. She had a puzzled look. "I didn't tell her. I should have never let her ride." She shook her head. "I knew she had a blackout spell. Why didn't I stop her?" Britany pleaded. "She could have been killed! Maybe if I had been more insistent she would have gone to a doctor and we would have found it sooner. I should never have let her ride. Why didn't I stop her?" The emotion welled up, and Britany trembled with fear.

"Britany, I want you to get rid of that guilt right now," Dr. Hanson said. He got up from his desk and sat in the seat beside Britany. He touched her shoulder and waited until she looked up to go on. "Brain tumors have very vague symptoms until they become quite large. Common symptoms are headaches, which people blame on stress, or vision changes. Jeanne is a grown woman. She makes her own choices. You were very perceptive and responsible by urging her to seek medical help, but the choice to ride was hers. You know that, and she in no way blames you, so don't blame yourself. The tumor is in the early stages, when treatment is most successful."

"So you can treat it!" Britany said hopefully. She moved toward the edge of her chair.

"Don't get me wrong." He waved his arm in emphasis. "There is a very big risk whenever brain surgery is performed. We have had very good results with this type of surgery when the tumor is found in time. I want to do the surgery first thing Tuesday morning. I also want you both to be aware that she still may not be able to see after the surgery. We can't tell if the tumor is just pressing on the optic nerve or is actually growing into it. The biggest risk other than damaging surrounding tissue is swelling of the brain after surgery. We will keep her heavily sedated until the risk is past."

"Why would the blindness happen a day after the fall?" Britany asked, puzzled.

"We really don't know. Swelling doesn't always happen right away."

"She was on the floor when I found her. She had fallen out of bed."

"She may have been going to get a drink or something and had another blackout spell. It is hard to tell since she doesn't remember events surrounding the blackout spells." Dr. Hanson remained caring and frank while he talked. Britany noticed that he looked haggard. The stress was affecting him, too.

"Have you talked to Jeanne about this? Is she willing to have the surgery so soon?" Britany asked. It seemed to her Jeanne might want some time to adjust to the idea and mentally prepare herself.

"Yes, I have. Since she can't see she wanted the surgery right away. She doesn't want to adjust to being blind if she doesn't have to. The sooner we do the surgery the better the chances, especially if there is bleeding or the tumor is growing into the optic nerve. Without the surgery she has no chance at all. Only several months in which time she will lose more and more abilities. As I said, the surgery is risky, but it's the only choice."

"Britany," Dr. Hanson continued, "from what she has said, you two have been through a lot together. You are her major support. I know this is hard, but be strong. She needs you." He patted her shoulder and left Britany alone in the room.

She felt as if the walls were closing in on her. She needed some air, but she desperately needed some time to think before talking to anyone. If she left the room Amy and Crystal would have lots of questions.

"Oh, Lord," she prayed quietly, "this can't be happening. Please let me wakeup. I must be in a bad dream. What do I say to Amy? How do you explain something like this to a child? Please be with Jeanne. She is my best friend, and I need her as much as she needs me. Actually I need her more. She has always been a support, even when she was grieving for her husband. Keep her safe. Give her back her eyesight. She is too young and active to be blind," she pleaded. "I'm sorry. I feel totally confused and at a loss on how to pray. Just please make everything normal again." She finished and wiped the tears from her eyes. She took a deep breath and lifted her shoulders a little higher. She had to go to Jeanne.

She left the room fully expecting Amy and Crystal to flood her with questions. They were nowhere to be seen. They must have gone to the cafeteria. Good, she thought. I'll have a chance to talk to Jeanne before explaining anything. They had taken Jeanne to a room on the neuro unit on the fourth floor. Britany took the stairs to the unit.

Britany knocked softly on the door. Jeanne responded for her to come in Britany was surprised to see Amy sitting on the bed beside Jeanne and Crystal seated on a chair across from her.

"Mommy is going to have surgery. They are going to try and fix her eyes She says they might be able to, but if they don't I can help her find things. She also said there is a possibility she may not wake up again, like Daddy, but that won't happen. My mommy would never leave me," Amy said simply, and Britany realized that Jeanne had already told her and, in her realistic way, was trying to prepare her for the worst. A lump caught in Britany's throat as Amy spoke.

"Crystal, could you take Amy for a walk? I need to talk to Britany alone," Jeanne asked.

"Sure," Crystal replied quietly with a weak smile.

"You were right, Britany," Jeanne began as soon as the door closed behind the two. "This is much worse than I let myself believe. I'm more than ready to die. I have everything to look forward to. Jesus is there waiting for me. I just hate leaving Amy. I'm not done raising her yet. She is so young...."

"Jeanne, please stop it," Britany interrupted her. "The doctor said there is a very good success rate. You aren't going to die! I won't let you!" Britany practically choked the words out as she sat beside her on the bed and reached for Jeanne's hand. "Please fight this thing, Jeanne. Don't give up!" Britany pleaded.

"Britany, I have seen too much in my life to not be realistic. Believe me, I will fight for all I am worth. I wouldn't leave Amy for the world, but I feel I need to be prepared, and you need to be prepared for the worst. When my husband died I made a will. Do you remember? I named you to be Amy's guardian in the event of my death."

"Yes, I remember, but it is not going to happen. Please stop!" Britany urged.

"Britany, listen to me! Amy told me my mother could be here anytime. I need to talk to you before she gets here!" Jeanne grasped Britany's shoulder firmly and continued.

"I don't want Amy to grow up under the same pressures I did. I want her to have a chance to have fun and be a little girl. Not a perfect little adult that my mother expects. My mother can be quite harsh with children, and I don't want Amy to have to deal with that. She will try and get Amy. I am sure of it. She is a very domineering person, and she would love to mold Amy the way she thinks she should be. The trouble is, Amy would be in boarding schools or with nannies all of the time. She has grown up with you and Crystal. Liz is much more of a grandmother to her than my mother is. Amy loves her pony and the farm. I know you would love her as if she were your own, because you already do."

"Oh, Jeanne, you know I would. But really you are going to be just fine Amy is like a daughter to me, but she needs her mother, not me!"

"Michael would make a wonderful and caring father, too. Please fight for her. She needs you!" Jeanne insisted.

"How in the world does Michael enter into this?"

"Sooner or later you will stop fighting yourself and see things clearly. You and Michael belong together," Jeanne continued with a resolve that Britany marveled at. Britany, who was still sitting at Jeanne's side holding her hand, was forced to turn away and look at the floor as Jeanne finished, even though she realized Jeanne couldn't see her.

"Right now I don't want to think about him." Britany turned back to face Jeanne. "We are talking about you and you're getting better."

"You don't want to think about him, or you won't think about him?" Jeanne asked frankly. "Be honest with yourself, Britany. If I don't make it through the surgery I want you to know I approve of Michael as a father. I don't want you using Amy as an excuse to come between the two of you. I have also made provisions for the horses. They are to go to you. If for some reason you can't keep Trigger, feel free to find him a good home Try to keep the pony for Amy. She means so much to her. I would hate for her to lose Sissy, too. I have set up a trust fund for Amy that the money from my estate would go into. You would have a monthly allotment to use for her expenses and education. She will get the remainder when she turns twenty-one."

"You certainly have everything covered," Britany said weakly.

The door burst open, and Britany turned just in time to see Jeanne's mother whisk into the room. The scent of a harsh perfume came in with her. She was dressed neatly in her cream suit and silk scarf with matching leather purse and shoes.

"Jeanne, darling, what has happened to you?" Monique Peirson asked as if she were talking to a little child. She squeezed her bony body between Jeanne and Britany, practically sitting on Britany's lap.

"I better go check on Amy and Crystal," Britany said quietly and took her leave.

The rest of the day passed for Britany as if through a fog. The scene of the doctor saying that the surgery would be tomorrow kept going through her mind. Liz drove in to town and spent the night with Britany to help with Amy but mainly for comfort and support. Britany was so glad to have her there. Britany didn't call Michael. When Crystal offered to call and tell him about Jeanne she sharply answered "No!" She was afraid to talk to Michael. She didn't want to run to him with her problems and she didn't want to feel dependent on him until he was ready to make a commitment. He didn't want a commitment, he had made that clear, and she didn't want to be a burden to him.

Satan attacked Britany full force. He filled her mind with lies and half-truths and she believed them. She was scared. She knew the fear of Michael was unjustified, but it wouldn't go away. Part of her wanted to talk to him and have him with her, but another part wanted desperately to avoid him. She felt responsible for Jeanne. Jeanne needed her, Michael didn't. Britany finally fell into a troubled sleep.

The night did pass, although it seemed an eternity. She was at the hospital before seven. The time in the surgery lounge competed with the night. Britany had never known that eight hours could be so long. Britany, Liz, Crystal and Amy made small talk and drank sodas as they waited. None of them spoke of the surgery except to comment on how long it seemed to be taking. Britany had been able to see Jeanne before surgery. The peace with which Jeanne faced the surgery was a sharp contrast to the dread that seemed to weigh on Britany's heart. Monique and Jeanne's father, Henry, were in the lounge. Monique talked nonstop and continued to bring up the subject of those dreadful horses. Henry tried unsuccessfully to reason with her about the real cause of Jeanne's surgery, but gave up after being totally ignored, and he walked away. Liz tried, also unsuccessfully, to talk with Monique, after which they all left her to her constant pacing and nonsensical chatter. Britany tried to be sympathetic in her heart toward Monique, but knowing how Jeanne had always said her mother ignored her most of her life made it hard to feel sorry for her.

Finally Dr. Hanson entered the room with a smile on his face. Britany felt hope for the first time since she had heard about the tumor.

"We were able to get the tumor without injury to the optic nerve. There was a small amount of bleeding, but we were able to get it under control. It looks as if she will regain her sight. We had to manipulate the brain to get to the tumor. I had hoped we wouldn't have to. That increases the chance for swelling. We are keeping her in a deep sleep state so the brain will require less blood. That decreases the chance of more swelling. No one will be allowed to see her for several hours, and then just one at a time and for only several minutes. I want to warn you, she is still on a respirator."

"Does that mean my mommy is OK?" Amy asked, pulling on the surgeon's lab coat.

"Yes, honey, that means your mom is doing fine. It will be a little longer until you get to see her, though." The surgeon bent down to Amy's level as he spoke to her. Amy squealed and gave him a big hug. Britany was sure she saw him brush a tear from his cheek as he rose back to his full height. She felt a rush of warmth toward him as she realized that he must have felt a great deal of pressure through this ordeal. It must have been a tremendous strain to do a delicate surgery on the mother of a darling six-year-old.

Liz suggested they go to a local restaurant and eat a real meal since none of them had eaten much in the last twenty-four hours. Every one felt like celebrating and agreed heartily. Monique even liked the idea.

Britany felt ecstatic. Suddenly she wanted to talk to Michael. She could tell him about what had happened without depending on him. She had gone through the worst on her own. But when she called him the phone rang and rang, and no one answered.

Later in the evening Britany got a chance to see Jeanne. She looked pale but peaceful as she slept. Britany held Amy as she looked down on her mother.

"Night, night, Mommy." Amy bent down and kissed her mother's peaceful face. "Britany is taking me to her house to go to bed now, too." Amy talked to Jeanne as if she were fully alert. Britany smiled and held Amy close. Then they left quietly. Britany took Crystal and Amy home.

Britany felt lighter than air and hurried to call Michael as soon as Amy was quietly sleeping. She was disappointed when he didn't answer. She imagined he was gone on a business trip.

Britany kneeled beside her bed and thanked God over and over again for bringing Jeanne through surgery. She then sank wearily into the deepest sleep she had been able to get for several nights. As she slept she dreamt of Jeanne. They were riding their horses across a meadow. It was a beautiful meadow with flowers blooming and birds singing. Suddenly Jeanne turned her horse and started riding in a different direction. Britany stopped and turned her horse, but when she tried to follow, Jeanne was gone She searched frantically, but Jeanne was nowhere to be seen. She was breathless and panicky when the phone interrupted her dream.

"Hello," she said trying to regain her composure.

"Hello," a shaken female voice came over the receiver. "I think you should come to the hospital immediately." The voice continued as Britany listened in horror. "There has been a drastic change in Jeanne's condition Please come as soon as possible."

Britany trembled as she quickly dressed and then went to wake Amy.

"We are going to the hospital," Britany explained softly. "They called and said something has happened to your mommy. They want us to come right away." Britany was speaking as much to Amy as she was to Crystal, who had awoken when the phone rang.

Dread as strong as she had ever experienced filled her. What has happened? she asked herself. She knew it must be drastic or they would not have called. Amy remained silent. She looked as white as a ghost. Britany held her little hand as the three of them went to the car.

They arrived at the hospital. None of them said a word. The walk to the neuro unit seemed an eternity, with each step a major effort. The halls were dark and empty. Various beeps and machine sounds penetrated the silence as they passed several rooms. Finally they reached the nurses' station. A midnight nurse that Britany knew looked up and immediately came to her side.

"Oh, Britany, the swelling has increased, and we aren't able to control it," the nurse said. "The pressure inside her head is rising out of control!"

Britany felt as if she was going to collapse, but, strangely, her legs seemed to be holding. Amy remained pale and still. At age six it was impossible for her to fully understand what had happened. She knew something was desperately wrong.

"I guess all we can do is...." Britany's sentence was cut short by a loud shout at the end of the hall.

"Where is my daughter! I demand to know what has happened right now. Where is the doctor? He needs to be here. Where is he?" Monique shrieked.

The nurse hurried to meet Monique.

"Mrs. Peirson, please calm down. We have very sick patients who will be scared by your shouting. Come with me, and I will explain. You have to stop shouting or I can't talk to you," the nurse explained, taking her arm to lead her down the hall.

"Release my arm this instant! I am perfectly capable of walking myself. Who are you to say I am shouting! I am not shouting! I just want to find out what has happened to my daughter." Monique failed to lower her voice and briskly shook her arm loose from the nurse's grasp. She continued her deliberate walk down the hall with the nurse half running to keep up. Monique was as impeccably dressed as always. Her thin nose was tilted slightly in the air as she walked.

"Britany, you tell me what has happened. It seems you always find out these things before I do," Monique said in her demanding manner, stopping to stand directly in front of her. She had her hands on her hips, and one toe was tapping impatiently on the floor.

Britany looked up at Monique with pain written on her face.

"Uh, I, they....," Britany faltered and looked down at Amy, unable to continue.

The nurse came to her rescue and explained.

Britany lifted Amy and carried her the short distance to a quiet lounge. There they waited, Amy on Britany's lap, Crystal beside them looking totally helpless. Britany put her arm protectively around Crystal's shoulder.

Monique and Henry had insisted on waiting at the nurses' desk so as not to miss anything. Britany actually felt sorry for her. As harsh as Monique came across, Britany knew she loved Jeanne. Britany couldn't even bear to think what she would feel if something this tragic were to happen to Crystal.

"Mom, I will watch Amy. You go call Michael. He would come and be with us. I know he would," Crystal said to Britany, tears sliding down her face.

"He's not home," Britany said quietly. "I already tried."

Monique moaned loudly from the hall. Britany froze. She knew what the surgeon, Dr. Hanson, was going to say as he entered the room.

"I'm sorry, Britany." His shoulders heaved and an involuntary sob escaped his lips. Taking a deep breath he continued, "We did all we could do, but the swelling was too involved."

Collecting Amy in her arms, she crossed the room to put a comforting arm on his shoulder.

"We know you did all you could do. Her life was in God's hands. I guess He just called her home. She told me she wasn't afraid to die. I think she knew she was going to. She tried to prepare Amy and me, but I wasn't ready to accept it." Britany said the last words more to herself than to Dr. Hanson.

A myriad of thoughts was going through Britany's mind, but she would only let one surface, and that was Amy. She lowered her arm from the doctor's shoulder and wrapped them both securely around Amy. She realized he was speaking again, and now he was trying to comfort her.

"Britany, no one can prepare herself for this. Amy will need you now, but don't forget you have needs, too." Dr. Hanson patted her on the back and turned to leave.

Crystal, who had been watching from a short distance, came over, and Britany wrapped her free arm around her shoulder. Britany wasn't ready to give in to tears just yet. There was too deep a flood of emotions inside. Amy remained silent, and Crystal cried softly.

CHAPTER 15

Monique took care of the funeral arrangements. Britany and Liz took Crystal and Amy shopping to get black dresses for the funeral. The dresses all looked the same, to Britany, so there was no need to be choosy. Britany went through the motions woodenly until they were choosing Amy's dress. The lady waiting on them was sweet and helpful. She was totally caught off guard along with the rest of them when Amy tried on her dress.

"Does it look nice? My mommy died, and I want to look nice for her funeral," Amy said innocently. The lady gasped and looked shocked.

"I am so sorry, honey. Yes, you look beautiful," she managed to say as Liz and Crystal were trying unsuccessfully to hold back the tears. The lady's eyes filled with tears as she helped them get their items together.

"We should have told you," said Britany, reaching into her purse for money. "It's just been so difficult to talk about it. I'm sorry to have shocked you like this. You have been most helpful with the dresses. It's made the task a little more bearable. Thank you."

"She must have been young," The salesclerk handed Britany her change and shook her head. "How tragic to leave a little girl behind. I am so sorry. If I can be of more assistance, please let me know."

Britany nodded in response, and they left the store.

Many people came to the funeral home; nurses and Doctors from work; friends and family. Most of them Britany knew. Jeanne was loved by many, and her absence would be deeply felt. Amy didn't cry at the funeral home, but she cried herself to sleep that night. It broke Britany's heart that was already shattered. She walked out of the bedroom after Amy finally fell asleep and sat on the couch. Crystal looked up.

"Mom," said Crystal. "Michael is probably home from his business trip. You should try and call him.

"No," was Britany's brief reply.

"OK. Then let me go call."

"No! I don't want him here," Britany said quietly but with resolve. She crossed her arms in front of her and wore an angry, determined expression.

"Mom you can't mean that!" Crystal gasped in amazement.

"But I do. We have each other. We don't need him."

Britany refused to call Michael despite Crystal's insistence. She was angry with God. She had trusted Him to take care of Jeanne, and He took her away. What good had it done to pray? God didn't care anyway. She had prayed, Jeanne had prayed and still she was left without a friend and Amy was left without a mother. She couldn't explain why she felt the way she did. She hadn't taken the time to reason it out. She just didn't want to be dependent on God when He had let her down. She didn't want to be dependent on anyone and that included Michael. She saw him as a gift of God and as much as she wanted to see him she was more angry with God and didn't want anything involved with Him.

Britany proceeded numbly through the funeral and to the dinner following. Friends and family talked about Jeanne with love and respect. They talked of her faith in God, and of how she was in heaven were everything was beautiful. Britany felt like shouting at them to shut up. Couldn't they see she was needed on earth to take care of Amy? How could they talk so lovingly of a God who just took away her best friend? She didn't feel like eating, and sat silently with Amy.

Liz sat beside Britany and said, "Britany, Jeanne isn't gone forever. She's in heaven with God. I know it's hard to have her gone, but she's in a better place."

"I know mom," Britany said solemnly. "But it doesn't help."

Liz looked at her daughter with loving concern. Charles cast Liz an anxious glance and Liz shrugged her shoulders.

Phillip stood beside Britany and gave her a tender hug. "Hang in there Sis. We all loved Jeanne. We love you too. You'll make it through this."

"Do you think I can take Amy and go home now?" Britany asked her mother.

"Sure," said Liz. "I'll go say good-bye to Monique.

Britany collected her purse and told Amy they were leaving. Liz walked toward Monique, but Monique brushed past her and hurried toward Amy.

Monique took Amy's hand. Britany thought she was coming to say good-bye Instead Monique started to walk away with Amy in tow and said in a sugary voice.

"Come on, Amy. We are going back to your house and collect your things so you can come live with us."

Amy shrieked and flew back to Britany, wrapping herself around her legs.

"No! Mommy said I was to stay with Britany. I won't go!" Amy shrieked at the top of her lungs, clinging to Britany with all her strength." Britany, please don't let her take me."

Britany looked at Monique with a surprised, angry scowl.

"She is right. Jeanne said she wrote a will that named me Amy's guardian. It was her wish for Amy to stay with me!" Britany said angrily.

"But I am her grandmother! Why wouldn't she want Amy to go with me?" Monique said smugly.

Britany wanted to list all the reasons Jeanne didn't want Monique to have Amy, but as she became aware of all the others around them, she held her tongue. Most of the people were relatives of Monique, and she didn't want to make her look bad in front of her family.

"I think we both know why. Besides it doesn't really matter. The will is made, and I am her guardian. Leave Amy alone. We are going home!" Britany spoke and turned to leave with Amy at her side grasping her hand.

"Wills can be challenged! Amy will belong to me!" Monique yelled to their backs.

"No!" Amy screamed and clung to Britany.

Britany reached down and took Amy in her arms and carried her out. Crystal ran to catch up.

Liz walked up to where Monique was and stood face to face. "Don't you think that little girl has been through enough pain! Stay out of the way. I am sure Britany will see that you get time with Amy if you stop threatening them," She said. Then she turned, and hurried to join Britany and Crystal.

Britany was shaking despite the heat that hit them as they left the building.

"Can she do that?" Britany whispered as her mother walked up to them.

"She can try. We may need to find a very good lawyer," Liz replied seriously.

"Britany, please don't let Grandma take me," Amy pleaded. "I want to stay with you and Crystal and Grandma Liz." Amy looked to Britany with sad, tear-filled eyes. It was the most Amy had spoken since her mother died, and against her better judgment Britany assured her, "No one will ever take you away!"

The pain Britany felt that night was like a deep dark pit. She had never been aware before how much sorrow could actually be a physical pain. As she finally let the thoughts of Jeanne's death begin to surface, it felt as if someone had kicked her in the stomach. Jeanne had known she would die. How could she be so calm? How in the world could she be so trusting in God? He had left her only daughter with no mother and a wicked grandmother who was going to do everything in her power to make Amy's life miserable.

"God, how can You do this!" Britany's heart screamed. "How can You take Jeanne away from us when we had faith that You could heal her! Is this Your idea of a sick joke, or some stupid test to see if I would pass! Well, I didn't. If that is how You handle us; how You say You love us--then I don't want any part of it. What about Michael? I felt for sure You gave him to me to love and be my husband. If You can be so uncaring to do this to a little girl, then I don't want any part of Michael either. You might just snatch him away right when I start to depend on him." Anger totally consumed Britany, and, strangely, it felt better than the pain.

Britany slept fitfully the next several nights and she couldn't eat. All her energy went into Amy and trying to make her life a little less sad. They both were afraid Monique would try to get Amy, and on a week after the funeral their fears were confirmed. A registered letter came addressed to Britany. Britany accepted it and then hesitantly opened it.

It was a court order stating that until the will was probated the guardianship of Amy was to go to Monique. It went on to say that Monique would be there that day to pick her up.

Britany collapsed on the couch. How was she going to tell Amy? She had never felt so alone in her life. She had always depended on Gods strength to get her through tough times. Here was the toughest time she had ever been through, and she could only turn away from Him. Despair filled her. She didn't have the strength to answer the phone when it began to ring. Amy came into the room to ask Britany why she didn't answer the phone and stopped short when she saw Britany's face.

"My grandmother's coming to get me isn't she?" Amy asked in a low voice with the perception of a small child.

Britany could only nod, and Amy fell into her arms in tears.

"I won't go. She can't make me."

"I am afraid she can, or else they will put me in jail. I am going to fight this, though. We will get a lawyer and get you back, but for a short time you will have to go."

"OK, Britany. I will go, but you fight hard to get me back." Amy looked at Britany with a resolve that Britany had once seen in her mother. Little did Britany know that Amy wasn't totally helpless. Amy had a plan of her own that could only be coerced by a six-year-old.

Amy's big brown eyes looked bigger than ever as she looked up at Britany and said good-bye later that afternoon. Her brown ringlets bobbed as she walked to the car. The scene burned an image into Britany's memory as Amy took off with her grandmother. The house was unbearably empty and the knife burning pain rekindled itself. Crystal came home that night to a quiet house and a distraught mother.

"Mom, we have to fight. The will says she is to stay with you."

"Crystal, I know, but Monique is a very rich and powerful person." Britany sank into a chair. "I have no idea who to even get for a lawyer. If we get the wrong one and he looses, she will be gone forever. Monique would make sure we never see Amy again."

CHAPTER 16

Michael determined that he was going to stay away from Britany for a while. He needed time to think, but it was hard. He wanted to call every evening when he came home from work, but he restrained himself. He secretly hoped she would call him, but, when she didn't call by the end of the first week, he felt dejected. He had rather dominated her time during the last several weeks, and she had certainly been through an emotional time with the graduation. He figured that Britany probably needed some time. He was glad that at least she had called to show her concern that he made it home safely. She had been a little formal when she called and not her usual cheerful self. He had told himself to give her time and not to expect anything, so he would wait. Maybe she would call this week. If not, he would try to call her the next week. Meanwhile work was always demanding. It had served well to keep his mind off things in the past.

Michael's Hunger for God steadily grew. He searched for a church that talked about Jesus the way Britany's pastor had. He went to a large church in his neighborhood and was impressed with what he heard. He joined a men's Bible study and eagerly searched scripture to learn more about Jesus.

Britany went to work the day after Amy left. Margaret, her department head had told her to take several weeks off to help Amy adjust, but, since Amy wasn't there, it seemed useless to take the time off. Britany wasn't the only one in the nursery who had hurt deeply from Jeanne's death. If the wounds had healed a little, they were opened back up with Britany's presence. Shelly was unusually quiet, and all the doctors were a little too patient and kind. Britany appreciated their thoughtfulness and could see that they were dealing with their own pain. It helped some to know she wasn't alone.

The next week continued with Britany sleeping little and eating even less. She knew that if her mother found out she wasn't eating she would be very upset, but as hard as she tried she just couldn't. There was a hopelessness in her life now that she suspected wasn't entirely due to Jeanne's death.

Britany sought her brother's help in finding a lawyer in Dayton. He recommended a friend of his, Mr. Fitzpatrick, and she drove to his downtown office. The building was old but wonderfully preserved with marble floors and massive columns. She entered his office to see a tall lanky man sitting at a desk. He was talking on the phone, and excused himself from the conversation on her appearance.

"Please come in and have a seat Miss Becker." He motioned to the chair across from the desk. He took a seat in his leather chair. His manner was pleasant as he listened to her story.

"From what you have told me, I think there is some hope that the will would stand since Jeanne was in a good frame of mine when she wrote it. I want to warn you that it is hard to break up blood relatives. The fact that they could financially offer so much would make it even harder." He leaned forward and rested his elbows on the desk, his fingers laced together. "The hearing will be rough. Monique will bring up anything about her past that she can. You mentioned a friend--Michael. You are an attractive, eligible female, and these people may use your relationship with Michael and make it look bad. I will take a look at the will and do some research. I will get back with you to confirm my findings."

Britany felt sick inside. Even when Michael wasn't around he was affecting her life. How could she possibly fight all these difficulties?

Mr. Fitzpatrick looked at her, rose to walk around the desk and sat on the edge facing her.

"Britany don't lose hope. I didn't say it was impossible, just tough. I want you to be aware of the difficulties before they surface. I'll definitely work hard for you and do more research."

Britany left his office feeling confused and desperate. She had thought he would help her get Amy back right away, but he had suggested waiting until the hearing in ten days. It agonized her to think of Amy alone with Monique. Britany wanted so much to hold Amy close and offer a little warmth and protection from the cruel cold world she had suddenly been cast into.

Britany didn't go to the farm on Friday even though she had the weekend off. She had lost weight, and her face looked drawn and sad. It shocked her to look in the mirror. Her eyes were sunken and looked almost gray instead of their normal green. She could wear loose clothes to hide the weight she had lost, but it was hard to hide her face. She knew her parents would be very worried if they saw her. She didn't have the strength to face them, or to see the horses again, with all the memories they brought. She felt guilty because she knew the horses desperately needed the exercise, but she couldn't bring herself to go.

Crystal begged her mother to call Michael. She secretly hoped he would pull her mother out of her depression. Britany refused to even discuss the matter and wouldn't allow Crystal to call. Crystal was concerned as to why Michael hadn't called Britany more. He had tried several times but her mother wouldn't talk to him. Surely he wouldn't give up that easy, unless something had happened between the two of them. She knew it wouldn't help to ask Britany. Crystal was quite concerned and wanted to call Michael herself, but remained loyal to her mother's wishes.

Fortunately Crystal had her summer job to go to and was able to get away from the house, which now days seemed drab and empty. She had always loved to come home to the warmth and protection of their home. She loved to tell Britany about the day's events and laugh together. It seemed like ages since her mother had even smiled, much less laughed. Crystal noticed that they never had devotions together anymore. When she suggested it to her mother, Britany would find a reason not to. She suspected that Britany had stopped praying. Crystal prayed often, and her mother was the subject of all her prayers.

Crystal had been shocked when Britany looked so hopeless after seeing the lawyer. Any other time Britany would have resolved to pray about the situation and stop worrying. Crystal contemplated calling their pastor and telling him, but she decided to give her mother more time and see if she could work this out on her own. Crystal was sure her mother wasn't sleeping very much. She heard her at all hours of the night wondering around the house, or cleaning cupboards, or numerous other odd tasks. Britany was looking awful. Crystal was sure that was why she wouldn't go out to the farm for the weekend. If only they could get Amy back she was sure her mother would snap out of it.

Britany spent Saturday cleaning and going through some closets. She went to Jeanne's home to see if she could collect some of Amy's belongings. She hadn't been able to face the task, but she needed to do something positive toward getting Amy back. She thought if she did something, by getting her things ready. It would help her attitude. She returned to the house around five and began sorting Crystal's closet to make room for Amy's clothes. "Maybe I had better use my closet instead," she thought. "Surely there would be more room than I am finding in Crystal's!"

Britany heard a car pull in and thought it was probably Crystal. She was surprised when the doorbell rang. She hurried to answer it. To her amazement it was Amy and her grandfather.

"Amy, sweetheart!" Britany exclaimed as she dropped to her knees and fondly embraced her.

"She managed to go through two nannies and practically drove Monique out of her mind," Henry Peirson said in a deep elderly voice.

"Does that mean she gets to live with me?" Britany asked hopefully as she stood and faced the elderly man. Amy stood in front of her, facing her grandfather, with Britany's hands protectively on her shoulders.

"For the time being Monique felt it would be best and the hearing will be delayed, but she is trying to find another nanny. She will still fight for custody. The boarding school starts in several weeks, so she thought it best if Amy could stay here until then."

"She's sending her to a boarding school? Why is she sending her to a boarding school? Does she even want Amy?" Britany asked in despair.

Realizing he had said too much, Amy's grandfather turned and left without comment. Britany could only stare after him.

"Oh Amy, I missed you so much!" Britany said, giving her a big hug, once again down on her knee facing Amy, "I've been trying to make room in my closet for your clothes. Crystal's closet is much too crammed to fit anything into it. I thought if I got things ready it would help you come back, and you did! What in the world did you do to your grandmother? You have always gotten along with baby-sitters so well," Britany said as she rose and led Amy into the kitchen to find her a snack.

"I thought if I could be awful enough it would make her want to give me back. It worked."

"I can't imagine you being awful. You must have tried very hard. What did you do?"

"Do you mean like writing on the windows with Grandmother's lipstick, or hiding the keys, or sneaking out at night and setting off the burglar alarm?"

"Yes, that would definitely qualify. Oh Amy, we are going to get you for keeps somehow," Britany said, holding Amy tightly in her arms.

"My mommy would have prayed. She also would not have liked all the things I did to Grandmother," Amy said honestly.

"Your mother would have prayed, but she would have been as happy as I am that you are back. Come. Let's see what we can do with your toys."

A car pulled into the drive. It was Crystal. Amy ran to meet her at the door and threw her little arms around her in a giant hug.

"Amy! You're back! What did you do? Make Monique so miserable she had to bring you back?" Crystal asked with a teasing smile on her face.

"How did you know?" Amy asked in awe.

"That's what I would have done. It's a good thing Monique is no expert in child behavior. She wouldn't have given you the very thing you were trying to get," Crystal responded cheerfully.

"I may have to go back when school starts. Grandmother wants to send me to a boarding school," Amy said softly, looking at the floor. The happiness drained from her face.

Crystal looked up at Britany with an astonished look. Britany nodded that it was true.

"Mom went to see a lawyer, and he is going to help us fight to keep you," Crystal said in an effort to put some light back in Amy's eyes. Crystal put her arms around Amy's shoulders and walked her to the kitchen for a snack.

They spent the rest of the evening arranging Amy's belongings. Britany would have liked to move Amy's bed and dresser to the condo. She wasn't sure if she would be allowed to, so she just made do with what they had. At least now Amy had a space of her own and things felt more permanent, even though the situation hadn't changed.

The next morning Crystal got ready for church and urged Britany to go too. Britany argued that she just couldn't go and didn't give Crystal a reason. Amy wanted to stay with Britany, and Britany relished her company. When Crystal came home from church, Amy begged to go out to the farm.

"There is really no reason not to," Crystal reminded her when Britany tried to back out.

"I guess you're right." Britany gave in to their insistence.

Britany sighed and went into her room to try to make herself look more presentable. She was dabbing some concealer under her eyes when there was a soft knock at the door. Crystal walked on in and stood behind Britany to view her in the mirror.

"You know, it would help if you would just smile a little," she said quietly.

"I know, but I just can't!" Britany said hopelessly as tears filled her eyes and rolled down her face.

Crystal reached over and put a supportive arm around Britany's shoulder.

"I'll try," Britany said drying her tears with a cool washcloth, "For you and Amy."

"I guess I had better start over with the makeup," Britany mumbled.

"You could just let Grandma and Grandpa see you as you are. Someone needs to know that you aren't eating or sleeping," Crystal said firmly.

"They would be worried over nothing. I will be OK, it just takes time,"

Britany spoke with more conviction than she felt.

Britany's parents were concerned, but they didn't say much. Liz prayed in her heart that Britany would come around and once again look to God for guidance. She knew only too well, that it was up to Britany. No one else could do it for her.

It was nice to be out in the fresh air. Britany was sure it would help her sleep a little better, but once again she had a bad dream shortly after going to sleep, and couldn't sleep the rest of the night.

Michael called after they had returned on Monday evening. Crystal took the call. When Britany found out who it was, she froze.

"Tell him I'm not feeling well and already went to bed," she whispered.

"Mom, I can't tell him that! You owe it to him to talk to him. He needs to know what is going on!"

"NO! I can't!" Britany pleaded.

Crystal gave in and told him that Britany was ill. He didn't seem very convinced.

Michael's heart ached when Britany wouldn't take his call.

"You know Lord I deserve this," Michael said a loud while he was alone in his room. "Britany has never been anything, but open and honest with me. She showed me love and respect. I could see You through her yet I kept pushing her away because of my fear of commitment. She is not Linda. She is not going to treat me the way Linda did. I need to open up and trust her. I want to tell her about You and how I've grown in my desire to serve You. Please help me know what to do.

Britany requested the week off work since Amy was back with her. Margaret, her supervisor readily agreed, hoping it might do her some good to get away for a while. The days passed slowly. Britany seemed to cling to Amy for some sense of security. Michael called each night, and each night Britany found another reason not to talk to him.

On Thursday Crystal went to a college orientation that was to last until Friday evening. She would be meeting her roommate. They would find their classes, and get the books they needed. The phone rang Thursday after Crystal left. Amy was asleep, and Britany refused to pick it up.

Britany could not understand why Crystal rang the doorbell when she returned on Friday evening instead of using her key. "Maybe she lost it," she thought as she hurried to the door. She had already prepared for bed and was wearing her floor-length, rose-colored velour robe over her T-shirt and stocking feet. She opened the door to reveal Michael standing tall and determined in the doorway.

"Michael," she said weakly. She knew what little color she had was draining quickly from her face. "What are you doing here?" She took a step backward at the sight of his face that wore an angry, determined look.

"I came to find out what in the world is going on!" He spoke angrily as he walked past her into the room. Turning back to look at her, his face suddenly changed expression. She looked pale and barely able to hold her own weight as she stood there. Her eyes were dull, and her beautiful hair had lost some of its shine. Even with the robe on it was plain to see that she had lost weight. She seemed small and frail, like a little bird.

"Britany, what in the world has happened to you! What has been going on?" Now it was his turn to be shaken. "I'm sorry I didn't believe Crystal when she said you were sick."

"I'm not sick. It's Jeanne. She died!" Britany managed to choke out.

Michael was unable to respond for some time. He stood where he was with his eyes wide and his mouth open.

"Britany, no." He finally managed a moan and swiftly closed the space between them to take her in his arms.

He was strong and compassionate. Britany needed so badly to draw from his strength.

"Britany, why didn't you call me? I would have come to be with you," he said with emotion, tilting her chin up with his fingertips, staring into her eyes to find an answer.

"I know you would have come. That's exactly why I didn't call," Britany replied honestly, lowering her eyes from his penetrating gaze.

"Britany, I love you! Look at me and tell me you don't love me!" He demanded, once again lifting her chin to look at him, this time a little more forcefully. He was trying to be patient, but he was confused, and frustrated.

"I do love you, Michael. More than I could ever imagine. You are in my every thought and I can't imagine my life without you but it is so hard to explain. I'm scared." Britany looked at him while she spoke, and the pain she saw reflected her own.

Britany withdrew from his embrace, walked over to the couch, and began to explain as she sat wearily down.

"Michael, this is hard, and I hope you can understand, because I certainly don't. Soon after we met I realized that I was feeling things for you I had never felt before. I didn't understand at first, but sometime between the time we met and the weekend on the boat I realized that I had fallen in love with you."

Michael walked over and sat beside her, taking her hand in his, looking at her with a special gentleness as he spoke. "That's when I knew I loved you but I was too stubborn to admit it to myself or to anyone else."

She sighed and continued while looking down at the folds in her gown. "When I was a little girl I used to look in the sky and pretend there was a special star just for me. That star was a symbol of the man who would be my husband. When I would get a new boyfriend, I would ask Jesus if he was the one for me, then I would look to see if the star would shine brighter. It's funny, I knew it was silly of me to expect such a thing to happen, but in my heart I truly believed it would. The star always stayed the same. When I looked in the sky on Easter morning I noticed this bright star that I hadn't seen before without realizing any significance. Something woke me up in the night around the time of Crystal's graduation. I went to the window to look out. Everything was quiet, but I noticed the same bright star. Suddenly it all came back, looking for the star that would be God's confirmation of the man I would marry. I realized God was showing me that you were indeed the one He intended. It was wonderful. Then, when we were on the boat, I started getting scared. Every time I thought of marriage, of getting too close to you, or depending on you, this horrible fear would surface. I told Shelly and Jeanne about it."

"What did they say?"

"Shelly said to give myself some time. There would be a lot of changes, and I needed to adjust a little slower. Jeanne said it was Satan trying to steal the gift God was giving me."

"Jeanne was very perceptive," Michael said in a soft voice, almost a whisper.

"Oh, Michael, how could she be gone! How can God be so cruel as to take both her and her husband and leave little Amy without a mother or father!" Britany pleaded for an answer that she knew he wouldn't have.

"Is that why you didn't call me? You thought if God would take Jeanne away from Amy then how could you trust Him to not take me?" Michael probed.

"Michael, if God is that mean and that uncaring, then I don't want His gift. I don't want anything to do with Him," Britany retorted.

"So you just want to mope around, not eat or sleep, and run yourself into the ground?" Michael said firmly.

"No! It's just that I can't eat. I try, but I just can't!" she pleaded. "Every time I get to sleep some horrible dream comes. I wake up, and then I can't get back to sleep. I don't mope around. I'm taking good care of Amy. Jeanne named me legal guardian. Even that is going wrong," Britany threw her hands up in despair. "Jeanne's mother is bound and determined that she wants Amy. She is a mean, domineering person who doesn't understand children. Jeanne pleaded with me before she died to be sure I kept Amy; to fight for her because her mother would try to get her. She was right. Monique took her by a restraining order a week and a half after Jeanne passed away. Before the week was over she brought her back to stay with me until school starts. It seems that Amy pulled some strings of her own and made life very miserable for her grandmother. I have a lawyer, but he said it will be a hard struggle. It's uncertain which way it may go. Monique has made some very unfair accusations about me and my lawyer says she will even try and make our relationship look cheap. It makes me feel sick just to think of it. I just can't loose Amy. Jeanne was right. I love her. I can't bear the thought of her gone, much less the thought of her struggling to survive under her grandmothers expectations."

"Britany, darling, you have been through so much. Why in the world did you think you had to do it on your own? Having someone to help you through things is not depending on him. It's sharing your life with him, good and bad," Michael said, cradling her in his arms as if she were a little child.

"I've been dealing with some issues of my own. That's probably where some confusion came from before Jeanne died. My first marriage was tough and I was scared to make another commitment. It's gotten to the point where the fear of loosing you is worse than the fear of commitment. After the boat trip I recommitted my life to Christ. Britany, I could see Him through your life and I wanted the same love for God that you had. God has reached down and helped me Britany. I'm scared too when it comes to sharing our lives together but God will help me with that. I can see that now.

"You know Britany, I am not the only one who wants to help you through these times. I know you are angry with God, but He is waiting for you to accept his arms of comfort, too. You helped me find God. I want to help you return to Him. You are wrong to try and go through this on your own."

"I have my parents and Crystal. I'm not trying to go through this alone," Britany said quickly.

"Have you told them what you told me?" Michael continued.

"No."

"Then you are still alone. You know, you are not the only one who has gone through hard times."

"I certainly don't need that lecture!" Britany retorted.

"I'm not giving you that lecture. I simply want to tell you a story about a person who could relate to your feelings very well. Do you have a Bible I can use?" Michael asked.

"It's in my bedroom." Britany rose and went to get the Bible. While she was in the bedroom she took a moment to go into her bathroom, and put on a light touch of make-up. Her eyes were gray and sunken instead of their normal green. It was a wonder that Michael didn't run the other way when he first saw her. At least now she knew he could accept her at her worst.

She returned with the Bible. Michael sat in the corner of the couch, resting against the arm, flipping through the pages of the Bible. She really wasn't too eager to hear what he had to say. She didn't want someone to preach to her. How could anyone possibly understand the reason for her anger? She didn't want him to defend God. If God was so powerful, then why should he need to be defended? She went to the kitchen. She filled two glasses with ice and pop and returned to the living room. Though reluctant, she politely handed him the glass and sat beside him on the couch.

Michael didn't lecture. Instead he turned to the book of Job and started reading.

"Are you really going to read the whole book? It's a long book, and I've read it before," Britany asked, perturbed.

"Where, exactly, do you need to go? Just relax. Maybe if nothing else it will put you to sleep. You said you haven't been able to sleep."

Michael started over.

Britany listened and thought as he read about how Job was righteous and good. How God thought highly of him, so highly He made reference to him to Satan; asking him if he had seen how loyal Job was. Satan complained that God had blessed Job so much, that of course he would be loyal to God It seemed strange to think of God and Satan having a conversation. Then he read that God let Satan attack Job in any method he chose, except he couldn't hurt Job physically. God claimed that Job would still not curse Him.

"How could God do that? See, I was right. God must be cruel to allow Satan to do that," Britany interjected.

"Just keep listening," Michael instructed firmly and calmly, as he kept reading. He read of how Job first lost all he owned in various disasters. Then, before the stories were even told, all of his children were killed. As he read, Britany started to relate with Job. She started to empathize with the pain he had experienced. How comparative to the pain she felt, yet Job didn't blame God. He proclaimed that anything he had ever owned came from God. God had the right to take it away.

Michael read on with Satan wanting to afflict Job more, and prove to God that Job would curse Him.

"Wasn't that enough! The poor man has nothing left, and he still didn't curse God," Britany lamented.

Michael continued in his reading.

Job was covered with sores, and his wife begged him to curse God so that he would die and escape his torment. Job refused. He questioned his existence and the reason he was born, but he didn't curse God. Three of his friends came to help him. They were certain he had done some terrible wrong, or God would not have allowed this to happen. They spoke in depth of how he needed to confess his grave sin, and then the Lord would stop this suffering. Job went into great detail of his anguish and torment, but he stood firm in the fact that he had not committed any grave sin. Britany sensed that Job, like herself, was questioning why these things had happened. He had remained faithful to God; yet it looked as if God were punishing him. That's what his three friends went to great lengths to tell him. The anger and resentment that Britany had felt began to dissolve as she let the pain that Job spoke of replace it.

Michael read in Job 6:14, "A despairing man should have the devotion of his friends, even though he forsakes the fear of the Almighty."

That was where Britany was, alone. Her friends were loyal, but she had shut them out and turned her back on God.

Page after page Michael read of Job's friends accusing him and Job responding back. It was bleak and hopeless, both Job's descriptions and their replies. Bleak and hopeless, that's how she felt. Yet she hated the feeling. If Job felt it useless to go on, why should she struggle to go on? Surely there was more than this to life! There had to be! She found herself wanting Michael to hurry to see if the end had answers, but he kept up his steady pace and didn't skip.

A young man was speaking to Job now. He had kept quiet out of respect for his elders, but he knew he had words from God. Now it was time to share them. He was angry with Job for justifying himself rather than God. He was angry with Job's friends because they didn't find anything wrong in Job, and yet they continued to condemn him. He pointed out that God cannot do evil. How could He judge if He himself were not righteous? He refuted Job for thinking his righteousness could profit God. He warned him to be careful, not to turn to evil instead of bearing the afflictions. He continued to point out the majesty of God in the things of nature and the insignificance of man. He challenged Job to compare his wisdom with the wisdom of God, to see just how short it would fall. The descriptive way he spoke of God's power in the rumbling of thunder and the clashing of lighting was awesome. He described the most powerful forces of nature, down to the smallest raindrop, and gave God the glory for all. God didn't need Man's help to create all these things. We can't even look directly at the sun. Michael continued with Chapter 37, verses 23 and 24: The almighty is beyond our reach and exalted in power; in his justice and great righteousness, He does not oppress. Therefore men revere Him, for does he not have regard for all the wise in heart?

Britany felt as if she had received a blow in the stomach. Who was she to question what God had done? She certainly had no right to accuse God of being mean and spiteful.

Michael noticed a change in Britany's attitude as he read. He prayed silently as he read that God's Word would speak to her. Instead of sitting stiffly and interrupting, she now sat with one arm around her waist and a hand to her mouth, her head slightly bowed. He guessed she was feeling a new reverence for God, and a bit ill at the thought of how she had perceived Him.

Now it was God's turn to speak directly, and Britany, like Job, was ready to listen. God quizzed Job on his knowledge, specifically how the world was created. Since Job was so wise, surely he must have been there. God described in vivid detail the world and the heavens. Creatures that inhabited it and how He cared for them. He spoke of the majesty of the horse and eagle, the smallness, yet integrity of a little bird. Then God demanded Job to answer. Job, like Britany, felt totally inadequate and incapable of a response. God challenged Job to capture an elephant or wrestle a crocodile. If he was not strong enough to do these things, then what made him think he was strong enough to challenge God?

Job's final reply came in Chapter 42 verses 5 and 6: "My ears had heard of you but now my eyes have seen you. Therefore I despise myself and repent in dust and ashes."

Britany sat with her head bowed and tears streaming down her face. Michael closed the Bible and placed his arm around her shoulders.

"Michael, how could I have been so mean? So mean, selfish and uncaring. I have been awful. Can you ever forgive me?"

"Britany, I love you. Yes I will forgive you, if you forgive me." He took her hand and held it tightly.

"Forgive you for what?" Britany looked up through the tears with puzzlement on her face.

"Britany I wasn't fair to you. I was so afraid of commitment that I let that shadow our relationship. Please forgive me for that, and for thinking the worst and coming here to demand an explanation. For not giving you the benefit of the doubt that something drastic could be wrong, like it was. For not being more sympathetic when Jeanne fell off her horse," he answered.

"Oh Michael, you had no way of knowing. It was all my fault. I am just as guilty as you when it comes to fear hurting our relationship, but yes I do forgive you." She gently caressed his face.

"You know there is someone who is waiting for you to ask forgiveness. Someone who is much more important than I," Michael quietly reminded her cupping his hand over hers.

"Oh, Michael, I have been for the last three chapters. I truly don't understand how he could still be watching out for me when I have been so cruel. Thanks be to God He is. He brought you here when I desperately needed you to help me find my way back," Britany said. She felt a peace and joy that sharply contrasted the anger and fear that had filled her heart.

"Britany, I know it is late, and you are near exhaustion, but do you think you could let me know what happened with Jeanne?" Michael asked softy.

"Of course. I will try."

She dropped her hands in her lap and with a deep breath and a sigh she began. She went through the whole account, starting with the first blackout spell. She took him step by step through the blindness, Jeanne's mother, Amy and her own part. Listening with much emotion, Michael reached his arm around her, pulled her head against his chest, and stroked her hair as she struggled though.

Crystal arrived home after midnight to find Michael sitting on the couch leaning in the corner with his feet propped on the coffee table. Britany stretched out beside him with her head cradled in his lap, sleeping. Michael smiled in greeting to her astonished look and placed one finger over his lips to signal her to remain quiet. She readily obeyed. It was the first she had seen her mother sleep in weeks, and she had no desire to wake her.

Britany stirred with the first light of dawn. She lay in silence contemplating were she was, why she felt so at peace and loved. At first she thought maybe she had dreamt a wonderful dream, and then the events of the night slowly came to her. It wasn't a dream but, it was wonderful! She couldn't remember what exactly had happened at the end. Michael had been there. Where had he gone? Then she heard deep, steady breathing and opened her eyes to see his knee. She had fallen asleep on his lap! The poor guy. He had spent the entire night sitting up while she slept comfortably. He must be terribly uncomfortable. She could tell from the rhythmic breathing that he was still asleep, so she closed her eyes. She felt the hard muscles of his leg under her head and the gentle movement of his breathing. She gently squeezed his arm that was resting on her waist and went back to sleep.

"Michael!" Amy's excited yell startled Britany as two little knees flew into her face.

Amy had flung herself onto Michael for a hug, not noticing that Britany was there. Michael lifted her quickly to the side to give Britany a chance to get out of the way.

"Hey, munchkin! I think you just about gave Britany a black eye," Michael said, pulling her back on his lap as soon as Britany was out of the way. He tickled her while she laughed and begged him to stop.

"What are you doing here?" she asked as he gave her a reprieve from the tickling.

"I came to see you, Britany and Crystal. Is that all right with you?"

"Yeah, I like it when you come. Maybe you can make Britany laugh again."

Britany felt the sting of her innocent comment.

"You mean like this?" Michael asked as he reached over and began to tickle Britany in the ribs. She gasped in surprise and then began to laugh along with the two of them. Britany reached over and grabbed Michael's foot tickling the bottom causing him to laugh and beg for mercy. Soon the three of them were frolicking on the couch, each trying to tickle the others.

"What is all the noise out here?" Crystal emerged from her bedroom, half awake, with her long blonde hair tousled over her shoulders.

"Michael is making Britany laugh!" Amy piped up.

"Good! It's about time someone did! Do you need some help?" Crystal asked as she grabbed Amy by the waist and tickled Britany with the other hand.

"I'm the one who needs the help! Get Him!" Britany managed to get out between peals of laughter.

"Stop! I'm bushed," Britany begged, then asked. "Is anyone hungry besides me?"

"I am! I am!" yelled Amy.

"I could use something to eat. I'm not sure when I ate last," said Michael. Britany went to the kitchen to make pancakes, with the rest of them following to help.

"When do you need to get back?" Britany asked as they were seated at the table.

"Tomorrow."

"Would you like to spend the night again tonight? You can sleep on the hide-a-bed in the living room. It would probably be a bit more comfortable to lie on than to sit on all night. Crystal and Amy will be here, so I think we are adequately chaperoned."

"I would love to. I want to see your beautiful face as much as possible," Michael said with a smile.

Amy giggled and put her hand to her face. Crystal looked at her mom and smiled. Britany wasn't use to getting compliments like his, but she liked it. She reached over, squeezed his hand under the table, and smiled.

After breakfast they worked together to clean up. Britany wanted to be together as a foursome and suggested that they go to the zoo for the day instead of going to the farm.

It was a beautiful summer day. After the zoo Michael took them for a ride on an old fashioned riverboat. Supper was served on the boat, followed by entertainment. Britany and Michael went up to the upper deck at dusk and watched the sun fade into the horizon while Crystal and Amy stayed below to watch the comedian. The lights along the shore began to appear as darkness blanketed the river.

"Britany, I have something for you," said Michael reaching into his pocket to bring out a small box. "You know I've been avoiding commitment like the plague. Well God helped me to see I needed to stop running. I promised myself that before I left to go back I would give this to you, if you would accept it." He opened the box for her to see a beautiful solitaire diamond ring. "Britany, will you marry me?" he asked. His eyes sparkled more than the diamond and Britany felt she would melt from their intensity.

Britany looked to the ring. A smile touched the corners of her lips. She looked up steadily into his brown eyes. Two days ago she would have run the other way. Now she knew with a strong assurance that they were to be together. It was part of God's plan.

"Yes, Michael, I will marry you. I love you more than I ever would have imagined possible."

Michael took her hand and placed the ring on her slender finger. The diamond promptly slid around to the bottom side of her finger. They laughed.

"I didn't do too well guessing the size of your finger. We can get it sized so it will fit."

"But I don't want to take it off!" said Britany sliding the ring back around and holding it in place by closing her fingers together against it. "It took me thirty-five years to get it!"

"I'm glad you waited!" said Michael, lifting her chin and kissing her firmly on the lips.

"Me, too," whispered Britany, reaching out for another kiss.

"I knew it. We can't trust you two for a minute. I thought at my age it was supposed to be my mother keeping an eye on me, not the other way around!" Crystal said from behind them.

Britany reluctantly released her hold on Michael's shoulders and turned to face Crystal and Amy. Her face was glowing as she showed them the ring.

"Michael and I are going to be married," she said quietly, looking back over her shoulder at Michael, her emerald green eyes shining.

"I'm going to get a daddy!" Amy screamed. She jumped up and down, then ran to give Britany a hug.

"Me, too!" said Crystal hoarsely. Britany looked up from embracing Amy to see tears forming in Crystal's eyes. She had forgotten that this decision was affecting Crystal as well. She was well aware that as a child growing up, Crystal wanted nothing more than to have a father. She hadn't realized that it still meant so much to her, even at seventeen.

Michael didn't miss what Crystal had said or the look on her face. He reached over and drew Crystal into a fond embrace.

"And I get two daughters!" he said. Still holding Crystal he, reached down to take Amy's hand. "Don't forget, you both get a brother too!"

Britany looked at the three of them. Her heart filled with love and admiration for this man who was to be her husband, a father to her two girls.

She would have a son, Britany thought. Panic started to grip at her. Then she remembered that God was in control of this situation. He would be there with her. She may not know how to handle a son, but God did. She would leave the worry up to Him.

"Can I be the flower girl?" Amy asked.

"Yes, certainly," assured Britany.

"When are you getting married?" Amy asked as she continued holding Michael's hand. Crystal was drying her tears and stood at his side with his arm on her shoulder.

Britany looked at Michael with a startled looked. He returned her look with a shrug of his shoulders.

"I don't know. We hadn't gotten that far yet. Any suggestions?" asked Michael.

"How about in three weeks. That way, if I do have to go back with Grandmother, I will still be here for the wedding," Amy said.

"Oh, my goodness! I didn't think about the custody battle. Jeanne wanted you to be Amy's father, but I don't know what kind of effect our marriage would make," Britany said. A frown crossed her brow as she looked at Michael. The moment had been wonderful, but suddenly it felt as if someone had thrown a rock into it. Why did Amy's grandmother have to be so stubborn!

"I will stay until Monday," Michael said. "We can go talk to your lawyer and see what he has to say. Ben will be fine. I will call the family he is staying with and be sure it is all right."

"Oh, Michael, I would appreciate that so much. I am tired of doing this alone," Britany looked to him with gratitude showing on her face.

Britany woke early the next morning feeling the peace she had felt the morning before. It was Sunday and she knew she needed to be in God's house. She liked the church in town, but her heart was in her parent's church were she had grown up. She eagerly arose and went to get the others up to prepare for church. They would have time to drive to the country if they hurried.

During the drive Britany and Michael discussed how they were going to tell her parents about the engagement. Britany placed her engagement ring in her purse. She would show them later. She didn't want them to see it before they were told about the wedding. Michael wanted to take the family out to eat following the service. He suggested they tell them at dinner.

Britany's parents stood at the top of the cement steps of the church. It was a simple white building with a tall steeple. The wide flight of stairs led to a landing and two wooden doors that were propped open. The bells in the steeple were ringing a welcome as the car turned into the cobblestone drive. Several ladies were milling around Liz. Charles spied them as they turned into the drive. He reached over to nudge Liz's shoulder. Her face lit instantly as she saw the little red car with her daughter in the passenger seat. She was still waiting on the top of the stairs as Britany, Michael, Amy and Crystal approached.

"Britany, you're smiling!" Liz exclaimed and opened her arms for a warm embrace.

Amy was quick to step in and wrap her arms around Liz's midsection. Crystal gave her grandmother a peck on the cheek.

"Doesn't she look great!" Crystal added and Liz was quick to agree.

Michael greeted Britany's father with a warm handshake and politely said "Hello, Ma'am" to her mother. The group was being welcomed by other members of the church when an usher reminded them the service was about to start. They filed into their familiar pew, led by Charles. Liz sat beside him, and Britany sat beside her with Amy between them. Michael followed with Crystal behind him. They filled the entire pew.

The music started, and the church rang out in song. Michael reached his arm over Britany's shoulder and she slid closer to his side. She fit perfectly beside him, and though she concentrated on the words of the hymn and lifted her thoughts to God, she was very conscience of his presence. This is how it will be every Sunday once we are married, she thought. The warmth of his body seemed to permeate into her side. She placed a hand on his muscular leg and glanced up into his smiling face.

"I wish Ben were here," she whispered up into his ear.

"Me too," he whispered back and gave her shoulder a light squeeze.

Britany listened to the sermon. She opened her Bible to the scripture he was reading from. She glanced at Amy as the pastor read. Amy was drawing quietly on the back of a bulletin with a pen Liz had given her. Liz was whispering a comment to Amy about the picture. Britany glanced over to see what she had drawn. There on the paper were two crudely drawn people. One was slightly larger than the other. It was clear to see that the smaller person was a girl with a long dress and something on her head. The larger person was a boy, or at least had short hair and was wearing pants. Beside the two people was a smaller person, a girl. She appeared to be wearing a long dress and carried a bunch of flowers in her hand.

Britany's eyes opened wide and her mouth fell as she realized what it was. She quickly covered her mouth with her hand to keep from laughing. She squeezed Michael's leg and motioned slightly for him to look at the picture. Liz was asking Amy what she was drawing, and Amy was telling her very innocently that it was a picture of her being a flower girl in Britany and Michael's wedding.

"Oh it is? How beautiful. Do you thing they will let me be in their wedding too?" Liz whispered with a twinkle in her eye.

"Of course. You are Britany's mother. Mothers are always in weddings," Amy answered back.

Liz looked over at Britany, smiled and winked.

Britany was shocked. She wasn't sure what she had expected her mother's response to be, but she didn't think she would take it quite this calmly Maybe she didn't realize why Amy had drawn the picture! She looked up at Michael with a puzzled look on her face. He shrugged his shoulders.

Following the service Britany's parents walked with them to the car.

"Are you going to tell us a little more about Amy's drawing or do we just have to keep waiting?" Liz spoke up as soon as they were away from the crowd.

"Maybe I should be the one to do this." Michael moved a step closer and announced, "Mr. and Mrs. Becker, I would like to ask for your daughter's hand in marriage and your blessing." He finished in an air of formality.

"Congratulations son! She's a great girl. The best, in my mind," Britany's father said boastfully and pumped Michael's hand in a hearty handshake.

"Welcome to the family, Michael. From now on it's Mom and Dad, or at least Liz and Charles. None of this Mr. and Mrs. stuff," Liz said lovingly and drew him into a warm embrace. She then turned to Britany with misty eyes and hugged her. Charles reached over and engulfed her in his strong arms.

"Congratulations, Britany! He seems like a fine man," her father said with emotion.

"One thing has me puzzled. Why didn't you look surprised when you saw the picture?" Britany inquired.

"Your mom and I have bets going on whether or not you two would get married before Christmas. We knew you would be getting married. We just didn't know how soon. By the way, when are you getting married? I want to know if I get my apple pie or not," Charles said, his blue eyes twinkling and a huge grin spread across his face.

"What is this? Did everyone know I was getting married except for me?" Britany blurted in mock anger, looking around her accusingly.

"We sure did, Mom," Crystal joined in, putting her arm around Britany's shoulder. "I must admit, though, you sure did give us a scare for a while."

"What are we going to do with these people?" Britany addressed Michael.

"We just gotta love em!" said Michael, grabbing Britany around the waist and swinging her in a circle, lifting her off the ground.

Monday morning Michael drove Britany and Amy to Mr. Fitzpatrick's office. The lawyer was pleasant and enthusiastic about their marriage. He felt that it would be in Britany's favor to be married, and he assured them not to let the custody battle come in the way of their plans. They left his office cheerful and relieved.

"Well, it looks like we are back to the three-week mark again. Do you have any objections?" Michael asked as they drove.

"Michael, it all sounds too wonderful to be true. I guess I'm not sure I can be ready in time, but I don't want to wait," Britany said thoughtfully. "It is still nice weather, and we would be taking a chance, but I would really like to have a small wedding in my parents' back yard."

"That sounds great to me. You have the two girls stand up with you, and I will have Ben stand up with me."

"We have to have my brother and his wife. And, of course, Shelly and Stan."

"Of course, Shelly and Stan. I think Shelly had this planned all along," said Michael with a chuckle.

"I'm sure of it!" Britany exclaimed. "What about your family?" Britany asked.

"I guess I'd better tell them soon. I don't think they will be much more surprised than your parents were. My mom is pretty quick. She knew something was up. I will check in town for motel space. My family is too big to expect your parents to put them up. Besides Liz will have enough to worry about. My sister and her family will want to come too," Michael said as he maneuvered the car through traffic.

"Britany, I am going to arrange for tickets to fly you and the girls down to Nashville this weekend. I want you to see where we will be living, at least temporarily, until we find a bigger house," Michael said.

"Michael, you are wonderful!" said Britany reaching, over against the pull of the seat belt to give him a kiss on the cheek.

Britany thought about the last few weeks. Would her life continue to change at such an amazing pace?

CHAPTER 17

Tuesday morning Britany went to work a changed person. The sadness from Jeanne's passing was still there, but it was just that, sadness. It wasn't an overwhelming hopelessness. She found Shelly in the locker room before work and told her briefly what had transpired over the weekend. Shelly was as excited as Britany.

"We are getting married at my parents' farm. It will be a very small ceremony. Michael and I would like you and Stan to be there. You were partly responsible for this, you know," Britany said, putting arm around Shelly's shoulder.

"Oh, Britany, I am so happy for you. Stan and I would be honored to be at the wedding," Shelly said lovingly and gave Britany a warm hug.

"What is going on in here?" asked one of the other nurses as she walked in the locker room.

"Britany is getting married to Michael in three weeks!" Shelly exclaimed. Two other nurses and the secretary were behind her. They rushed forward to congratulate Britany.

"I suppose that means you are going to leave us and move to Tennessee?" asked Robin, one of the nurses Britany had worked with for several years.

"Yes. It is going to be hard to leave," said Britany, her eyes beginning to mist up.

"Britany, don't be sad. We are going to miss you, but this is wonderful You deserve a good husband and a family. I hope Michael realizes what a prize he's getting," Robin said and put her arm around her Britany's shoulder.

"Why do you think they are getting married in three weeks! He doesn't want her to get away," said Shelly, laughing.

The news spread throughout the entire hospital in no time. Friends from all over the hospital congratulated her. The atmosphere of the nursery was bubbly, bringing a striking contrast to the sadness that had prevailed the last month.

Later in the day she took time to talk to her boss, Margaret. She took a deep breath to steady herself. After fourteen years she was going to resign. Britany had planned on working until retirement in the hospital, and to think of leaving was hard.

"Hi, Britany, have a seat. I've been expecting you," said Margaret.

"I guess I've been putting this off until the end of the day. I'm excited about getting married, but it's going to be hard to leave," said Britany as she sat down.

Margaret looked at Britany. "You've worked here a lot of years and worked hard to improve the quality. That's not easy to walk away from."

"I feel like I am letting the hospital down in some way. I planned on being here another twenty years!" said Britany.

"We are going to miss you, but you have someone else to be devoted to now, and I am sure he will appreciate you. Who knows, maybe you will end up working at a small rural hospital, and they will get the benefit of your expertise. I'm really glad for you, Britany. We will be fine here. You be happy, OK?"

"Thanks," Britany said and smiled.

"How long do you plan on working before you leave?"

"Two weeks. That will give me a week before the wedding to pack and get ready for the move."

"That is very considerate of you. Good luck Britany," said Margaret.

Britany left the office and walked slowly back to her work area. She looked around her at all that had been so familiar; all the people she had shared her life with. How could she possibly leave and start all over again? She took a deep breath and pushed those thoughts aside. She would be leaving, but she would be gaining not losing. God was in control. He would be with her and help her through.

During the next few days she spent every spare moment planning the wedding.

On Friday she left work at two o'clock to pick up Crystal and Amy and go to the airport. Amy talked non-stop in her excitement. Britany and Crystal looked at each other and grinned.

"You used to talk the same way when you were excited!" Britany chuckled.

"You have got to be kidding! Why didn't you tell me to be quiet!" asked Crystal.

"Sometimes I did! But for the most part it makes life more exciting. I'm excited, too. It's fun to share it," said Britany.

Crystal laughed. "Yeah, your right. She sure is cute!"

"There's a plane!" Britany pointed to a plane coming in for a landing directly in front of them as they drove along the highway.

"Are we going to be on a plane as big as that?" asked Amy, her eyes wide.

"I hope so! I've heard the smaller ones aren't as smooth. We won't know until we get there," Britany replied.

Britany watched the big green signs closely as she entered the turn off for the airport. Traffic was very heavy, and she needed to be sure she was in the right lanes. She knew where she wanted to go since she had been there several times with Michael. They turned into the long-term parking lot and unloaded their things. They each had one suitcase and a carry on bag to keep with them on the plane. She had fixed a backpack for Amy with toys and crayons.

They had arrived early, but by the time they got through baggage check it was time to board the plane.

Amy continued to talk nonstop. Britany listened happily. The excitement was building up and she felt as if she couldn't keep silent either. Soon the plane would be sweeping her away to meet Michael again. Two weeks was a short time in some ways, but it seemed an eternity in others. In two hours she would be seeing his smiling face again.

The taxi down the runway was amazing! The Landscape went by faster and faster until suddenly they started to get farther away.

"We're flying!" squealed Amy.

"That we are," said a smiling stewardess who was walking by. "Could I get you something to drink?"

They each gave their order and settled back to enjoy the flight. Britany had brought along some books to read to Amy, but they spent their time looking out the window. It was truly amazing. They could see the ground through the clouds. There were tiny farms scattered everywhere. The landscape was divided into squares by the roads that ran through it. At places there were tiny lines so close they could barely be made out. It wasn't long before the farms disappeared and dark lush patches of varying green took their place as they flew over Kentucky. The flight went fast, and Britany would have been disappointed to have it end so soon except that she knew when they landed Michael would be waiting for them.

She could see him peeking above the heads as they stepped off the deboarding ramp. His eyes lit up as he saw her. He waved. Britany motioned for Crystal to follow and took Amy's hand to hurry and meet him. Ben was standing beside him.

Her heart thrilled at his sight. She was soon to be his wife and would look at his face every day. What a wonderful thought!

Michael heard the announcement that Britany's flight had arrived. He stretched as high as he could to get a better look. Unfamiliar faces appeared as one by one the passengers came through the exit. Then he saw her. Her face looked radiant as she immediately recognized him. She had regained much of the glow that had been missing on his last visit. She was beautiful, and if he had any previous doubt about his love for her, the doubt was totally diminished. She was rushing toward him holding Amy's hand with one hand and a large flowered bag in the other. He thrilled at her softness and fragrance as he reached out and drew her near.

His arms encircled Britany and the familiar scent of his cologne touched her senses. The warmth and strength of his embrace filled her being as she returned his embrace.

Michael would have held her close for much longer, but voices brought him back to the fact that others were present.

Amy was giggling and Ben was looking very embarrassed. Crystal was talking, "You'd better get used to it. It's kind of surprising how mushy two adults can get."

Michael laughed and reluctantly released Britany. He turned to hug Crystal. Then he turned to lift Amy into the air and hold her in his arms. "Oh, Ben, it is so good to see you again," said Britany as she gave him a big hug. Ben smiled shyly.

"No need to stay around here. Let's go!" Michael said and escorted them through the airport with Amy in his arms. The airport terminal seemed alive and bubbling with excitement. Large posters with country western singers, displays of western apparel and Grand Old Opry advertisements adorned the isles. Plants and flowers were abundant; lights glittered as they rode the escalator down to the ground floor. In the middle of the glistening tile floor was a shiny new car on display.

"Britany, look, a car just like yours." Amy pointed.

"They make them down here in Tennessee. Not too far from where we live." Ben offered his knowledge.

Britany felt as she was floating on air. She loved it here, and she wasn't even out of the airport terminal! She knew it was silly, but she felt a hope and promise spring up from deep inside.

Michael couldn't talk fast enough to keep up. Every time he took a breath Amy would ask a question, or Ben would interject his knowledge of the area. They drove through a pass where both sides of the road were bordered by a cliff of limestone. Sparse, daring plants and flowers clung to its surface. As they drove out of the limestone tunnel, the roadside was covered with lush green grass and flowers.

"They've done a beautiful job making the city pretty," commented Britany.

"I knew you would love the flowers. This side of the city is a bit prettier than other areas. Not all of the city it is so nice. I like to drive through here except for the traffic. It gets unreasonable at times. Friday afternoon at rush hour is one. We may get held up a bit in traffic. We live about twenty miles south of here."

It wasn't long before they could see large mounds of hills in the distance. The sides went sharply up, curved and then descended just as bold.

"The mountains are beautiful!" said Crystal.

"They aren't really mountains. They are just big hills. You need to go to Eastern Tennessee to see the mountains," said Ben.

"It doesn't matter to me. They are beautiful and are taller than any hills I have ever seen. If you don't mind I think I will still call them mountains," commented Crystal.

"You can call them mountains if you like. I don't mind. Even some of the locals call them mountains, although most of the time they are referred to as hills," said Ben.

"I think those hills look like the hump on a camel," Ben pointed to the hills Britany had been looking at.

"They really do!" Amy agreed.

Michael took them to his house before going to eat. He wanted them to have a chance to relax first. Besides, Britany had insisted that they had eaten on the plane and were really quite satisfied.

Michael's home was in an impressive sub-division that was less than five years old. The house was two story covered in light brown brick. The thought that the house was to be her home in just two weeks was both startling and comforting to Britany as she walked through it. The house reflected Michael's taste. She felt a kinship to it as she looked about, knowing that it was a personification of him. It was clean and tidy, but lacked the little extras that a woman adds. Britany was glad for that aspect. He had bought the house after his divorce, and it was comforting to know that no other woman had lived here with him.

Saturday, Michael took them to several stables. The barns were immaculate with acres of beautiful grass for the horses to graze on. They chose the closest one to where they would live since all of them were nice.

"Britany, I have something special to show you still this afternoon. The country side is beautiful and if you don't mind I would like to take you for a little drive," Michael stated as they were leaving the stables.

"Our time is yours. We came to see the area, so we are game for whatever you have to show us," Britany answered lightly.

Michael drove them through mile after mile of beautiful countryside. He drove past two mansions on meticulously kept lawns, surrounded by fertile farm land. Michael pointed out that the area had been quite prosperous before the Civil War. The massive residence of the Chears Mansion was built of stately native brick. It had an immense yard with large shrubs that would have looked too big for a smaller home. Giant old oak trees were scattered throughout the yard. Britany could almost picture a horse and carriage rolling down the narrow drive and through the black iron gate that led to the buildings in back.

"It's going by too fast!" Britany moaned.

"You'll get to see it again many times. We can possibly tour the mansions on special occasions."

Michael looked over at her and gave her hand a squeeze. It pleased him to see that she shared his love for the countryside.

He drove through a quiet town and then out winding roads that seemed to be going nowhere in particular. He came to stop in front of a small farm with white horse fencing surrounding it. A large Cape Cod home sat on top of the hill that graced the property.

"I want you to meet my friend, Brad Moore. We work together and he has been wanting to see you," said Michael as they pulled into the drive.

"Your friend lives here? I love it! If I had a dream home in mind this would definitely qualify. The house even has a darling front porch!" Britany said, admiring the home they were approaching.

"Yes, this is Brad's house. He wanted me to bring you here and see if you like it," Michael answered.

"What's not to like? You can assure him I love it. Brad must have had good foresight to plan this. It looks like you can see horses grazing from any window in the house. The view is spectacular! Miles of rolling pasture with hills in the background--it's just beautiful! I would love to just sit for a while on the front porch and admire the view!" answered Britany. Crystal and Amy heartily agreed.

"I think he would be glad to have three lovely ladies grace his porch," said Michael as he brought the car to a stop at the top of the hill and assisted with car doors.

Ben had been unusually quiet during the exclamations and had a sneaky look on his face. Britany took note of it and began to wonder if Michael might be planning something.

Brad was a gracious host and amiably showed them around the house. It had a large spacious kitchen with bright shinning floors and white cupboards. The eating area was accented by a bay window and lace curtains. It opened into a formal dinning room from one end and an open family room on the other. A fireplace was centered on the outer wall of the family room. The mantel was constructed of dark cherry wood with intricate designs carved into it.

"The mantel looks old, but the house looks new!" commented Britany thoughtfully.

"The mantel was taken from an ante-bellum home and is quite old," Brad explained with pride. "I looked hard to find it and am rather fond of it."

"I can see why. It's quite lovely," Britany replied.

The tour continued into the master bedroom, off from the family room. Elegant French doors opening onto a wooden deck caught Britany's eye.

"This is just too wonderful!" She exclaimed as she walked out the door onto the deck. The deck overlooked the back pasture and down the hill to a breath taking view below, where a little stone bottom creek flowed.

"It must be wonderful to wake up in the morning and simply walk out your door to this beauty all around!" exclaimed Britany in honest admiration.

"Britany, look! A pool!" Amy blurted out.

A large above ground pool was off to the left. The deck wrapped around it and French doors opened onto the deck from the kitchen.

"Can we go swimming? Can we please?" she begged.

"Let us take a tour, and then maybe that can be arranged," Michael assured Amy.

Britany looked at him in puzzlement.

"What do you plan on her wearing?" Britany asked. "She is a little too old to swim in her panties."

"I hope you don't mind. Ben and I kind of took the liberty of going through your suitcases and getting your swimwear out. I wanted to surprise you," Michael said meekly.

"So that's what all the secrecy was about! I thought you and Ben were up to something," Crystal interjected.

Michael escorted them away from the deck to show them the rest of the house. The master bedroom opened into a luxurious bathroom done in light pink, with marble floors, and a matching Jacuzzi. Large roses were stenciled in a border across the top walls and into the bedroom.

There were three large bedrooms and a bath upstairs with an extra room over the garage.

They descended the stairs to the formal living room and then walked out to the porch. Michael remained sure to his promise and went to get their suits from the car.

"I'm sorry my wife and kids are gone. They went away for the weekend. They will be back about the same time you leave," explained Brad while they were waiting.

"Tell your wife she has a lovely home. She must like it here a lot," said Britany.

"Actually she likes it better in town. She doesn't enjoy the country."

"I'm sorry to hear that. It looks like you put a lot of time and effort into this place," Britany replied as Michael was taking the last step in a giant leap.

"Anyone ready to swim!"

"I am! I am!" yelled Amy and Ben in unison.

Britany helped Amy change her suit in one of the bedrooms and then put hers on with her blouse over the top.

The water was warm and felt good. They swam and played for a while, then Britany and Michael sat on the deck and watched the children. Their host excused himself to attend to something in the house.

"Britany, Brad has been transferred to Florida," Michael began as they sat beside the pool sipping lemonade. "The reason he wanted you to see his place is because he really wants me to buy it. My plan for the future was to find some land and build you a unique house of your own. This place is nice so I thought I would bring you here and see what you thought. Not to mention that Brad was quite insistent that I bring you. He was sure that you would fall in love with it," Michael said.

"He is scheduled to move in two weeks whether the house is sold or not. That is actually where his wife is this weekend, getting some things ready in their new home. He feels a bond toward this place. He thought he was going to be here a long time and he put a lot of extras into it that he wouldn't have otherwise. That is why he is trying hard to convince me to buy it. It is a little further away from work than I had planned, but it has a lot of other pluses that would make it worth the drive. There is a good Christian school just a couple of miles down the road. The public school is also very good in this county. I don't want you to feel pressured either way. This place is nice, but we can always build a nice place of our own," Michael finished.

"Michael, this place is lovely. I can't think of anything I could possibly want that would be half as nice as this. It must cost a fortune," said Britany. "I don't want you to spend this much on us. I like the place you already have."

"Britany, I have the money. You don't have to worry about that. I know you don't ask for much, but I am going to get us a nice place. The kids need space to roam, and we want the horses to be with us, not at a boarding stable. This would be a much nicer atmosphere for Ben and Amy to grow up in."

"We could be happy in an old farmhouse on a few acres somewhere. I really don't want to see you spend so much. I love you, Michael, and I love being with you. We don't have to live in a luxurious place to be happy," Britany replied honestly.

"This place doesn't cost very much more than what I can get for my place. Land value goes down a lot as you get away from Nashville. Where I live the cost of housing is very high. People want to live there, so they are willing to pay it. Do you think you could like it here and be happy?" Michael asked. "I want you to also consider the idea of building our own place. We can build whatever kind of house you would like."

"I can't even imagine a place I would like more than this. It is lovely!" Britany said with emotion as she moved beside him and sat on his lap. Wrapping her arms around his shoulders, she said. "I just want you to be perfectly honest that you can afford this place, and it is not too much money. I will have some money from selling my condo, but it won't go too far toward a place like this."

"Believe me. I have the money. That is no problem. You do like it, then?"

"I love it!"

"You wouldn't be happier building a home?"

"I have no desire to build a home," Britany assured him.

"You don't have to decide today," Michael explained wanting to be sure she wasn't making a hasty decision.

"Michael, what is not to love? I would love it for the view alone even if it meant living in a tent!" Britany said laughing.

Michael gazed at Britany and breathed a sigh of relief. Linda was never happy no matter how much he gave her. Her discontent always left him feeling inadequate. Britany didn't expect things. She didn't need possessions to make her happy. He smiled to himself. Her attitude made him want to provide for her, and her thankfulness was very fulfilling.

"Michael, your gal has good taste. I like her attitude!" Brad said, returning from the house.

"This is really too much to believe. Can I tell the girls?" Britany asked removing herself from Michael's lap and once again taking a seat.

"Sure. Ben knows a little bit about it, but I told him it was our surprise and he's done well to keep it," Michael said.

"He certainly has. I thought he had a sly grin on his face when we got here," chuckled Britany.

"Amy, Crystal, Ben!" Britany called, moving to the side of the pool to be heard above the splashing water. "Come out for a minute. Michael and I have something we want to talk to you about."

The three got out and grabbed their towels.

"Michael is thinking about buying this place for us to live here. Do you think you could like it here?" Britany asked.

"It is so big!" said Amy. "Does that mean we could keep my pony here with us and I could ride her every day?" she asked.

"I want the bedroom with the Jacuzzi!" shouted out Ben.

"Ben, the bedroom with the Jacuzzi will be for Britany and me. You can have one of the bedrooms upstairs, and Britany and I will decide who gets what so there won't be any fighting. You can each have your input into which one you want," Michael spoke firmly.

Britany felt a thrill run through her when Michael spoke of the two of them sharing the bedroom. The realization that in two short weeks they would be married struck her once again. They would be sharing a bedroom, and the rest of their lives! This was one of those times when two weeks seemed like forever!

"Does the pool stay? Do we get it, too?" asked Amy innocently.

"Yes, Amy," laughed Crystal.

"Yea!" she yelled, jumping up and down.

"I'll race you to it," challenged Ben bending into a starting position.

"Go!" yelled Amy already running for the side.

"That's not fair!" yelled Ben as he raced toward the pool easily overtaking Amy and tucking his knees to his chest as he jumped high over the water doing a cannonball. He hit the water with a big splash that soaked the floor of the deck and managed to spray water over Britany.

"I don't think they like the idea of living here one bit!" laughed Britany teasingly.

"You know, Mom, it isn't fair. I am going to be in college and won't even be able to live here with you guys," Crystal said in dismay.

"You get a short break the end of the first term, don't you?" Michael asked.

"I get Thanksgiving and Christmas."

"Do you get any time off before then?"

"I might get a three-day weekend, but I'm not sure."

"If you do, we will fly you down, and you can enjoy a little time with us. I can pick you up from the airport on my way home from work," Michael offered.

"That would be wonderful! I would really like that," said Crystal.

"Would you mind if I changed and took a walk around the property. I am anxious to see what it looks like and to see that stream up close," Britany asked.

"I would like to, too," added Michael. "I'll see if the kids want to go."

They went for a walk after changing. It seemed like a dream to Britany. She didn't know exactly what she had expected this weekend but certainly not all this. She prayed silently as they walked, thanking God for His goodness to her and also His guidance. The land and house seemed wonderful, but she wanted to be sure it was what God wanted for them and not just what they wanted for themselves. She asked God to place a peace in her heart if He did want them to get the home. She asked Him to give her a definite no answer if it wasn't His will. As they walked she felt the peace and an awe of the beauty around them.

The sun was getting low in the sky when they finally left. Michael took them to "Fred's", one of his favorite restaurants in the area. He said they would get an authentic Southern meal. The restaurant specialized in catfish and cracklin' corn bread. Britany was rather leery but tried the catfish. It was good, and she loved the cracklin' cornbread. The children weren't quite so daring. They had the "all you can eat" southern fried chicken. Britany didn't think Ben was ever going to stop eating.

"They would have charged you for the adult portion if they had known how much you were going to eat!" Britany said to Ben.

"You're just used to girls," teased Michael. "Ben is a growing boy. He makes sure he's got plenty of fuel to work with. You'll have to get used to it. Believe me, sometimes I think he's going to eat us out of house and home." They all laughed, except for Ben, who was still eating a chicken leg.

They returned to Michael's house and helped Ben and Amy prepare for bed. After they had them tucked in bed and bid goodnight to Crystal, Michael and Britany sat in the living room and made plans for the coming move.

"I think it would be best if you only bring what would fit in the car temporarily. Hopefully within two or three weeks of the wedding we will be able to move into our new home. That is if you are for certain you want the house."

"Yes, Michael, I do without a doubt want the house," she assured him once again.

"We can get a moving van to move your things," suggested Michael.

"It would probably be a good idea to keep my furniture in the condo while we're trying to sell it. Places show better when they have furnishings in," said Britany. "I haven't had time to contact a Realtor yet."

"Since we aren't going to build, I think at least we can buy new furnishings after the wedding. So if there are some things you don't want, go ahead and sell them. It will make the move easier." They spent several hours going over details and discussing plans.

"There is a lot more to merging two house holds than I ever would have imagined," Britany said wearily.

"Britany, I'm sorry. I've kept you up much too long. I get carried away when it comes to things like this. I always want things to run smoothly," Michael said softly pulling her close and smoothing her hair. "Don't get discouraged. It will all fall together. It's not so hard as it sounds."

"I'm not discouraged, just tired. I'm glad you're good with details because I'm not and there are so many things I hadn't thought about. I think we will be good for each other, don't you?" Britany said with a slight yawn.

"I'm sure of it. Right now you need to get to bed," he said and gave her a soft kiss.

"You could do that some more and I could just drift off to sleep," she said dreamily.

"Sure you would. I'm afraid it wouldn't quite work that way. Now go to bed," Michael commanded in a mock sternness.

"Oh, all right, if you insist, but I really do need another kiss first," said Britany reaching over to embrace him and give him a full kiss. As it ended, she quickly jumped up and headed for the bedroom.

"Britany, you little tease! See you in the morning."

In the morning Michael escorted them to his church of several hundred people. Britany had never been to a church as large as his before. She enjoyed it. The pastor gave an inspiring sermon.

The day passed quickly, and before they knew it they were standing in the airport terminal saying good-bye.

"I don't know whether to be happy or sad. I can't bear the thought of leaving, but in two short weeks we'll be back together to start our new life together," Britany lamented.

"Never be sad when you can be happy. The next time we will be coming back together!"

"Oh, my goodness! I completely forgot about a honeymoon! Michael are we going to have a honeymoon?" Britany exclaimed, almost in a panic.

"I'll call you. They are calling your flight. Goodbye, soon-to-be-Mrs. Kaiser," Michael said, gathering her into a full embrace.

He released her and turned to hug Amy and Crystal while Britany hugged Ben. They hurried to the plane waving behind them as they went.

As the plane took off Britany's heart felt heavy. The plane seemed to be taking her away from her new home and family. She wished it could turn around and go back.

CHAPTER 18

Michael worked hard the next week securing the paperwork on the new home. Everything went smoothly, and they set a temporary closing date in four weeks. Unbeknownst to Britany, Michael made arrangements for a honeymoon. He booked a four-day cruise to the Bahamas. He had asked Liz to watch Amy and Ben while they were gone. She was as excited as he when he told her about it and gladly kept his secret. He wasn't sure how long he would be able to put off telling Britany, but he wanted to surprise her after the wedding. He was concerned about the timing with Amy, but he wanted to get their marriage off to a good start and he really felt they needed some time to be together with no other responsibilities. He and Britany had never been completely alone together for more than a few hours.

He made arrangements for his mother and father to come from Michigan to attend the wedding. His sister and her husband and three girls were driving down from Michigan, too. He found a motel within ten miles of Britany's parents for them to stay. He planned on staying there, too, so he wouldn't see Britany the day of the wedding.

In retrospect, Britany wasn't sure how she actually accomplished all the details of the wedding, but by the time the day of the wedding arrived she was ready. She had spent a last week at work and then managed to pack and help her mother clean. Crystal was ready for college, and Britany had an offer on her condo.

Britany had heard nothing from the Peirsons, nor did she know when the hearing was to be held. The thought of it felt like a heavy cloud hanging over them. Amy was bright and cheerful most of the time, but every once in a while the topic would come up, and she would become quiet and subdued. Britany called her lawyer. He told her to hang in there and he would call if he heard anything. He told her to enjoy her wedding, and offered his congratulations.

Michael found it hard to stay at the motel Friday night and not drive on out to the farm when he arrived at the motel just before midnight. His parents and sister were just getting in. It would be rude of him to leave them in a strange place. Not to mention the fact it would be very late before he could get back to the motel. He didn't even give in to the urge to call Britany. As far as he knew the cruise was still a surprise, and he was afraid if he called he would blow it and tell her. Ben needed to get to sleep and so did he. He would have to be patient and wait. The drive had tired him out and he fell asleep much easier than he had expected. The next morning went slowly, but he enjoyed the visit with his family. He was eager for them to meet Britany. They went to a leisurely breakfast and then back to the motel where the adults watched the kids swim until it was time to go.

Saturday morning looked promising to Britany as the sun was made its appearance on the horizon. There wasn't a cloud in sight. Britany felt calm and peaceful as she arose from her bed in her old room at the farm. She quietly went through the house and out to the barn. An early morning ride sounded wonderful. She wouldn't be seeing Misty for several weeks unless they moved the horses down before the rest of the things. Britany laughed to herself at all the little things she hadn't thought to talk over with Michael. She didn't even know what they were doing after the wedding. Oh well, she thought it didn't matter. The important things had been seen to, and as long as she was Michael's wife, she didn't care what they did. She didn't even care if they just packed up and took off for Tennessee. She was ready.

Misty whinnied a welcome as soon as Britany was in sight. The cows were quietly chewing on the leftover hay from the night before.

"Well, girl. Today is the day of my wedding. Isn't it wonderful! I think you'll like it in Tennessee. It may take you awhile to get used to climbing hills, but Michael says the winters are mild, and the grass grows almost year around. You'll like that, fresh grass in winter," Britany said, stroking Misty's soft nose.

They rode through Britany's favorite spot where she had taken Michael on their first ride. She fondly remembered the time. She rode on through the woods and down some paths and then headed back to the barn.

When she entered the house Liz looked up in surprise.

"I thought you were still in bed! I thought you were sleeping in a long time for the day of your wedding," Liz said with her rural Midwest accent.

"I went riding. It's a beautiful day!" commented Britany as she crossed the room and gave her mother a big hug.

"You'd think it was a beautiful day if it was raining cats and dogs like it did the day your brother, Phillip, got married. The thunder roared so loud in the middle of the ceremony that you couldn't hear the vows. I don't even think he heard it!" Liz laughed as she spoke.

"You're right. I wouldn't have cared if it was raining but it will make things easier this way."

Around ten o'clock everything started to happen at once. The florist van arrived with the flowers, and the lady who made the cake showed up. Britany's cousin came with the keyboard to set it up, and her father went to the church to get chairs.

Everyone needed to know where to set things up at the same time. Britany directed them to the front yard under the shade of the spreading maple trees. Britany's mother quickly got the table prepared for the cake, and Britany showed the florist where she wanted the archway and the large bouquets of red roses. The yard looked beautiful when everything was in place.

Britany grabbed a quick bite to eat and went upstairs to prepare for the wedding. She wanted plenty of time to get ready and pamper herself a little. She had gotten perfumed soaps and lotion from the bath shop to make it seem more special. She finished her bath and fixed her hair. She wasn't sure whether to put it up or leave it down. She compromised by pulling it up loosely and letting the curls fall down to her shoulders. She had Crystal pin the halo of flowers in place. She helped Amy bathe and wash her hair. Then she dried it and curled it with the curling iron to make ringlets. She pulled a section up and put the flowered barrette securely around it. A small rosebud and baby's breath on the barrette matched the flowered halo in her own hair. They fixed Crystal's hair to match their style, although Crystal's hair fell in curls down to the middle of her back.

It seemed rather early to put on their dresses at one o'clock. The wedding wasn't to begin until two, but they decided they would put them on and then paint their nails while they waited.

Britany's simple cream silk gown was high-waisted with a length between the ankles and knees. It flowed loosely around her hips and legs and looked soft yet elegant with the satin slippers. The v neckline was set off with her mother's pearls which brought out the golden tan of her skin. The girl's dresses were similar in style to Britany's. They were cream-colored muslin cotton, with pink rose buds. The neckline was accented by a cream crocheted lace collar. The same lace edged the sleeves and draped over their forearms. The skirt flowed out from the high waist to stop between the ankles and knees. They each wore pink ballet slippers with ribbons winding up their legs.

Liz came into the room a short time later to let them know that Michael and Ben had arrived, along with Michael's parents, his sister, and her family. Britany's heart raced wildly. She wanted to meet his family, but what if they didn't like her?

Another knock came a short time later and Liz entered. A sweet-looking lady in her early thirties stood at the door.

"Britany, this is Michael's sister, Sarah and his mother, Mrs. Kaiser." Liz informed her. "They were anxious to meet you and wondered if they could come in."

"Of course," Britany said, holding the door open wide in welcome. She extended her hand to his sister and mother. It was easy to see where Michael got his height. His mother was fairly tall with dark hair and a warm smile. His sister was Britany's height and bubbly. Britany liked them immediately. Britany introduced Crystal and Amy, and the five of them talked comfortably. Britany wanted to see Michael's three nieces, so Liz went to find them.

When she returned she had three perfectly groomed little girls with her. The children were polite and looked like stair steps in size. The youngest, Lesa was a darling two-year-old with chubby hands and dimples in both cheeks. Britany found out the tallest one, Libby, was actually the middle child; she was five. The oldest of the three Lesley, corrected Britany when Britany thought Libby was the oldest.

"I wish I weren't so short," Lesley complained.

"My grandfather always said that the best things come in small packages," said Britany. Lesley giggled and looked pleased.

The music started downstairs. Michael's mother and sister gave Britany a hug and left to be seated. Britany looked up at her mother.

"The time is finally here. Do I look OK? Is my makeup too dark or light? Is my hair in place?"

"Britany, you look as lovely as ever. Everything is perfect. I'm going to go now. You father will be waiting for you at the bottom of the stairs," Liz said, reverently giving her daughter a soft embrace so she wouldn't wrinkle anything.

Crystal walked from the bedroom to the top of the stairs with Amy carrying a basket of rose petals behind her. Britany followed.

Crystal gracefully descended the stairs and stood at the opened front door. She looked out across the yard, to the archway, under the trees where Michael and the minister stood. The keyboard poured forth a collection of beautiful music in the sound of an organ. Through the upstairs window Britany could see Michael standing in front of the archway with Ben at his side. She hadn't seen him in two weeks and she wanted desperately to run to his side. Instead she shifted impatiently and tried to concentrate on what she was to do. She glanced down the stairs at the door where Crystal was getting ready to start the walk down the aisle bordered with pedestals of roses.

Crystal looked up and gave her mother a thumbs-up sign as the music changed. She turned back and started out the door. Amy took her spot at the door and waited momentarily. Britany descended the stairs. At Britany's nudge Amy started out, daintily dropping rose petals with each step. Britany smiled up at her dad who gave her a light kiss on the cheek. She took his offered arm and waited for the music to change again. Amy was dutifully dropping petals one at a time. Britany felt a fleeting stab of pain as she thought of how cute Amy looked, and how proud Jeanne would have been of her. Britany pictured Jeanne, and she smiled at the thought of her looking down on the wedding.

The music changed into the bridal march as Amy took her place beside Crystal. Britany's mind was jarred back to the present. She looked up at her dad with a smile. Together they stepped out the door and down the brick walk to the front of the yard. She looked around at the small group of guests: Phillip and his family; Stan and Shelly, who wore a big smile but had a trace of a tear on her cheek; Michael's parents; Sarah and her family; and her Mother, Liz. Britany smiled at each one as she made her way down the aisle. The soft cream silk of her gown swished softly against her legs as she walked. Then her eyes met Michael's and all else seemed to fade into the background.

Michael had arrived at the farm before one. He made introductions and tried not to show his impatience at not being able to see Britany. He was envious of his mother and sister when they went to meet her. He fidgeted impatiently as the music played and he and Ben took their places. He caught a glimpse of Britany as she moved past the upstairs window and saw her smile down at him. He quit fidgeting and stood straight and tall as the music changed. At the same moment Crystal started out the door. She was tall and graceful as she walked along. Amy looked adorable as she followed Crystal. It was hard to keep a straight face as she dutifully dropped the petals one by one.

Then he saw her standing in the doorway. The image of her burned into his memory as she descended the stairs from the porch, holding lightly to her father's arm. She had the grace of a deer as her slippered foot touched the earthen bricks. Her curls swayed softly and glimmered like gold as the sun touched them. Her flowing dress touched her body lightly and gave a hint of the feminine shape beneath. Her dark eyes met his and held them firmly as if in a trance. The power of her gaze sent tremors down his spine. She was the picture of beauty, and in a few minutes she would be his.

Charles and Britany stopped in front of the minister. The air was hushed. The minister spoke, and Charles answered. He then placed her hand on Michael's arm and turned to sit beside Liz.

The pastor spoke on the sanctity of marriage and the grace of God, Who ordained it. Britany drank in the love she saw as she gazed into Michael's eyes. They exchanged vows and then rings. The pastor spoke words of encouragement and then announced loudly, "You may kiss the bride!"

Michael took her in his arms and kissed her for the first time as her husband. She held him close and soaked in the magic of the moment.

The organ began its loud peal. Britany looked out at her family and friends and smiled. The pastor raised his arms, "I present to you Mr. and Mrs. Michael Kaiser." They were immediately showered with rice and shouts of joy. Britany was lifted off her feet by Phillip and twirled around before she realized what was happening. His robust congratulation was heart warming. Shelly was quick to embrace her as Phillip put her down, and Stan gave her a warm kiss. Shelly stepped up and boldly gave Michael a kiss, who hugged her in return.

Michael introduced his father, John Kaiser, and brother in law, Tom Edwards, to Britany. She loved his father from the start. He was jovial and gave her such a big hug she felt herself once again being lifted from the ground. He was a large man, taller and bigger than Michael but with the definite resemblance to Michael in his face.

The photographer wanted them to pose for some pictures. Then it was time to cut the cake. Britany had time to visit with her family and Michael's. She was enjoying the small wedding. It was warm and personal. Liz and Michael's mother, Dianne, had a chance to get to know each other, as did Charles and John. Britany went over to her father when things were quiet and gave him a big kiss.

"Britany I am really happy for you. I like Michael. I never thought there would be anyone good enough for my little girl, but he seems like a swell fellow. You've done well caring for yourself and Crystal these years and I have always been proud of you, but I am glad God sent someone to be with you. It's not good to be alone. Especially as you grow older. I would be lost without your mother and I hope you and Michael will be as happy as we've been," Charles said sincerely.

"Thanks, Dad. That means a lot to me. We will be most fortunate if we are as happy as you and Mom," replied Britany with moist eyes.

"And don't worry none about the kids while you are gone. Your mom and I will take good care of them," he continued.

"What? I'm sorry but I don't know what you are talking about!" Britany gave him a puzzled look. "The kids are going to Tennessee with us, aren't they?"

"Well, yes, they are, kind of," he stammered. "Liz! Michael! I think you had better come here. I think I said a little more that I should have," Charles called out.

Michael and Liz came over immediately with suspicion on their faces.

"I simply told her we would take good care of the kids. No one told me she didn't know."

"Of all the times for you to pay attention to me. I didn't tell you it was a secret because you never remember anything I say anyway!" Liz said accusingly.

"Well now you know I do!" he retorted back.

"Mom, Dad! Would you stop arguing and someone please tell me what this is all about! Apparently everyone knows but me!" Britany said in exasperation, her arms moving in animation as she spoke.

Michael grasped her hand. "Honey, I planned a trip to Florida and then a cruise to the Bahamas. Your mom and dad are going to keep Ben and Amy. You are right. Everyone did know except you. Amy did a wonderful job to not let the secret slip. We just forgot to tell your Dad it was a secret. I wanted to wait and surprise you," Michael explained.

"Just exactly how long did you plan on waiting until you told me?"

"Well, I wasn't, sure but your Dad kind of helped me out with that." Michael and Britany had everyone's full attention. Shelly held her breath waiting for Britany's reaction.

"Michael, it sounds wonderful, like something out of a fairy tale, but I just can't up and leave!" Britany protested as she looked around. "I need to pack. And what about Amy? We haven't heard from her grandmother. What if she comes to get her?"

"If she comes to get her she will take her whether we are here or not. I talked to the lawyer and he said nothing would take place that couldn't wait for one week and we will be back by then, "Michael assured her. "You've told me yourself Amy thinks of your parents as her own grandparents. She will be fine. Crystal is coming the end of next week as she gets everything organized and she will be here to help. I've talked to both Ben and Amy and they are thrilled," Michael said reassuringly.

"He's right Britany," said Liz. "I went to the lawyer myself and made sure he felt it would be OK. He said to give you his blessing and that he is very happy for you. Crystal and I have been doing a little packing on the sly and have a suitcase ready with things we thought you could use on the cruise. You already have your makeup and things ready," she added.

"If there is something you need that's not packed, we can buy it for you on the cruise. I've heard there are great shops in the Bahamas and there will be stores on the ship with anything you could possibly need." Michael turned her toward him and put his arms around her waist as he spoke, looking deep into her eyes.

"Michael, what am I going to do with you? Are you always so full of surprises?" she asked softly.

"It makes life more interesting."

A clinking sound filled the air as Stan and Shelly started tapping their glasses with their spoons. The rest of the guests followed their lead. Michael reached down and gave Britany a warm kiss, and everyone clapped.

"So, it's going to be all right with you to go?" Michael asked tentatively.

"I need to double check with Amy," Britany said and turned to bend down to speak with Amy. "Amy I know Michael has talked to you about this, at least someone has. Is it OK with you if I go on a cruise for a week with Michael? I don't want to go if you are going to be scared."

"Ben and I are going to have fun. We already have plans to ride Sissy every day, and Grandma Liz said she would let us gather eggs. She's going to teach us how to bake cookies. Ben likes to bake, too. He says he has too because his dad isn't very good at it. He wants to learn to make cookies like Grandma does. Grandpa is going to take us a ride on the tractor and he even said Ben could help him bale hay!"

"OK," laughed Britany, turning back to Michael. "I guess we're going!" she said joyfully. She clasped his shoulders and gave a big leap. Michael caught her and everyone gave a joyful shout. Ben and Amy ran up and embraced them.

CHAPTER 19

The newlyweds' flight to Florida was scheduled for six-o'clock that evening. Britany resisted the urge to double-check the things her mother and Crystal had packed. It was hard saying good-bye. She wanted to have time with Michael but she was eager to get settled into her home in Tennessee. She waved good-bye, and they were off to the airport.

"Take care and have fun!" she called back as they drove out the drive.

"Well, this is it. It's hard to believe, isn't it, Mrs. Britany Kaiser!" Michael said with a sigh as he took her hand.

She clasped his hand firmly and smiled back a worried smile. She was concerned about leaving Amy, but her hesitancy disappeared as soon as their plane left the ground.

Michael explained the agenda to her. They were leaving port in the morning for a four-hour cruise that would take them to the island. They would stay there for four days and then go back to Miami where they would stay for another two days on the beach. They would be back in time to go to church with her parents on Sunday and then start to Tennessee the next day.

"You certainly did have things planned out well!" Britany said with admiration in her voice. "I was so busy with the wedding, it was hard to plan beyond that. It kind of worked out nicely that we will have a few weeks before I actually move my things down. It wasn't so hard just packing clothes. I wasn't sure if we would need fall clothes, though," commented Britany thoughtfully.

"As long as you packed a couple of pairs of jeans, a jacket, and sweater, you should be fine. Normally you can wear shorts until the middle of October, except for the occasional cool day that comes along. We should be able to move before then." Michael looked at her fondly. "I wanted to take care of the planning after the wedding. I knew you would be busy with enough things. Besides, I wanted desperately to surprise you with this trip. I couldn't ask you any questions for fear that you would guess what was going on. Fortunately, you didn't ask me any questions."

They enjoyed a light dinner on the flight, after which Britany relaxed and took a short nap. When she awoke, the plane was circling and she could only see water through the window.

"I guess we're here," she said, straining to get a better look.

"It looks like it, unless they are going to keep going and take us directly to the Bahamas," Michael chuckled. "I could have gotten a direct flight there but a friend of mine said we would enjoy the cruise to the island."

"It sounds more romantic. I like that." Britany said dreamily.

The plane landed, and they hurried out of the plane and down to the luggage belt to retrieve their things.

"This is a little more rushed than it was in Nashville," commented Britany as she hurried to keep up.

"I guess everyone is eager to start their vacations," laughed Michael.

They hailed a taxi, which took them to a very fancy motel. The driver stopped in front and helped them with their luggage.

Britany stood looking up at the pretty, pink building with its green, tinted windows. She could smell the salt air, and the wind blew briskly against her dress. Between the buildings she could make out the Atlantic Ocean just beyond.

"Oh, Michael, this is beautiful! I could stay here the entire time," she said wistfully.

"We'll come back here at the end. The rest of the trip will be just as beautiful, don't worry. I think maybe we should get these bags up to our room," he said, reaching down to sling a strap over his shoulder and pick up another bag with his hand.

"I'm sorry, let me help." She took two suitcases and her beach bag.

They were able to get checked into their room easily.

The room was large and plush with a hot tub in the middle and large bed along with a couch and chair. The room was done in light pinks, oranges, blues and greens. A sliding glass door led to the balcony overlooking the ocean. Britany quickly deposited her bags and stepped out onto the balcony. The sun was going down leaving faint pink orange glow in the sky.

"Oh, Michael, let's hurry and go for a walk on the beach before the sun is completely gone!"

"Let me change into some shorts. I don't really want to wear a suit on the beach."

"That's fine, but I am going to wear my dress. It seems more romantic. It's my wedding day, and I want to wear it for as long as possible," Britany said, lightly sliding off her shoes and stockings when they were back inside.

Britany practically flew down the stairs and out to the beach as soon as Michael was ready. The waves were lapping on the beach. The roar of the tide was loud in their ears. A group of pelicans flew overhead in single formation, swooping down over the water close to the surf and then back high in the air again. The leader turned sharply to the west and the rest of the formation followed. They looked regimented and orderly. Britany was amazed.

Michael said, "They are making one last round, and now they will head to an island on the river where they nest for the night."

Britany walked barefoot close enough to the water that the waves rushed up over her ankles. It was surprisingly warm. She was accustomed to the Great Lakes which were always cold. The colors from the sky reflected on the water, turning the waves the same pinkish orange color mixed with the blue green. Tiny fish swam away from her feet. She saw something flopping in the water and pointed it out to Michael. They hurried over to where it was. A flash of silver broke the water and she thought it was a fish caught in the tide. As they got closer she could see it was a small skeet. Several other skeets were splashing around beside it.

They walked along following the skeets down the coastline, when one turned and swam straight at Britany. It fluttered against her leg and felt soft like silk. She screamed and ran out of the water. A deeply tanned elderly gentleman dressed in a white golf shirt and tan shorts laughed. "There is no need to be afraid. He is as curious about you as you are about him. He just came up for a closer look. The skeet meant no harm."

"Thank you," Britany said, but she stayed out of the water.

She and Michael walked hand in hand down the coast. Buildings and apartments lined the coastline for as far as they could see. The sand and surf seemed to create a buffer between the buildings and the ocean. It gave them the sensation that they were all alone with nature as they walked along the shore.

"What a day! From a wedding on a midwestern farm to a walk along the ocean. It must be an illusion," Britany said dreamily.

"Believe me, Britany, this day has been very real, and it's only just beginning," Michael said huskily and took her in his arms. He kissed her like he had never dared kiss her before, against the background of darkness that was settling around them.

Britany awoke the next morning to the steady, even sound of Michael's breathing. She could barely see the rise and fall of his bare chest as the sun was just beginning to add some light. She was curled around him slightly, and she carefully stroked the hair on his chest. She thanked God silently over and over again for the glorious gift He had given her. She closed her eyes and basked in the softness of Michael's bare skin beneath her cheek. She was torn between the desire to watch the sunrise from the balcony and the pleasure of lying there next to him.

The ocean seemed to beckon to her, and, ever so gently so as not to wake him, she slipped out from under the covers. Her mother had graciously packed a pale blue silk nightgown and matching robe in Britany's bags. Britany reached for the robe that was on the chair where she had left it the night before. She slipped into it, took the Bible from the nightstand, and went to the balcony. Her bare feet padded softly on the carpet.

She stood against the railing with the salt air blowing against her face, tugging playfully at her hair. She couldn't quite see the sun yet. She took a seat in one of the lounge chairs and opened her Bible to I Corinthians 13. The pastor had read it at the wedding. She could barely see the words. She stopped at verse four and reread it:

> (4) Love is patient, love is kind. It does not envy, it does not boast, it is not proud.
> (5) It is not self seeking, it is not easily angered, it keeps no record of wrongs.
> (6) Love does not delight in evil but rejoices with the truth.
> (7) It always protects, always trusts, always hopes, always perseveres.
> (8) Love never fails....

Britany prayed that God would fill her marriage with the perfect love described in these passages.

She stood by the railing. The sun was large and bright as it rose. The reflection from the water made it hard to see because of the brightness. It was beautiful and majestic. Two arms reached around from behind and pulled her close.

"Isn't it beautiful!" Britany said with a touch of awe as she relaxed into Michael's embrace.

"Very beautiful," Michael said as he reached around and kissed her cheek, her neck and then her shoulder.

"I meant the sunrise on the ocean," Britany laughed.

"It's nice, too, but no match for you," he said softly, continuing to caress her with his lips.

"Michael, I love you," said Britany, turning to face him and lifting her arms to his shoulders. "I didn't realize love could be this way."

"Neither did I until you came along. Come back to bed for a little while longer," he coaxed.

"Do you expect me to leave this magnificent view!" she teased lightly.

"We can see it from the bed. It will be even better!"

They turned to go back in as the gulls squawked, the waves roared onto the shore, and a few fishermen dotted the shoreline. The sun continued to make its spectacular appearance on this grand day.

Britany insisted on another walk on the beach before they headed to the dock to board the cruise boat. The walk made them later than they had planned. Passengers were boarding as they got out of the taxi. They checked in and were welcomed aboard warmly. The ship was huge. They walked the length of it and watched the commotion on the dock as the workers prepared to set sail. A whistle sounded, and the loudspeaker warned all those going ashore to do so. Twenty minutes later the speaker announced all passengers to go below deck and check their passports. The men working at the passport desk were stern. Britany felt nervous, even though she knew everything was in order. She was afraid she forgotten something, or that her passport wouldn't be right. They passed inspection. It turned out to be quite simple, to Britany's relief. They hurried topside as soon as possible. It was awesome to see the large ship slowly get underway. The ship moved effortlessly in the water, gliding smoothly along.

Miami was beautiful from a distance. The tall buildings looked white against the blue sky. Britany relaxed in a lounge chair and Michael sat be side her. She closed her eyes and let the breeze and warm sun bathe her. She was too excited to take a nap, but the sun felt relaxing. They walked the deck again, and then the porter called them to dinner.

Below deck they shared a full course meal prepared with luscious fresh fruit, seafood, and tasty deserts. The waiters were very professional, although their English was limited. The table service was elegant as they dined with another couple who were also on their honeymoon.

The cruise was wonderful and over much too quickly. The chaos that greeted them as they left the ship was a drastic contrast to the order of the ship. They had to dig through bags that had been dumped in a pile. The sun was hot, and they were cut off from the ocean breezes by the metal buildings surrounding them. A line of beat-up cars labeled, "TAXI" waited to take the passengers to their destinations. Horns were honking, and people were yelling. Michael and Britany shuffled through the masses of bags. Satisfied that they had the right ones, they headed toward one of the taxis.

"That one looks full. Let's try the next one," Britany suggested and Michael agreed.

To Britany's alarm the taxi driver grabbed the bags from her hands and tossed them onto the roof of his taxi.

"Plenty of room! No problem!" He said in a crisp British accent.

"I guess we take this one," Michael said with a half-hearted chuckle as he tossed his bags beside Britany's.

"But where do we sit?" Britany asked in dismay.

The driver opened the front passenger door and motioned them to slide in beside the two people already seated there. Michael slipped in and pulled Britany down onto his lap. The taxi driver seemed pleased and closed the door behind them.

The driver squeezed in and immediately whizzed around the car in front of them going down the left side of the road. He drove fast along the country road. Suddenly it seemed as if four roads merged together instead of the typical perpendicular intersection. There were no stop signs or stoplights. Britany could see no logic in which car was to go first other than simply the most daring and determined. Their driver seemed to fit that category perfectly. Britany was tossed about on Michael's lap, bumping her head on the window glass as the taxi swerved in and out of traffic. Britany was sure they were going to wreck. She suspected that if they did the traffic wouldn't even slow down. What would happen if they did wreck? Did they have ambulances here? What were the hospitals like? If they were anything like the roads, she would rather not find out. She gave Michael a worried look, and he squeezed her gently and laughed.

"I think we'll make it through this ride, but I'm sure we will never forget it!" he whispered in her ear.

Britany laughed and relaxed a little. It was funny if she could get past the fear and look at the humor in the situation.

They arrived at the motel and were unloaded in the same haphazard fashion. Britany and Michael gathered their bags and entered the motel to check in. The lobby was nice, but was a long way from the elegance of the motel they had just left in Florida. It was hotter in the motel than it had been outside, and Britany noticed windows and doors were open to allow any breeze that might happen by to come in. Apparently the air-conditioning was broken. Britany suspected it had been that way for quite some time. They signed in for their room and were told that the rooms were not ready yet. There would be a slight wait.

The slight wait turned out to be several hours. They were hot and tired and beginning to wonder if they would ever get a room. The front desk finally announced that the rooms were ready. There was a scramble as people got to their feet and quickly gathered their belongings.

Britany cringed as she walked into the room. It smelled must and the carpets were dirty. She looked at Michael in distress. He looked devastated and Britany quickly said, "Who needs a nice room when you're on the Caribbean Ocean. We'll be outside most of the time anyway."

"Britany, you really deserve better. I'm sorry about this," Michael said sadly. He was feeling like his wonderful plans were crumbling and he didn't know what to do. He wanted this marriage to be different, but he was already being a failure and they had only been married for one day!

"Michael, it's Ok, really it is." Britany put her bags down and reached up around his shoulders. "You are here. That's what I really want. We are together, alone. We don't have to have a perfect room to have a perfect time!"

Michael held her close. "Thank you, Britany. I love you," he said quietly.

Britany awoke to rain and her heart sank. She dreaded staying in the dingy room, but remained cheerful; determined that a little rain wasn't going to dampen their spirits. She pulled her hair into a ponytail and put on her swimsuit with a pair of casual shorts and T-shirt over the top. Michael threw on a T-shirt over his cut offs, and off they went into the rain.

Britany was surprised by how warm the rain was. It was actually quite pleasant. The rain bouncing off the palms made a pretty pattering sound. They walked the short distance through the main part of town and out to the country on a road that led to the beach.

The beach was beautiful with white sand and a gentle surf. Docked offshore in a small marina was a replica of a pirate ship. They walked across the beach up onto the boardwalk that led to the ship. A sign announced that the boat sailed the next day for an all day party.

"Michael, that sounds like fun!" Britany exclaimed.

"It looks like you sign up here," said Michael, pointing to a nearby shop. "Let's go for it!" They entered and registered, then browsed through other shops in the area. At noon they stopped for lunch and then made their way back to the beach. The sun was beginning to shine, and the island started to feel like a sauna. The breeze coming off the ocean felt refreshing. Britany stripped down to her suit, sat in a lounge chair on the beach, and was soon soaking in the sun and drifting off to sleep. Michael watched her peaceful rest until he found himself falling asleep.

"Michael, Michael," Britany said softly and stroked his arm. "I hate to wake you, but I'm afraid if we stay here much longer we may get burned. This sun is really strong."

Michael looked at her with a smile and nodded in agreement.

"This brochure we have says there is a beautiful garden on the other side of the island. I would love to see it," said Britany, showing him the pictures.

"Do you think you are up for another taxi ride? I think that is the only way to get there."

"Oh," groaned Britany.

"Maybe all the drivers aren't as wild as the one we had," said Michael.

"Wishful thinking!" Britany laughed. "I guess I'm willing to chance it. I do want to go."

Fortunately this taxi driver was a bit easier on the gas pedal. In fact he was in no hurry at all. He leisurely drove them the ten miles to the garden, which was a magnificent collection of flowers and tropical plants. The foliage around them made it seem as if they were alone and had the entire garden to themselves. Britany would never have believed how close she could feel to someone as she did now to Michael. Hand in hand they walked, enjoying the beauty surrounding them.

Michael asked Britany to sit on a quaint stone bench while he took her picture against a backdrop of flowers. He snapped the picture, and Britany screamed and jumped to her feet. He ran to her side as she stood staring at the bench, holding her hand.

"A lizard ran right over my hand!" Britany exclaimed in distress.

"Oh, honey, I don't think they would hurt you," he said gathering her in his arms.

"I know, but it was creepy. I didn't even see it until it ran across. I think I am ready to go now," she said as she shook her hand.

"I think we've seen it all anyway. It might be a little while before another taxi comes to take us back."

"I don't think you need to worry about that. He didn't seem in too much of a hurry. I think he waited for us. He probably left the meter running."

"He never turned the meter on," Michael chuckled.

"Oh," laughed Britany. "It probably wouldn't matter anyway!"

They spent the evening casually touring shops, and then went to one of the shows offered. It was fun walking the streets at night in the warm breezes without even a sweater.

The pirate ship turned out to be more fun than they had hoped for. It cruised for an hour over the crystal blue waters and then put down anchor over a reef. After a brief explanation snorkeling, equipment was handed out to everyone who wanted to try it. Britany looked at Michael.

"I had no idea we were going to get to snorkel!"

"Sounds great! What do you think?" asked Michael.

"I'd love too!"

The water was only waist deep where they descended a ladder at the stern of the boat. One large, very muscular black man got out with them. He had a knife strapped to his leg and Britany presumed he was watching out for the safety of the passengers. It made her a little more comfortable. Although the instructor had insisted that the sharks in the area would not attack them, she was still fearful of them. The muscular man soon was out of sight and Britany wasn't too sure how much help he would be in case of trouble.

Michael adjusted right away to the use of the snorkel, but Britany panicked when she tried to breathe underwater with hers. She swam around using the mask alone. The scene underwater was so beautiful that soon she tried using the snorkel again. She tried to relax and took a breath. It worked! She tried again and found that it wasn't so hard. The beauty underwater was amazing; hundreds of beautiful fish in all shapes and sizes. There were brightly colored blue fish, green fish, orange fish and yellow ones, too. She saw striped angel fish and beautiful bright purple and green plants. It was an entirely different world under the water.

She was so engrossed in the view underwater that she lost sight of Michael. She surfaced to find that she was also quite far from the boat. Many passengers stood on the deck and many more were close by, waiting patiently for their turn on the ladder. She looked for Michael and saw him several hundred feet to her right. She ducked underwater and swam in his direction. He must have been swimming toward her, too, because they almost bumped heads. They turned and swam side by side toward the boat. As they swam Michael motioned for her to look off to the left. She looked and couldn't believe what she was seeing. She started to panic. It was definitely a shark. He was swimming idly in a large circle. She would have surfaced and screamed for help, but she felt Michael's strong grip on her hand and looked over to see him put his finger to his mouth. He motioned to her to swim easily, and she followed close beside him as they slowly made their way back to the boat. The shark never looked their way. He acted as if they didn't exist.

Britany sank to the floor of the boat as soon as they got on board. She was shaking all over. Michael sat down beside her and took off his equipment.

"Wow, that was great wasn't it?" he exclaimed as he removed his mask.

"It was great until we saw the shark! Then it was just plain horrifying!" Britany lamented, still shaking.

"You saw a shark!" one of the passengers exclaimed.

Soon they were surrounded by a crowd of people all asking them questions; wanting to know how big it was; what it did; if they had been scared.

"It was great! It must have been four feet long! It was only fifteen feet away from us. It circled lazily and never even looked at us," Michael excitedly told the crowd. "We swam slowly back to the boat, not wanting to draw attention to us. Man, the teeth on that thing were awesome! I'd love to see one again!"

Britany looked at Michael and cringed. She was too shaken up to speak, but after a while she did enjoy the attention and concern of the other passengers. Soon she began to relax, knowing she was safe on the boat. After a while the ordeal started to seem a little exciting to her, too. She certainly had enjoyed herself before the shark appeared.

Later she spoke to the black man who had escorted them while they were snorkeling.

"Did you see the shark too?" she asked.

"Yes, I did," he said in his crisp accent.

"Do you carry that knife in case one of the passengers gets into trouble?" she asked.

"No, I fish. Knife is for my protection," he said simply and showed her a large fish he had in a net.

"Oh," she murmured. She felt her face go pale even under the redness from being in the sun.

The ship took them to a small deserted island. A large barbecue pit was ready and food was set up on tables under a tent. The crew let out a boisterous yell and motioned for the passengers to enjoy the food. After eating there was a volleyball game. They were divided into different teams and had challenges and play-offs. Some of the crewmembers joined in, too. The ones that didn't sat on the side and watched. Britany had the feeling that they were enjoying watching the girls in their bathing suits more than the game. Between games Britany and Michael spent time swimming in the sparkling blue water. The water was bluer and clearer than any she had ever seen. She didn't actually swim and wouldn't go out too far, even with Michael's prodding.

Sunset was approaching settling as they left the island. The crew set up a game of limbo and held a dance contest. Britany fell the second time under the bar of the limbo contest because she was laughing too hard, but she and Michael won third place in the twist contest. The boat was alive with music. People were dancing on every available spot on the boat. Michael and Britany stood on a platform around the mast that was high above the ship. Several other couples were with them, and it was crowded but no one minded a bit. The scene was breathtaking as the sun disappeared in the horizon and left a dazzling display of color reflecting on the water. Soon the stars began to appear, and the moon came out in half crest.

Michael held her close as they sailed for shore and watched the stars come out. It was a magic moment. They savored it until the ship docked and the crew began urging people to leave the ship. Michael slipped each of the crewmembers a dollar, and large smiles lit their faces. Britany and Michael had learned earlier that saying "thank-you" wasn't the proper way of showing appreciation on the island. The dollar spoke much louder.

Britany woke during the night. She had the strange sensation that someone was standing at the foot of the bed. She stared intently, but it was pitch dark, and she couldn't see. She reached her hand over to be sure Michael was sleeping next to her. He was there, and she shook him slightly. He stirred. Britany heard a scurrying noise and the sound of rattling metal. She reached for the light beside the bed and switched it on.

"What is going on?" Michael asked, suddenly awake.

"I think someone was in here," said Britany, quietly fearing there still might be someone in the room. "I had the strangest feeling that someone was standing at the foot of the bed. It was too dark to see, but I'm sure someone was in here!"

Michael got up and checked the bathroom and under the bed to be sure no one was still around. As he looked under the bed he noticed that the panel beside the air conditioner was lying on the floor. In its place was an opening to the outside big enough for a person to slip through.

Britany looked over to where his eyes had stopped and saw the hole. She gasped.

"There was someone in here!"

"It looks like they are gone now. Check your things and make sure nothing was stolen," Michael ordered. Britany quickly slipped out of bed and checked her money and passport. It was all there. Her jewelry was still in its place, too. They couldn't find anything missing.

"I think you must have scared him away before he could get anything. I'm glad you are a light sleeper. You're just as good as a watch dog," Michael said jokingly.

"Thanks, I think," Britany said weakly. "I'm just glad we are going back to the States tomorrow. The ocean is fabulous, but I'm not so sure I like the island. I don't think I will be able to sleep the rest of the night."

"We'll leave the light on. That will help discourage any more attempts. Besides, I'm sure you scared them off. They are probably running fast in the other direction. There are only a couple more hours until light comes. Then we get to go snorkeling again!"

"That's supposed to make me feel better!" Britany exclaimed. "Now I know

I won't get to sleep."

To her surprise she did sleep. Snuggled securely beside Michael she soon fell into a restful sleep and woke long after the sun had made its appearance.

"I guess you didn't have so much trouble sleeping after all," Michael said lightly as she opened her eyes.

"No, I guess not," she said with a smile.

They went snorkeling right after breakfast. This time they shared a small boat with six other passengers. Britany overcame her reluctance to swim and was soon in the water with Michael. The boat had taken them to a reef where the water was ten to twenty feet deep. Michael loved it and soon learned to blow out of the snorkel as he surfaced so he could dive down and take a closer look at the bottom. Once again Britany felt as if she was in a different world, and her fear and anxiety were soon lost in the excitement. She kept Michael in view and followed him closely. When she finally surfaced to check the position of the boat she found that the wind had picked up, and the waves were getting rough. Underwater they hadn't noticed it. The others were in the boat waving frantically for her to come in. She dove down and got Michael's attention to go back. When they got to the surface she tried to swim back. A large wave splashed her in the face, and she swallowed a mouthful of salt water. It gagged her, and she tried to spit it out. She coughed and struggled to catch her breath. She finally started to swim again when another wave caught her and tossed her around. She got her bearings and looked for Michael. He was already in front of her on his way to the boat. He had left his snorkel on and was having no trouble. She tried to put her snorkel back on, but it was full of saltwater. She tried to blow it out but the waves kept fighting her. Britany started to panic. She reminded herself that she could swim and would be all right if she just relaxed. The waves kept pelting her in the face, and she had to struggle to keep water out of her mouth and eyes. She tried doing a sidestroke instead of going straight into the waves and slowly she began to make progress.

Michael reached the boat and looked back for Britany. He was surprised to see she was far behind. He unloaded his mask and snorkel and started swimming back after her. By the time he reached her she was close to the boat. He swam beside her and held the ladder so she could climb in.

No one in the boat seemed to realize that she had been having problems. In fact they were angry that Britany and Michael had gone so far and that the weather was getting bad. It started to rain, and their spirits dampened even more. Britany wasn't sure what the others were so upset about. They were already wet, and the rain was warm. It really wasn't uncomfortable. When the boat had returned to shore and they were out of earshot of the others, the captain explained why the other passengers were angry. They had gotten into the water and were afraid to use their snorkels. They swam around for ten or twenty minutes and then got back into the boat. They were just angry because Michael and Britany caused them to wait. Otherwise they could have gone back. He assured them that he was not upset. They had paid for a two-hour trip, and he was glad they had enjoyed themselves.

The rain ended as quickly as it had started, and soon the sun was out, once again causing a sauna effect. Britany was starting to get used to the heat and enjoyed basking one last time on the beach. They returned to the motel. They quickly showered and dressed and were more than ready to leave by the time the taxis arrived.

They were heaped back into the cars and vans. This time Britany held fast to the door. She was back on Michael's lap. They laughed as the taxi sped through the city.

The cruise was once again elegant and enchanting. They dined on an elaborate supper and enjoyed entertainment throughout the three levels of the boat. As the ship neared shore Britany and Michael found themselves standing at the rail watching the stars. The lights of Miami were beautiful as they neared the coast of Florida.

Britany was delighted to find they had the same room for the next two nights that they had stayed in the first night of their honeymoon. It felt as if they had returned home when they switched on the lights to the room and walked in.

"Michael, I loved the four days on the island. It was an adventure I'll never forget, but I am delighted to be back, and I am really looking forward to the next two days alone here with you," Britany commented as she eased her body into the hot tub.

"I couldn't agree with you more. I almost lost you to a shark, a robber, the waves, but the worst of all was the taxi driver!" With his comment they both burst into laughter.

CHAPTER 20

The next several months passed in a whirl of activity with very little time for Michael and Britany to be together, especially not alone. Looking back, Britany was thankful Michael had been insightful enough to plan their honeymoon. It had given them some time alone together to start their married life. The move into their new home went without many problems, but it was a much bigger job than Britany had expected.

Jeanne's will was read and was not contested. Amy was elated, but Liz and Britany looked at each other with hesitancy. They both knew Monique, and neither felt secure that the matter was totally settled. Fortunately, Amy was living with them and would be able to start school with the rest of the students.

Britany and Michael chose to send Amy and Ben to the Christian school that was just two miles away from their new home. Britany drove them the forty-five minute drive to the school until they moved. Her days were consumed with taking Ben and Amy to school before the move, and after the move there were more things to do than Britany could have imagined.

As summer changed into fall, Britany was in for a pleasant surprise. The days remained warm, and Ben and Amy were able to use the pool long into September. Britany rode bikes with the children to the school in the morning, and then back in the afternoon to ride home with them.

She loved her new home and the area. The church they attended was the same one that supported the school and was just down the road from their house. The people were caring and considerate. There were several ladies she found easy to talk to. She started going to a Bible Study on Tuesday mornings and took the children to the Wednesday evening service. The pastor Daniel Shepler and his wife Jewell were wonderful. They were about the age of Britany's parents, and she felt a warm bond with them soon after she met them. Jewell attended the Tuesday morning Bible study. She had raised six children and Britany found her comments during the study to be a big help.

Michael was on the road at least three to four nights a week, leaving Britany alone with the children much of the time. She soon found to her discouragement that the disciplining was left up to her. Britany tried to plan supper when he was in town, so Michael would be there and they could eat together, but as several weeks passed she found that Michael was never home at a set time. After quite a few cold, late meals she stopped trying to wait supper and fed the children when they got home from school.

Amy started having problems with school soon after they moved into their new home. One morning Britany noticed that she was quiet during their bike ride to the school. When they got there, Amy stood beside her bike and wouldn't move.

"Honey, what is wrong?" Britany asked.

Amy didn't respond, but tears welled up in her eyes and started to roll down her cheeks.

"Do you not feel well?" Britany asked. Amy shrugged her shoulders. Britany reached out and gathered her in her arms, and held her close. Do you want to go back home? Amy looked at her with big brown eyes, shook her head no and cried harder.

"Let's go to the ladies room and dry your tears then," suggested Britany and took her by the hand to lead her into the building. When Britany had dried Amy's tears she tried to talk to her again.

"Are you ready to go to class now?" Britany asked. Amy nodded her head yes, but looked as if she would start crying again any time. Britany walked her to her class and waited until Amy put her things in her locker and found her desk. Britany spoke to Amy's teacher, Mrs. Brown, and told her to call if Amy seemed to have any more problems. Britany worried about Amy the entire morning and was relieved to find when she went back to pick them up at two that Amy was fine.

The crying continued for the next two weeks and it was hard for Britany to take Amy to school, but Amy insisted she didn't want to stay home. One day when Britany picked the children up from school Amy was ecstatic.

"Look Britany, I got a one hundred on my math paper," She waved the paper proudly over her head. "Now I don't have to worry about not being able to learn in first grade."

Britany looked at Amy in puzzlement. Was that what she was so afraid of? Britany wondered. "That's wonderful honey. We will put it on the refrigerator and you can show it to Daddy when he comes home," she said.

Amy squared her shoulders and smiled the next day when it was time for her to walk in the building. Britany gave her a hug good-bye and there were no tears. Britany was thrilled and relieved.

Ben seemed to be doing well at school. He was making new friends, fitting in well. At home it was an entirely different story. Many nights he would come home angry. He yelled at Britany and Amy about some trivial thing. Britany didn't know what to do. She had never faced this problem with Crystal. His outlook on life and his attitude about himself seemed to be poor. She had no idea what to do about the anger, but she didn't feel it was appropriate for him to yell at her or Amy. She explained to him that he would have to find another way to express his anger. Some nights she played ball with him just so he would have something to hit and release frustration. Other times his outbursts were so uncontrollable she had to physically set him in a chair until he calmed down.

He yelled at her that she wasn't his mother and she had no right to tell him what to do. She responded by saying that she knew she wasn't, but she loved him and she was responsible for him. She loved him enough that she wasn't going to let him hurt himself or others. She made it clear that whether he loved her or not, he still needed to respect her and listen to her.

Michael was never home when Ben had his little blow ups. She didn't tell him about them because she felt it was something she and Ben needed to work out. She didn't want to bother Michael with it. Besides, it seemed like Michael was never home. The only day they could plan on him being there was Sunday, and that was only if he didn't have an unexpected weekend trip.

The weeks were turning into months and Britany was starting to get discouraged. She missed Crystal. She missed her parents. Most of all she missed Michael. She wanted so much to see him and to share more of their lives together. He didn't seem to have the same need. That hurt her deeply. She told herself she expected too much from this marriage and she should try to be happy the way things were. It was a time for adjustments, and she needed to be patient. Things would get better.

One Saturday in late October when the weather was still beautiful, Britany took Amy and Ben riding for the day. They packed a picnic and took off across the field and over the hill to see what they could find. Britany had been working with Ben to teach him to ride Trigger. He was doing well, but Britany thought it wouldn't be too safe to let him ride alone on trails yet so he and Amy doubled on the pony.

Michael was home when they returned, and both children ran to him.

"Daddy, Daddy, we went on a picnic!" yelled Amy.

"Yeah, we rode the horses and saw a snake skin and a bunch of squirrels," added Ben.

"They were collecting nuts for the winter. We tried to gather some nuts, too, but the squirrels had taken them all," Amy said.

"Well those little stinkers," said Michael.

"But the squirrels need them more than we do," said Ben. "They need them to survive the winter."

"It sounds like you had a good time!" said Michael.

"Can we go again tomorrow, Britany!" asked Amy.

"Can you go too Dad?" asked Ben.

"I'm awfully tired," said Michael. He looked at the two fallen faces in front of him and then up at Britany.

"But I'm sure that would be fun," He smiled and leaned on the counter.

Ben and Amy yelled with delight and jumped up and down. That evening Britany grilled hamburgers, and the four of them ate outside. Then they played ball until dark.

The next day Britany got up early and prepared another picnic lunch, then dressed for church. As soon as they returned from church they changed their clothes and took off on the ride. It was a beautiful day. The leaves were beginning to change just enough to add color. For the first time since the wedding Britany was beginning to feel as though they were a family. Amy and Ben were full of enthusiasm, and Michael joined in their fun. It was good to see him and Ben have fun together. It was nice to see Ben smile and not have to argue with him about something. They rode and chatted and stopped near a stream for lunch.

After they had eaten Amy and Ben searched for crayfish and salamanders in the stream and under rocks. Britany sat on a large tree trunk that had fallen across the stream. Michael sat down beside her.

"This is great. You are so good with the children. You think of nice simple ways to have fun. They both need that. It's starting to feel like we are a real family," commented Michael.

"I was thinking the same thing. You make a wonderful father and they need that, too." Britany looked up at him as she spoke honestly.

Britany's comment, though meant in a good way stung. Michael knew the children needed a good father and Britany needed a good husband, but he didn't feel like a good dad or husband.

"I'm not a very good dad," Michael said looking down into the water. "I never have been. My first wife and I fought so much I took refuge in my work. Now I am so involved in it I don't know how to be a Dad. I'm too caught up in my work. I know that, but I don't know what to do about it," he finished with a touch of sadness in his voice.

He had always felt inadequate as a parent, but when his first marriage broke up it was like an affirmation that he was a failure. Britany was caring, but he didn't feel she totally understood how he felt. He wasn't sure he wanted her to know just how much of a failure he had been. Work was where he was good and very successful!

"Michael, I love you. I always will. I miss you too, as I know the children do. We will pray about it. God sees your desire. He will help you see clearly."

"Britany, it seems so easy for you to pray. I love God but it isn't easy for me to ask Him for things. I hate to feel as though I am always asking, as if there were no end to the things I ask for."

"God says to ask Him for our daily bread. It seems to me, if He didn't want us coming to Him, He would say to ask once for all the bread you will ever need."

"Britany sometimes you can be really cute," Michael said with a laugh.

"That's why you love me so much, right?" Britany asked, putting her arm around his waist and tucking her shoulder under his.

"Only partly. Actually I love you for your body!" he said tickling her and practically knocking them both into the water.

They stayed for a while longer with their feet dangling, watching the water gurgle over the rocks. The children searched diligently for hidden treasures. Then they mounted the horses and continued the ride.

Britany popped popcorn for the evening as they settled in and played a board game. Britany and Ben teamed up against Michael and Amy. They played until it was time for bed. Together they tucked the two children in, saying prayers and giving out hugs and kisses. Britany loved the way Ben good-naturedly gave Amy a kiss each night. He was always careful to give Britany one too. A lot of boys his age would have protested loudly to such a routine, but Ben had joined in with no reservations, right from the start. Britany could just imagine the hurt Amy would feel if he ever protested, and she was very grateful that he didn't.

"Ben is such a loving child. He must get that from his lovable Dad," Britany commented as they went back down stairs and she curled up beside him on the couch.

"He always has been. You're so good for him, Britany. His own mother doesn't have much to do with him anymore. It's getting worse as he gets older. She says he is obstinate and won't do anything she asks. She also says he yells at her and throws fits. I won't deny he can be a handful at times, but I think she is just giving excuses because she doesn't want him around. I'm sure he feels that way."

"I'm afraid I'm not doing too well in that area myself. He gets so angry with me and Amy sometimes that I don't know what to do," Britany confessed.

"Britany, I didn't know that!" said Michael.

"I love him dearly, but I need his respect. I've told him he doesn't have to love me or like everything I do, but he does need to respect me. I tell him I won't tolerate his behavior, and I make him either go to his room or sit in a chair until he can speak to me in a tolerable fashion. I didn't want to bother you about it. You are so busy, and I figured it was all a part of the adjustment period. If he is doing the same thing to his mother, there may be something more than I realized going on," Britany said thoughtfully.

"Britany, I'm sorry. Please tell me these things. I know I'm not around much, but I really do care about what goes on. You are right. He does need to respect you. I thought his mother was just telling me those things and that they weren't true," Michael said earnestly.

"I'm just never sure I am doing the right thing, and it makes me feel insecure. So far he hasn't had a problem with it at school, so that is good."

"Are things going OK with Amy?" Michael asked.

"She is fine at home and seemed to be doing better, but she was crying every morning when I left her. It just broke my heart," Britany confessed.

"Why didn't you tell me these things earlier?" Michael asked with concern in his voice. He felt hurt that she hadn't shared the problems with him.

"I didn't want to bother you. I think it's partly because I've always had to deal with these types of things on my own. I just didn't want you to worry. You have enough to worry about the way it is."

"Britany, we are a family. You have someone to share these things with now. I care about what happens and how things are going here at home. My family comes first. Please don't leave me out," Michael said gently and earnestly, his dark eyes looking deeply into hers.

"I'm sorry, Michael. I never thought about it that way before. I'll be more careful in the future. I love you so much, and I do so want to be a family."

"I know you do. I love you too. I guess we have a lot of learning to do together, don't we?" he asked. She shook her head in agreement, her eyes moist. He gently took her in his arms and kissed her softly.

The next week seemed to go like clockwork. Ben was polite and happy. He didn't have an angry spell the entire week. Amy cried once when Britany dropped her off, but quickly got herself under control. Britany was sure the improvement was due to the special family time they had on Sunday. She wished that they could have more times like it.

"Britany," said Michael one morning as he put on his tie, "I have business trips scheduled for the next two weekends."

Britany's spirits sank when he told her the news. He looked at her and could tell she was disappointed. Why couldn't she understand that this was the way his work went and that he would be gone a lot? He thought.

"Why don't you take Ben and Amy to visit your parents one of the weekends I'm gone?" Michael suggested. He hoped it would lessen her disappointment. Her face lit up and he felt relieved.

That sounded wonderful to Britany. Suddenly she was terribly homesick and missed Crystal. She called Crystal and Liz the next morning. She wanted to be sure Crystal would be able to leave school and be there before she made further plans. The weekend worked into both Crystal and Liz's agenda.

Britany took Ben and Amy, out of school on Friday so they would have more time to get to her parents'. They left as soon as they got out of school on Thursday. The drive went quite smoothly. Britany had gotten some book tapes from the library and the three of them enjoyed them. They stopped for supper half-way. It wasn't too long after that when Amy fell asleep. Ben stayed awake and talked to Britany as she drove, but by the time she arrived at her parents' he was asleep, too. The quiet gave Britany time to think as she drove.

Britany was tired as she pulled into her parents' drive, but pleased with the ease of the trip compared to what she had feared it might be. The outside light came on as she opened the car door, and both her parents stood at the door to greet her. Ben drowsily looked up and yawned. Amy didn't stir so Britany carefully lifted her and carried her to the house. Her mother met her at the door and helped her get Amy into bed. Charles helped lead a groggy Ben to his bed, and then Britany came to help him get settled.

When the children were in bed, Britany sat down at the table to a glass of milk and some cookies her mother provided, and they talked.

"I guess Crystal will get out of her last class at noon tomorrow and be here some time around two," Britany said as she sat down.

"She called here yesterday and told us the same thing," Liz agreed.

"It's hard to be this close and not see her right away," Britany said wistfully.

"I suppose it is, but it's great to see you! It's kind of hard for us to wait to get to talk to the children now that you are here, too," Liz replied.

"I hadn't thought about that," Britany mused.

"Tell us about the drive here, and how Michael is doing. Then you had better go to bed and get some sleep. You must be tired after that long drive."

"I'm more excited than anything," Britany said and then proceeded to go into detail on the trip and their new home.

The next day Amy was the first to see Crystal. She was out of the door in a flash. Britany was close behind. Amy jumped up and down beside the car as Crystal opened the door. She flew into Crystal's arms as soon as it opened.

"I missed you, Crystal. I hope you can come and see our new home real soon. There are lots of places to ride, and I found a new friend. I have a new school now, and my teacher is real nice," Amy rattled off as fast as her little mouth would go.

"Well, I hope to real soon," said Crystal gaily as she lowered Amy to the ground and let Britany get her turn to give her a hug.

"If you didn't already notice, you're very much missed," Britany laughed to disguise the tears that were threatening to fall.

"I miss you guys, too. I don't have a lot of time to miss you, though. They keep us snowed under in studies. I am going to have to study some this weekend to keep up," Crystal replied.

"That's too bad. I won't complain though. It's great just to have you here," Britany said quickly.

"Thanks Mom," Crystal said giving her another hug. "How is my little brother?" said Crystal turning to address Ben, who was coming from the barn with Charles.

"Fine," said Ben, his one dimple highlighting his face as he gave her a hug.

"Are you behaving yourself and doing well in school?" she asked.

"He gets mad at me and hits me," Amy spoke up before Ben had a chance.

"Only when you do something stupid," Ben shot back at Amy.

"Ok you two. That is enough," said Britany sternly.

That was the end of the argument, although Ben gave Amy a mean look.

"They're starting to act like brother and sister," Crystal laughed. "Maybe I'm better off at college."

"They only act like that some of the time. Most of the time they get along pretty well," Britany defended them.

"I remember some of the fights you and your brother had when you were younger. You could go at it pretty well," Liz chuckled.

"Yeah, I don't know if you noticed or not, but they stopped when he got bigger than me. I got beat up during one of those fights, and that was the last time we fought. At least when he was near enough to reach me!" Britany laughed.

The weekend was fun. Britany enjoyed being the center of attention when she went to visit work and church. She received some more wedding presents which people had been leaving at her parents' until she came for a visit. Britany relished the time spent with her parents and Crystal but felt a tug at her heart to be back home with Michael. She was anxious to start back to Tennessee as soon as church was out. Michael's flight was due back some time after five and with the time change she should get home shortly after he did.

Both Amy and Ben were very tired from the weekend and slept a lot of the trip. It went quickly and smoothly, but as Britany pulled into the drive her heart sank. Michael's car wasn't there and she could tell from the solitary light shining in the house that he wasn't home yet. She wasn't sure if she was more disappointed or scared. She told herself to relax--his plane may have been delayed. She unlocked the door to the house and then carried Amy in with a drowsy Ben following behind. She put them both to bed and then went to check the answering machine which was flashing.

It was a message from Michael. Due to some complications he had to stay through Monday and would be home sometime Monday evening. Fatigue and disappointment swept through her as she sat heavily in the nearby chair. She sat staring for some time and then went to tackle the task of unloading the car.

The phone rang as she brought in the last load. She hurried to answer it. It was Michael apologizing for the delay and checking to be sure she had arrived home safely. He was talkative and wanted to know all about the trip. She told him about Crystal, her parents, and the presents they had received. She could tell he was lonely and suddenly felt sorry for him. He would be alone in a motel room and had been all weekend. He wanted to be sure she wasn't upset about the delay. She lied and told him it was fine, although she missed him and would be glad to see him. She didn't have the heart to tell him how she really felt. She didn't want him to feel guilty about something over which he had no control. He was concerned that she didn't seem her usual cheerful self, but she assured him it was because she was tired from the trip.

When she hung up the phone she suddenly felt lonely. She had been right when she said she was tired from the trip. She was exhausted. Between disappointment; anger at his job; loneliness and tiredness she felt a bit overwhelmed and went to bed to fall into a troubled sleep.

Monday went quickly, and soon Michael was back home again. Fortunately he got home before it was time to put the children to bed. She was dreading trying to get them to bed before they had a chance to see him. Once again things seemed complete; they were together as a family.

Ben's mother called on Tuesday.

"Hi, this is Linda, Ben's mother. You must be Michael's new wife?"

"Yes, this is Britany."

"I'm calling to tell Michael I will be there Friday to take Ben for the weekend. He can pick him up on Sunday."

"I'm sorry, but Michael isn't here now, and I would feel a lot better about it if you would talk to him. I will have him call you when he gets home from work." Britany had never talked to her before. It was the first time Linda had called and wanted Ben since Britany and Michael had married. Britany wasn't sure what to say.

"Good, you do that but it won't make any difference. I'm entitled to see my son. Good-bye."

Britany called Michael's office as soon as she hung up the phone. She felt shaky and insecure as she called, not knowing quite why. He was in the office, and she got to speak directly to him. He told Britany not to be concerned that he would take care of it. He also told her he would tell Ben's mother to call him at the office and not at home unless she wanted to talk to Ben.

Ben went to stay with his mother for the weekend. She picked him up from the house on Friday after school. Britany wasn't too pleased to be meeting her for the first time when Michael wasn't there. There wasn't much else to do considering Michael was in Chicago for the weekend.

Linda Abernathy was polite and reserved. Her blonde hair was pulled up in a bun. Britany felt a sting of jealousy when she saw how pretty and petite she was. Britany assessed that her outfit was probably by some designer name, but since she wasn't into that type thing she didn't recognize the look, but Linda wore it perfectly. She realized she should have been expecting Linda's good looks, but it caught her off guard. Britany was relieved when she stayed only long enough to get Ben's things.

Britany bent down to give Ben a kiss good-bye and was surprised to see a look of distress on his face. She gave him an extra hug for support and looked up to see a mean glare sweep over his mother's face. It was amazing how quickly her pretty face changed into one of harshness. Britany's heart went out to Ben as they walked to the car. She and Amy stood on the porch as they left. She wanted so much to tell Ben he didn't have to go if he didn't want to but that was between

Michael and Linda. She wasn't to be involved, it wasn't her place. From the look on the Linda's face when Britany gave Ben a hug she could tell his mother was more than a little jealous of Britany.

Britany said a prayer for Ben as they drove away. Then she turned to Amy and said, "Well it's just you and me for a couple of days. Is there anything you would like to do?"

Amy looked up at Britany, her eyes sad. "He didn't want to go. He said his step dad is mean to him, and his mother doesn't really like to have him around. He said they always talk mean about Michael and that they think it is silly to believe in God."

"I didn't think he wanted to go. I hated to let him, but he needs to spend some time with his mother, too. Maybe she will be nice to him this time," Britany said trying to reassure Amy. "Let's go riding and then maybe we can go and get ice cream!"

"I'll race you to the barn!" Amy yelled as she took off.

The house was quiet, and Britany was reminded of the many evenings it was just she and Crystal alone. So much had happened in such a short time. If anyone would have told her a year ago how much her life would change, she would never have believed them.

Michael called and checked on them after Amy was in bed. It was good to hear from him. She told him what Amy had said. He said he suspected something like that, but Ben had never told him much of what went on at his mother's.

Michael brought Ben home with him when he returned from the airport on Sunday evening. Amy ran to give him a hug and he looked glad to see her. There wasn't much of the evening left by the time they got home but it was nice to have the family back together again.

"Crystal will be home a week from Wednesday and stay with us over winter break until after Christmas. She hasn't gotten to see our home yet. Ben, you and Amy can help me get her room ready," Britany said as they sat at the table.

"How many days is that?" Amy questioned.

"Nine. See, we are here, and this is when she comes," Ben explained, pointing to the days on the calendar.

"Yeah! I'm going to mark the days off so I can tell when she is coming."

"Britany," said Michael, taking a bite of salad. "I was thinking of seeing if my parents might like to come down for Thanksgiving. Would that be OK with you?"

"That would be great! That's why we have this big house. We may as well put it to good use! I think I am going to enjoy not working the holidays. It's the first time I remember not having to plan Thanksgiving and Christmas around my days off," Britany commented cheerfully.

"Maybe if my parents come for Thanksgiving we can go to your parents for Christmas," Michael continued.

"It sounds like you have been giving this some thought," laughed Britany. "It would be nice to be with them on Christmas, but if you don't mind, I would kind of like to have our first Christmas right here. Maybe we could go up the day after."

"Sounds like a winner to me. I guess I just need to see what day Christmas falls on and when I go back to work. Some of us do need to plan around our work schedule. I will check with my parents and we can make plans from there," Michael finished.

"I know two children who need to get ready for bed," Britany said, noting how tired Ben looked.

Ben seemed quiet and reserved the next morning as he prepared for school. Michael wasn't home by the time Ben and Amy were ready for bed that night.

"Ben, Amy, it's time for bed," said Britany.

"You're not my mother, and you don't need to tell me when to go to bed!" yelled Ben. "I will go to bed when my dad gets home!"

"I will have your dad come in and say good-night to you when he comes home, but you do need to go to bed," Britany said firmly.

"You're mean! You don't love me! You don't even like me!" he screamed.

"Ben, I do love you!"

"No, you don't! No, you don't!" he screamed and ran to his bedroom and slammed the door. Britany followed and listened to him cry from behind the door. She checked on him shortly and he had fallen asleep. Britany breathed a sigh of relief. She told Michael about the outburst when he got home and he went in to tell Ben he was home. Ben woke just enough to give his father a hug and then drift back to sleep.

Britany got a call from the school near the end of the week. It was Ben's teacher, Miss Wagner. She said Ben had thrown a fit when she asked him to rewrite a paper he had written sloppily. It had concerned her so much she wanted to let Britany know about it. Britany thanked her and assured her she would speak to him about it. Britany did talk to him about it, but she didn't get much of a response. He mumbled something about the teacher not knowing what she was talking about and that's all she could get him to say. Michael didn't have much luck when he tried to talk to him either.

Michael was out of town the next night when Ben blew up at Amy and punched her in the stomach. Britany was in the next room and could hear the force of the blow. She went running in to find Amy doubled up on the floor, her face twisted in pain. Britany ran over to see if she was all right. When she was convinced Amy was all right, she lit into Ben.

"What in the world were you thinking!" she yelled. "She is half the size you are, and you could hurt her badly. This is serious, and I won't tolerate it. You do not take your anger out on Amy. You can hit the bed or punch a pillow, but never hit her like that again!"

"She started it!" he screamed, his face red and contorted in rage. "She was in my room and I didn't tell her she could be."

"I wanted to borrow his crayons," Amy whimpered.

"I don't care what she did," Britany spoke firmly. "You do not punch, kick, or hit her. Do you understand me?"

"You hate me! You only like Crystal and Amy. Nobody loves me!" Ben screamed, totally out of control of his emotions.

"Ben, that's not true. You know it's not true. Your dad loves you very much, and so do I. You just cannot go around beating up Amy. That doesn't mean I don't love you," she explained trying, to reach out and give him a hug.

"If my dad loves me, why isn't he here!" Ben jumped back from her and ran to his room slamming the door behind him. Britany could only stare at the door in disbelief at what had just happened. She had no idea what to do next.

"His mom told him that. She told him that his dad only keeps him because then he doesn't have to pay her. She told him that you are just nice to him so Michael doesn't get mad at you. She told him there is no God and if there was He wouldn't love Ben anyway because he is so bad," Amy said through teary eyes. She quietly put her arm around Britany's neck as Britany stayed kneeling on the floor.

"She did?" Britany asked weakly. "How do you know?"

"He told me when he came back from her house. I think that's why he doesn't think anyone loves him. Now he doesn't love us either," Amy whimpered.

"Amy, you are precious. That was an awful thing for his mother to say. He still loves you very much or he wouldn't be so upset. We just have to let him know we do love him and that his mother is wrong."

"How do we do that?" she questioned.

"I don't know, Amy. I don't know. I guess we just keep loving him and showing him in whatever way we can. Love always wins out over hate. Let's get you ready for bed," Britany coaxed.

"Will you read to me?"

"Of course. Let's get your jammies on and brush your teeth."

Britany helped Amy, all the while praying silently for God's guidance. She felt Ben needed to at least hear his dad's voice. She would call Michael. She didn't want to tell him all that had happened over the phone, but at least she could call him and tell him Ben needed to know his father still cared. She put Amy to bed and read her a short story, giving Ben time to calm down a little. Then she went and telephoned Michael. He answered the phone on the second ring to her relief, and she relayed just a portion of what had transpired. She then gently knocked on Ben's door and told him his father was on the phone and wanted to talk to him.

Ben opened the door and took the phone from Britany. It seemed to calm him some to talk to his father and he smiled slightly as he handed the phone back to Britany. She thanked Michael and then went to help Ben prepare for bed.

During the night Britany woke to a horrible scream. She was up in a flash. It was coming from Ben's room, and she ran in to find him thrashing wildly in bed.

"Ben, Ben, wake up! You are dreaming. It's OK. You are all right," Britany said, shaking him gently.

He opened his eyes and wildly looked around. Then he clung hard to Britany.

"I had a nightmare," he cried.

"I know," said Britany. "You are fine. Everything is OK. You are at home and safe. How about if we go downstairs and see if we can find you some milk and cookies?"

"That would be nice."

Britany took him downstairs and helped him calm down. He was afraid to go back to his room, so she let him sleep with her the rest of the night.

Britany didn't know which was best for Ben, but to her relief his mother had no further contact with them except to request to have Ben for Christmas.

CHAPTER 21

The holidays were delightful. Crystal was enthralled with everything about their new home. Michael had extra time off from work with no long trips during that time. Britany enjoyed having his parents come and stay for Thanksgiving. It was the first time she had ever been responsible for entertaining anyone, and she was a bit nervous. She soon found she had no need to be. Dianne joined to help in the kitchen. Between her and Crystal and Amy's cheerful help the time spent in the kitchen cooking was quite enjoyable.

The time between Christmas and Thanksgiving gave Britany and Crystal plenty of time to be together, and Crystal was anxious to learn all she could about the countryside. She even got involved in some of the youth activities at the church. There were several other college students home for the holidays, and Britany soon found Crystal going out for the evenings with the other youth.

Since Ben was going to be with his mother Christmas day, they celebrated Christmas with a special meal on Christmas Eve. Michael started a fire in the fireplace. Britany put Christmas music on the stereo, and they sat down in the evening together to read the Christmas story out of the Bible. Their church had a special candle lighting service that they attended. It was a beautiful time, even without snow. They drove to a neighboring church following the service where there was a live nativity scene. The entire evening drew the family close, surrounded by the love of Jesus. Michael carried a sleeping Amy. Britany helped Ben into the house and up the stairs when they returned home.

Sitting alone with Michael, staring into the crackling fire, Britany was totally happy and content.

"I love being a family," she said quietly as she was seated on the couch beside Michael with her head on his shoulder.

"It sure beats living alone and raising a son on your own. I love having the girls around, too. I'm glad Crystal was able to come. It was special having her here. There is one thing I worry about, though," Michael said thoughtfully, staring into the fire also.

"Ben is going to his mother's tomorrow," Britany reflected for him.

"Exactly. I wish we could just say no and not let him go. I'm not sure which is worse though. She is his mother and it's important that he spends time with her. I just don't know what to do about the things she says."

"Neither do I. I'm just glad we have Amy to at least help us get a little insight into what is going on. I hope he keeps talking to her so she can fill us in," Britany added.

They decided it was safe to play Santa Clause since everyone was asleep. They brought the presents out of hiding and carefully placed them around the tree.

The next morning they awoke to an excited Amy jumping on the bed at five o'clock.

"Wake up! Wake up!" she screamed, "Santa has been here, and I have some packages under the tree!"

"OK," Britany laughed. "We'll be out in just a minute. Give us some time to get ready. You can go wake up Crystal while you're waiting."

"Yeah!" Amy gleefully exclaimed and took off.

"Crystal's going to love you for that!" Michael said sleepily.

"I know. I couldn't help thinking of all the times she did the same thing to me in the past. Now she can see what I went through. Besides, I wanted to officially say Merry Christmas," Britany laughed, embracing Michael warmly, giving him a soft kiss.

"I like this Christmas already," Michael whispered back.

When they entered the living room, Ben and Amy were busy sorting presents into piles. Crystal emerged from the stairs, looking half awake.

It was fun watching the joyful shouts and the excited faces as the presents were opened. When they were finished, Britany went to the kitchen, and Michael gathered wrappings and started a fire with them in the fireplace. Britany was just getting started with breakfast when the doorbell rang. She startled and quickly went into the living room in time to see the color drain out of Ben's face. They knew it was his mother. They just hadn't expected her so early. Michael welcomed her in and Britany went to help Ben get ready to go. She wished so much she could let him stay with them. She gave him a hug and said a short prayer with him before he left. He gave her a weak smile and went to greet his mother.

The day seemed to lose its cheeriness. They reread the Christmas story and enjoyed playing games they had gotten that morning, but the atmosphere was subdued.

Ben returned at bedtime with a new bike that his mother had gotten him. He was quiet and not too excited about the bike. Michael read a story to him and Amy and then tucked them into bed.

January seemed quiet and lonely to Britany. Crystal returned to college, Ben and Amy were in school, and Michael was once again busy with work. She felt like everyone had something special to do but her. She decided it was time to go back to work. Michael had noticed she seemed a little depressed and agreed with her when she suggested it. Since she had worked in the nursery most of her fifteen years of nursing, she decided she would start by seeing if they had an opening in the nursery.

She checked out the local hospital. They had an opening on days for a nurse to float between Pediatrics, Post Partum and Nursery. Britany took it with enthusiasm. Any other position would be nights or afternoons. She liked the idea of working in a smaller hospital, and the challenge of working all three units sounded exciting.

There was a long orientation of three weeks in each unit. Then she would be free to develop her schedule around the needs in each unit. Britany left the hospital in high spirits. She made a cake for supper to celebrate.

The first few days of her orientation was mostly in a classroom, and explained information concerning details of the hospital and how it ran. She did some competence testing and was taught on the use of the computer and the different paperwork used.

It was exciting to be back in the hospital. She had missed it more than she realized. On Thursday she worked in the nursery. The nursery was different than what she was used to. It was small and secluded. There was one window, and it opened to the hall. There were no windows to the outside. The one window was for visitors to view babies, and the shades were drawn except for two hours a day. The day went slowly, and it was hard to learn procedures with only five healthy babies who were eating well. Britany left work that day feeling a little disappointed that she didn't get to learn more.

The next day didn't go much better. She had questions about procedures and how different situations were to be handled. The problem was she didn't seem to be getting any answers.

Ben was very reserved after his return from his mother's. He also became angry easily. Britany was especially concerned when she received a phone call from his teacher requesting a conference. She set it up for Friday after work.

When the time came for the conference, Britany was nervous. She wanted Michael to come, but he had been called out Wednesday and his plane wasn't due in until Friday night.

"Hi! You must be Mrs. Kaiser. I'm Katherine Eberhard," said a pretty, young lady as Britany entered Ben's classroom.

"Yes, I am. Glad to meet you." Britany extended her hand in greeting and then took the seat offered her.

"I wanted to talk with you because I am very concerned about Ben's attitude toward school. He did well the first half of the year and got along well with the other students. Recently he seems to be having a hard time concentrating. His grades have been considerably lower on recent tests. He doesn't join in with the other boys as he used to," She finished.

"We've noticed some difficulties at home, too," Britany said, sitting on the edge of her chair, a worried frown across her forehead. "I don't know if Ben told you, but I am his stepmother. His father and I just married in August, and moved here soon afterward. There have been a lot of adjustments to make for him and all of us. I've been having problems with him at home, but was relieved that up until now things have been going well at school. He gets angry at times and flies off into fits of rage. He seems to become worse after visiting his mother. The last time he returned he was very quiet and wouldn't talk to us about what happened. I am at a loss as to what to do for him. If you have any insights, I'm interested in hearing them."

"Ben has never mentioned anything of what you just told me. I thought you were his mother. Britany, is Ben a Christian?"

Britany stared at Katherine in amazement. "I don't know!" Britany stammered. "I guess I just took for granite hat he is, but I really don't know! I talk about Jesus all the time, but he has never really said too much."

"You know there is a possibility he isn't and that would make a great deal of difference," Katherine said. She looked around the room and seemed to be thinking, then she said, "The teachers have a time to get together and pray for the students. If you don't mind I will put Ben on our list."

"I would be very grateful for the prayers of the rest of the teachers. I will reevaluate Ben's relationship with Jesus. Thank-you for the insight. I guess I am so involved in the situation I overlooked the possibility that Ben may not be a Christian."

"I'm glad to have this chance to talk to you. Maybe with what you've said it will help me understand things a little better. I will watch him a little more closely and see if there is anything I can find out or anyway I can help," the young lady spoke with concern.

"I would appreciate that. God has brought me through a lot in my life, and I know the power of prayer. Thank you for being concerned and sharing these things with me. If anything new develops please let me know," Britany finished as she got up and went to the door. She felt perplexed. She needed to find out if Ben had accepted Jesus as his personal Savior. She looked back and smiled as she closed the door.

Michael had the weekend off. The time together was good for all of them, although she didn't talk to Ben about Jesus. She prayed that God would help her find a way.

Britany felt refreshed and full of energy as she headed for work on Monday. Her enthusiasm once again dwindled to frustration. She had a lot of quiet time which she would have been grateful for in her old job, but now she was finding it quite boring and frustrating. There were a lot of things she wanted to learn, and the opportunity just didn't present itself. It worried her because in the future there would be times when she would be the only RN on the floor. She would be expected to be in charge. It scared her to be in charge without first getting more experience in more situations. There was no intensive care unit for babies in this hospital. In case a baby stopped breathing, or the heart rate stopped, they would have to stabilize it for several hours minimum. The nearest intensive care for newborns was an hour away. She had been in emergency situations before, but it was just a matter of two or three minutes before help arrived. There had always been a neonatoligist or resident in the hospital. In this hospital she would be on her own until the doctor could get there. The other nurses assured her that the doctors lived close and could be there within ten minutes. She still wanted some firsthand experience, which just didn't present itself.

Fortunately, they did admit several babies during the week, and Britany was able to familiarize herself with the procedures for admissions. She started to feel a little more comfortable.

She was glad when the orientation in the nursery was over and it was time to go to pediatrics. She had never worked in Peds before. The change was challenging and new. She found that the nurses were more open to her being there. The unit was busier, and Britany seldom found a time with nothing to do. It was great, and she loved it. The three weeks went fast. She was finding it hard to keep up at home by the end of the six weeks. It seemed like the laundry was never done and it was difficult to keep the house clean. On days when Michael was gone she let the housework go and took the kids riding or played games with them. Ben was getting more skilled at riding Trigger. Britany was thrilled to find they could ride in January and not freeze or have to worry about warming the bits before they put them in the horses' mouths.

Ben's attitude wasn't changing much. Britany had watched Ben closely and asked him several questions, from which she determined he was not a Christian. At times he started to relax and enjoy himself, but for the most part he was resentful and angry. The anger was hard for both Amy and Britany to deal with. Britany kept a close eye on Ben and Amy when they played. Ben had continued to hit Amy occasionally, and several times she had gotten hurt. Britany agonized over what to do. Ben still didn't display his anger in front of Michael, and although Britany told him about it, she didn't feel he quite understood what they were dealing with.

In early February Ben's mother called and asked to take Ben for the weekend. Britany once again referred her to Michael's office. When Michael came home he informed Britany that Ben would be going to his mother's for the weekend.

"Michael, isn't there something we can do so she can't take him? I know she is his mother but she must be doing something awful to make him act like he does," Britany pleaded.

"Britany, if we went to court they would think his behavior stemmed from our marriage not, from his mother. I had a hard time getting custody the first time. I don't want to risk it a second time," Michael sighed in defeat. What was she expecting of him, he thought. He knew she would be disappointed in him eventually. He wished he could be a good father and husband, but he couldn't. So he might as well face the fact.

"Well I'm not going to do nothing. We can pray for Gods protection while he is there," Britany said with resolve.

Michael smiled slightly, "Sure. That we can do." He wished he could do something more to ease Ben's situation and to make Britany happy, but he just didn't know what to do or where to turn. It made him feel inadequate, a feeling he didn't care for very much.

The next week went fast. There were a lot of sick children and Britany found herself learning something new every time she turned around. The head nurse praised her for learning fast and doing a good job, but Britany felt there was so much still to learn.

It was hard for Britany to concentrate on her work when Friday morning came. She could only think of Ben. By noon it started to snow. It was the first time it had snowed since she had moved to Tennessee. It snowed hard and fast. By two o'clock there was a weather advisory issued. When the next shift came in, they said the roads were getting bad, and it was even worse in Nashville. Britany drove home slowly and carefully. There were several cars in the roadside ditches, and a lot more that couldn't stop and ran into the bumpers of the ones in front of them.

The children were playing in the schoolyard when Britany pulled up. They were delighted with the snow. They were both bubbly when they got in the car. It was hard for Britany to share their excitement. She would feel much better when Michael got home safely.

When she got to the drive she decided it would be safer to park at the bottom and walk up. She was afraid to drive up the steep hill. It wasn't cold in the soft fluffy snow. She relaxed a bit as they walked, and she joined in their snowball fight. She heard a car at the end of the drive as they reached the house, and turned to look.

"Daddy!" yelled Amy.

To Britany's surprise it was Michael. He must have gotten off work early. He parked the car beside hers and opened the door to get out. He looked powerful and handsome as he emerged from the car. Her concern was replaced by a flow of love.

Ben and Amy ran toward him. Britany watched as they threw themselves on him with excited shrieks of joy. She waited as the snowball fight continued, and they made their way up to the house. Ben and Amy begged to stay outside but Britany urged them, "Come inside and get warmer clothes on first. Then you can play until supper."

She was hanging her coat on a hook in the entryway, and Michael was stomping the snow off his boots when Ben said with excitement. "Does this mean I don't have to go to my mother's tonight?"

Michael glanced at Britany with a startled look and then grinned.

"No one is going anywhere tonight. I just hope Britany has enough food in the house so we don't starve," Michael answered in a jovial tone.

"We have enough to last almost a week. I think we will do just fine. We even have hot-dogs to roast in the fire place and hot chocolate for when you come in from the snow."

"Yeah! Come on Ben, let's go get changed," Amy urged.

"OK," said Ben. He looked up at Britany. "You prayed for me didn't you?" Britany nodded. "Thanks," he said.

"Ben. Come on!" coaxed Amy.

"I'm coming!" called Ben, but before he took off he gave Britany and Michael each a firm hug and big smile.

Britany's eyes were moist as Michael said in awe, "God sure does work in mysterious ways. You're teaching me a lot about prayer, Britany."

"Yeah," she laughed weakly, "but what about the next time?"

"We will worry about that when the time comes. Right now what I'm thinking about is you and how romantic the snow and a warm fire can be," said Michael, drawing her close into a savory kiss.

The snow melted off the roads by noon the next day, and Britany was concerned that Linda might still come for Ben. Michael told her not to worry until she called. She didn't call. The snow remained on the ground long enough for the four of them to build several snow men and a large fort. Britany reluctantly left the happy group to go in and do laundry while the rest of them continued their adventures.

"Dear Lord," she prayed as she folded laundry. "Thank-you for helping Ben realize you control our lives, and please help him to find You!"

CHAPTER 22

Britany hated to leave pediatrics, but she found post partum fun and exciting. The three weeks went fast.

Britany didn't have a regular schedule following her orientation. The children were off of school for spring break. She checked with the supervisor to see if it was all right to start a regular schedule the week after spring break. Since Britany wasn't committed to any particular days as a float, she didn't have any trouble getting the time off.

Britany took Amy and Ben with her and went to Ohio for a visit. While she was there she set up an appointment with Dr. Anderson, the pediatrician who had taken care of Crystal as she was growing up. She had been wanting to talk to him about Ben. He had always been helpful in the past when she had had a problem with Crystal, and he seemed to have good insight into problems. The situation with Ben hadn't gotten any worse, but it wasn't getting any better.

Dr. Anderson welcomed her warmly and offered her a seat in his office.

"It's great to see you again! How is your new life in Tennessee?" he asked.

"For the most part it is great, but there is an area we are having difficulties in. That is why I came to see you."

"I'm disappointed. I thought you came because you missed me so much and just had to see me," he said with a twinkle in his eyes.

"Well, I do miss you. I miss all the gang back at the hospital, but unfortunately that's not why I am here."

"I was just giving you a hard time. What can I try and help you with?"

Britany explained to him Ben's behavior. She explained the visits with his mother and what Amy had told them. She also told him about how hard she was trying, but nothing seemed to be working.

"Joining two families together is hard, and you are actually putting together three. That's an awesome responsibility. How is Amy doing?" He questioned.

"She seems to be doing great. We talk often about her mother, and we are going to put flowers on her grave tomorrow. Through all his anger Ben and Amy have a special bond. They help each other," Britany said.

"Britany, I've known you a long time. I know your mothering skills, and I know your love for people," said Dr. Anderson. "I hate to tell you this, but I don't think there is any more that you can do than what you are already doing."

Britany felt a sinking feeling. If she couldn't do anything then what was supposed to help this situation?

"See, a mother gives a child unconditional love," the doctor continued. "In a healthy home children know their mother is going to love them no matter what they do. A father gives a child a sense of self-worth and self-respect. Ben has two things going against him. His mother isn't giving him that unconditional love and from what I suspect Michael isn't giving him the sense of self-worth that he needs," The doctor spoke sternly.

"Michael loves Ben very much!" Britany protested.

"Does Michael spend a lot of time with Ben?"

"As much as he can. He works six days a week and travels a lot over night. Some of his travels include week-ends." Britany explained.

"It's important for Michael to spend more time with Ben, just the two of them. If he could spend five to ten minutes a day with him, I guarantee you would see remarkable results."

"I don't think Michael quite realizes that the problem is as bad as it is. Ben doesn't throw his fits of rage when Michael is around. Besides, what do we do about Ben's mother telling him these things?" Britany asked, starting to feel very discouraged.

"If Michael would spend the time I was talking about, the things Ben's mother says wouldn't have such an effect on him. Right now he is insecure about himself. She reinforces that insecurity. You just keep loving Ben, and he will soon decide for himself that his mother is wrong in what she says about you. I have a feeling he has already come to that conclusion by himself. Britany, brighten up a little. Ben has a lot to adjust to. Just convince Michael to do what I said."

Britany left his office discouraged. How could she tell Michael what the doctor had said without making him feel guilty? How could Michael even change the situation when he was gone all the time? Michael didn't know she had made this appointment, and until she could figure out what to do he wasn't going to find out.

Britany felt tired the entire time she was at her mother's. She found herself making excuses to go to bed early, and she slept past the time she normally got up. She also took several naps each day.

"Britany you are working too hard. You have a family now. Why don't you work part time instead of full time. You are worn out," Liz said with concern near the end of her stay.

"I think the trip tired me out. I'm just having a hard time catching up I really haven't been tired although it is different working full time, cooking and cleaning. I don't have you to fall back on for the weekends," Britany said with a chuckle. "The position I am working is a float position and I can work part time easily enough. I just don't have to schedule myself for as many days. I'm not guarantied to be able to work a certain number of days anyway. It just depends on when they need the help."

"How many years have you been in nursing, and when have they not needed help? Be realistic," said Liz.

"OK mom. If it is too much I promise I will cut down on my hours."

Britany and the children traveled back that Thursday to be with Michael on the weekend. Britany had been driving around four hours when she started having trouble keeping her eyes open. "It won't hurt if I just close my eyes for a second," she thought. Suddenly she snapped alert, realizing how close she had been to falling asleep.

"Ben, I am so tired. I am going to stop at the next rest area. I need you to be the big boy that you are and watch out for Amy."

Soon a rest area sign appeared, and she stopped. She opened the car door and spread out a blanket on the grass beside the car door.

"Amy and Ben, could you two play here while I take a nap? Don't go anywhere and wake me if anyone comes too close," she said. Amy nodded her head and Ben agreed.

"Don't worry, Britany. I will watch out for her," Ben said trying to look grown up.

"Thank you. I am so tired," she said. Britany reclined the seat. She prayed for God to take care of them while she slept because she was too exhausted to do so. She woke up forty minutes later with Ben and Amy both quietly sitting on the blanket beside the car making houses with twigs they had collected.

"I feel much better now. Let's get started again, Britany said to the two of them. Ben and Amy took the event in stride as if everything were normal. Britany felt fine after the nap.

To her dismay, the tiredness continued through the weekend. Michael noticed it and urged Britany to stay in bed Sunday morning while he took the children to church.

"That sounds very inviting right now. I'll just sleep a little more and then get up and come for the morning service following Sunday school," Britany said sleepily.

"If you feel rested. Otherwise you stay in bed and sleep. We will be fine, and I will bring something home for dinner," Michael said with concern as he sat on the edge of the bed and reached over to give her a kiss.

"Thanks, Michael," Britany said warmly. She rolled over and promptly went back to sleep. She woke again at ten. She decided she would get up and shower for church. She got up and walked toward the bathroom. Suddenly stars started dancing around her. It seemed as if someone had pulled a shade down in front of her eyes, and things started to go black. She reached out for anything she could get hold of. She grasped the dresser as she was about to fall. She buckled, but was able to keep herself from falling by holding firm to the dresser. The lights started to come back, and she timidly made her way back to bed. The next time she awoke she realized the rest of the family would be back soon. She wanted to shower and get dressed. This time she sat on the edge of the bed a short time before trying to get up. She did fine, but felt a bit light headed after her shower.

She heard the car as it pulled into the drive and soon she heard happy laughter. She walked to the living room as Amy burst into the house.

"Britany! Guess what!" she shrieked excitedly.

"What honey," Britany laughed.

"Ben received Jesus in his heart today!"

Britany looked at Ben in wonder. "You did?" she asked.

"I wanted to be able to pray to Jesus like you do," said Ben in a very serious manner, but his face was full of happiness. "And when the pastor asked if anyone wanted to know Jesus I raised my hand. After the service Dad and I went into the pastor's office and we prayed. I can pray to Jesus now too, Britany, just like you do. I felt Him come into my heart when we prayed."

Britany gathered Ben in her arms and stroked his sandy colored hair. "Ben, that is so wonderful," she said softly and held him close. Silently she prayed and thanked God for the miracle.

"This calls for a celebration! I'm going to make a birthday cake for your new birth in Jesus!" Britany announced.

"But honey, you've been so tired I think you should rest," Michael coaxed.

"I'm not anymore," Britany laughed. "Come on Amy. Let's get to work on that cake!"

She gave herself extra time in the morning to get ready for work in case she felt light-headed again. She did need to sit for a while after her shower, and she used that time to do her Bible study. She didn't tell Michael for she knew he would make her stay home from work. She hated to call in sick on her first real day at work.

To her dismay when she arrived they needed her in the nursery. She had hoped to work on Peds. Her dismay didn't last long. During the week she had been gone they had received three premature infants from the neonatal hospital. The infants were basically stable but needed a lot of care. They ranged in weight from two and a half to three and a half pounds. They were adorable babies and it had been awhile since Britany had cared for a preemie. She had cared for them quite frequently back in Ohio; because she had worked occasionally in the neonatal unit when they needed help. She was thrilled and excited to get the opportunity again. Since they were so small, these babies would be staying in the hospital for a long time. There was a good chance that Britany would be spending most of her days in the nursery for the next several weeks.

Britany was standing at the isolette getting morning vitals when she suddenly felt very hot and nauseated. Sophie, a sweet older nurse that Britany was especially fond of, looked up and saw her.

"For land sakes, girl, you look as white as a sheet. You best have a seat before we have to scrape you off the floor," she said as she came over and closed the door to the isolette so Britany could sit.

Britany followed her advice and started to take a seat in a nearby rocker. Suddenly she jumped up and ran for the bathroom. She hadn't eaten much for breakfast, but what she had came back up in a very unpleasant way. She sat on the floor for a while until she felt better and then returned to work. The rest of the morning she did her work sitting on a stool or chair at every opportunity. She managed to keep working.

The busy morning passed into a quiet afternoon and she found herself sitting with Sophie at the nurses' desk.

"You're looking a mite better than you did before," Sophie acknowledged. Sophie was sitting in a chair feeding one of the preemies from a little bottle. Her feet dangled as she held the infant in a sitting position on her lap to burp it. She wore her ever present smile. Britany felt Sophie's heart must be as big as she was small because she always had a kind word for everyone and was genuinely concerned about them.

"I feel a lot better too. Thanks a lot for helping out. I guess I might be trying to come down with the flue or something. I haven't been sick until this morning but I've been extremely tired. I hate to miss work when I just got started."

Sophie laughed and Britany looked at her perplexed.

"Britany, how long have you been working with mothers and babies? I can tell you, I've been working with them for twenty-five years, and the only flu you have is the three-month kind. I can spot that look you had this morning in a minute."

Britany sat in her seat stunned. She had never thought about the possibility that she might be pregnant.

"Don't tell me there is no way. You're married. Those things happen. I'll bet you're two weeks late with your period," Sophie continued with motherly wisdom.

"You're right, I am. I thought it was just stress," Britany admitted.

"You go down to the lab. We are caught up for now. They can do a pregnancy test, and we will know officially before you go home," Sophie urged.

"They will do that?" Britany asked hesitantly.

"Sure. It's one of our privileges as employees. They will be excited for you. Everyone loves it when an employee is expecting. You go on now. Quit sitting there, and get going."

Britany followed her instructions and soon returned to the floor.

"They said to call in an hour for the results. I feel kind of weak and shaky. This isn't something I had thought of. I don't know if I hope you're right or not. I want a baby very badly, but I didn't really plan on one yet. The timing isn't right. There are so many things going on right now. I don't know if our family can handle more changes," Britany confessed. She was glad to have Sophie there to confide in.

"Babies have their own timing, and it's never when we plan for them. They always seem to find a way of fitting in though. The family will do just fine. Those young'uns of yours will be tickled pink to have a new baby. That little girl will mother it to death. The baby won't be lacking for attention, that's for sure," Sophie spoke with her cultured southern accent, endearing herself to Britany as she did so.

Britany could think of nothing else for the next hour. She busied herself with little tasks, but her heart was thinking about the lab result. She wasn't even sure what she wanted it to be! Somehow, as Sophie had spoken, she had begun to contemplate the idea and began to realize that Sophie was right. She did have a lot of the same physical feelings that she had had when she had been pregnant with Crystal. She was surprised she hadn't noticed them before. All the symptoms were there.

The hour passed, and she called the lab. They confirmed the fact that she was indeed expecting.

"Of course, now you know the whole hospital will be busting with the news. You had better not waste time in telling that husband of yours, or he will find out from someone else."

"No, I guess not," laughed Britany. "Thanks for being so excited for me. You are wonderful," said Britany, giving Sophie a big hug.

Sophie was quick to let the rest of the staff in on the news, and suddenly Britany was the center of attention.

"How are you going to tell Michael?" they asked.

"I have no idea. I'm open for suggestions!" she said. They all laughed.

Before she left work that evening Britany felt a new appreciation for the ladies she worked with.

Britany felt enthusiastic as she left work but as the evening wore on some of the enthusiasm died a bit. Cooking supper made her dreadfully ill, and when she finally got it to the table she had to go to bed before she could eat any of it.

Michael came home early, and she heard him enter the house.

"Something sure smells good," she heard him say as he entered the kitchen. She could hear his conversation with the children, but felt too sick to get up.

"Where is Britany? It doesn't look like she's eaten yet," he asked Ben and Amy.

"She didn't feel good again and is in bed," explained Amy. She sounded worried.

Britany heard his footsteps approach the room and she sat up just enough to elevate her head to see him better without getting too ill.

"Britany, I knew you shouldn't have gone to work today. I want you to stay home tomorrow until you get over this flu bug and get your strength back," Michael said as he entered the room, and sat beside her on the bed looking very worried.

"Michael, I appreciate your concern but, this flu bug isn't going to go away for another two months if it's like before, and it's not exactly the flu." Britany wasn't at all sure how she had wanted to tell Michael or how he would respond, but given the way she felt she thought she should be straightforward and let him know so he would stop worrying. "I got sick at work today, and one of the nurses convinced me to get a pregnancy test. It was positive. We are going to have a baby!"

"Oh, Britany! That's wonderful!" said Michael, his face lit up with excitement. "I was worried that the stress was too much for you, and I shouldn't have brought you down here to a whole new way of life. Here, instead of something bad, it's wonderful! I hate to see you feel so bad, but I'm glad you're all right."

"I wasn't sure how you would react to the news of another child. We really hadn't talked about it. It seems kind of soon in our marriage," Britany said hesitantly, giving him an opening to voice any misgivings he might have.

"You are right, we hadn't talked about it. But I love you so much, and this baby is a continuation of that love. How could that possibly be bad or ill-timed?" Michael said softly, gently taking her into his arms.

"Michael thanks," said Britany.

"For what?" he questioned.

"For being happy and excited," she said with a sigh.

"Thank you," he responded.

"Why?"

"For having my baby. Do you think we can call the kids in and tell them?" Michael said with excitement.

"Now?"

"Sure, why not. They need to know why you are feeling bad too. Amy might start to think you are really sick like her mother was."

Britany could only smile up at him and nod her head in approval. Her feelings were too overwhelming.

Michael left and soon returned with Amy and Ben. Amy's face was ashen.

"Oh, Amy, come here," pleaded Britany. She cradled Amy in her arms.

"Britany, please get better!" Amy cried.

Britany looked at Michael with tears in her eyes. Michael bent down and lifted Amy's chin with his finger. "Amy, Britany is feeling sick, but it's good, not bad."

Amy looked at him with a puzzled look.

"What do you mean Dad?" asked Ben.

Michael looked at both of them with a big smile and said, "We are going to have a new baby. You are going to get a new brother or sister.

"A baby!" marveled Ben with his eyes large. "But you are too skinny. He said looking at Britany's stomach.

"The baby is tiny right now Ben, but believe me it will get bigger as it grows," laughed Britany and dabbed at her eyes.

"Britany," Amy said looking up at Britany. "You mean the baby is making you sick, and you are not going to die?"

"Yes, Amy," Britany explained. "The baby is making me sick, but so did Crystal. It's worth being sick to have a baby. You even made your Mom sick at times but she loved you very much." Britany stroked Amy's soft curls.

Amy's face suddenly changed to one of excitement and she asked, "Can I feed the baby when it gets here?"

Michael smiled, "Sure. We can all help take care of it! That means changing diapers too."

"Yuk!" exclaimed Ben turning up his nose. Then he became excited also and yelled. "It's got to be a boy! I want a brother. I have two sisters and I want a brother."

"I want a brother too!" exclaimed Amy.

The both started jumping up and down on the bed and giggling.

Britany felt herself getting very sick. Michael came to her rescue, and grabbed both Amy and Ben around the waist.

"Come on kids," he said. "Let's go eat supper and let Britany rest."

In the following weeks work was difficult for Britany. Several times she felt the world go dark and realized she was about to pass out. Each time she was able to sit until the sensation passed. Work was hard, but she enjoyed it. Holding the tiny newborns helped Britany appreciate the life growing inside her. She began to appreciate the slower pace the nursery offered.

She found she was getting worn down. On many days, by the time she got home from work she had no energy left. She went to bed as soon as Amy was asleep. Some nights when Michael wasn't there it meant Ben was responsible to get himself to bed. She felt she was cheating the children of some much-needed attention. She worked the scheduled days of five days a week for the two weeks already posted and then she put herself down for two to three days a week.

Spring was in the air, and on the morning of her day off Britany took a long walk. The fresh air was invigorating, and the walk provided quiet time for her to think and sort things out. Most of the time her thoughts were jumbled up and busy. It was hard to sort through and make order of them. The day was warm, so much so that she didn't need a jacket. The sun was shining, and the warmth it created on her back felt good. Green leaves were trying to burst forth from the swollen buds, and many trees were in blossom. She breathed deeply of the spring air and walked briskly, her arms swinging in rhythm with her step.

Ben was still her major area of concern. Katherine, his teacher was worried because, although his grades were good but she felt he was doing just enough work to get by. His teacher felt he could do much better if he would apply himself a little. His behavior at home hadn't worsened but neither had it improved. The difference was that Britany felt ill most of the time and her tolerance level was much lower.

Now as she walked, she felt anger and frustration. She was thankful to God for the new life growing inside her, and she loved the baby; but at the present this pregnancy seemed to complicate things. She knew she was more irritable than normal, and found herself upset at things that probably wouldn't have bothered her at another time. She was angry with Michael although she was not about to tell him. Britany hadn't talked to Michael about the pediatrician's advice. She felt resentful that Michael couldn't see for himself that he was needed at home more. Ben was his son! Unconsciously she clenched her fist and walked faster. It seemed to her that Michael could be a little more attentive without having to be told. Besides, she wasn't sure how she fit into the picture. She had been reading her Bible in Ephesians on how a wife should act. The Scriptures clearly stated that she should be submissive. It didn't seem very submissive to be telling Michael he should be spending more time with his family. She wished his job was a little less demanding.

The sun was shining and birds were singing, but tears glistened on Britany's face as she walked. Why was life so complicated? Why weren't things as wonderful as she had wanted? Why did she have to have morning sickness that lasted all day? It would be so much easier being pregnant without feeling sick all the time! She walked some more and prayed as she went. She was frustrated and confused but she hadn't given up on God. She remembered the darkness following Jeanne's death and the despair she had felt when she turned away from God. She knew God was working in her life. She just wasn't quite sure what she should do. She turned the corner and headed back to the house. A quiet peace began to surface through the midst of her despair. She felt God's warm touch. He was there, watching and caring, whether she knew what to do or not. She got back to the house and dropped onto the couch, were she slept.

By the end of May the nausea started to subside, and Britany was relieved. She felt good and had more energy. Her abdomen was growing fast, and she had to find some clothes to wear.

School would soon end for the summer, and Britany was looking forward to having the children home. She attended the last Bible study for the season one Tuesday morning. Jewell led the study which had nothing to do with husband and wife relationships, but Britany's thoughts were on that subject. She hadn't told the group the problem with Ben but she could think of nothing else.

During discussion time she opened up and talked. She had been careful in the past not to say anything because she didn't want anyone to think badly of

Michael, but the Holy Spirit was speaking to her, and it was hard to keep quiet. She shared with them Ben's behavior, the pediatrician's suggestion, and her reluctance to share it with Michael. She sensed care and concern coming from the other members as she spoke.

Discussion went back and forth in the group. Some shared that they had similar concerns, while others knew someone who had been in there, too, and had advice to offer. After a few minutes Jewell began to speak.

"Britany, I'm getting the message that there are several different things going on." She slipped her reading glasses on and thumbed through her Bible. "Let's look at the scripture you referenced about being submissive Ephesians 5:22. It does speak clearly about being submissive to our husbands, but it gives the husbands a command also--to love, feed, and care for their wives. It is hard for husbands to be caring if they have no idea of what we need." Her voice carried across the room, and Britany listened intently. "I would like to take you all back to Genesis 2:18. God speaks of man being alone, and that He will make a helpmate for him. He made woman and then saw that it was good, and together they were complete." She paused and looked up at Britany. "I think there may be a little resentment on your part that Michael can't see what is going on by himself. After all, Ben is his son."

"That's for sure," said Britany. "I want to talk to him about it, but then I get defensive and think: 'Why can't he see that on his own? or 'Why isn't he as concerned about the situation as I am?' I also feel hurt that he isn't home more. I know his job is strenuous and demanding but sometimes I would like him to think we are more important than his job and take some time off to be with us," Britany said sadly.

"Those feelings are perfectly normal, and I don't know a one of us who hasn't experienced them in one form or other," she replied. A few "yesses" and "that's for sure" could be heard around the room.

"The problem is, Satan likes to get in and make us feel sorry for ourselves instead of seeing the problem from the right perspective and doing something about it. Let's go back to Genesis. God made us to be a helpmate. Men sometimes have a hard time seeing things that we find easy to pick up on. We are different than they are, and oftentimes we perceive a situation in a different way. When that happens, I feel we have a responsibility as a helpmate to share our insights. That is not being nonsubmissive when it is done lovingly and with God's guidance. We do have to remember, though, that just because we share our insights doesn't mean they have to do anything about it. I have found from past experience that it takes a while for my insights to sink into my husbands' thinking. Sometimes about six months. That's where prayer comes in. We have the responsibility to share with them, but they need to be in close communion with God to do the right thing with the information. It is impossible for a husband to be the man God asks him to be when he is out of communion with God. We need to be constant prayer warriors supporting our husbands in prayer." She paused and reached over for Britany's hand. "Britany, I want us as a group to pray for you as you share with Michael. I also want to warn you, things probably won't change overnight. We are going on God's timetable, not our own. It will take time for Michael to see for himself what is going on and the need present."

The group of ladies held hands in a circle and prayed for Britany. She was touched by their simple heart-filled prayers as they lifted their voices to God. She could feel the warmth of the Holy Spirit present as they prayed.

"Thank you so much," Britany said. "You have been very kind."

"Just remember," Jewell said. "God's in control no matter what the circumstances look like."

Britany left feeling refreshed and happy.

Ben started practice with his Little League team and was thrilled when it was finally time for his first game. Michael was working, but Britany and Amy were an avid cheering section. Ben played left field. It was near the end of the game before he got his first ball hit to him. It was coming hard on the ground and bouncing at precarious spots. Ben ran up to it just as it bounced. The ball went flying over his head, and he had to turn and run after it. He got the ball and threw it to second base. The throw was wild and went high above the second baseman's head. Britany could tell Ben was mad at himself, and her heart went out to him. His hitting didn't go well either. He hit one ball into the outfield but was thrown out on first base. He struck out two other times. Their team lost, and Ben was a very defeated team member as they came off the field.

Britany and Amy tried unsuccessfully to cheer him up on the way home. When they got home, Britany succeeded in talking him into letting her and Amy help him practice. She pitched the ball to him, and Amy ran after it when he hit it. Then she hit some balls to him to give him practice in fielding. He was appreciative and in a much better mood the next day. Michael was home on Sunday and Britany encouraged him to help with Ben's practice. The practice with Ben, Amy and Britany turned into a daily routine, and Britany could see and improvement in his playing. Most of all there was a great improvement in his attitude toward her and Amy. In the next game he caught a fly ball and got the man out. Britany and Amy yelled excitedly from the sidelines. After the game he was thrilled and couldn't wait to tell his father.

Several weeks passed, and Britany still hadn't told Michael anything. She knew it was time, and one night, after the two children had gone to bed, she sat down beside him to talk. She looked at him hesitantly and began.

"Michael, I went to see Dr. Anderson, Crystal's pediatrician, when we went to visit my mother. He was always helpful whenever I had a problem with Crystal as she was growing up. I was concerned about Ben and his behavior and I was interested in any advice he could give me to help Ben's situation. He was quite receptive, and I think he had some good insight," Britany began.

Michael's eyes darkened. He felt irritated with Britany. She should have talked to him before discussing their problems with someone else. He asked "Did he think we should try to keep Linda from seeing him?"

"No, actually he suggested something quite different." Britany saw the look in Michael's eyes, but decided if she was ever going to talk to him about Ben she should continue. She gestured widely with her hands as if trying to help Michael comprehend. "He explained that children get their self respect and a high self esteem from their fathers, and the way they interact. He suggested you make a conscience effort to spend time with Ben one on one, even if it is only five minutes a day. He said Ben will see that he is important enough that you would want to spend time with him. He feels as Ben's self concept improves so will his attitude. He stated Ben's anger is partly from the fact that he doesn't feel worthwhile and really doesn't like himself right now. What Linda says reinforces that. He felt if Ben could see that you really do care that what Ben's mother says won't have as much effect. He said he suspects that Ben doesn't really believe what she says anyway but is searching for a reason not to believe her."

"Britany how could you do that! How could you tell our problem's to someone I don't even know!" Michael jumped up and paced across the room.

"Michael, I'm sorry," Britany stammered. "I didn't think you would mind."

"You're just like Linda! You blame me on our problems and expect more than I am able to give!" he yelled, running his hand through his hair. "I work hours and I'm tired when I get home. Then you want me to spend time with you and the kids, and make me feel guilty when I don't." He continued to pace.

"Michael!" Britany said sternly as she stood to her feet. "Get a grip! I am not Linda and don't ever compare me to her again!" Britany exclaimed with her fists clenched at her side. "Take your frustrations out on her, not me. I just asked you to spend a little time with your son. I didn't ask you for the world. Just five minutes of it. Is that such a horrible thing?"

Michael blew out through pierced lips and walked to look out across the deck. He stood there for several minutes and Britany waited for him to answer.

"I guess I will try, but I don't see what it will help," he said with an edge of resentment in his voice.

"Thank you Michael. I'm tired and I am going to bed now," Britany said and stood quietly. He continued to look out the window then turned toward her. He stared at her in bewilderment and then turned back toward the window. "I'll be in shortly," he said. Britany turned and left the room. Michael couldn't shake the feeling that Britany was blaming him for Ben's problems. Maybe it was because he was blaming himself. He knew he wasn't being the father or husband, that he should be, but he just didn't know how to do any better. He heard a quiet voice inside speak to him. Michael, stop trying so hard and let me help. He ignored it.

Britany knelt beside the bed as soon as she entered the bedroom. "Dear Lord help Michael sort through this," she pleaded. She fought the urge to be angry toward him and tried to sympathize with him. "I know he was hurt deeply in the past, and it must be hard for him to put it behind him, but please help him. Help him to see that Ben needs him and he needs You. He can't do it on his own and yet he won't give up trying. Help me to be the wife I need to be." She finished her prayer with anguish. She fought hard against the resentment that wanted to flood over her. She had not wanted to speak to Michael about Ben, but Mrs. Shepler had encouraged her to along with the entire Bible study group. She had also felt strongly that God had wanted her to say those things to Michael. She had prayed and had done what she felt God wanted her to do. The results seemed ominous at best, but she had to hang on to the faith that God was in control and in His time he would work it out.

Michael avoided the subject the next several days but he did make an effort to take time with Ben. Ben was thrilled with the attention.

"Why can't I go out and play with Dad?" Amy complained.

Britany explained, "I'm sorry, honey. They need some guy time together. Could you be a big girl and help me make biscuits? We will have some girl time."

"Sure," said Amy and ran into the kitchen.

Britany was amazed at the improvement she saw in Ben's behavior. He seemed happier and threw less temper tantrums. His attitude improved, and he helped out when asked without as much protest. He was nicer to Amy and appeared to like himself more. Britany was delighted at the change. Now that the children were home with her for the summer she was especially grateful for the improvement.

Life was good, and Britany thanked God for His grace. Little did she know of the tempest ahead.

CHAPTER 23

Britany looked into Amy's brown eyes. She hated leaving her.

"If anything goes wrong please call me," Britany said. "If your Grandmother doesn't bring you back in one week, I will personally come and get you," she promised.

"I will be fine Britany. Remember last time?" Amy said with a twinkle in her eye.

"Yes I remember," Britany laughed. She took Amy in her arms and held her tight.

"You take care of my little sister!" said Amy reaching out to pat Britany's stomach that was starting to protrude.

"I will. I promise! But I thought you wanted a brother."

"Oh that was last week. Now it's a sister!"

A stewardess approached and said, "You must be Amy. I am going to take care of you while you fly with us. Would you like to come with me and see the captain?"

"Yea, that would be fun," said Amy and followed happily. When they reached the door, Amy turned and waved to Britany, then she disappeared into the plane.

Britany was in anguish about Amy spending the week with her grandmother but that was the agreement that had been made at the last hearing. Britany had retained temporary custody but Britany was afraid Monique would try again to take Amy. Why was it the planes were always taking the ones she loved away from her? Fortunately they had always brought them back.

Ben was at his mothers for two weeks. The first few days without Ben and Amy went smoothly and Britany was able to wallpaper the baby's room. After several days she started to feel lonely. Michael worked long hours and seemed distracted. He even went to the office on Sunday.

On Wednesday, Michael came home from work late and stated he had already eaten. Britany sighed and cleaned up the meal she had prepared.

"I am going on a business trip to Seattle. It looks like a big account and has a lot of possibility," Michael said as he settled on the couch to read the paper.

"Seattle is a long way away," Britany said hesitantly. "Is it for several days?"

"I'm sure it will last through the week-end, and possibly into next week," Michael said shuffling through the paper.

Britany looked at him and suddenly felt very sad. The children were gone. Her family was hundreds of miles away, and now Michael was going on a trip.

"I was kind of hoping we would have some time alone together while the kids are gone," Britany said, as she sat down beside him on the couch.

"Well, the trip can't wait," said Michael. He knew she would be upset about the idea of him leaving, but he wasn't too happy with her. She had blamed Ben's problems on him, and she constantly wanted him to spend more time at home. He felt as if she was trying to control his life.

"Maybe I could go with you," Britany suggested and caressed his hair.

"No, Britany!" he said sternly. Britany drew back and looked at his stormy eyes.

"Michael! What is wrong?" she asked.

"Just leave me alone," he said, and jerked the newspaper closed. "First, you want me to give up my job and spend more time at home. Then you blame Ben's problems on me. Britany, I have been alone for seven years, and I don't want to be strapped down. Don't I do enough by working hard and giving you a home and providing for you?" He stood and looked down at her angrily.

Britany felt sick in the pit of her stomach. What was happening?

"I like my job, and I like to travel. You seemed to think my job was just fine when we first met!" he yelled.

"I do like your job. I love you Michael. I just want to be with you," said Britany. She reached out toward him. His eyes glared, and his fists were clenched. She drew her hand back. It was the first time she had ever been afraid of him, but he was very angry.

"I'm sorry," Britany mumbled looking down into her lap. "I'll not ask you to stay home again. Enjoy your trip. I'll see you next week," Britany got up and went to the barn to feed the horses.

She was shaking when she got there. She didn't know what had happened but she wasn't going to give Michael the satisfaction of seeing her cry. She took a deep breath and threw some hay over the fence. She had been self reliant and independent before in her life and she could do it again. If Michael felt closed in then she would give him some room. When she went back into the house he was already in bed. She could tell he had packed his clothes for the next day. She prepared for bed and crawled under the covers being especially careful to stay on her side.

Britany awoke during the night. She could hear Michael's steady breathing. She got up and went to the window. She looked out at the shinning stars. There was peace in the heavens in the midst of the turmoil. She dropped to her knees and prayed silently, "Dear Lord, This is not like Michael at all. Something is troubling him deeply and I have a feeling it is Satan. Hold him tight for me as he is going through this. I don't understand it or what to do to help, but You do and You can guide him through. In Jesus name, Amen." She finished and crawled back into bed. She didn't feel as angry and she softly curled beside him being careful not to wake him.

The alarm went off early. Michael turned it off and went to shower. Britany went downstairs and prepared breakfast. Michael thought about the night before. He was very angry and he didn't know why. He needed to get away for a while. He was feeling trapped by too much responsibility of being a husband and father. He didn't like the demands Britany was making on him, and now he was facing the responsibility of a new child. He had made a mess of Ben's life and he was scared to try again. Seattle was a safe place to go. He didn't tell

Britany he had purposely planned the trip.

He went downstairs and grabbed some toast, but didn't touch the rest of the breakfast she had prepared. "I don't have much time and they will serve breakfast on the plane," he said in explanation. He knew he should apologize for the night before, but he didn't want to humiliate himself, so he hurried to go. "I'll see you next week." He gave her a quick hug. She embraced him lovingly and he almost gave in to her warmth. Instead he stiffened and pulled back. "Why don't you go visit your mother for a couple of days?"

"I might do that," Britany said and braced herself enough to give him a big smile. The last thing she wanted to do was to make him feel more tied down, and with every ounce she had, she was not going to break down until he was gone.

"Good Bye, I'll call you when I get there. I called Linda and told her I was going to Seattle in case something happens to Ben. We'll take care of him. There is no reason you have to stay here by yourself."

Britany cringed with his parting words. It was as if he was saying he wanted her to get out of his life in Tennessee, and that included Ben's life too.

Michael drove to the airport and felt a touch of triumph. He had done it. He had broken away, and even though he wasn't exactly leaving Britany, temporarily he was putting her out of his life. For one week he could be himself without the pressures of being a husband to Britany, or father to Amy and Ben. When his plane arrived at the airport he heard his name called.

"Michael,"

He turned and smiled at the gorgeous blonde lady waving to him from the aisle. "Victoria!" he called and waved back.

"I saw your name on the conference list and got your flight number," Victoria said as she came closer. "I wanted you to feel welcome back in Seattle. Do you have time to take an old friend to lunch?" she asked in a seductive voice. She wore a silk blouse and tight cream skirt that revealed long slender legs.

"Vicki, it's nice to see you, but I think I need to tell you that I'm married now!"

"Oh, what a pity," she said coyly. "You can still take an old friend to lunch can't you?"

Britany dropped to a chair as soon as she heard the noise of the car disappear in the distance. She didn't know what was happening. She felt numb. She gently put her hand over her abdomen where the baby was and said, "Oh little one, what have I done? What is going on? What is going through Michael's mind that is making him act this way? I guess we may as well pack and go to Ohio. There is no one keeping us here now." Britany slowly got to her feet and went to get dressed. She packed her things and fed the horses. She thought about staying just in case Michael changed his mind, and came back, but from the way he left it seemed pretty final. She called her mother and told her she was coming. She didn't tell her about Michael leaving. She decided she should call Linda and talk to Ben before she left. She wanted to remain involved in Ben's life. She loved him as her own, and she was concerned about him being with his mother for two weeks.

She was glad when Ben answered the telephone. "Hi, Ben, this is Britany."

"Hi Britany!" he said with enthusiasm. Britany's heart was thrilled to hear his voice that sounded excited to hear her.

"I wanted to call and see how you are doing. Is everything all right?"

"It's ok. I miss Trigger though, and I would lots rather be home," he said in a dismal voice.

"Ben, don't let you're mother hear you say that!" Britany said.

"Oh, she's with the baby. Is Dad ok?" Ben asked.

Britany's heart sank and she struggled to speak, "He went to Seattle for a few days."

"Yea, I know. My mom told me. Britany, Mom is right here now and wants to talk to you."

Britany didn't want to talk to her but she found herself listening. She could hear Linda through the phone telling Ben to go outside and play.

"Britany, I know we don't get along very well, but I wanted to warn you. Michael has a friend who he visits when he goes to Seattle. A very young, beautiful, attractive friend, get the picture?" Linda said.

"Linda, I trust Michael. He can take care of himself. Why are you telling me this anyway?" Britany was getting angry.

"I know there is no lost friendship between us Britany, but I despise that Victoria and I wanted to warn you about her."

"Did she come between you and Michael?" Britany asked suddenly curious about Michael's past.

"No, for all the things that I didn't like about Michael, the one thing to his credit was that he was loyal. At least to my knowledge." Linda said.

"Then why do you think I should worry now?" asked Britany.

"Because you haven't met Victoria. I'm sorry Britany I guess I shouldn't have said anything. Just keep you're eyes open for anything suspicious. If it were me, I would make a surprise visit to check things out in person."

"Thanks for your concern, Linda, but our marriage isn't worth a lot if I can't trust Michael. I called to tell Ben I'm going to my mother's for a couple of days. Please watch out for him. I will call when I get back Good-bye," said Britany.

"I'm glad you trust him, but I will keep my eyes sharp for you. Good-bye," Linda said.

Britany was shaking when she finished the phone call. She quickly dialed Shelly's phone number.

"Hello, Britany! It's great to hear from you," said Shelly in a sweet voice.

"Hi Shelly, I'm coming up for a visit and was wondering if you are going to be home this afternoon. I thought I would drop by on the way to my mother's."

"Sure, I'll be home. I'd love to see you!"

Britany was tired when she pulled into Shelly's drive. Shelly ran out to greet her.

"My stars girl, what is the matter? Where is that happy glow of the newly wed?"

Britany looked up at her and the tears started to flow.

"Come on inside, and tell me all about it," said Shelly soothingly putting her arm around her shoulder, and leading her into the house.

Shelly looked at Britany in disbelief as Britany explained what had happened.

"Oh, Britany," said Shelly and held her tight as Britany cried.

Britany leaned back on the couch and said as she dried her eyes. "I'm not even sure that he is coming back. He made everything seem so final," she sighed and took a deep breath. "I may be raising this baby on my own too."

"Britany, don't think that way! You and Michael will work through this. I'm sure Michael is feeling like a jerk right now and he has probably already called your mother to apologize to you," Shelly said and patted Britany's hand. "Hey, by the way that baby is really growing," added Shelly with a chuckle.

Britany smiled, "You are a wonderful friend, Shelly. I didn't realize how much I've missed you."

When Britany was rested, and had composed herself, she drove to her parent's house. It was still light outside when she pulled into the driveway and she was disappointed to find her mom and dad were in the field making hay. She knew that if Michael had tried to call no one would have been in the house to answer. She dialed her own number to retrieve messages from the answering machine. There were no messages. Her heart sank and she walked to the kitchen to get a glass of ice water. She sank into a chair momentarily and then went to the field to greet her parents. She smiled bravely. It was nice to see them again. She went back into the house and started supper. Her mother soon joined her in the kitchen.

"It's great to see you Britany. You are looking tired. I hope you are taking good care of that grandchild of mine," Liz said as she entered the kitchen.

"If you mean the baby, she or he is doing just fine. I'm not so sure about the other two. It worries me having them gone," Britany said with a slight wrinkle showing faintly across her forehead.

"Honey, they will be fine. You call them and let them know you are here in case they need you for anything."

"Thanks mom, but I already called as soon as I knew I was coming. By the way, where is Crystal?" Britany asked.

"She will be here shortly. She is working today. She normally works evenings, but was able to get someone to trade with her so she could see you when you got here," Liz explained.

A little while later Britany heard a car enter the drive and she hurried outside to greet Crystal.

"Mom, you are growing!" shouted Crystal as she got out of the car.

"I'm afraid I have a lot farther to grow!" said Britany as she approached the car and gave Crystal a hug.

"Man it sure is different seeing my mom pregnant. It's just not something you think about when you are eighteen. After being an only child for such a long time, and then to get a sister and brother and new baby in a little over a year is quiet a lot. How are my little brother and sister doing? I wish they could have come with you."

"They are doing just fine I hope. At least they were doing just fine until this week. Amy will get back on Monday, and Ben has another week to stay. I worry about them," said Britany.

"I'm sure they are doing just fine. Amy is pretty adept at looking out for herself and I would be really surprised if Ben's mother keeps him the entire time," Crystal said.

"Oh Crystal, you always know how to cheer me up. I miss you so much," Britany said.

"I talked to my boss and the restaurant I work at has a chain near you. I could possibly transfer. Then I could spend the summer with you in Tennessee."

"Oh Crystal that would be wonderful!" Britany said excitedly. She wondered with dread what Michael would say to having another person around. It didn't matter. Crystal was her daughter; she had as much right as anyone to live in their household.

"What about all your friends that are here?" asked Britany. "You won't know anyone your age in Tennessee."

"I have a whole new family I hardly know. I would kind of like to spend some time with them. Besides, give me a little credit. I make friends fast. I already know some of the teens from youth group and they seem like a nice bunch of kids to hang around with. There are some cute guys too."

"I love you," said Britany wrapping her arms around Crystal.

"That baby sure does pop right out there. Are you sure you are only four months along?" asked Crystal looking at Britany's abdomen.

"It's almost five. I got big pretty fast with you too. Its just the way I carry them, all out front." Britany took Crystal's arm and walked her to the house where supper was waiting.

Michael went to lunch with Victoria, where she sat across from him and kept a constant stream of conversation going. She was beautiful, and he used to be very attracted to her, but now he saw her as boring and shallow. Suddenly her lovely face seemed worn, and lost, in a world were beauty was skin deep, and anything was done to keep it. Britany was beautiful too, but her beauty would last forever. Britany's face kept picturing itself on Michael's mind. The hurt she showed the night before tore at his conscience. What was he doing here? He wondered. Victoria didn't care anything for him, and he knew it as he watched her. She wanted whatever the world had to give, and she would use Michael to her advantage. Michael had known that before, and he knew it now. He asked the waiter for the check and excused himself before the meal was over. Victoria gave him an angry glare as he turned to leave. He made his way to the conference room and waited for the meetings to begin.

Britany visited the hospital where she had worked on the next day of her visit. The building itself seemed to welcome her as she stepped into the old familiar hospital. A flood of memories rushed in as she entered the nursery. She could almost here Jeanne's voice call across the room. She heard a voice, but it wasn't Jeanne's.

"Britany, it's great to see you!" called Shawn, as soon as Britany entered the door. "How's married life?"

Britany wasn't sure how to answer her. "It's been an adjustment, but we are already multiplying to help replenish the earth!"

"I see that," she laughed.

Betsy rushed up to give Britany a hug and Margaret walked up to welcome her. Britany told them about Tennessee and her new job. She felt herself relax in the company of friends. They visited as much as possible around the work that needed done. Britany was getting ready to leave when she turned around to see David.

"David!" Britany exclaimed in surprise. "I didn't expect to get to see you. I'm so glad you are still here."

David wore a big smile, and his dark eyes were filled with warmth. He gave her a gentle embrace and then took a step back and looked at her.

"Pregnancy becomes you Britany. You make a splendid picture of motherhood," he said.

Britany laughed, "Thanks, I think. How have you been?"

Shawn and Margaret were busy with some orders and the rest of the nurses where working frantically to catch up on morning tasks. Britany realized they were alone in the midst of the busy nursery.

"Do you have time for coffee?" David asked.

"I do, but do you?" In a natural gesture Britany rested her hand on her stomach, where the baby lay below. "You're usually back at the office by now."

He escorted her toward the door as he said with a smile, "I don't have to be there until noon today. I really have been wanting to talk to you. It was perfect timing that you stopped by."

The hallway was quiet compared to the noise of the hectic nursery.

"Are you being good to yourself and the baby and getting enough exercise that you can walk the stairs?"

"Sure," she answered.

"You know Britany, I'm a pediatrician, not an obstetrician, but you look as though you really should get some more rest," he commented as the descended the stairs.

Britany moaned inwardly and was glad he couldn't see her face as they walked. She didn't want to tell him that Michael was upset and things were not going well.

"It was a long drive and I'm still tired," she said as an excuse.

They went to the cafeteria and Britany got some juice. They found a table and Britany let David lead the conversation. She was quite curious as to what he had to say.

"Britany," said David as he sat back in his chair. "I wanted to tell you in person. Do you remember that night in your apartment when I got very angry about Jesus?" he asked and leaned forward.

"Yes, I remember," Britany said hesitantly. How could she forget? She thought.

"Jesus is important to me now too. I was miserable after we broke up and I just couldn't seem to get over it," he looked down into his coffee.

"David, I'm sorry," Britany said softly and reached out to cover his hand with hers.

"No, don't be sorry. There was something missing from my life. I had known it for a long time, but when I was near you I felt a presence that left when we broke up. I didn't know it then, but I realize now that what I felt was Jesus," he said with confidence. Britany looked at him in puzzlement and the crease appeared in her forehead.

"It took awhile, but I finally stopped fighting God's call and gave in. I found Jesus and now I feel as strongly about Him as you did that night you turned me down. I wouldn't give Him up for anything in the world," he said. His face beamed with delight.

Britany clasped his hand tightly, "Oh David, That's wonderful. I never would have dreamt that's what you wanted to tell me."

"I also wanted to say I'm sorry for the way I reacted when you spoke of Jesus. Now that I'm a Christian, I realize how you felt. I was blind then," he said with emotion. "I've read the scriptures for years. Now they are so alive it's like reading them for the first time. I just can't get enough."

Britany smiled in wonder, but her smile faltered a little.

David chuckled, "I'm sitting her telling you about my miraculous conversion, and you're sitting there thinking about your fight with Michael."

"How could Shelly tell you that!" Britany exclaimed.

David patted her shoulder. "Calm down Britany. Shelly didn't tell me anything. It's written on your face."

"Oh," Britany said meekly.

"He'll come back Britany," David said softly.

"But you don't know that! I don't know that!" Britany said sadly.

"I do know because if he doesn't I'll tell him to get his stupid head on straight, and look at what he has, a wonderful wife, two healthy growing children with one on the way. I'd trade him in a heartbeat. He'll come back." This time he reached out and squeezed her hand. "Just believe me," he said with reassuringly.

"Thanks," Britany said and gave him a smile.

Britany thought about David as she drove back to the farm. She couldn't believe the change he'd experienced. It truly was a miracle. She thought about Michael. He knew Jesus, but he hadn't totally subjected his life to Him yet. He still tried to live his life by his own power. Britany sighed. Did she make a mistake? She thought with panic. She suddenly felt very stupid. Of coarse she didn't make a mistake. She thought with confidence. God had reaffirmed her decision many times and she wasn't about to waver now. "Thank You Jesus for being with me and guiding me. Continue to hold tight to Michael and help him through this time," she prayed as she drove along.

Her parents were still in the field when she arrived at the farm, so she went to the kitchen to prepare supper for the evening.

Michael lay awake in his room It was four o'clock in the morning, but he hadn't been able to sleep. He turned over and reached for the light. The Bible on the nightstand caught his eye. He remembered back to the night in the other motel room when he recommitted his life to Christ.

"Boy, I sure am making a mess of things. Lord, how could I be so stupid?" He prayed. "I'm sorry for being so mean and selfish. I was so afraid that I would fail again that I made it happen. Britany never demands things of me like Linda did. It was just me thinking that she was, so I could blame her for my problems instead of facing them myself." Michael dropped to his knees beside the bed and continued his prayer, "Lord, please forgive me. I will try harder to be a good father and husband."

He crawled back into bed. "I need to apologize to Britany. I can't believe I've kept her in distress for so long. Maybe I went too far and she won't forgive me," he chucked as he thought to himself. One thing he could count on was Britany's loving spirit and faith in God. She would be happy for him and gladly forgive him. How could he ever have resented her? "Maybe I can wrap up business tomorrow and fly home," were his last thoughts as he drifted to sleep.

The next morning Britany got up and helped her father with feeding the cows as much as he would let her. Later in the morning she hung some clothes out on the line for Liz. It was only around ten, but already the sun was hot, and she could tell it was going to be a very warm day. She was disappointed not to hear from Michael the night before, but she had given the situation to God, and she was trusting in Him. As she reached up to secure a clothespin, she felt a sharp twinge in her abdomen. She was sure she must have twisted the wrong way without realizing it. It didn't last, so she continued, being careful not to twist the wrong way again. The same thing happened again, and this time strong enough to make her moan and grab her stomach. Liz looked up and came quickly to her side.

"What's wrong?" she asked with concern in her voice.

"I guess I must have stretched too high. I got a pain. It's gone now. I'm fine," Britany assured her mother although she felt a little uneasy.

"You go in the house and lie down for a while. I will finish up here," Liz insisted.

Britany followed her advice and went to the house. Just as she raised her leg to step up the back step she felt a warm gush of fluid stream down her leg. She hurried to the bathroom and was panicked to find her shorts saturated with blood with more running down her legs.

"Mom!" Britany screamed.

Liz was at the door in an instant. She had heard the scream through the open window.

"Something is terribly wrong!" cried Britany, who was afraid to move and stood hunched over the bathroom counter.

Liz moved quickly. She ran to get her some clean shorts and warm wet towels to clean up with.

"Britany calm down. It's going to be OK," Liz assured her.

"I'm losing the baby. I'm too early to be bleeding this much, and not lose the baby," Britany cried softly. The pain was in her abdomen again and this time went around to her back.

"We are going to get you on the couch and call the doctor. Just calm down and pray for God's help. It won't help to get so upset!" Liz said sternly.

Crystal came downstairs and was alarmed to see Liz helping Britany to the couch.

"Go get some pillows," said Liz. "We need to get your mother into a comfortable position. She is having some problems with the baby."

Crystal ran back upstairs and quickly returned. Charles entered the house and turned as pale as a sheet when he saw Britany and Liz.

"Put the pillows on the couch," said Liz. "Put them so she can lean on two and put one under her feet," she instructed. She helped Britany onto the couch and then went to get the phone. Crystal and her grandfather stood nearby. Neither were sure what had happened or what to do.

Liz handed Britany the phone. "I would call, but I'm sure you know more about this area than I do," she said.

Britany took the phone. Her hand shook as she dialed. She called the labor and delivery unit where she used to work. The nurse she talked to was warm and sympathetic and went to get one of the obstetricians present at that time.

The doctor listened carefully and asked her a few questions.

"Stay off your feet totally. If the baby is going to miscarry, there is nothing we can do here at the hospital. You are better to stay where you are. There is a good chance it will miscarry, probably within the next twenty-four hours. Don't lose hope, though. Sometimes you get bleeding without losing the baby. The best thing you can do is to stay put, and stay off your feet. Call us back in the morning, or if something more happens before that," the doctor finished.

Britany hung up the phone and quietly told the information to Crystal and her parents. Her dad looked so shook that Britany managed a brief smile to try and assure him that she was fine.

"Mom I am going to call Michael," Crystal said. "Do you know how to reach him?" Britany started to speak and Crystal interrupted. "You are not going to stop me!" Crystal said with determination.

"There is nothing he can do and he will only worry," Britany protested. She thought about Michael, and pictured his face when he left. He was feeling trapped. What would he feel when he got a call saying Britany was loosing the baby. Would he think it was a means of control to get him back? She was afraid what would happen.

"Mom I am going to call Michael, and you are not going to stop me!" Crystal said with determination. "It's his baby too and I know he would want to know," Crystal insisted.

"Crystal, Mom, Dad, I may as well tell you," Britany said taking a deep breath and leaning back. Michael and I had some words when he left on his trip. He made it very clear he doesn't want me to tie him down. What would he think if I call him now!" Another pain seized Britany and she grimaced in pain. Liz held her hand and waited until it passed.

"He would think that as a husband and father he needs to be here with you," Liz said quietly. Tears threatened her eyes. "If he thinks anything differently, God will deal with him."

"And if God's not convincing enough, I'll help out! He'll see where he belongs!" Charles said standing beside Liz.

"OK, His work number is in my purse. He isn't there but they will know how to get hold of him," Britany said and laid her head back on the pillow. She hurt badly. The pains continued in rhythm. She wasn't sure how much of the discomfort was from pain and how much was from fear. She had never once in her pregnancy thought of the possibility of something going wrong. Now all she could think about was a picture of a little baby and the dread of that little baby not being there any more. Somehow she had the picture of a little boy.

Crystal returned to say she had gotten hold of the office and they would get word to Michael.

Michael had fallen asleep, but was awaken at six by the telephone ringing. "Hello," he said sleepily.

"Michael, I'm sorry to wake you," said Denise, one of the secretary's from the office.

"Denise?" he asked, trying to wake up and figure out what was going on.

"Michael, you're daughter Crystal called and said Britany was having some problems with the baby. She wanted me to call you. I know it's early out there, but I thought you would want to know." She paused, but she heard no reply. "Michael, are you there?"

"Yea, yea I'm here. Is Britany alright?" he asked with fear.

"I don't know. She is at her mother's. Do you want her number?" Denise replied.

"Yes, please," said Michael scrambling for paper and a pencil. "Ok, go ahead. Thank you, Denise," he said as he wrote the number.

"Call us when you find out what is happening, Michael," Denise said.

Michael scrambled to dial the number as soon as Denise hung up. His body shook and he prayed, Dear God let her be all right. As he waited Crystal answered the phone.

"Crystal, what is wrong?" Michael asked painfully as soon as she answered the phone.

"Michael, mom is having some bleeding and the doctor says she might loose the baby."

"NO!" groaned Michael in agony.

"Michael, calm down. She hasn't lost the baby yet and she may not," Crystal said through the phone.

"Crystal, I'm going to find a flight there. Do you think you could pick me up from the airport?" Michael asked as soon as he could speak.

"Sure!"

"I'll call you back as soon as I find out when my flight will arrive," He said. She agreed and he hurried to call the airport.

"Mom," Crystal said as she walked into the room. "I don't think you have to worry about Michael being mad. He sounded pretty upset. I just hope he can manage. He seemed pretty shook!" She sat down beside Britany. "He is going to call back and tell me when I can get him from the airport."

"I can't believe he's flying home!" Britany said in amazement.

"He needs to be here," said Liz. "I knew he would try and find a way to get here. I just hope he can find a flight on such short notice," said Liz. She went to get Britany some tea.

Liz returned and handed her the tea. "Are you still in pain?" she asked.

"Yes, sporadically. It's more scary than painful. I can't believe Michael is actually finding a flight to come here. I feel so helpless. Everyone is so worried, and there is nothing I can do!" said Britany.

"Don't feel bad. We are just worried for and about you. You are doing something. You are staying off your feet just as you are supposed to. Now stop worrying. Your dad is doing enough of that for you!" said Liz.

Michael called back to tell them he would be at the airport around five and asked if Crystal could meet him there.

"She is scheduled to work, but Charles can pick you up," Britany could hear Liz from the other room as she spoke to Michael on the phone. "That will be no problem. He needs to feel like he is doing something to help. She is doing a little better. She is quite anxious and I am glad you are going to get to come," there was a pause as Liz listened to Michael. "We will see you around six then if everything goes all right." Britany could hear the receiver click, and then shortly her mother was in the room to relay the message.

Britany felt awkward, but Liz insisted that she let Liz and Crystal carry her to the bathroom when Britany needed to use it. They locked arms and carried her sitting between the two of them as Britany used to do as a child in gym class. They insisted that Britany wasn't heavy with the two of them working together, but Britany felt she was being a big burden. She was glad her mother was in good shape from working on the farm. It wasn't unusual for her to lift a one hundred pound grain sack. She knew it was no problem for Crystal, who was also in good shape and very strong. To Britany's relief the bleeding had subsided a little.

Liz brought Britany some more tea as they arranged her back on the couch Britany was hesitant to drink anything more. She didn't want to make her mother and Crystal carry her again to the bathroom. Liz was insistent she drink it. She tentatively obliged.

"Are the pains still present? You are looking a little better." Crystal asked.

"My back is still sore, and my abdomen is tight, but it has let up a great deal, and the pain isn't coming in waves anymore," Britany answered.

"Hopefully that is a good sign," Crystal replied, and Liz nodded in agreement.

"I think the main improvement is that the panic is gone. I still dread the thought of losing the baby, but God will help us, whatever happens," Britany said.

Liz smiled, and Crystal hugged her mother.

"Mom," said Crystal. "I don't know if I can ever be as strong as you."

"I remember saying that about Jeanne," said Britany. "Remember, honey, it's God's strength, not mine!"

Britany managed to sleep for a while, and the rest of the household carried on routine chores. Crystal talked to Britany for some time before she left for work. Britany was touched by her concern. Crystal helped Liz carry Britany to the bathroom one more time before she left.

"Maybe that will get you through until Michael gets here in the next hour or two," Crystal explained cheerfully, trying to make her mother smile.

"If you can get your grandmother to stop forcing me to drink, I might be able to make it," Britany answered.

"You need to keep your fluids up, but I guess it wouldn't hurt for a little while to not drink so much. You really aren't that big. I'm sure I can carry you by myself." Liz proposed.

"Mom, there is no way you are going to do that. I will draw the line there. I don't want you to end up getting hurt," Britany answered emphatically. "Crystal you go ahead and go to work. We will let you know of any change. It will do you good to get away for a while and stop fussing over me. Give me a hug, and thanks for everything."

"Take care of yourself, Mom. It's going to be all right. That baby has our blood in it, and it's bound to have a fighting spirit," Crystal said as she gave her mother a gentle hug.

A lump immediately rose to Britany's throat, and all she could do was to nod in agreement.

Liz went to the barn to feed the animals and start the milking. It gave Britany some quiet time and she read a book. It was hard to concentrate, but it did help to get her mind off her distress.

Britany heard the dog barking and could hear the faint roar of her dad's truck as it turned into the drive. Soon Michael appeared at the door and immediately crossed the room. He knelt beside her, gathered her in his arms and cried, "Britany, I am so sorry for doing this to you. I was selfish and mean." Sobs racked his body and Britany caressed the hair on his head and rubbed his back. "Shhh, Michael, it's alright. You didn't do this to me," she said soothingly. It was wonderful to hold him in her arms again. The movement had caused her stomach to tighten and Britany cringed.

"Oh, Britany I'm hurting you," Michael said in horror and backed away, looking at her with sorrowful eyes.

It took several seconds, but the tightening stopped and Britany was able to relax again.

"Britany, can you ever forgive me?" He took her hand and held it in both of his. "I've failed you. I wanted to be a good husband and make you happy, but I've blotched things up bad. The very thing which I feared I have caused to happen. I'm sorry for blaming you and telling you that you expect too much of me. You've never asked for anything, but love and that is exactly what I withheld. I'm a terrible husband and a terrible father," tears streamed down his face as he spoke and the site tore at Britany's heart.

"Michael, I forgive you. Would you stop blaming yourself?" Britany asked. She stroked his cheek with her free hand. He hadn't shaved. It was the first time Britany had ever seen him unshaven. "The only thing you did wrong was to try and be a good person on your own. We can't possibly be good on our own. We need God's help. I don't expect you to be perfect and neither do Ben or Amy. We all love you and all we want is your love in return."

"But Britany, that is what I'm trying to say. I've tried and I keep failing." He buried his head in her shoulder.

"That's just it Michael. You tried. You can't do it. Seek yea first the kingdom of God and His righteousness, and all these things will be added unto you. You recommitted your life to God now you have to let Him use it. The only thing you have to do is seek Him."

He shook his head in her shoulder. "But you don't understand. I'm the reason you are losing the baby. I upset you and caused this to happen. I was afraid to be a father to our baby and now you're losing it, and I won't get a chance to try."

Anguish tore at Britany when he talked of losing the baby and she bit her lip. Tears stung her eyes.

"Michael stop!" she said sternly. "You have to stop! You didn't do this to me anymore than I caused Jeanne to die! Remember how you talked to me about Job?" She took his face in her hands and made him look at her. "You said then that God is in control and we have no right to think we know better than He does or question His authority. All week I've been dealing with the possibility of losing you and now the baby. I've had to face the fact that you and the baby are in Gods hands and he knows best. All things work out for the best, but in His time, and in His way."

Michael blew out in a big sigh and shook his head. "You're right Britany. I've been afraid to put things in His hands and let Him take care of it. I thought I could do it on my own and I didn't want to ask for help. I was horribly mistaken."

"I think we should pray," Britany said quietly. He nodded his head and took both her hands in his.

"Dear Jesus," He prayed. "I need you. I need you to show me how to be the father and husband You want me to be, not the one I want to be. If it is in Your holy will I ask that you spare our child and give us the joy of raising it. Thank you so much for Britany and the three children we already have. In Jesus name, amen."

Michael looked at Britany and smiled. He rose from the floor and carefully sat on the edge of the couch beside her. He reached down and kissed her face. "I love you," he whispered.

"I love you too, Michael," she smiled back.

"You look tired," Michael said.

"I am. It's been a rough day."

"How bad is it? Are your hurting? Will we lose the baby?" His voice was taut as he spoke, and it tore at Britany's heart to see the look on his face.

"So far there has just been a lot of bleeding. The baby is still all right as far as I know. The doctor said there is a good possibility the baby will miscarry, but not always. He said if the baby doesn't miscarry in the next twenty-four hours, it will decrease the risk. In the meantime I'm to stay off my feet," Britany explained. "I was having pains like labor pains. My back is still sore and my abdomen hurts, but its much better than it was."

"I'm sure your mother is doing a good job of taking care of you," Michael said.

"That's for sure. She and Crystal wouldn't even let me walk to the bathroom. They insisted on caring me. Mom said she would carry me by herself when Crystal went to work, but I told her you would be home soon, and she would do no such thing."

"Britany, I am so glad to be here with you now, finally, after that agonizingly long wait. It's going to be all right. I just know it is," he said stroking her cheek. She smiled back weekly.

Liz came in from milking with Charles following behind her. She was speaking to him as they entered. "You are just like a blister, showing up when the work is done," she said good-naturedly.

"We didn't leave all the work for you, Mother," Charles replied. "Just calm down a bit. We brought home chicken so you wouldn't have to get supper. See, I can be thoughtful."

"That was sweet of you," she responded reaching up to give him a big kiss on the cheek.

Britany and Michael looked up and smiled.

The family spent the evening playing cards. No ones mind was on the game, but it passed time. The family quietly understood when Britany lost her place or played the wrong cards. She read in everyone's face that they were concerned for her. She was concerned for the baby, but tried valiantly to be somewhat optimistic and cheerful.

Even with the extra attention the night seemed to last an eternity for Britany. She slept fitfully, waking often in the middle of a bad dream. She feared every time she used the bathroom, afraid of what she might find. She couldn't imagine what it would be like to find that the precious little body had passed from her, yet it seemed that was all she could focus on. The pains started again several times, but were light in intensity and lasted only briefly. By morning the bleeding was only a trace, and Britany breathed a sigh of relief to have made it through the night.

Britany and Michael stayed the weekend with her parents. For each hour she made it through with no problems, she thanked God. She prayed for His grace and mercy for the baby, and started to let herself be a little hopeful that the baby would live.

Britany called Amy's grandmother in Michigan to arrange for Michael to pick her up on Sunday afternoon at Monique's instead of having her take the plane to Nashville. Crystal rode with Michael to keep him company.

Britany reclined on the couch and read a book in the afternoon. Her parents had gone upstairs to take a nap. Michael and Crystal were still on the road. As she sat reading, she felt a funny tingling sensation in her abdomen. It felt like a butterfly fluttering lightly for a moment. It was very soft and quick. She startled, a little puzzled at what it might be, and then continued reading again. Shortly she felt it again. This time she realized that it was the baby moving. Tears of joy and thanksgiving welled up in her eyes. Her baby was alive! She wanted to run and tell her parents and somehow call Michael, but she knew she needed to sit quietly. She gently reached down and touched the spot where she had felt the movement. She prayed for the baby's continued safety. Overwhelming joy surged though her as she waited to tell Michael and her parents.

Several hours later she heard the dog announce Michael's arrival. Amy came running into the house and stood in front of Britany. Her face was serious. "Britany, you can not lose the baby," she said sternly. She folded her arms and looked at Britany accusingly.

"What did you guys tell her?" Britany questioned Michael and Crystal.

"I'm not sure, Mom," said Crystal. "We were trying to break the news gently. We told her you were not feeling well and might lose the baby."

"Britany, if you lose the baby I will find it, because he's my brother," Amy said sternly.

Crystal laughed, and Michael looked at her in surprise.

Britany wrapped her arms around Amy and said, "We are trying very, very hard to not lose this baby."

She looked up at Michael with her arms still around Amy. It felt wonderful to have her back. "The baby moved. I felt it move while you were gone," she said softly.

Michael knelt beside Britany and Amy and laid his hand on her abdomen. "Really?" he whispered. She nodded. He embraced both her and Amy and kissed her.

Crystal came over to her other side and kissed her cheek. "Mom that is so wonderful. That has got to be a good sign."

On Monday Michael drove Britany to the Doctors office of the obstetrician who had been on call during the weekend. Since she was no longer having pains and the bleeding was minimal he wanted to get an ultrasound.

The ultra sound showed the baby moving and the heart beating strongly. Tears of joy flowed down both her and Michael's faces as they watched the dark tracing that showed up on the screen. The technician agreed that the baby looked quiet healthy and was very active. Following the ultrasound the doctor talked to them. He explained that the placenta had grown over the cervix and had come loose. That was what had caused the bleeding. He said things looked good and as the uterus grows the placenta usually moves up moving it out of danger. He instructed Britany to continue staying off her feet. He felt it would be alright for them to travel back in the morning but he wanted them to make the trip in two days and stay over for the night somewhere. He informed her that he would send a copy of the ultrasound with her and that she was to take it to her doctor as soon as possible. His suggestion was for her to stay off her feet for two weeks and then get another ultrasound to see if the placenta had moved enough to be out of danger. Of course it was dependent on what her doctor said when he examined her.

Britany was ecstatic and found it hard to contain herself. Michael was concerned that she might do something she shouldn't in her state of excitement but he need not have worried. She was very careful in her movements.

Her parents were thrilled with the news when she told them. Her dad tried to tease her by saying that Becker's are tough stock and he knew that baby would hang in there, but Britany could see a spot of moisture in his eyes. Her mother hugged her and let the tears flow. Britany wouldn't have wished the incident to have happened for the world but it was wonderful to see the closeness of her family as they together had faced the ordeal. Amy jumped up and down for joy and had to be reminded to not jump on Britany's lap.

After supper Crystal arrived home and she and Britany had a chance to talk.

"Mom I am so happy for you. I was worried about you but deep inside I really want you to have this little brother or sister of mine. I know we can't see it yet but it seems like it is already a part of our family. I didn't want to say anything before because you already felt bad enough," Crystal said with love and continued. "Michael and I talked about it on the drive to pick up Amy. We also talked about some other things. One of them was the possibility of my coming to live with the two of you for the rest of the summer as you had mentioned when you first came. I talked to my boss at work and they called the bosses of the chain in your town. They are in need of workers. My boss gave me excellent praise and they accepted my transfer on the phone. I can go back with you tomorrow if we can fit my, yours and Amy's things in the car.

"We will fit them in if we have to tie them on the top! Oh Crystal that is wonderful. Michael had conspired to get me to try and talk you into coming back with me, but with all that happened I had forgotten. I'm glad the two of you were thinking straight." Britany reached out and gave Crystal a squeeze.

"You are going to need some help around the house for a few weeks also. Maybe longer. This way I can be there with you."

"Crystal, I don't want you coming down for that reason. We can manage. I don't want you to feel responsible for raising my children. You are young and have a life of your own."

"That isn't the reason. I have a brother I hardly know and another sibling on the way. I want some time to be with the family and be part of it. I knew you wouldn't want me to come down just to take care of you. You are too independent for that. Don't you think after living with you all this time I don't know that by now?" Crystal answered with determination.

"You always have been an insightful child. Well I'm glad you're not coming because you feel I need taken care of, but I am glad you are coming." Britany smiled pleased.

It was hard for Britany to watch the rest of the family pack their things the next day without being able to help. She stayed totally away so she wouldn't be tempted to do something she shouldn't. The drive made Britany nervous. She hoped the doctor was right that it wouldn't hurt and make the bleeding start again. The bleeding did start up a little but it was light and there were no more pains associated with it. She started to relax a bit more as they neared the destination for the night.

There was still a big portion of the day left as they checked into a motel. Britany sat near the pool as Michael, Amy and Crystal swam. Later Crystal took Amy to an outlet mall to do some shopping and Michael and Britany were left with some time to themselves.

"The circumstances surrounding this little vacation are certainly not great, but I am thoroughly enjoying this time together," said Michael as they sat by the pool.

"The girls are certainly making the best of it," laughed Britany. "Sorry I can't go any where or do anything. It makes things rather of slow," she continued apologetically.

"I think it is kind of nice actually. There is no pressure to go anywhere or do anything. It's relaxing. It's enough simply to be together. Watching you go through this ordeal has made me appreciate you even more. I know you were not in danger yourself, just the baby, but it made me realize how easily you could be. I guess now I am satisfied to simply sit back and smell the roses, as they say, and enjoy our precious time together," Michael said reaching over to hold her hand.

"Michael, you're wonderful. I'll tell you I have felt like a queen the last several days. I feel the same way you do. I would never have asked to go through that experience or want to again, but it certainly does impact the way a person thinks. Like you said, it has been a blessing in the way our family has had to take time together, and Crystal is coming back with us. I guess it just shows how God uses bad things at times to bring blessings. I wish Ben could be with us though," Britany said with love in her eyes.

Michael found a quiet little restaurant for supper and then the four of them played cards and watched TV for the evening.

The following day went well and they arrived home by noon. Michael went to work for the rest of the day and surprised the family by bringing Ben home with him in the evening. He explained that he had called Ben's mother from work and she was more than happy to let Ben come home a few days early.

"Oh Ben! I am so glad to see you! I missed you. Now we are all together! Isn't it wonderful!" exclaimed Britany wrapping her arms around Ben in a firm embrace. Ben returned her hug and appeared pleased with her reaction. Maybe just maybe he is beginning to realize that I do love him, no matter what his mother says. Britany thought hopefully.

CHAPTER 24

The two weeks passed quickly with no more major incidents. Britany found it hard to watch others do her work when she felt fine, but for the baby's sake she stayed off her feet. Crystal was a big help and practically took over the household chores. Ben and Amy helped where ever they could. Michael got Britany a high stool so she could sit at the counter and cook and wash dishes. Even though she was off her feet she still managed to do quite a lot. The kids brought her the laundry to fold as it dried and she cooked most of the meals with their help to run for supplies.

The four of them spent a lot of time at the poolside and Britany enjoyed watching Ben and Amy play in the water. She found she was spending all of her time with the children and thoroughly enjoyed it.

The doctor felt it would be safe for her to return to work when the ultra sound at two weeks showed the placenta had moved enough to be out of danger. He wanted her to still continue to be careful and limit her activity. Britany had mixed feelings about going back to work. She hated to leave the children after being with them constantly for the last two weeks; yet she missed the fun and excitement at work.

On her first day back she was excited to see they had three preemies that had transferred in from the regional hospital to their care. One infant was a tiny little black girl Cecilia. She weighed only two pounds four ounces. She had scant curly black hair that clung to her head in ringlets. She lay quietly on her side as Britany walked up to examine her. She had oxygen tubing around her head with two tiny probes that went into her nose a short distance. Her arm wasn't any bigger around that Britany's index finger, and was about the same distance in length. Britany watched her to observe her breathing and then gently reached in the issolette to listen to her heart and lungs. Her lungs were clear and her heart was strong with the faintest of a soft murmur. Her eyes popped open as Britany checked her stomach. She had bright observant dark eyes and quietly watched Britany as she changed her diaper and prepared her for the feeding. The infant wasn't big enough yet to bottle-feed. She sucked vigorously on the tube that Britany gently passed down her throat to her stomach. The infant never cried but was very attentive as Britany passed the formula down the tube for the feeding. Britany felt a bond toward the tiny infant. She wrapped her after the feeding and sat to hold her and rock. Britany thought about how close in size the tiny girl was to her own little child growing in her womb.

Each time Britany worked she requested to care for little Cecilia. It was endearing to see how much she changed as she grew. Her little legs started to fill out and her bottom even started getting a trace of baby fat on it. Her cheeks that were so thin at the beginning supported a tiny dimple on the left side as she grew. Britany was as excited as the mother when the time came for Cecilia to eat out of a bottle. Cecilia looked up at her mother with her big bright eyes as she slowly sucked the bottle. The mother grinned, delighted to be able to feed her baby.

Britany was enjoying the summer and having the children home. It would soon be time for them to go back to school and Britany cherished the time they were home. She especially hated to see Crystal go back. Crystal was getting to know some friends between work and the other youth at church. Britany secretly hoped Crystal would decide to go to a college nearby and live at home for the next year. She didn't say anything to Crystal. Crystal needed to feel she was on her own and not pressured from her mother.

Michael took his vacation the first week of August. They spent it at home. He stated he did enough traveling during the year that he wanted to spend his time off at home with the family. Britany couldn't have been more pleased, although she felt his decision might have had something to do with the problems she had earlier in the pregnancy. Ben and Amy were happy to stay at home too. They had the pool and horses. They also had friends in the neighborhood who came by almost daily to ride bikes or swim.

Britany couldn't ride horses anymore but she insisted the rest of them go on a trail ride and packed a picnic for them one day during Michael's vacation.

"We don't want to leave you here while we go off and have fun!" Michael lamented.

"Don't be silly. The kids need your time too. I will be just fine. Now go and enjoy it!" Britany insisted.

Michael smiled, "You can be pretty demanding when you want to!"

"You're right, I can. You ride Misty and let Ben ride Trigger. I have been coaching him all summer and he is doing quiet well on him. Just warn him not to try and jump Trigger. I think he needs a little more experience first."

They returned a tired but happy group.

"Britany! Ben fell off Trigger! Amy yelled as soon as they were in earshot. Britany had seen them coming and had gone to the barn to meet them.

"Are you all right?" Britany asked in concern.

Ben looked at her sheepishly and said, "Yea, I'm fine."

"Don't feel too sorry for him. He did exactly what you told him not to. He took Trigger over a log. He could have gotten hurt bad but he landed on some old leaves that broke his fall. He got right back on though. I was real proud of him. That is, once I was through being mad at him!"

Britany took Triggers reins and held them while Ben got down.

"Are you sure you are OK?" She asked again looking him over to assure herself. "You need to get a little more experience riding, and then I will teach you how to jump. Promise you won't try that again." she said sternly.

"I won't." Ben answered without hesitation.

"I think the fall was enough of a scare to put a damper on his adventurous spirit. I don't think you need to worry," Michael said as he dismounted and crossed over to where the two of them were. "You take care of Trigger Ben. Britany shouldn't be around these horses." Michael instructed.

"It's hard enough to not be able to ride. Please don't expect me to stay away from them. I have been around horses all my life. I know how to be careful. I rode quiet a long time into my pregnancy with Crystal." Britany urged.

"Oh, all right. I'm sure it wouldn't make any difference if I said no anyway," said Michael brushing her cheek with a kiss.

The next day they took the family and went to an amusement park. The landscaping and flowers in the park were beautiful. Crystal and Michael rode all the fast and scary rides they could find. They took Ben on several of them, but Britany wouldn't let them take Amy even with their urging. Fortunately when they got to the front of the line they found out she was too small so Britany didn't have too worry about a fight. There were a lot of rides for Amy and Ben was small enough he could go with her. He said he went just so she wouldn't be alone, but Britany suspected he liked the smaller rides too. Britany and Michael talked while they watched Ben and Amy ride.

"Michael, I feel like we need to make the situation with Amy stable," said Britany. "School starts soon, and I'm concerned that Monique may have boarding school in mind for Amy."

"Do you think she would still try and get her?" asked Michael.

"Monique doesn't give up easily," said Britany, "and there has been nothing final stated."

"What do you have in mind?" asked Michael.

"I don't know Michael. I just feel very strongly that God is urging me to take action."

"You know I'm behind you whatever you decide," said Michael.

"Thanks, I know you are," said Britany just in time to catch her balance as Amy ran into her, clasping onto her legs.

"That was great Britany! Can we ride it again?"

"I think maybe we had better be heading home. It's getting late," said Michael.

"Do we have to?" echoed Ben and Amy.

"You heard Dad. I'm getting tired whether you guys are or not!" said Britany.

"That was a lot of fun." Britany commented to Michael as they were on their way home.

"It sure was. We may be able to do that more with the new job I'm getting. I won't be working week-ends anymore except for an occasional one for a fill in," Michael said casually.

Britany looked at him in amazement. "What new job?!" she asked.

"I wanted to wait to tell you until everything was finalized," Michael said as he took her hand. "I called this morning before we left and it was approved."

"You are serious?" she asked, squeezing his hand hard. "You did this for me?"

"For all of us!" Michael said looking deep into her eyes. "I know it has been hard on you and the kids having me gone so much. It has been especially hard on Ben. I've been praying about what to do. With the new baby coming, I hated the thought of being gone so much. I went and talked to my boss and told him the situation. I told him I was seriously thinking about a new job unless I could be off weekends and stop traveling so much." Michael shrugged his shoulders.

"He agreed I had worked a lot of years with that schedule, but he thought I liked it. Then he told me the company is expanding, and he needed someone in management. He had considered asking me, but he thought I liked to travel and hadn't said anything. He offered me the new position which is actually a promotion. I will get a slight raise." Michael shook his head and smiled. "I was expecting a decrease in pay and was ready to take it so I could get off of that crazy schedule. Instead I get the job with a raise! It's enough money so that you won't have to work after the baby comes. You really don't have to work for financial reasons anyway, but I want you to do what ever you feel is best for you."

"Michael, I can't believe it! That's wonderful!" exclaimed Britany. She thought back to when the ladies had prayed with her, and how the pastor's wife had said to be patient, it may take a while. She had been right. Michael did take to heart what she had said about being home more. It just took him a while to realize the importance and decide the best way to correct the situation. She thanked God over and over again, first for opening Michael's eyes to the problem, and next for providing the solution so easily. Her heart was so full she felt it would overflow.

Britany prayed and fasted the following Monday. She felt troubled about how to approach Monique about Amy. She prayed earnestly, searching for God's direction on what to do.

Later in the day Britany was cleaning Amy's room, and the sight of Jeanne's diary caught her eye. Amy kept it on a shelf above the dresser.

"Jeanne, I could really use your help. I just feel Monique is going to try to get Amy again. School starts in a few weeks and I'm sure she has found a boarding school for her," Britany thought out loud as she sat on Amy's bed. She thumbed through the diary. She felt guilty to be looking through it, but she needed to be near Jeanne even if it was through the words written in the diary. She read several inserts and chuckled.

"I remember that," she said out loud. "We used to have fun teasing Jeanne's husband."

She flipped through a few more pages and realized that she was reading Jeanne's entries following the death of her husband. Britany's throat tightened. "It's easy to forget the hard times Jeanne faced. She always drew on God's strength to help her through," Britany said solemnly.

"Oh, my word!" Britany exclaimed and hurried to read more of the words written by Jeanne.

"I just need an escape from the darkness. I feel like I'm trapped. I have this closed in feeling like when my mother used to lock me in the closet."

"Lock her in a closet!" Britany exclaimed. "Jeanne never told me about that. No wonder Jeanne didn't want Monique to get Amy! Don't worry, Jeanne. Monique will never get Amy as long as I have breath to fight. I think you've just given me a tool to fight with!"

Britany hurried to the door as soon as Michael arrived from work and showed him the insert.

"Wow!" he said and rubbed his chin thoughtfully. "I never would have guessed."

"I'm going to have my lawyer draw up papers for permanent custody of Amy," said Britany, her words tumbling over each other. "We will adopt her if you agree to it." said Britany.

"Of course I agree," said Michael. "I want Amy too. Just how are you planning to get Monique to agree?"

"I'm going up to Michigan and talk to her face to face. I will tell her exactly what I know and not let her deny it!" Britany said angrily.

"Oh, no, you're not!" Michael towered over her as he looked sternly into her eyes. "We almost lost the baby before when you traveled, and I don't want you to run the risk again!"

"Michael, I need to go! Can't you see?" Britany's eyes pleaded with Michael's as she spoke.

Michael looked down at Britany's protruding abdomen and placed his hand protectively over it.

"Britany, let's wait for awhile," he said and moved his hand to her shoulder, looking directly at her. "Maybe nothing will happen. We haven't heard anything to make us think Monique is going to try and get Amy again."

She touched his cheek and smiled. "I know you are worried about the baby. We can wait and see what happens. I really feel I need to go and that the baby will be fine, but you need to be comfortable with the decision. Please promise to pray about this," she said.

He smiled and nodded his head.

The next day Britany went to the lawyer's office and asked him to write out the legal guardian and adoption papers.

Not long after she got home the doorbell rang. Britany answered it. It was a registered letter. Britany knew before she opened it that it was a court date. Monique had arranged it for two weeks from Friday. Britany showed it to Michael when he got home.

"Now we know. We both know what I need to do," said Britany.

"When do you plan to go?" asked Michael.

"The lawyer will have the papers done by Friday. We can go as soon as you get out of work. Crystal will be around to take care of Amy and Ben."

"Britany, you know I don't want you to go."

"I know."

"But you are sure you have to," he stated simply.

"I'm sure."

"And I'm sure you've prayed about it," he said.

"Every minute."

Michael smiled, "how can I argue against both you and God, Just promise me you will take it easy and not push yourself."

"Michael, I promise. Besides you will be right there with me to make sure I'm alright," she said, and gave his a warm embrace, as much as the growing child would allow.

Britany held tight to Jeanne's diary as she rang the doorbell of the Mansion in front of her. A Butler answered the door. Michael watched from the car wishing he could face off with Monique, but Britany had wanted to face Monique by herself.

"May I help you, madam?" he asked.

"Yes. I would like to speak to Mrs. Peirson," Britany said firmly.

"May I ask who is inquiring of her?"

"Yes. I am Britany Kaiser."

"Please have a seat," the butler said, motioning to a chair in the foyer. Britany didn't feel like sitting and remained standing.

It wasn't long before Britany heard the quick snap of Monique's heels.

"Hello Britany," said Monique coldly. "I see you got the notice. Have you come to give her up early or are you looking for trouble?"

"I've come looking for trouble, because I will never give her up to you or anyone else," Britany stepped toward her and squared her shoulders. "Do you have a quiet place we can talk?"

"The library will do fine. Follow me. I assure you Amy will belong to me." Monique turned and led the way.

They walked to the library, and Monique closed the door behind them. "Now what is the meaning of this? I really have nothing to say. The whole messy matter will be taken care of in court, and Amy will no longer be infested with your rude country ways."

"I have brought papers granting me legal guardianship and a release to allow Michael and me to adopt Amy. I want you to sign them now so as to avoid a very messy matter, as you say," Britany said showing her the papers.

"What on earth makes you think I would ever sign that? I suggest you leave now, Britany." Monique pointed toward the door. "I have important people to see."

"I wonder what the judge would say when he hears that you use to lock Jeanne in her closet?" Britany stepped toward Monique.

Monique looked startled momentarily and then flared with anger, "How dare you accuse me of such a thing! That is exactly the reason I want to get Amy away from your influence. What other lies have you told that child?"

"I haven't told Amy," Britany said calmly. "I don't want her to hate you. I just want to love her and care for her. I won't take her away from you either. She can still come for visits and you can visit her. Grandparents are important to their grandchildren and I don't want to take that away from her. You are the one who is trying to do that. Just enjoy her and love her, but don't try to send her to boarding school and lock her in closets. You know you don't have the patience to have children around all of the time."

Monique's face was red and enraged. "I don't know what you are talking about! Get out of here now! I will see you in court and if you even hint that I locked Jeanne in a closet I will sue you for slander for so much money you will never get out of debt. Now get out of here with your false accusations!" Monique yelled.

"Monique, I have written proof that you locked Jeanne in the closet. I was written by Jeanne's own hand. It's all in this diary," said Britany holding it so Monique could see. "Here is a photo copy of the page so you can see I am not lying." she handed the copy to Monique and showed her the original in the diary. Monique grabbed for the diary, but Britany quickly moved it.

"You fabricated this! How could you stoop this low?" Monique grabbed the copy and crumpled it. She threw it on the floor and struck out to punch Britany. Britany easily caught her wrist and held it tightly.

"I'm not a little girl who you can strike and lock in closets!" Britany said between clenched teeth. "Monique, I can take this to court," she said. "I came to the house to spare you embarrassment. Right now Michael and I are the only ones who know. If it goes to court it's hard to tell who will find out. I promise that if you sign the release I will never tell anyone. The diary is still Amy's and I won't destroy it. But isn't it easier to have her read about it, than find out about it first hand?" Britany pushed the paper under Monique's nose.

Monique glared at Britany. It seemed like an eternity but Britany didn't back down. Finally Monique grabbed the paper, signed it, then threw it back at Britany and left the room.

Britany picked up the paper and gladly let herself out the door. Michael jumped out of the car as soon as he saw her. She smiled and waved the paper in the air. Michael ran up the stairs and reached around her waist to support her.

"Are you all right?" he asked.

"I'm shaky, but elated. At last Amy will officially be part of our family! Praise God! He certainly answers prayers in mysterious ways!"

Michael made Britany rest by the poolside of their motel as soon as they got back. She was tired, but the trip back the next day went smoothly with no ill effects on the baby.

Britany curled Amy's hair and Ben dressed in his Sunday clothes for the trip to the courthouse. Britany held Amy tightly as the judge finalized the adoption. She held her so closely that the baby objected and kicked hard. Amy squealed, "Even my little sister is glad I'm officially part of the family!"

"So am I," said Michael, taking Amy from Britany to hold her close. "Just remember, your sister may actually be a brother."

"I don't really care if the baby is a boy instead of a girl. I just like to pretend it's a girl. I already have a brother and a sister so, it really doesn't matter," said Amy cheerfully.

Crystal smiled at Amy and said. "We've been sisters for as long as you've been around haven't we?" Amy nodded. "Now every one else knows it too," finished Crystal.

School started up again, and Britany reluctantly sent the children back. Amy looked so much older than she had the year before. Britany watched her with mixed emotions as Amy hopped out of the car and ran to the door. A group of children were there to greet her. They were excited to see each other again after the summer break. She wondered if she would always see glimpses of Jeanne when she looked at Amy. She hoped she would. It was a wonderful way to preserve Jeanne's memory.

The hardest of all was saying goodbye to Crystal. They had just gotten used to having her around. Crystal hugged her mother before boarding the plane and assured her that she would come and visit when she could.

"If you time it right, I might be here when you have the baby. The baby is due close to the end of fall term," She laughed as she grabbed her bags and headed for the boarding ramp.

Watching her plane take off reminded Britany of the times she had watched

Michael take off. I guess the ones we love always will bring us a touch of joy and sadness at the same time, Britany thought as she watched the plane disappear from sight.

At first the house seemed empty and the days long. It wasn't too long before Britany fell into a routine, and the time alone felt good. It gave her time to do laundry and clean. With no one to bother her, the tasks went quickly. When the school day ended, the house was once again filled with commotion.

Michael was now getting home in time to eat supper with the family. It was wonderful to see him actively involved with the children. Before it had seemed he was a separate entity from the rest. He had always been loved and had given love in return, but now he was in the midst of them, making decisions when problems arose, or giving a word of encouragement when needed. Britany had yearned for that very thing, and as the months evolved she saw her prayers being answered.

They had been in their new home for a year, and, looking back, Britany was amazed at the changes that had taken place. She felt a strong bond with her new friends. She was enjoying work, even working in the nursery. She laughed to herself as she thought back to the first weeks on her new job and how much she had disliked it. She was sure her coworkers must have been as frustrated with her as she had been with the job. She was grateful she had stuck it out and given it a chance. She truly enjoyed it, although the weight of her fast-growing infant was making it a struggle to get through each day.

Britany came home from work one afternoon in the middle of November totally exhausted. Her legs ached. Her back was sore. The skin encompassing her abdomen was so tight it hurt from the pressure. She dropped into her favorite chair. It had become her favorite in the last two months because it was easier than the others to get out of. She let the tears flow. She needed to pick Ben and Amy up from school in a few minutes, but she desperately needed to get off her feet. She awoke with a start to the ringing of the phone.

"Britany, are you going to pick us up? School has been over for half an hour," a disgruntled Ben said as she picked up the phone.

"Oh Ben, I am so sorry. I will be there right away." Britany spoke apologetically.

She must have fallen asleep. Her body still ached, but she managed to get herself out of the chair and out to the car. Both Ben and Amy wondered what had happened as they got into the car but neither seemed too upset. They filled her ears with talk of homework and their plans for the evening.

Britany wished she would have picked something up for supper on her way home from work, but she hadn't so she struggled through preparing a meal. She had just finished as Michael walked through the door.

"Britany, you look awful! Get off your feet right now! Go lie down! I will finish up here and bring you something to eat!" Michael exclaimed as he entered the kitchen.

Britany looked up and tried to force a smile. Instead of a smile tears stung her eyes, and she spoke a weak "OK." She had already forced too much today, and she was ready to give in for a while.

It wasn't long before Michael appeared in the bedroom with a tray of food.

"Thanks, that was really nice of you," Britany said softly.

"You're more than welcome," said Michael as he came to sit beside her and gently kissed her forehead. "You may not like what I have to say. I want you to call work in the morning and tell them you won't be able to work anymore until after the baby."

"But it's another two weeks before the baby is even due!" Britany protested.

"I don't care. You need to be sensitive to what you body is saying. From the way you look it is trying to tell you to stop working. They will understand. Many women aren't able to work up until their due dates. You don't need to push yourself so hard," Michael spoke with resolve, but in a caring, compassionate way.

"I do feel pretty sore. I guess you are right. Did the kids tell you I was late to pick them up?" Michael shook his head "no" and looked at her questioningly. "I fell asleep in my chair. Ben woke me up when he called to see where I was. I hurried to get them, and they wondered where I had been. They were very understanding when I told them what had happened."

"They are pretty good kids. Ben has been much happier than I have ever seen him, and is thinking more about others." Michael kissed her cheek. "You eat now and get some rest. I am going to make sure Ben and Amy are behaving themselves and clean up after supper." Michael gave her another kiss and then left the room. Britany was too tired to eat more than several bites, and then she drifted off to sleep.

Crystal's plane arrived the following Wednesday. She was on break for Thanksgiving and was spending it with Britany and Michael. Britany drove to the airport to pick her up. They had a wonderful drive home, both of them anxious to catch the other up on all the news.

"I'm glad you waited until I came to have the baby," Crystal said as they drove.

"It's not like I had anything to do with it. I'm getting anxious to have this baby, and if it had decided to come, believe me, I wouldn't have tried to stop it! I just hope it decides to come before you have to go back," Britany answered.

"It will, Mom. Don't worry."

"I'm glad to hear that. This little fellow was due two days ago and I am getting quite anxious to see what he or she looks like. Not to mention the fact that it is getting hard to sit, stand, or lie down," laughed Britany.

Britany woke later that night to Amy's cry. She hurried out of bed as fast as the baby would allow and went up the stairs to see what was wrong.

"Amy, honey. What is the problem?" Britany asked as she entered her room and turned on the light.

"My stomach hurts really bad," Amy whimpered holding her arms tightly against her stomach.

Britany grabbed the plastic wastebasket and carried it with her to the bedside.

"Did you feel bad at Lucy's house?" Britany asked. Amy had gone home with Lucy after school, until Britany and Crystal had gotten home.

"No. We had fun. We made chocolate chip cookies."

"Did you eat a lot of cookies?" Britany asked.

"We ate a lot of them before we even cooked them. They were good, but they don't sound so good now," Amy moaned. "Please make it stop hurting."

"There isn't much I can do, but I think you will feel better shortly."

Amy let out another moan and then the cause of her suffering decided to come back up.

Britany was bending over Amy, holding her shoulder with one hand and the wastebasket with the other, when she got a strong sudden pain throughout her stomach and back. She had been having small contractions on and off for the past two days. This one was stronger than the rest had been. She was glad that she didn't have to straighten right away. The pain passed, and she went to get Amy a cool cloth and a drink.

"I think you will feel better now," Britany said soothingly to Amy as she helped her lie back in bed.

"I already do. Will you stay with me for a while?" Amy asked with big brown eyes.

"Of course," Britany said as she wrapped her arms around her, and gave her a kiss.

"Do you think it was the cookies?"

"I think maybe so." Britany soothingly stroked Amy's hair. "We will know by morning. If it was you should be able to sleep now and not feel bad anymore."

Britany felt another contraction just as Amy drifted off to sleep. She sat quietly in the room until she was sure Amy was asleep. She had another contraction just strong enough that she was sure something was happening. They weren't too hard yet, and she had been in labor for a long time with Crystal, so she took a shower. During her shower another contraction occurred, and she could see her abdomen tighten and stand up like a rock. She felt a rush of excitement and fear at the same time.

"It looks like this is it, baby. Hang in there. We both have some hard times to go through before this is over." She touched the spot where she usually could feel the baby's bottom to give it a pat. Her abdomen was so hard it was impossible to feel where the baby's bottom was.

"Dear Lord," she prayed quietly as she finished and dried off. "Be with me and the baby. I would like to pray that you would spare me from this pain I am about to go through, and make it easier. I know that isn't fair though. You endured pain for us, and I will go through the pain for this child. Please be with us both and bring my child safely into this world. Amen," she whispered.

Britany quietly got her things ready to go. The pains still weren't close, and she wanted Michael to get as much sleep as possible. She went through the house and made last-minute checks to be sure everything was in order. By the time she walked through the house the pains started to make it difficult to get back to the bedroom. She decided it was time to wake Michael.

"Michael," she said, quietly sitting on the edge of the bed beside him. He stirred and she continued. "Michael, it's time to go to the hospital."

He looked up at her with a confused expression on his face and then quickly sat up.

"Are you all right?" he asked.

"I'm fine, but I think it is time to go to the hospital. The pains are coming closer and a little harder. Don't panic. We still have plenty of time. You get dressed. I will go wake Crystal."

Crystal was at the top of the stairs as Britany reached the staircase. Britany was relieved, since she hadn't wanted to climb the stairs, and she didn't want to wake Ben and Amy.

"Mom, are you OK? I heard voices," Crystal asked in concern.

"It is time to go to the hospital. Michael is getting ready. Stay with Ben and Amy. I don't want to wake them up. It will be a long time before the baby gets here. When they wake up in the morning, you can bring them to the hospital. There is a room were they can wait. If anything happens sooner, I will call." Britany answered in a whisper as Crystal descended the stairs.

"I'll call Grandma."

"No, not until a decent hour. There is no need for this baby to keep everyone from getting a good night's sleep." Britany wanted to get through her explanations before another pain came. She didn't want Crystal to see her during the contractions. She quickly brushed off any protest Crystal might have had and made her way back to the bedroom just in time. It was hard to stand upright during the contraction, but it was impossible to sit, so she just hunched over slightly and did her relaxation breathing. Michael came out of the bathroom to find her in that position.

"Britany, we are getting you to the hospital right away. I didn't realize they were getting so strong." Michael said hurrying to her side.

"They have a long way to go before we need to get too concerned, but I am ready as soon as you are. I gave instructions to Crystal." Britany said as soon as she could resume normal breathing and talk again.

When they got to the hospital they learned that Britany was much farther along than what she had expected.

"It looks like we are going to see a new baby in the next hour or so," Dr. Harrison announced when he finished his exam.

"You have got to be kidding. I don't feel nearly as much pain as I did with Crystal at this point," Britany responded in surprise. Michael looked at her and grinned widely.

"Second babies are often a lot easier than first. Don't get too relieved yet. You still have a way to go," the doctor answered and then left the room with the nurse standing by.

The hour passed with no baby. The contractions were coming faster and harder. The room became a blur of gray as Britany focused all her energy on breathing. The unrelenting pain seized her whole body like a vise, starting out tight and gripping harder until Britany was sure she couldn't take any more and then it would let up for a few short seconds. She could hear Michael in the background telling her to breathe, but all she could see was the steady movement of the second hand as it swept endlessly across the face of the large black clock on the wall.

"What is wrong?" moaned Britany at the end of two more hours. "I thought the doctor said the baby should be here by now. Please go get him. Something must be wrong." Britany was staring up at Michael.

Her beautiful face was now puffy and twisted in pain. Wisps of hair clung to her forehead which was covered in beads of sweat. Michael felt empathy for her. He would gladly trade places with her. How he wished she didn't have to go through this part of labor. He didn't want to leave her side, but she had sounded desperate. He breathed a sigh of relief as the nurse entered the room, followed by the doctor.

"I thing we need to check things out and see what the hold up is," The doctor spoke with concern but maintained an air of confidence.

Britany let out an involuntary scream during the procedure, and Michael cringed. He squeezed her hand and held it as she clung desperately to him. Tears stung his eyes.

"Britany," Dr. Harrison said as he stood by her side. "I'm sorry but you are not progressing as well as we would like to see. I am going to have my nurse start some medicine in your IV, to see if it will help you along. If it doesn't help, we may need to do a cesarean section."

"Is the baby all right?" Britany asked. She worried about the baby and fear started to fill her as the next pain started to wrack her body. Everything went dark and hazy. Britany could barely hear the doctor's words.

"Don't worry, Britany. The baby is doing fine. If anything at all were wrong with the baby, I wouldn't wait. The heartbeat is strong and steady."

"Thank you," Britany breathed a sigh of relief as she heard his words and the contraction ended. Tears of gratitude stung her eyes as she reached out and squeezed his hand. He smiled back at her.

The contractions came faster and harder. The room became a complete blur. The clock wasn't even visible. Grayness seemed the only thing Britany could see. Grayness that was getting darker, turning black.

"Oh, Lord, help me!" Britany cried out.

Suddenly she could now see a light in the middle of the darkness. A soft, warm glow that broke through the grip of the pain. Then she felt a strong urge to push.

"Get the nurse!" Britany yelled.

Michael startled at the panicked plea. Britany looked alarmed. He looked at the door with a sigh of relief. Apparently the nurse had been close and was running in to see what was happening. To Michael's dismay she ran out just as quickly. Before he had time to get off his chair there were three nurses running into the room with the doctor close behind, fastening on a surgical gown.

Britany started to push. The pushing seemed to drive away the pain and the harder she pushed the less she felt the pain. She was vaguely aware of the commotion going on around her as the nurses put the final preparations to the room for the delivery.

"Britany, blow out. You can't push right now. Your body isn't ready," the doctor said sternly, almost harshly.

"I can't! I have to push!" yelled Britany. Yelling helped her to blow out instead of push. She didn't know if the doctor and nurses realized that. Michael certainly didn't.

"Britany, you have to," he pleaded, fear etched in his face.

The contraction ended, and Britany fell back into his arms. Michael smoothed back her hair.

"Here. Put this on." A nurse was putting a surgical mask around his face and fastening it for him. Britany could no longer see his mouth, only his eyes that were filled with concern.

"It's coming again!" Britany shrieked.

"Blow, Britany, blow!" the doctor exclaimed right back.

Britany blew, but through the blowing she still pushed.

"Britany, you're still pushing. You have to blow. Hold on just a little bit. I have to go in and turn the baby slightly."

Britany blew hard, but the pressure wouldn't let up. She could feel the hand inside her, and she blew hard, but her body continued to push against it.

"Britany, blow, you can't push now." The doctor was yelling now, too.

"I'm trying!" Britany screamed.

Suddenly something broke loose, and the pressure released.

"OK, Britany, you can push now," the doctor instructed with relief.

Britany pushed for all she was worth and let out a loud groan in the process. One of the nurses came to stand on the opposite side of Michael and help him hold Britany's back up so she was partly sitting.

"Push, Britany, but don't groan. Use all your energy to push, "the nurse instructed."

With the next push Britany could see a mass of hair appear.

"The baby! It's coming!" Britany exclaimed in utter amazement looking at Michael. He nodded his head in agreement.

"Push, Britany, don't talk," the nurse continued to instruct.

Britany fell back into their arms at the end of the contraction, totally exhausted.

"Get ready, Britany. It's time to push again," the doctor instructed after Britany had a minute to catch her breath.

Britany pushed for all she was worth. She could see more of the baby's head now, but the next two contractions failed to get much farther.

"You have to push harder!" the doctor demanded.

"I can't," Britany moaned and fell back once again against the supporting arms.

"Yes, you can! Push!" the doctor ordered.

The nurse spoke quietly to Michael, instructing him to help her give Britany more support and get her back up higher.

"OK, Britany, here it comes. Now push!" she urged as the next contraction came.

Britany took a breath and pushed.

"Good! Good! Now take a breath and breathe again," the doctor encouraged.

Britany could feel the head moving. The pain was intense, but not as strong as the urge to get the baby out.

"One more deep breath, and push!"

Despite her effort not to, Britany let out a loud groan and felt a sudden release as the baby's head popped out.

"Don't push! Don't push!" The doctor was once again saying as he swiftly suctioned out the baby's mouth. Britany took the moment to look into Michael's face. His eyes were shining brightly and she squeezed his hand.

"OK, easy now, I need to turn the shoulder slightly with this next contraction."

Britany pushed, and the baby gushed out in one swift movement.

"It's a boy!" the doctor said, but Britany could tell that for herself. The slimy purple bundle was wiggling. It looked amazingly large to have come out of her.

"My baby. My baby!" Britany exclaimed. "He's beautiful!"

The doctor briskly rubbed the squirming body with a towel and handed him to Michael. The nurse wrapped a towel around the baby in Michael's arms. Michael surrounded the baby with his arms, and sat beside Britany, holding the baby's cheek next to hers. She looked exhausted, but had never looked more beautiful to him. How could he ever express the love he felt for the two of them?

"I want to see him and make sure he has all his fingers and toes," said Britany.

The nurse laughed and carefully unwrapped him while Michael held him. He was purple and pink, but the most beautiful thing Britany had ever seen. The nurse tucked the unwrapped baby under Britany's blanket and helped position him to nurse. The baby eagerly started sucking.

"He is so beautiful," said Michael, stroking his back. The doctor finished and the nurse bustled around cleaning the room and keeping a close eye on the baby.

"Someone is here to see you," she said quietly.

Crystal peeked her head in the door and Britany exclaimed, "Crystal! Come see your brother, Andrew!" The baby had finished eating and was looking intently around. Amy beat her through the door and hopped up to curl up beside Britany and the baby. Crystal kissed Britany on the cheek and touched the soft down on the baby's head. Ben stood hesitantly beside his father.

"You can touch him, Ben. He wants to see his brother. He has been hearing your voice these past nine months," Michael urged. Ben reached out and gingerly touched Andrew's hand.

Britany looked at her family. Michael, with all the pride of a father in his eyes; Amy's glowing face; Ben's look of amazement; and Crystal's eyes of love.

The door opened again, but Britany was too absorbed to notice.

"I told you those Beckers have a fighting spirit. This one looks like he's ready to carry on the tradition!"

"Dad!" Britany exclaimed. "How did you get here?"

"I think he broke the sound barrier. Fortunately there isn't much traffic in the wee hours of the morning," said Liz.

"Oh Mom. This is so wonderful! I'm glad you came. Isn't he beautiful!" exclaimed Britany.

"You know, Britany," said Liz, leaning close so only Britany could hear. "I recall that just a little over a year ago you thought your life was coming to an end. It seems to me that it was just Beginning!"

Britany smiled and looked at the amazing love surrounding her.

Printed in the United States
25529LVS00004B/271-351